FARQUHARSON'S PHYSIQUE
AND WHAT IT DID
TO HIS MIND

FARQUHARSON'S PHYSIQUE AND WHAT IT DID TO HIS MIND

by

DAVID KNIGHT

STEIN AND DAY/*Publishers*/New York

A NOTE ON YORUBA:

Accents show tones: high, low, mid, rising, and falling (fẹ, kò, lọ, yĩ, nâ). They are used here only in speech, and not for written words, names, or words taken into English, like *oyibo* and *agbada*. Vowels are as in Italian (ẹ and ọ are open, *e* and *o* closed), nasals as in French, but with no glide into an *n*-sound before vowels. Ṣ is the same as *sh*. *P* is pronounced *kp*. Both *kp* and *gb* are single sounds.

N.B.: This book is fiction, set in a real place, at a real time. None of its actors are real, and no actual people, living or dead, are represented among them. Nor are the cars they drive, the rumours they discuss or believe, or the riots they see, actual. The weather and the houses are. But because the history is real, unchangeable, and in newspapers, the framing events, and names on the periphery, *are* real: these people, and these people alone—in the Federal Government *Azikiwe, Balewa, Okotie-Eboh, Ironsi*; in the government of the North *the Sardauna of Sokoto*; in the government of the West *Akintọla, Awolọlọ, Adegbenro, Esua* and *Fajuyi*; at the University of Ibadan the Vice-Chancellor *K. O. Dike; Wọle Ṣoyinka* the playwright, and finally, by permission (for which I thank him), *Brother Patrick*. Nevertheless, any links between these people and the various actors in the book are fictional, and no representation is intended of any actual events.

First published in 1971
Copyright © 1971 by David Knight
Library of Congress Catalog Card No. 73-149824
All rights reserved
Printed in the United States of America
Stein and Day/*Publishers*/7 East 48 Street, New York, N.Y. 10017
SBN 8128-1362-6

CONTENTS

FARQUHARSON'S PHYSIQUE
AND WHAT IT DID
TO HIS MIND

Introduction: Prologue or Epilogue

IN the early hours of July 29, 1966, certain units of the Nigerian Army mutinied, and the Nigerian Revolution passed over into its second stage. At Ikeja, among the Lagos suburbs, they took over the airport and threw up a roadblock at the corner by the Mogambo nightclub, where a white man from a shoe factory was killed in the crossfire. White deaths were scarce, almost unheard of: there is said to have been a second, elsewhere and later, a man shot in his car by a group of fleeing soldiers. Beyond these two, they say, no whites were killed in the whole of the second stage, between the mutinies in the barracks and the secession of the East, as Biafra, more than a year later. This isn't true. There were two white men killed when the army took over the Lagos Airport, and though one of them was where all the accounts said he was, the other was in the airport itself, near the stand-up desks of the immigration officials and about ten feet in from the doorway into the main waiting room. He lay with his hands under him, against his stomach, where there were two bullet holes, and there was a third among the short hairs at the back of his neck, against his skull. The man who fired that shot had been crouching over; the gun, when it went off, had been wavering slightly against the skin. One man's body got into the newspapers; the other's didn't. One death was an accident, the other not. And one man had a name, and the other, for about four days, didn't. No one appeared to claim him; there were no papers in his pockets, and no money, and none of the other passengers, when their plane left, had acknowledged him. The clean-up put his body into a Lagos hospital, and there it stayed, until a visiting doctor from

Ibadan was brought into the morgue by a young Yoruba intern, with the words, "And perhaps, sir, you will be enabled to enlighten our mystery," and the body was drawn out and the cloth peeled back from what remained of the face, that is, the forehead, the eyes, part of the cheeks, and the top half of the nose. The forehead was unlined, the ears big, hard, and bunched together, the hair, looking like old fur, a colourless straight pale brown. The eyes had been duly closed. "Yes, I've played tennis with him," the visitor said, finally. "He's from Ibadan. I can't tell you his name. But I *can* tell you he's got a wife and a small boy."

"We have been sent no other victims," the intern said, staring out of anxious and aggressive eyes. "And how is it that if you know him you do not know his name?"

So the doctor phoned an official in the Arts Building in Ibadan. "I've identified him," he said, "but I haven't got a name. Spell it. F. A. R. Q. U. H. Oh, Farquharson. Right. No, I haven't got time to hunt for Mrs. Farquharson. See here, Ogundele, he isn't going to keep forever. He's got to be buried, and he belongs to your university. Please, he's been shot at point-blank range through the back of the head: now think about it. Well, if his wife comes afterwards, he can be dug up and sent home, can't he? *Cut* the damned red tape!" And he hung up, full of rage.

"You might as well dry him out and mummify him," he said to the intern. "You're going to have him a long, long time." But in fact the university did send a car with a box, and have him buried, as if where they could keep a not-too-close eye on him, in the cemetery on the north side of Ibadan, and the cost of the funeral was added to his unpaid account. So there he was, under a wooden marker, uprooted from his house, that said "Prof. & Mrs. H. J. Farquharson" (the " & Mrs." now blacked out), and underneath, on a separate little tag of wood, the figure "1".

PART ONE

I

To September 14, 1965

His name was Henry John Farquharson, and he avoided the problem of "Harry", "Hank", or "Hal" by being to almost everybody, and even to his wife, "Farquharson", or, upon occasion, as when someone needed to yell, "Farq". He was happy, thirty-seven, married; without relatives, but a father; healthy, a lazy athlete, an unimpressive scholar, and a more-than-satisfactory teacher, if occasion gave him the chance. He liked people.

He had heavy sloping shoulders—underwear tops always looked too small on him—but his body wasn't something he believed in much, or particularly worked on: it was what he had. At home it stood in front of classes in a grey suit with two buttons of the coat done up, while he lectured in a ratty black gown that had been given to him, and put on and took off a pair of very round-lensed spectacles with steel frames. He had grey eyes. He also had straight wide eyebrows that seemed not long enough, big ears, a long, rather broad chin with a dimple in it, round cheeks, solid pale lips, and a large grin. But his nose was a clown's nose, with a straight, strong bridge and a tip that from the front looked almost like a rubber ball. With the dimple, the nose, and a forehead that looked as if it had been untouched since childhood, the face was genial but not especially important, and people, even his wife, took him at times for a sort of child-man, which was a mistake. He wore his hair short now, clipped for the tropics into near-stubble at the back, but he had kept a long straight forelock against the front of his skull, like a fallen cockscomb. He had done his doctorate in "Themes of Innocence and Experience in English Literature Before Blake", and there were days when the Fall of Man made a kind of perambulating landscape within which he moved, he felt, comfortably and without illusion, in a quiet bodily contentment that should have been despair, but had been let not be. He was a happy man. He had few friends; his wife only partly liked him. Yet parties opened, people chatted; his grin fetched grins. After five minutes of him everybody liked him; after five years they felt exactly the same. And his wife, in bed, first grabbed him and then shoved him away, each time they met. If he had wanted a confidant, there wouldn't have been one person around to listen. He was the everlasting acquaintance, the guy with the grin on the tennis court, the half-conspicuous young man with the big teeth and the martini, who could do the hula, and did. He should have been miserable. But at some time, without ever having thought of it, he had trained himself to count on nothing. Therefore everything was a surprise, and whatever came was a gift. Equally, of course, everything was superficial, a sliding skin, never trusted. Something held back, conglobulated under the surface like Dr. Johnson's swallows in wintertime: the encysted state of innocence, or of experience, unlabelled for him either before or after Blake. With a typewriter under his fingers, and a lecture haltingly to prepare, there might be communication out of this depth, gross bits of wry insight or upsetting bland remarks, but that was for worktime only, and the psychiatrist-couch safety of the classroom. He had encountered death in hospitals—his parents and two grandparents at intervals—and, having stayed safely too young for the war, had lost a brother in it. Death was thus orderly, and mainly a theme for class. And his wife had had a daughter and it had died before its first birthday, also in the hospital, which it had hardly ever left. "And the Virgin," he had written on a card, "fled back unhindered until she came to the caves of Har."

And so to Africa, with a trim workable wife and a two-year-old.

"I don't know," he said. "I saw pictures in a magazine once," and he sang the start of *Vissi d'arte* under his breath (he had never been known to get beyond the first few bars), said, "Joan? what would you do if we went to Nigeria?" and tried to kiss her as she turned her head.

It wasn't Joan's fault, he thought, even if he wondered sometimes, not what she thought about him, but what she might be able to feel. She was so set in prettiness, with blue eyes and short black hair, as if she were young and royal but didn't know too well how to sit for photographs. "Poor Joan," he thought—so longing for his sex, so quick to take it and so quick to lose it, unable to give anything back because as soon as she had come she disapproved, and besides, she hurt. And she came quickly. Well, the rest of her life wasn't like that, but still, there she was. He had fished two children up out of that stung disapproval; he'd kept one of them. "*Wá sí mi*," he would say, practising his Yoruba out of a book in the living room, with Jamie stumping around the floor on private errands. "*O fẹ́ bá mi wá?*"

Come with me (pitching his light voice into an unnatural bass). *You wish with me come?*

And Jamie clumped up to him and said, "Up!" and was therefore picked up, proud.

At least Joan loved *him*, almost as much as his father did.

There were times at night, on the edge of sleep, when his wife lay curled into herself like a closing hand, when he tried to pretend that his back was relaxed and warm, while he stilled his breath and his unfinished flesh stood achingly unable to fade, and he didn't want her to know that he had anything left; times when he thought he had fooled her by pretending to come, times when she knew quite well that he was being kind to her, times when he might quite openly have walked into the bathroom to use his hand and finish, times when he could only lie there, and wish them both asleep, so that he wouldn't make judgements on her. A man's sex life took up only a few minutes a day, and then there was all the rest.

"And we go tonight," he had said, "to a 'Now-we-get-rid-of-the-Farquharsons' farewell party." And that was the kind of party it had been and they had had a good time, and now here they were.

Nobody came to see them off at the airport: there were no relatives except Joan's elder brother, and he wasn't the sort of person who would come from Hamilton to look at a plane. It was the grief and innocence of the bullet, Farquharson thought (as if he had a class beside him), to have no ties. "Think that a rusty piece, discharg'd, is flown / In pieces, and the bullet is his own, / And freely flies." London came out of the morning like an unbelievably detailed collection of models on a concrete floor, and they were on their way.

Farquharson, with Jamie clutched to his shoulder, sailed stepping down the unfathomable escalators, the coat tight across his shoulders, leaving his wife behind. "Yes, of course I'll go to Africa," she had said. "Would I stay at home?" Once they saw two massive African women with dense gold earrings and their heads in clouds of thin brocade, their hips draped in velvet. Farquharson said, "They're Yoruba. Remember that article about what the women wore?"

The women were staring into a store window. To pass them the Farquharsons had to creep past power, wealth, and perfume.

Joan said, "I guess that's what happens when they get loose in the fancy fabrics."

He took Jamie into the American Express office once, while he cashed a cheque. In the hubbub and confusion Jamie cried till he was purple. Farquharson had to crouch and hug him till he was only sobbing, and then the people on the Haymarket saw a man with a grey suit and a sombre homely face pushing a green empty stroller with his left hand and carrying a delighted miniature of himself, awkwardly, on his other arm.

On the flight to Venice, for some reason, Farquharson was afraid. They had bungled getting aboard the plane and were separated; Joan had Jamie and he could only just see her head. So he held his hands in his lap and tried not to anticipate, in spite of having seen those women in their abundant arrogant finery.

That night he marched them to Florian's and bought Joan Carpano, and tiny roses in silver paper which she held just beyond the edge of the table, while the night glowed. She let her husband see a withdrawn flicker of honeymoon dread around the lips where the kiss should go. They had a room overlooking one of the streets behind the piazza. He left the shutters wide open and then came upon her in the spongy semi-dark. After a while she said, "I'm sorry."

They stayed two weeks. Then one night Joan pleaded exhaustion and went to bed, and Farquharson walked out into the piazza with Jamie on his shoulders while a band played overtures on metal scaffolding. A dozen people, including one of the musicians, saw and remembered the proud motionless image of the man, with his mouth partly open and his eyes shining as if somehow wet, and his hands gripped on the ankles of the awestruck and delighted small boy who held his forehead.

And then they went to the Accademia and saw the pictures, and Jamie trotted among martyrdoms and Bellini landscapes and almost kept his father from seeing anything, while Joan fed her eyes. About the only picture Farquharson got time to remember was a smallish Tintoretto in which a white-robed God stampeded the birds and fishes across a turmoil of blue canvas. The picture had an uncanny, exultant overspill of mortality: what was being created were the things that were going to die, and that was what they were all so excited over. He tried to buy a reproduction of it, but there wasn't one.

Rome was only a place to spend one night in. They holed up in a tiny bedroom at the top of a hotel and that night there was a storm so violent that the skylight broke, and water was running down the stairs.

"Europe," Farquharson shouted, after he had scrambled barefoot to the washroom downstairs and back again, "is washing herself clean of us, all right!"

Joan was hugging Jamie because he didn't like thunderstorms. "Do you wish we weren't going now?" she said.

"I do not! Besides, we're going to be met by the High Commissioner's representative."

They had one light-bulb burning. She thought he looked unnecessarily nice without his glasses and with his hair rumpled from two attempts to go to sleep. Then the commotion faded and Jamie was asleep again. "Do you think you could hold back," Farquharson said, "if I came in?"

And because it was the last night before Africa, she tried, and left the light on and her eyes open, gaining the kind of dull tension that would keep her down. She succeeded sometimes: this was one of the nights she did. Her husband probed and shifted, drew himself this way and that, had what passed sometimes for a good time in their bed, and came to a natural convulsive orgasm and was, she supposed, glad of it—and she couldn't help feeling he was selfish and that therefore she was right to hold back his welcome from him. If she didn't, if she rode with him, she would be like fire in birchbark, she couldn't help herself. Then after the one great flare-up all the nerves would transmit was pain. And then he couldn't finish. She would try to keep him in and he could tell he was hurting her. Whatever happened was going to make one or both of them selfish: honour said it was his turn this time. So he had to be bemused and sorry because she hadn't come at all, and he couldn't make her. "Watch your step on the stairs," he said finally, when he had pulled out and had patted her as much as seemed necessary to take the regret out of both of them (which it didn't do). "They're as slick as glass."

She went down to wash, and when she came back he was asleep.

A happy man. They rode the bus to Fiumicino Airport in the companionable silence of conspirators. And then at last there was the plane they had to walk to and a Negro stewardess at the top of the hot metal stairs.

Farquharson had the seat by the window—his wife had made him take it. The big man with the smooth-backed head and the alert, tough ears, the man who had laboured in the cause of his own sex and been rewarded, the father who had sealed his off-spring between a cushion and the safety belt, was being given the view of busyness and the horizon outside the window. Like a boy, he took it. The many Negro passengers seemed overdressed. There were too many white shirts, grey suits, dark ties, black shoes, all spotless: no African clothes. The white men and women were rather more rattily dressed.

Someone with purple lipstick gave them candies, and the plane took off.

Farquharson looked at porphyry-coloured hummocks sliding like a map below. Europe was gone, Canada gone still further. He wanted to say "Look!" to Joan, and then thought that it wasn't necessary to force any mind down to that, took Jamie on his knee and let him bash the glass. "You're going to have paw marks all over the window," Joan said. "Wipe his hands, at least."

He had to make out the landing cards. Oddly, he didn't like to, and he set the naked identities down on paper with a sort of nervous intensity, lest he should make any mistake. Purpose of travel: "To teach"; "Accompanying husband"; "Accompanying parents". The sky got dark.

He had thought of Kano as miles of gold-brown ground, dotted with oases and a labyrinth of houses, but when they broke through the cloud he saw only an unbelievable rain-fed green on dark ground, and they circled, in storm and rough air, for more than half an hour; Jamie was crying with the jolting and said, "Bump!"

"That's wind out there!" Farquharson said. He never realized that he used enthusiasm sometimes to calm his son. "It's got bumps in it."

"Oh, Farq," his wife said, "a wind doesn't have bumps in it."

"Sure it does," he said. "Smoothness is simply a function of relative size and speed. *Wump!* Corduroy road. If we were a rocket, smooth. If we were a bird too, maybe. The slow lives get the little bumps. Hey, I can use that!"

"Where?"

"*Lear.* Goneril and her father. She wouldn't even notice the big things go by: she'd just crest them. And Lear wouldn't notice the little fusses. That isn't his scale. It isn't any wonder they yelled at each other."

"And the Fool?"

"He can be a gadget for shifting scales. Why not?" He squirmed contentedly to get away from the safety belt, proud of a moment of professionalism.

They landed forty-five minutes late, and the Lagos passengers were made to stay in the plane, without ventilation. He pulled the cellophane off one of the sweets the stewardess had dropped into Jamie's chair. Joan walked up and down the aisle to make her legs right.

"It would be unnatural," a voice said over his head, "not to be delayed," and was answered by a dry Canadian voice quoting Sterne. Farquharson craned his head to look up beyond the seat back and saw, upside down, a black face with pouting lips and a tiny chin, and a razor-scraped red face with pale eyebrows shining in the tiny spotlight over his head. "Good evening," the black man said. "Why don't you stand and stretch?"

Farquharson pointed to the dozing Jamie. "I'm on guard."

"I was about to observe to my friend that a man should confine his wanton acts of quotation to his own discipline. Is this your first trip to Africa?"

He was evidently faced with friends. He twisted around, cramped by the pushed-back seat in front of him, and, as they made talk, wondered if he was going to have African friends, and if so, whether they would be suave and bouncy like this or whether Henry Farquharson would be like the other man, signalling his security because he had this friend. Farquharson held his name back. They were anonymously at a party for a few minutes, talking politics. Demonstrations in Lagos were demanding the dismissal of the Finance Minister. "Well, the next time they have a state of emergency," the white man said, "I hope they can have it in the East or somewhere. We've *done* that!" Then Joan came back, and Farquharson sank into the dictatorial contours of the seat and dozed to Lagos, his head held stiffly upright, dreaming—in a plane—of flying, and knowing it. The real plane touched, pulled, roared.

They walked through steam into the Immigration and Customs shed, Jamie riding his father's arm. Joan fished in her bag for the documents; Farquharson took a breath and realized that he didn't know what he was smelling, or even where he was. Scraps of words hit his ear in accents he couldn't fit to English. Joan tried to fix the passports into his other hand. He was dangerously close to spilling blessings wholesale, wary as an interloper, spinning with the earth.

The man from the High Commissioner's office got there just in time. Farquharson was locked in an argument over his entry permits. They were photostats. Someone from the university was supposed to be meeting him with the originals. He wasn't there. Farquharson said, "I'm sorry. I can't do anything more. That's all I've got." Then he hung on the edge of the obstinate lack of composure of the official behind his lectern; his face got very solemn and he said to the newcomer, "We're stuck."

The officer turned towards the arrival of (perhaps) authority, and while the new man took Farquharson's hand and said, "I'm Bill Thomas of the High Commissioner's office," held out the dirty-looking photostats, mustered his dudgeon, asked, "What am I to do with these?" and was subjected at once to one of the most ruthlessly offhand bullyings Farquharson had ever seen ("Well, who else's documents are they if they aren't yours?"). Then they were ushered through. Farquharson said "Thank you" as he got the photostats and put them into his pocket until his wife could take them, and then they were past the customs, unexamined, and Mr. Thomas had demanded and got a room at the hotel since their plane to Ibadan didn't take off till tomorrow morning. Farquharson kept a hand in his pocket, and wanted to pull the binding underwear down away from his crotch but was embarrassed to.

They were in the dark, on red concrete steps, among a dozen faces; a black station-wagon beyond. People in khaki shorts threw their possessions through the tailgate. "How much do I give them?" Farquharson said.

Mr. Thomas said, "Leave it to me." A black driver ushered them into the car.

They dropped into the night, following a grey road. A single billboard with an immense elephant leaned out of the darkness into the headlights and then went away.

Concrete steps. Doors opened. They were in a lobby with steps across it. Jamie pressed against his legs as they signed in. Then Farquharson asked where he could change a pound note into coins and was given twenty shillings in a stack, so brusquely that when he thought he might want sixpences or something smaller, he found he lacked the authority to go back. Mr. Thomas said good night. Four or five people picked their suitcases up, and they were taken across a huge sultry courtyard under a dead sky like a dome over them. Wet grass crowded against a path. The air was fresh and close. They were stopped on white concrete, under a light-bulb, by a wooden door. There was the embarrassment of tipping with his shilling, and then they put themselves to bed and had to listen, eyes open, to the blanketing, undefinable, almost-silence.

Farquharson woke in the near-dark with an aching bladder and had to feel his way to the bathroom. He was muddleheaded and sharp together, and at first the noise of falling water wasn't his. Then he put his face to the blind and stared between the slats. He saw the flat end walls of a couple of pale three-storey houses, a few silhouetted and attenuated palms, a light in one window, and the blank backs of what were probably garages: commonplace suburbia, mysteriously near, with a dim brightening overblue sky and nothing moving. He thought: "Africa."

They had breakfast in what felt like a morning-after bar, and were hurried along to the airport in the hotel station-wagon. Jamie's stroller had been stolen, and they had to get more change for tips. Then they waited in a wide, dusty, shallow hall like a small hangar, among metal-armed couches with slit plastic upholstery. From time to time somebody took orders and brought them beer. Farquharson felt spruce, trim, ridiculous.

Finally the plane took off, and for about half an hour Farquharson fixed his nose to the window and stared at green complicated miles of the tops of trees. His wife and child, in the seat in front, were far away. Ibadan came up on the wrong side of the plane. They bounced onto the ground and strutted up to the control building.

Sun splashed as if heat were something painted on. They stood with their possessions all about them, in a sparse modern room, and were met by a lean-faced man with almost wanton eyes and a shaving rash. He said he was Ogundele, the executive assistant, apologized that Professor Ormford, as Professor Farquharson probably knew (he did), hadn't yet come back from his leave, and explained in a whirlwind of confidence that the house they were supposed to be going to hadn't been vacated yet, and wasn't going to be, but that there would be something ready in a few days, and in the meantime . . . all this time getting them into the station-wagon, commanding the driver to load their luggage in the tail-gate, and gesturing to the surprisingly unexotic surroundings of the road, until they swung off the highway past a gate with a coat-of-arms. Then the bewildered Farquharsons, with no idea how they had got there, were taken around a confusion of short roads and brought to a dead-end circle in front of a white block of flats. "Bottom left, number one," Ogundele said. This time servants took their luggage.

The screen door had a vicious spring. Farquharson helped Jamie up the high step into the hall, and as he turned to talk to Ogundele the door walloped him. He took his bruised side into the apartment and sat down. "There'll be a car for us at three," he said.

There were two bedrooms, a bathroom with a hot-water tank, and a big living room. Outside, between the flats, was a concrete hall and a bare stairs, and a dining room behind, like the tiny stem of a T. They were given an English lunch heavy with pota-toes and pastry, and fell on to the beds without even bothering about the bathroom. They had to be wakened by the driver, and Farquharson went bleary-eyed to the door.

2

September 14–15, 1965

THE driver had the face of a converted demon, so they all rode in the back seat, Jamie on his father's knee. They were going into Ibadan, and there was a Shell station at the first highway corner. Later, the road turned at the bottom of a dip, and they saw a man crouched naked on a stone, in the middle of a muddy pool, bathing himself with splashes of his hands. Farquharson tried, almost involuntarily, to see whether he was a bull or not, and couldn't tell. Legends of giant African equipment surfaced briefly in his mind, and he touched himself through his trousers and was content about comparisons, amused at himself, and well at home.

They passed a cattle market on one side of the road, a slum on the other. Farquharson didn't know where to look, turned gawking from black beasts to smeared walls and vegetables—and when he swung his head he was suddenly staring into a thin face of power, almost frighteningly austere and devious, and caught in a flash the man's dull white robe and huge umbrella with segments of red, green, blue, and yellow, and then the crowding narrow sea of black heads and horns. They popped over the railway tracks.

"I suppose I ought to warn you," Ormford had written, "that you aren't going to find it very African. There's a hotel that's so modern they can't bear to finish building it, but the rest is North American suburbs. You'll have seen it all before. Except maybe Our Lady of Lourdes (I think), who stands in front of one of the schools in a tremendous amount of correct grey grotto next to a burning garbage dump. *That* I suppose is African."

26

"It wouldn't be African, the man said," Farquharson muttered as they raced between concrete ditches and came suddenly to a traffic roundabout with a view over a white gas station, and a billboard with pictures of money on it.

They raced on, veered to the left into a gully: the road was narrower, the ditches precipitous; people crowded the street; concrete terraces hung beside the road like decks as they descended; it looked as if everyone were posing and showing off his clothes. Then the car went up again, with pedestrians jammed against its windows. The sidewalk was filled with women selling things out of round trays and little tables, boisterous immobile women with many children. Farquharson saw tiny tins, miniature boxes of detergent, a few little bottles: stuff to play store with. A woman looked at him with a fierce grin. "Master! You buy from me!"

So he tried his Yoruba and said, "*Bẹ́ẹ̀ kọ́*," hoping to get the slide right on the first syllable: *thus-not* or, with a modest, enthusiastic twitch of the mouth, "No."

Words broke; another woman almost reached her hand into him; then the traffic moved, and they got up to the corner and were parked off the road in front of a large dusty store. They pushed a shopping cart on a grey concrete floor, buying liquor and treats for Jamie, who stood up in the cart and jumped. But one wheel stuck, and Farquharson kept steering into the shelves. At the cash register he couldn't help staring at the girl's hair, so she stared back. She had spider's legs all over her head. Her face mixed cold, sharp dignity and sulkiness, she spoke the prices as if she could shame him with the figures. His lips tucked inwards in a tiny moment of suppression; then he pulled his hand out of his pocket with the money in it, paid her with the four out-of-date pound notes that he still had (he could see the new ones sitting in the cash register, chalky-smooth red notes with a modern building on them) and got back a penny with a hole in it, two shillings, a green crisp bill and a little purple one like a muddy rag. He felt that she was almost challenging him to take this one, so he looked at it, smiled, and put it away.

27

They rode back the way they had come, and he saw a cemetery beside the road, behind bushes and trees. He grinned at it. Jamie was half asleep, his head tucked against his father's chest.

When they got back, Ogundele met them, showed them the Arts Building (it was raining), then told the driver to take them once around the compound and went back to the shelter of the porter's office to smile and wave at them. They were taken quickly past a lot of signs with names on them, and saw hedges and flowering trees, and long houses close to the ground. The road wandered among huge lots with garages and servants' quarters, dead-ending now at stripped ground and stark ugly flats, now by a romantic little sunken lake with a white tree standing in it. They bestowed a curse on the name plate of the house they hadn't got (they knew its address). Then they were swooped around, taken down a long road with a playing field beside it, driven slowly around a corner past a small theatre and straight up to a passage-way through the Administration Building. The driver said, "You get the mail here," so Farquharson asked for some, but there wasn't any. Then they were zigzagged through little streets and dumped off at the Catering Flats. They got out of the car feeling bruised, and as if they were going to be put into a cupboard.

Farquharson had expected twilight to be fast but not noisy. They sat at their table with their spoons in their hands, stunned. The air shrieked: insect legs, tree frogs, white noise breaking from everywhere simultaneously and shifting as their heads turned. Jamie said, "Birds?" and his eyes were wide, but very stolid. A woman at the next table said, "You get used to it. After a few weeks you won't even think you hear it."

So they threw pieces of conversation over their shoulders.

Suddenly the room was invaded by a round-faced, happy man in peach-coloured damask pyjamas, with a shimmering little matching cap forced on to his head. He pointed and said, "From the plane. I should have thought to ask if you were coming here. Forgive my incompetence, Dr. Farquharson. My name is Femi Balogun. I am Professor of Linguistics, and Dean of Arts for the moment. I have been informed that you are here, and you *are* here, and will you have lunch with me, all of you, at my house, and I'll send a car—or perhaps you have one?"

Farquharson said, "We haven't anything yet. Not even a house."

"Oh indeed, I heard of that." The man spread his hands, as if to encompass pride. "We are not simply incompetent, Dr. Farquharson. We are sometimes quite complexly incompetent. But there *are* reasons. I'm afraid a man with seniority absolutely refused to move out, after having said he would. Consequently there is at the moment nowhere else to put you." He looked as if he were going to challenge some North American realization about doing good, and then said, "An expatriate, I'm afraid."

"Forgive me for not recognizing you," Farquharson said, feeling as if this breezy formality was a kind of trap, "but, if you remember, on the plane you were upside-down."

"Nor was I dressed in quite such clothes." Farquharson, thus forced to acknowledge what he had been decently pretending not to see, nodded his head. "I go to dinner now," Balogun said, "to defend my system of Yoruba orthography to a visiting American professor with excellent connections whom I must therefore cultivate. And disarm slightly; hence the clothes. One-fifteen tomorrow? Sixteen Sankore. Any driver will know the way. Welcome to Ibadan." He bowed. "And Mrs. Farquharson. We will have food for the little boy. Ó d'àbọ̀."

Farquharson raised his hand and said "Ó d'àbọ̀" from the far side of the table, almost it, seemed, properly.

"You speak?" Balogun turned about in mid-flight, pleased, but still blandly challenging.

"I read a book."

"Ah! If you trespass into Yoruba with books, my friend, there will be trouble. The books require the Latin alphabet."

When Farquharson turned back he found Joan looking rather sadly at him. She said, "Don't *I* get to talk?"

Suspended time. Nothing attached to anything. Roads, houses, meaningless people, jostled for attention. "We're here," Joan said; then, "Aren't we?" and she looked indecisively around their room with its brown furniture clumped in the middle. "Didn't you buy some beer?"

"Scotch. Only we don't have water."

She said, "Yes we do," and took ice water out of a tiny refrigerator in the corner.

"Scared?"

"Maybe a little," she said, grimacing over her drink. (Joan recognized whiskey mainly as a medicine.) "It isn't Europe, is it? Well, the store looks manageable." She put the university's "Notes for Newcomers" on the seat beside her. " 'The Senior Staff Shop,' " she read. "We haven't seen that, have we?"

"Must be over by the Club. You want me to walk there tomorrow?" She couldn't go with Jamie, because the stroller was lost in Lagos, but he felt he had stepped across her territory. He leaned over. " 'Seven,' " he read. " 'Transport. A car is a necessity.' "

"We've got to buy a car."

"*And* hire servants," he said. He started laughing. "Look at us," he said, to her bewildered faint annoyance (she had to listen to the insects, if she wanted to hear him laugh—he had by far the happiest laugh she had ever heard: perhaps she had, not fallen in love, but steered into a marriage because of it—the man who could laugh so openly and without fuss had to be, perhaps, good for her). "Lining up all the things we have to do, and you're so tired you can't even drink your drink. Can we go to bed?"

"I have to drink it up," she said, evading him.

"Sitting in the bed."

But they had two beds, side by side.

She bathed, put on a green nightgown, brushed her hair. Farquharson lay on his bed holding the now-warm bottom of the glass against his stomach, spread his toes down to the corners, and eased his legs by stretching them and his stomach by sucking it in. He felt the hard pillow hot beneath the prickles of his hair and thought that he would change his shorts in the morning, but for tonight would leave them on. It would be more sensible to sleep naked and medieval. He didn't do it. He breathed, and the glass on his stomach rose and fell. "I never knew anyone," his wife said, "who was so damned pleased about being alive. Can we go to sleep without your admiring your diaphragm?"

"Actually," he said, at a moment's loss, "it was my kneecap."

He was fond of her. He reached his hand to the light and finished the whiskey in the dark.

Ogundele had to write a note to get them a car for the next few days: the first obligation was apparently finished with the first drive. So Farquharson spent one morning in trudging to Ogundele's office, to the Staff Store, which was indeed beside the Club, a tiny concrete box choked with enough heat and humidity to nauseate a man, to the bookstore for a map and a couple of Nigerian novels, and then back to the Catering Flats with Chinua Achebe in one hand and a half dozen of beer under one arm, to find the second driver scowling on the doorstep, waiting for him.

"How long's *he* been here?"

"One whole hour. We've had people wanting to be servants. I've sent three of them away. Look," she said.

"Dear sir," he read, skipping, "regarding my conduct and ability, I must frankly state that my Testimonials are here available to testify."

"Jamie was scared of him."

"And the others?"

"Well, one stood in the window and said 'Madam' about sixteen times. He looked diseased. And then there's 'my eleven years experience in the domestic work and I will surely discharge my duties very satisfactorily.' He kept looking at my purse."

The new driver took them behind the airport on a fast, desolate road over a railway crossing, then between distant back yards and the uninhabited ends of streets. At one point there was a formal entry into a suburb on the right, and Farquharson's eyes snatched at a name in yellow letters on the stone and he said, "Awoḷọwọ!"

"What?"

"The name on the post."

"Who's he?"

"Premier before Independence here," he said. "They put him in jail for something."

"Is big man, master," the driver said, keeping his head set.

"Well, what did he do?" He could feel his wife wishing him not to be too democratic.

"He go to Federal Parliament, master. Leave Akintọla here for premier. Akintọla have big big fight. That when they put Awolọwọ in jail. Very bad time, master. Prime Minister, he take away our government." He took a hand with a scolding finger off the wheel. "That something we remember, master."

A car swept closely past them. Joan said, "Farq, let him drive," and information stopped. They slowed at a long cheap bungalow of a building on their right and veered quickly up a driveway into a parking lot in front of a very modern bank. Yes, Mr. Farquharson's deposit from Canada had been received; yes, here was his chequebook, and his cash. He stood for a moment, looking at a huge airy room and at a man with a bile-green shirt, furiously arguing. Then he went to the car contented, slick bills in serial order held in his hands, saw a woman in a dirty wrapper climbing from the road below, and, embarrassed at the size of his wealth, put the money away and was driven to his lunch.

Balogun's living room was cool and huge, with a few masks on the walls, as if out of duty. Sherry and fellow Canadians were produced to make them feel at home, and they met Mrs. Balogun, who launched a strident noise towards a servant, then turned to them like a schoolmarm: "And would you meet Mrs. Isobel Eayrs," a North American small-town girl in a white dress, "and Professor Edward Eayrs, known here as Ted. Ted is in History. They are your compatriots."

"Were, Joseph, were," Eayrs said. "We don't go home."

"Joseph?" Farquharson said.

"Joseph Olufẹmi, Professor Farquharson. You'll find most of us here have the divided name. Two worlds in one: or in two. But it wouldn't do for a fighting Yoruba linguist not to have a Yoruba name." He was preening in ordinary clothes. "*J. Olufẹmi.* And the 'Olufẹmi' means . . .?"

"Something loves me," Farquharson answered, waiting to drink his sherry.

"God." He balanced. "And the other name means roughly 'master of the house of war'. 'Joseph' is no bad third—if it is the Egyptian Joseph. A bridge."

Joan looked at Jamie snuggling with luxurious competence back against his father's arm, and asked if Nigeria was a good place for children.

The Farquharsons had hardly had their sleep when there was a formal knocking at their door. They opened it to find the porter from the Arts Building, in his uniform, with a letter, and two men in the shadow behind him, as if hung from strings.

Joan said, "From Ogundele," and handed the letter to her husband, and Farquharson suddenly wished he had the "Notes for Newcomers" open beside him. All he could remember was "the employer provides uniforms".

"Come in, Jack," he said, having picked up the porter's name in Ogundele's office, and he turned to get the edge of the desk under his rump.

"I have asked Mr. Okpata," the letter said, "to find you some servants for your approval," and then a few words of praise, in advance, for his choice. Farquharson put out his hand for their testimonials. He didn't think of the gesture as arrogant, but his wife did.

"To whom it may concern: This is to certify that Mr. Elias Ateghie has been my steward for this last year. He is careful and honest, and quiet, and knows how to cook, but I am returning to England, and cannot therefore continue to give him employment. I recommend him. Malcolm Halloway, Assistant Professor of History, University of Ife." But the date was nine months old. Elias Ateghie waited.

"Stanley Ademu is a first-rate driver and mechanic. Therefore

33

it is with some regret that I acknowledge that I have now no necessity of him. He has been giving utter satisfaction in his performance and it will be pleasure to hear how he is suitably re-established. Sincerely yours, B. O. Ogunbọmẹhin.''

The driver raised his head as a shy boy might, pleased but subordinate. "They learn to drive," he said.

"Well, my wife doesn't drive," Farquharson said. "Of course, we haven't got a car yet," The driver smiled.

Joan said, "And we haven't a house."

Jack Okpata beamed at her, a bird-man, preening. "We are working on a house, madam. You will need these good men."

"Why should we hire people before we've got work for them?"

Jack Okpata said, "You are early, madam. Others come. They will hire."

Farquharson said, "Get 'em while the supply lasts!" and folded the letters.

"It'll last!" ("She was signalling, Don't surrender; back me up.")

But Farquharson had taken a liking to the driver. Ademu's eyes were uncommunicative, but he stood attentively, easily, and his face was intelligent. Joan had no choice but to address herself to the other, the eager, abased, old-looking Elias, who nodded with enthusiasm as if his head might be thrown at somebody. Okpata blessed them from a corner, looking half like a patriarch and half, Farquharson thought, like wild Prince Hal.

So they had two servants. Farquharson said, "I want a beer," and had one. Joan said, "I think we've been very foolish. We should have seen more people before we hired anyone."

And in the evening there was nothing to do. Farquharson lay beside Jamie's crib and sang to him, and Joan picked up an Achebe novel and couldn't like it. Against his will Farquharson found himself at the desk, with another beer, thinking of lecturing. Joan looked up and said, "What are you going to do without your notes?"

He had a big back solidly planted over the desk. That was what she had seen when she came down the aisle to marry him: the big triangular back of a man so confident that he didn't even turn around. As always, she wondered at him. She said suddenly, "I like you, Farquharson," and felt as dishonest as the words, even while she meant them.

He shoved a hand out behind him, as if to say, "Hold onto me."

So she tickled the palm of his hand with a fingernail. He said, "Coquette." He sounded warm, and pleased, and amused.

"Oh well," she said, "everything else is all right, isn't it?"

3

September 16–18, 1965

THE English Department was on the second floor of the Arts Building, on a long gallery of white pillars and pierced concrete railings. Farquharson's name was already up, and he ran his finger over the letters, pleased as usual with the amount of print required.

Ogundele had told him of a car. Joan wanted a barber, and he had shoved that to Jack Okpata for resolution. Now he was faced by the empty offices of his colleagues, and this corridor, or gallery, or whatever it should be called, lined with dark plywood doors and blue louvred windows that he couldn't see through. (He patted the door again, checking in his pocket that he still had the loose key for it.) He walked to the bridge that joined the two halves of the building and looked down into a lower courtyard with stepping-stones in the grass, across at a huge vine thick with purple flowers, then at the lecture theatre with its grille-work wall of concrete block, and at the library beyond, looking rather like a Zeppelin hangar. Well, there was no one around, except Ogundele in his office, thinking, perhaps, about the Farquharsons' house, if there was going to be such a thing.

His office had a hidden cubbyhole on one side with a desk, a view of an array of red-earth tennis courts, and a blackboard with the words "Lord David Cecil: Pathos" written on it; the rest was a largish room, with the continuation of the blackboard streaked deep in chalk, and far more chairs than he seemed to have a right to. To prove that he was there he had taken the few books that had travelled with him and put Chaucer, *Rasselas,* and *The*

36

Anatomy of Criticism on the shelves. Childlike ownership made him go back and look at them.

When he came out again, he saw somebody coming out four doors down, wearing turquoise plastic sandals. The man raised a hand and Farquharson noticed the arresting flash of the pale Negro palm. So he called, "I'm Farquharson."

"I am Oscar Nwonkwo. I am a poet. Have you a place to live?"

"Are those related statements?"

They were aware of sudden friendship like something nervous in the air. "It frequently takes the artist to be aware of practicality. Who have you met?"

"You. Professor Balogun. Mr. Ogundele." He pointed across the courtyard to the entrance. "And Smiling Jack. Oh. Eayrs."

"Poor Eayrs, perennially last in the catalogue. Where are you now?"

Farquharson told him. Nwonkwo said, "Then we must come and see you," and then, quite abruptly, went down the stairs and left Farquharson holding his door key, stuck in the corridor (or gallery) because he hadn't locked his door. Below, flowering trees stuck out of circular concrete benches, and a line of fire extinguishers crowded against a little wall across the courtyard. "They deliberated awhile what was to be done," he murmured leaning against the railing, as if he could mock himself, "and resolved, when the inundation should cease, to return to Abyssinia."

Ogundele's idea of a car was a wreck belonging to a friend. Farquharson turned it down.

"Professor Farquharson", the note said, "as discussed this morning, here is the barber."

A wizened, ice-cold scarred man in discoloured white, with a fish-net undershirt, sat Jamie, wrapped, on a chair, and cut his hair, chewing it with old clippers, while Jamie's eyes became very

37

large. Farquharson asked how much and on being told five shillings, paid five shillings and never thought to bargain Jamie's skull shone like dishevelled velvet.

"How's our house, Mr. Ogundele?"

"Sir, I have a line on one."

Nwonkwo called to him from the upper railing, "Do you have a car?"

So that afternoon, with Stanley Ademu and Oscar, he went to look at a withered Peugeot, and with the owner and yet another friend they all stood around in the Motor Transport Department and went through ceremonies of inspection and evaluation and indications of bargain, all of which Farquharson watched as a game which, to his delight, he wouldn't play.

"There is my friend's car," Oscar said. "What do you think, Henry? Should my friend sell it?"

They were on the roadway, walking under trees.

"I haven't been Henried for fifteen years."

Stanley said firmly, "I do not like that car." To Farquharson's relief, he didn't then say "master."

"Well, it was all very cheerful," Farquharson said, "but I *think* they were out to skin me."

"In this country," Oscar said, "you have been skinned already."

"Not Farquharson."

"Oh yes, my friend. You are an *oyíbó*, a 'peeled person'. You have been spelled out in Yoruba, and Yoruba is of course *the* language of the world. Yoruba, according to one student of it"— and his voice waved the words as if they were someone else's ridiculous and mislaid banner—" 'is an endless ocean!' So how can I arrange to have you skinned for the purchase of this car?"

"This friend's car."

"My poor friend! After all, he needs to sell his car, and *he* drives it. But do you need to buy? No."

So Farquharson said, "Thanks anyway," and walked back to the Catering Flats.

38

"If the master still wishes a car . . ." Stanley began.

"I've been 'sir' in classrooms for twelve years," Farquharson said, "I'll be 'sir' here."

"There is a man his wife works at the Clinic, sir. She has a car. Is good car, sir. I know this car." He added, "We can see tomorrow morning. I hope she is in Lagos now."

"Stanley, is this the car you want?"

"Sir had to see the car of his friend."

Therefore it was all set up.

"No car!" Farquharson called, but Joan looked a little scared and said, "Where were you?"

The university car had come to take them into town. "I wanted to buy a toy," she said, "but there weren't any."

Farquharson heard aggrieved disappointment, and wanted to put his arms around her. It wasn't an important sad moment, but she had been alone in a store he hadn't seen, and her little boy hadn't seen her buy a toy. He wanted to laugh for her, or cry, "Joan, it's a new country!" So he had to hug her. Otherwise he would have had to see her eyes. Then she said, "I had a man at the window. And he wouldn't go away."

Very solemnly then, because they were so far from home, Farquharson played with Jamie and told him a silly story.

"And oh, if you just weren't so magnificent in your own eyes!" Joan said.

"Something's wrong?" he said, when they were alone as adults in their living room.

"Ha," she said. "Maybe I won't like Africa."

So he told her about the cars, but if it was to cheer her up, it didn't. She said, "They cheat so!"

"You bought something, didn't you?"

Reluctantly, she gave him a necklace of long white translucent beads. He had to pull them out of her clenched hand and let them swing. "He asked three pounds," she said. "I got him down to two. Moonstones, he said. I'd be ashamed to put them on."

An attempt to like the country, he thought, feeling sick for her, as if he were supposed to become angry but couldn't make it. He put the beads over her head. "So you were had," he said. "*I almost bought a car.*"

But he lay awake that night wondering just how efficiently she was going to dislike the place, once she had started to.

When he woke, *very* early, Stanley was crouched on the small paved terrace outside his window; fine-boned, flat-cheeked, with tiny ears and a forehead cut with a few shallow even creases. His mouth was a small contented shape with lips no fuller than Farquharson's. His nose was small and wide, and the end turned under: "A Jewish nose," Farquharson thought, "only somebody flattened it. If you were in a classroom, I would have taught you three times over, in pink and brown." One of the fractious ones, he thought, who never have quite enough integrity that they can afford to stop presuming on it. "I wonder who besides him gets a cut if I buy this car?"

Stanley sat with his shirt open. Somehow it was a surprise that his chest should be also black. Quietly, lest he should be known to see, and thus as much seen as known, Farquharson got out of bed. The eyes outside the window moved and saw him. Farquharson made no acknowledgement, but, shaving in the bathroom, wondered what it would be like to look at bare pink skins if they were the one per cent exception, and your own was black, blue-black like Ogundele's or a black-cat brown like Stanley's. What would the white look like? *A Passage to India*'s "pinko-grey"? No, that was the unloving white eye labelling itself.

Something vulnerable and soft? "*Oyíbó: the peeled people.*"

While he shaved, he felt with the other hand along the defence-less forearm. It was sparsely furred, dry; it was his boundary, mottled pink, pale, brownish, ambiguous grey discolouration over the veins on the back of his hand—flesh colour, he thought, self-pleased, if you averaged it, generalized it, Platonized or eroticized it. But there was no armour in it, no defence. No clothing, either, for better or worse. He toyed with the possibility of a version of the Fall of Man in which Man changed colour, and thought of the fig leaves of the Vatican Museum. Green fig leaves on black, he decided, would only be tempting gaiety.

"Hi-hi," came from Jamie's bedroom, half sung, a morning praise.

Farquharson answered with a karate fighter's "*Hai!*" whereupon Joan called out that she *had* been awake, and the day started.

"Ormford's supposed to be coming in today," Farquharson said.

Sparse items, piecemeal. Personality was in abeyance, he thought, until it could assemble its materials: car, boss, house, trade, geography, something to do.

To get to the Clinic they had to walk a long way around. (Farquharson asked for mail: he didn't think Joan's brother had ever been known to write to her.) There was nobody at the Clinic, and no car parked, so they went to the back, and there was a huddle of people against the closed glass doors. Farquharson felt trouble, and started to explain about the car, with Stanley at his elbow like a mute interpreter.

A woman in a nurse's uniform suddenly spoke, but not in English. A much too handsome young man looked at them both. "Well, if she isn't here," Farquharson said, "we can come back."

"Mrs. Kayode has had an accident," a man said. "In her car. She has been killed. You will not buy this car." His voice was a stretched skin, drumming of itself.

They left, objects of unwelcome awe, and no apology would cure them of it. Across the road a drive went down to a house, a cheap lane on the littered edge of a forest. The house was a long way down. "That ends the car hunt for today," Farquharson said. "Let's just go home."

The street they walked on was a tunnel under trees. "She was pleasant woman, sir," Stanley said. Then, practically, "We have to go to Ijẹbu Bye-Pass now, to find a car."

They turned silently up to the entrance highway, and parted at it. "I think that God grants us no ill luck," Stanley said, and went away. Farquharson plodded toward the small cross-street that would get him back to the Catering Flats. It was a dull stale morning, full of sun. "Obong Road", he read, turning off the dual pavement and noticing the wide ditches on each side. "Here we drain by valleys and not slots." But bodies were in his mind, as if he could see Mrs. Kayọde there in the grassy ditch beside him. It looked like a comfortable ditch to lie in.

And because he didn't want to walk straight home, he went to the Staff Store and came home with candies and beer.

They had a long day then, with nothing but three books. In the late afternoon Farquharson and Jamie were rolling a pink ball back and forth on their narrow terrace, while Joan, reading inside, seemed to have faded into darkness. Then a small bright-red car whirled into the noose-shaped end of the driveway, and a man with a water-slicked wide fringe of rust-red hair got out of the front seat as if all labour was difficulty, showed a faded shirt covered with red-and-yellow ducks, and said, "So you're Farquharson! I'm Ormford. Welcome, if that's the word."

"Arrives the boss," Farquharson thought.

"Okay, Jamie, let's go in." He picked up the ball, rose to open the door, and found it locked.

Joan said, "You can come around," and was, Farquharson was afraid, grossly embarrassed when she found who she'd kept out.

Professor Ormford gave the impression of a weary man galvanized into walking only by an incurable gregariousness. He took a beer, downed it in no time, told them about Wimbledon, heard the whole story of their trip to Africa—talking, it seemed, at cross-purposes all the time, his voice dancing with a light, continual unembarrassed stammer, gagging occasionally—he never tried to change the impeding words. He noted the dilemma of their house, went directly to the problem of a car, knew Mrs. Kayọde, appreciated that Farquharson would have enjoyed the car, and said, "Oh, well, the Lagos-Ibadan road, that's *like* that: the most dangerous stretch of hh-highway in the world, I always tell myself that I ought to gg-go by Abẹokuta.

"You want to do something before term," he said to Farquharson. "Mark some scripts for me. You might as well have an

42

idea of what you're up against. I'll have them put in your office. Do you have a typewriter?"

"On the high seas."

"I'll get you one. Servants?"

"Two so far."

"Fine." He looked at the beer. "Only if I may recommend," he said, "*Top*, not *Star*. *Top* are new and terribly anxious for sales, and consequently they don't charge you a sixpence deposit on the bb-bottles."

Joan shouted, "Sixpence!" and never, Farquharson thought, would she be more completely the righteous image of a Western housewife.

"Bb-bottles are very, very scarce in Nigeria. If you gg-go for a prescription you have to take your own bb-bottle or pay for one—and it *could* be a bb-beer bottle. I'll bet the servants steal them, don't they?"

"No," she said, "but I wondered why they were wiping them so carefully and putting them beside the bookcase."

"The survival of bb-beer bottles is the beginning of honesty. Don't look for more, though. Don't *ever* look for more." Then he said, "Moonstones, I see? You've met a Hh-hausaman already."

"He called himself Mr. Quality."

"Oh for hh-heaven's sakes! No, we have a manageable one. Maybe I can ask Peg to send him round to you. Well, I must gg-go. Come to tea tomorrow. I'll have to send for you." He pointed. "We're at the far end.

"On second thought," he said, "I'll send Nicodemus with the scripts. He has to gg-go to Abadina anyway. Or maybe the cattle market. I don't really know *wh-where* he lives, if he doesn't vanish in a flash of sulphur under an iroko tree. You'll want something to do, won't you?" The door closed.

"Well," Joan said, "there's your boss."

4

AFTER dark, Farquharson opened the door to a bullet-shaped head and a pair of small shoulders even more sloping than his own, and was handed a bunch of papers and a little Italian typewriter. This, Farquharson supposed, was Nicodemus, but the thick and too-smooth eyelids were turned down, so there were no eyes to see. By noon the next day he had gone through thirty versions of the views of marriage expressed in the Franklin's Tale, Othello's noble motives in killing Desdemona, and whether *The Playboy of the Western World* was a poetic play or not.

Peg Ormford seemed a pretty woman who was scrambling to remain twenty-five, which she hadn't been for ten years, and who had no conversation but housework and no housework to talk about. As the afternoon showed, she took it out in a proprietor's fussing about politics and the respective fixities of the tribes. Ormford shouted, "Michael!" and the steward seemed to possess the house so absolutely that Farquharson felt as if he should do homage for his glass. They sat in a Spartan living room astonishingly broken by a three-foot drop across the middle, unconvincingly railed. Outside was an unrailed high terrace and a view. Farquharson mounted guard, breathed air, and looked at a long sloping lawn and palm trees, shadowy near distances, and the cloudy sky. Had he been a cat, he thought, he would have purred. (Peg discussed the natives, Ormford the expatriates.) Palms were feather dusters made out of cheap painted metal. He thought of Mrs. Kayọde and wondered what colour the car had been. With beer and clean sandwiches, and silvery curling shrimp

44

chips, he was prepared to watch the scenery absorb the sun, to listen to the insects grind the night with carborundum wheels, to be content that nothing happened any more, that the state of hell that was neither innocence nor experience was manageably occupiable, an edgy, empty, and contenting state. But he wasn't able to sit there self-companionable for the night. They went home, to the Catering Flats, and ate English curry.

That evening the Ormfords suddenly appeared with a huge gaunt Scot in charge of housing. "We thought of Kongi or Bodija, but Ormford said you were promised the compound, so we have a house. There's a family moving from number one Jaja on the twenty-eighth. Can you stand nine days?"

Farquharson said, "If my stomach can. What are Kongi and Bodija?"

"Suburbs," Ormford said. "H-housing developments. They're all jerry-built. I used to live in Bb-bodija." He mimed a shudder; his wife didn't echo him.

"One thing," the official said. "The house is bigger than you need by one bedroom. If somebody throws rank"—he paused and thought—"then *you* can play the game of refusing to move out," and he was so pleased that he was still chuckling when the Ormfords took him home.

WP2471 entered Farquharson's consciousness on a pale sun-stricken used-car lot on the Ijẹbu Bye-Pass. "There's the British Council Building," Ormford said on their way there, with Stanley Ademu crouched in possession of the back seat. "Now left, and around the roundabout. There's the dental clinic down there, and the post office. There's Cocoa House." He had to name every landmark. None of them meant anything. They got out at a very dusty, very empty garage and showroom with a little lot of perhaps eight cars beside it. There was a white station-wagon, a few small sedans, a few cars obviously unsuitable whether wrecks or not, and a tan-brown Wolseley sedan with a highly polished grille and what looked like zebra-skin upholstery sealed under a plastic cover. Ormford amused himself by kicking tires, as if on a theory to annoy someone if he did it long enough.

They bargained, half-heartedly, took the car for a drive, bargained again.

Finally: "You are a professor, sir We can make a price for you of three hundred and seventy-five."

Farquharson had to see the chief accountant, arrange for a car-loan, haggle for its terms, submit to what he thought was an indecent querying; but he wanted the brown Wolseley, and if he had to fight to get a loan approved, he would.

So he bought the car. Suddenly, Farquharson thought, the roads began to make sense.

That night there was a small violent storm for celebration. When it was over they put Jamie into the front seat, went for a hesitant ride around the university compound, and then, feeling greatly daring, took the car out behind the airport, with Kongi on the left, and drove aimlessly through Bodija between the stripped lots and the houses full of electric light until they came out at the Ọyọ road, and so drove home, having made a circuit, and knowing where they were.

And the next day he went to get his licence and the transfer of ownership, and was taken somewhere in Ibadan to a huge green house made over where he waited as if in a stripped and desecrated living room while Stanley took Mrs. Farquharson to go shopping in the Kingsway. And when he had paid his money, signed his documents, and got ink all over his fingers, with much intruded help from bystanders, they went out to the car to put a paper circle on the windshield. Stanley pointed to a house in a wide lawn behind a locked gate. They were parked in front of it. "This Awolọwọ's house, sir," Stanley said. "His wife live here."

"The politician," Farquharson said to Joan. "The one in jail. He tried to boot Akintọla out as premier and there was a riot in Parliament. Is Awolọwọ a good man?" he said suddenly to Stanley.

"Sir, he build Cocoa House."

"There's Africa," Farquharson thought, "if I can understand it."

46

By some bewildering route Stanley brought them back to the store where Joan had been going shopping: a regular department store with a big parking lot and an edge-on view of the new slab of Cocoa House. When they got out Farquharson saw a beggar, in white, with withered limbs where the skin was drawn so tight it glowed. And then another, with one leg, leaning on a pole like a quarterstaff, looking like a happy king. The man at Farquharson's feet looked like a debased jester. He said, "Master, master."

Farquharson had never been so ruthlessly aware of the plain success of his own body. He was strong and without disease, beside a car he owned, and one hand was reached down to a two-and-a-half-year-old who took a stolid delight in things. So he said "No" to the beggars, sharply and without distaste, and walked Jamie between the cars, and in the process left Joan and Stanley to follow along behind. At the bottom of the steps somebody else tried to beg; at the top somebody tried to sell him a watch. He walked into air-conditioning.

Two or three African children were jiggling about at the foot of a little escalator. Somebody chased them off. He saw a luxurious book department, racks of North American greeting cards, toiletries, compacts, a travel agent's counter, office supplies, cheap scribblers, Scotch tape, drinking straws, gold paper doilies. The people moved as if they were on show: white women in cotton summer dresses, all rather faded; black women in lace and velvet or pillarlike ambiguous prints; white men in wilted shirts; black men in bunched exuberant robes or khaki uniforms; a cream-robed nun, smooth as a statue. Joan took him into the foods. "Look," she said, "you can get everything."

Chocolates, liquor, honey, tea, squash, milk; soup, jam; every possible cereal; tinned fruit and vegetables; tinned seafood, pies, hams, chickens; Austrian toilet paper; American peanuts; New Zealand meat, Nigerian meat, frozen everything miniature liqueurs, a huge bottle of champagne, and a rack of spices and herbs, all from Montreal. The cream-coloured nun went from sandwich spreads to caviar, to Swiss powdered soups. Stanley pushed Jamie in an extra cart and said to him, "I am your driver,

47

sir!" Farquharson felt as if he were pulling one of everything off the shelf to look at it. And Joan, who had shopped there and not gone home yet, started again.

"Cornflakes, four-and-six," she said. "What's four-and-six?"

"Did I see lamb chops at eighteen shillings a pound?"

"Then we won't eat lamb chops."

"Vodka thirty-two bob."

"Is that cheap or not?"

"It surely couldn't set us back more than the beer's doing."

"Okay, buy a bottle."

He came back saying, "There is also whiskey, gin, brandy, rum, and somebody's medicinal something, *all* thirty-two a bottle." He held out brandy: " '*Élaboré en Nigéria.*' I couldn't resist that."

They were checked through by an aristocratic, flirtatious girl with a running eye; three Kingsway boys quarrelled over who should carry their purchases. Farquharson settled the matter by giving the bag to Stanley and picking Jamie up, and they walked, unpopularly, through the lobby and out the door, which a doorman held for them while he quarrelled with someone outside who braced his hands against the stone rail behind him and quarrelled back.

WP2471 had a flat tire.

"I hope someone has removed the air," Stanley said, and sent them back into the store until he should get the tire changed, there being no air pump within sight.

They saw a sign that said there was a restaurant upstairs, so they sat with soft drinks and looked out through slots of concrete to see the town.

Soon they were at the window, craning their heads this way and that, to see beyond the concrete baffles.

They saw a pink church, a hill with a big yellow building on it. They saw the land roll and buck, covered to the horizon with pale rusted metal roofs. It was a *big* city. Jamie got restive, and they went down again. Stanley had the car canted at a great angle, and was labouring over the last of the replacement of the spare tire.

At the gate going out they were shouted at by a child with coat hangers, and a beggar spoke to them, incomprehensibly, in English.

They turned past Cocoa House, a tall thin hexagon with blue panels under the windows. They went around a roundabout, past a large service station, looked into a green hollow with a smoking pile of something at the far end below Barclays Bank, did another roundabout, and sped home up the Ọyọ road, past the sheds of Dugbẹ Market, the waiting buses, the neon sign mounted on the tower of a brown building, the hotel on the hill, the cemetery, Bodija, the railroad crossing, the cattle market, the airport, the Shell station, the university gate, and home. "I begin," Farquharson thought, "to own the world I move in." And his wife had a very careful face when they got home.

Her maiden name had been Dill. On occasion he called her "Pickle." He did now: "What is it, Pickle?"

"I'm afraid," she said.

"Of what?"

"That I'm not going to like it."

"Seriously not like?"

"Yes."

"Why?"

"Somebody let the air out of our tire," she said, "didn't they?"

"I don't know."

"That's just it. You'll like the place. Whatever it does."

"Oh, come on, you aren't going to go rushing me down a garden path of what I'm going to *have* to do, are you? What's wrong with liking it?"

"The beggars," she said. "The dirt. I bet you haven't even seen the dirt."

His feet were like soft rubber in his shoes. He kicked off the shoes, pulled the socks off from a point at the toe, wiggled knobby toes, and thought that that much of dirt at least was true: his feet stank. "All right, you saw dirty places. Tell me, how many dirty *people* did you see? I didn't *smell* anyone."

She said, in a small voice, "Why are you attacking me?"

49

"Because somebody let the air out of the tire." The hot water spat as if to rage all over the tub.

"I did a wash this morning," she said. "I've been in twice to town. I haven't *seen* anyone."

He was taking his clothes off. That had to be her signal to leave the room. They might have been married for six years, but they still kept each other's privacies. Joan left him.

Farquharson ran a deep bath and sank himself in it as if he could pump relaxation out of his guts into his toes. Here he was in a big slant-backed bathtub, in the middle of West Africa, in a private skin of oil and steam, with soapsuds in his armpits and a window at his shoulder looking out on crinkled grass and the kind of spread-out suburbia that in his city only the rich had. "Now, I am alone," he said. Oversize Hamlet in a bathtub.

Then he was signing *Vissi d'arte*, and cutting it short in the usual fashion.

Beyond one door: his bedroom, his wife; beyond the other (there were two doors squeezed into one corner, both opening against the toilet bowl): his son, and the other bedroom. He was happily lost, alone, loneliness tugging sideways. When he stood drying himself on the soaking bathmat—and the trouble about being big was that so much water could drip off—he was as solitary as a bachelor and as much without a place to go. He had a half-comforting show-off gesture, for himself. He wrapped a hand around his genitals as if they were something separate from him, and pulled down, once. He called it "straightening his tie". He thought he'd done it as a boy to make his prick get longer. If he had, it had worked. But it was a grooming gesture, like matching the knots in his shoelaces (that was important) or making a straight part in his hair. Straightening his tie, the way he always pinched and tugged the knot on his real tie until it was a little too tight for the bigness of his neck and made his collar buckle. The satisfaction of checking the wallet in one pocket, the keys in another: all present and correct, everything working, and in order, his balls hanging secretly askew, with the left one lower.

It wasn't a thing he did before making love; or at least it hadn't been, for a long time. It wasn't a particularly sexual gesture. It just confirmed that he was all there, every part of him, the attentive residence and the accommodated resider. Henry John Farquharson, as ever was.

He called out, "I'm losing weight!"

"Lord David Cecil: Pathos." He kept the words on the blackboard, hoping by some process to find out what they had been put there for. He was going to lead off the first-year lectures, apparently, with the great vowel shift and the Franklin's Tale, and since he hadn't fully expected this he caught himself at times in idle hope for his mid-Atlantic notes. In the meantime he drew the vowel triangle, annotated consonant changes, had tinkerer's delight for a while, then stopped and mapped:

"1: Language; 2: Fourteenth Century; 3: Love.

"Poet as 'Maker': a) Language (Dante &c); b) Craftsman of words; c) *grand translateur*; d) 'Olde Bokes'; e) influences: poet as conveyor of tales & ideas; f) literature as *re*-definition."

On another card:

"Love! Sight. Lady hard to be won ('drede'). Service (poems &c.); self-subjection (focusses manhood, &c.). *Declaration.* Refusal. Service & Proof. Acceptance. *Secrecy!*"

"Parallel to mystics?" he wrote.

"*Sic et Non?*"

"Abelard's entire technique, when transferred from theology, as it was by the Courtly Lovers, and from matters of Government, into the worlds of private experience, private personality, and *private* love, became a means to recover and define the state of Innocence by pitching the elements of the state of Experience against each other, without escape. Innocence, in any *débat*, becomes the logical consequence of the uttermost that Experience can do to and about itself. In the triple suggested *débat* of the Franklin's Tale, the outcome is the identification of Innocence and 'fredom': '*Whiche was the mooste fre, as thinketh yow?*' "

It was doubtless proof of his own limitations that he had the minor and weeded-out parts of his thesis memorized so thoroughly. Wonderfully, he enjoyed that. The notes grew.

Oscar Nwonkwo put his head into the cubbyhole and said, "I hear you have procured a car?"

"No harm intended."

"Perfectly, but do you know whose car you got?"

"Oh, his name was on the form. Ọrẹ-something-or-other. Why? Is he well known?"

Oscar said, "Secretary, I believe, to an assistant to the Premier of the Western Region," and sat down on a little table.

"Well, well," Farquharson said. "Don't erase my talisman."

Oscar shifted his shoulder from "Pathos".

"WP2471?"

"Yes."

"In your own words, well, well."

"Oscar," Farquharson said, leaning forwards, pleased, "in all truth, do I look like an assistant's secretary?"

Nwonkwo spread his hands. "You could," he said, "be perhaps more popular in other cars."

"Oh, well, I'm told the man whose house we're moving into is a hotbed enthusiast for the Opposition. Do you think that will balance things?"

"You must take us a little seriously."

"I'll take it seriously if they start running me off the road. Oscar, I had fifty people around me while I changed the registration, and every damn one of them knew what the licence was. I tipped three of them for some reason, I remember. It'll get around."

"You never 'tip', Henry, you 'dash'. That is the universal word."

"All right, then, I dashed them. So where is the gentleman?"

"He is in England."

It was Farquharson's turn to spread his hands. He said, "Well?"

"You do *not* take us seriously!"

"All right," Farquharson said, becoming annoyed and halfway enjoying it. "Permanent licence plates, and I haven't seen a single other Wolseley, fair enough."

52

"There is a black one, also two green, one with a broken front."

"But no other brown Wolseleys?"

"No."

"Fine. But I still cannot possibly be taken for a Nigerian politician, on whatever side of the fence. I'm an *oyibo*."

"Lo, the conquering hero?"

Farquharson grinned. "No. The unconquering professor struggling into the state of Innocence. I think I'm going to enjoy that car." He made his face look serious. He said, "But thank you, Oscar."

"I am Onitsha Ibo," Oscar said, leaning forward as if to impress Farquharson with his hands. "Therefore it shouldn't matter to me which Yoruba faction fights with which, but there are alliances. The alliance now is Adegbenro's people with my people, and Akintola's people with the Sardauna in the North."

"Who's Adegbenro?"

"I think you should be made to pass an examination, my friend, before you come!"

"I don't know," Farquharson said. "I read books, but they didn't seem to help too much. I keep forgetting the names. I haven't got an adjusted eye for African names." As an excuse, he thought, that needed an excuse itself. He said, "There are so *many* names!"

"True. We have too much politics. Just remember that the Western government is allied, at this moment, to the central government and to the government of the North, and the Opposition, which is an alliance in itself, is, *at the moment*, allied to the government of the Eastern Region—and that the natural ruler of the alliance, at least according to half of the Yoruba in the West, is a political prisoner." He looked slightly embarrassed and added, "In the East," and then brightened and said, "but, I think, in Calabar, not in the Ibo region. Henry, will you sell your car?"

5

THEIR house-to-be was the one across from the Clinic. Joan wanted to make arrangements with Mrs. Onyeama about moving, but when Elias took a note over, he came back without an answer. "I asked if we could see the house," she said. "It wasn't a rude letter. Just could we see the house, and could I know anything about it that I had to know before we moved." So she sent Elias out with a rather North American list of things to buy: brooms, buckets, furniture wax, and so forth. Then she worried her husband's coxcomb with her fingers and said, "I'm going to see that house. Good heavens, I can at least ask her what size the sofa cushions are. Then I could buy the material for covers."

But she didn't get into the house, or even, in a way, close to it. They drove up in the afternoon, riding in the back seat like royalty, and were stopped by a servant in the driveway. "Master not home!"

"I want to see *Mrs.* Onyeama," Joan said, out of her window. Is *she* home?"

A big woman's voice cried, "Kalu!" from somewhere out of sight.

But Joan said, "I have to see the house: we're going to live here!"

A woman appeared, lavish in brown and green. She said, "Kalu!" Then, without even glancing at the car in her driveway, she went away. Joan sat white-faced, clutching at a raised half inch of window glass. Then Farquharson made a gesture for Stanley and they backed up and went to the Administration Building. Farquharson got out of the car for mail.

Joan saw Peg Ormford, and called, "Do you know what just happened to me?"

"What you need," Peg said, after peering in the window at her, "is a bit of getting it off your mind. Mr. Farquharson?" she called. "With your permission I'm going to take your wife with me."

He held the door for Joan, then folded himself in and took Jamie on his knee.

"You'll find my husband at the Club," Peg said. "Tell him you're *his* guest." And with a nod a little too bleak to be quite arch she went away, leading Joan off after her. They were already talking.

Farquharson opened an envelope and an airmail letter. They had come a quarter of the way around the world. Funny that they weren't interesting. "Okay, Stanley," he said, "let's see this Club."

Stanley tucked the car under a tree near the corner of some tennis courts. Outside the Staff Store a big man sitting like an idol above some small vegetables said, "Master, buy tomatoes? Spinach? Very good."

Farquharson took Jamie on a sidewalk past tennis courts and an asphalt parking lot. They came to an inattentive young man sitting in an entrance at a small table with an open notebook, and thus found the Club: a swimming pool framed by attachments; trellis, tables, a noticeboard, and a sort of fountain with water boiling over to splash concrete flanges. The clubhouse was a one storey half-circle, focussing on to the fountain with open walls and a canopy roof that sheltered a semicircle of huge chairs.

He walked into a curved sitting room with louvred windows, a mosaic partition, and a bar backed with a bamboo wall. Ormford was at the bar, talking with high delight to someone, and in a glassed room to the left, people were getting tables ready.

"Farquharson!" Ormford called. "Don't come near the bar! You've gg-got a child. What do you want?"

"One large, long beer. I'm to tell you I'm your guest."

"Oh well, we'll remedy that. Kalu, gg-give me the forms, will you?"

Ormford filled out a form. "Fee for Swimming," he read. "Or do you bother?" Farquharson shrugged. "Tennis?"

"I play, Joan doesn't."

"Then that's six pounds ten, I think. Kalu, have I gg-got it right? Now sign that (that's an order to the bb-bank) and you can bb-buy *us* drinks."

"But how can I sign it," Farquharson said, "if I can't get near the bar?"

"Is she around, Kalu?" The barman shook his head. "We'll take a chance."

So Farquharson signed, got his receipt, and was a member of the Senior Staff Club of the University. "Your wife," Ormford said, "will *live* here."

Farquharson told him what had happened at the Onyeamas', and they sat down in the chairs to keep Jamie legal and let him run. "Sorry, Farquharson," Ormford said, pointing. "Allow me: Professor Charlie Spanier-Dodd, who has been here, complete with h-hyphen, since nineteen forty-eight and has not yet gg-gone mad."

Spanier-Dodd had pale eyes and short hair damp with sweat. He smiled at the introduction as if at the departure of an old friend, but merely said, "Onyeama is afraid. The man lives with more fear than he's got a right to, but still, he's Ibo. And political, as if being Ibo wasn't politics enough."

"But why is being an Ibo political?" Farquharson said.

"Oh Lord, where do I begin?" He said, "They're Ibo. Sorry. They get educated and they go everywhere and they get jobs. And they carry their society with them and put it down in clumps. And then they've got the money, and they're very, well, 'who-are-*you*?' and proud." He said, "*I* like them. But they're every-where. We've got an Ibo Vice-Chancellor. They had one in Lagos till they threw him out last year—*that* was a bad thing." He went on, "You see, the Ibos have been almost squeezed out of the central government. They're the Opposition. And we don't use

56

our oppositions very well here—look at Awolọwọ. Anyway, why do you want to see the house? Wait till you have to!"

Ormford added, "It'll bb-be bb-bad enough at the time."

"Why?"

"Bb-because it's been a village, probably," Ormford said. "Come, Farquharson, enlightenment and equality are all right in their way, but you're in Africa and these are Africans. Africans don't live in their h-houses the way we do. You get bb-bathtubs chipped all over on the inside, I still don't know why—maybe they pound yam there. You don't think the educated African comes into his education by himself? He's got a village with him. *Hh-he* moves in. They move in. You can't imagine the stranglehold of an African family on an African. Personally, I think Onyeama's moving out simply to gg-get away from them. You'll see quite enough of that house when you have to."

"He's going back to the East," Spanier-Dodd said, "so he won't have to be afraid."

"Of what?" Farquharson said. If his world was going to be full of the ghosts of political echoes, he wanted to know what they were.

"Oh, I don't know," Spanier-Dodd said, looking into the bubbles on his beer. "Thugs, beatings. It's just this, you see: why should he be brave and stay for them?"

"Ah, if you want to see genuine incompetence," Ormford said happily, "wait for an African gg-government-run insurrection! The rewards of being unable to vote," he said again, after a long time, "are inestimable." But in the meantime Farquharson had excused himself and taken Jamie over to the small playground, and was placing him partway up a slide and letting him coast slowly down. Ormford came after him. "Somebody said walking around with the gg-glass in your hand was a Canadian custom," he said, and raised his beer against the sky. "In your honour."

"*Is* it safe here?" Farquharson said, suddenly wanting to challenge what might be a silly man.

"Yes," Ormford said.

On Saturday they took two long drives trying to see Ibadan. But though they went to the steps of Mapo Hall and saw the land like solid waves covered with roofs (Cocoa House a tiny distant rectangle), though they were caught in a traffic jam on a big flat street where one huge gabled house jutted out of low shacks and shops; though they listened to shrill voices, flat voices, noises of almost Italian anger, they took in less of it, even, than on the first day. What was that long precipitous descent down an S of road with bare-earth sides and the houses falling down the hill? Farquharson realized suddenly that he wasn't seeing people. So he stared at the first face he saw, found nothing but blank weary anger and looked away. He was an unsocial, almost worried man when they drove back to the Catering Flats and found Elias, with a treasure cache of objects, beside their door.

Joan was able to approve the purchases and count her change. The brooms were long fistfuls of bound palm fronds, without handles. Elias with an anxious smile bent and showed how they were used, in fast strokes with the fronds almost parallel to the floor. Treating him as an ally, Joan made plans for moving in and house cleaning and how much time they would need, and Farquharson thought, partly with admiration, partly with fright, that she hadn't seen the place, hadn't been inside it, was planning an abstract game, perhaps to reduce a village to a house, and without knowing it. He poured a beer and on impulse gave Stanley one as well. "Madam knows full well," Elias said, looking at a small pail with a tin of wax inside it, "that this is much work."

So she said, "We could get somebody to help you for the first few days."

"Ah, Madam wants a small-boy," he said. "Good. Good."

Farquharson wondered how old Elias was. He seemed middle-aged, atrophied by anxiety. Was he married? Did he have children? His face thrust forward, anxiously, to an Arabic nose. The chin receded; the ears were wild, big. Oh, he was ugly enough. And Stanley stood, like a guardian, with his beer, waiting to be told to go, his arrogance held in a serviceable abeyance, even, Farquharson suspected, his humanity and his gender. These men would call him "Master". Could he feel Ormford tickling himself with pleasure at the power of command?

Could he feel Farquharson doing it? Because it was incongruous?

Sunday they drove to the Onyeamas' again, but there was no one there. Their car turned on the grass beyond the garage and they saw that the house came around three sides of a square patio, but everything was closed, and it all looked unfriendly.

On Monday, well-dressed students appeared on the university streets. Elias came with a small-boy for approbation. His name was Jacob. He was handsome, barefoot, and his hands and feet were too big. Elias said, "He is my cousin, madam."

Farquharson went to Ormford's office to ask him something about the timetable, but he was busy with a student, and there were two more outside his door. Farquharson felt the eyes measuring him as if he were a box, so he went back to his office and almost missed his next-door neighbour by not looking at him.

"Hi!" the man called. "Fisher. Jim Fisher. Jeremy, really. You must be new." Farquharson saw a curly-haired, stocky juvenile with a round face and flat blue eyes. A child of eighteen, a man of thirty-one or -two. "Has anyone invited you to a party yet?" he said.

They were swung into a moment of irrelevant acquaintance, then a massive red-faced Scot came from the other direction, said, "Fisher!" in a ringing voice, was presented as Sandy MacLachlan, bowed, and began to talk gossip from the summer.

"Farquharson!" Ormford called. "It isn't necessary to wait among the undergraduates."

Always beginnings, Farquharson thought, and never what began. He thought suddenly, almost fiercely, "I am *not here!*" shut himself in his office and stared out at the red tennis courts. A girl walked by on the sidewalk to the library, going with flat-footed ungainly militancy—the ultimate displeasure and unpleasantness of education, he thought, its face a peremptory stiff blank. He muttered, "This is the Kingdom of Wrath," and wondered why he'd said it, so almost against his will he went back out to the corridor and stared covertly at the new students. It felt for a moment, queerly, as if he had lost contact with the geometry of his own face, and yet he would have been ashamed to put a hand up to the once familiar contours of shaving.

"Can the Professor say where is the Chairman's office of the Department of English?"

He pointed down the corridor. "Can the Professor," Oscar Nwonkwo said, "say where he mislaid himself?" Then, formally, "May I present Mr. John Cord? Professor Henry Farquharson."

Farquharson shook hands with a man who seemed to be wearing pyjamas of coarse striped cotton, a man so tall that the first part of him Farquharson saw was a rough-skinned, very black Adam's apple and then the rest, receding upwards to the wide hair: the absolute Negro, almost a caricature. Farquharson was tall, just over six feet; he felt, with complete certainty, that Oscar was laughing at him. "Mr. Cord has come to us from New York. He is an American."

"Damn it, Nwonkwo, I left that country! I am a *repatriate*." The voice had been trained once to get out of a stereotype; now obviously it couldn't make the second escape into the percussive softness of the African. Cord was a cultivated audible white New Yorker for all time. And furthermore, he didn't see the joke, or hear it. Farquharson had seldom seen a face with less humour in it.

"Come, my friend," Oscar said, gathering Farquharson's shoulder briefly in his hand, "let us go drink some coffee and pretend that we three are the world."

But Cord cut "we three" to two by going abruptly back from them.

"What a man! But he is going to have to learn that one doesn't *always* talk to a white man for the sole purpose of disparaging *him*." And Oscar put the man out of his mind as visibly as if he had dropped a letter into a bag, and guided his friend over the bridge and through a barrier door on the far gallery, and so into the Senior Common Room, which was full of large sharp-cornered furniture arranged in squares too close together. Farquharson banged his shins twice getting to a white sofa half-way down the room.

Tuesday the twenty-eighth. They got up in the morning and marked time for what seemed a decent interval, then drove over to Number One Jaja, in time to see all the Onyeamas gathered about their cars, not looking like people being made to move away by fear. Elias was behind a tree, halfway down the drive. Someone ran to them and said, "Yes?" and a man who must have been Professor Onyeama looked at their car and its licence number and came towards them.

"We didn't mean to be too soon," Farquharson said, across his wife.

"You are moving in?"

Joan said, "If we can," sharply, and Farquharson pulled back from her, wishing he could get his face into a real shadow. "There is our steward," Joan said, pointing. "Will you give him the keys, please?"

"What got into you?" Farquharson said when they were driving to the Club.

"They were supposed to have left."

"Today. This *is* today. They were going, weren't they?"

"She never answered my notes. You know I sent more than one?"

He tried to explain that the Onyeamas were leaving because of political fear, but Joan said, "Oh, nonsense, they looked as if they were going on a picnic!"

"Be warned," Peg said. "It's going to be dirty!"

They found Elias on the patio, with all the doors and windows open. Elias held out the keys. "Madam," he said. Joan took them and entered in.

The house was in three parts, shaped roughly like a damaged H. The crossbar was the dining room; the left-hand upright the kitchen and the garage—but displaced, as if the whole line had slipped down. The right-hand upright had the living room and bedrooms. The rooms that faced the patio were walled with wide glass doors and were joined to the eye, though separated by a sideboard and a set of open shelves. There was a tiny refrigerator in the dining room, and big louvred windows looked down on to a blank garden from a living room full of pieces of big furniture. The painted concrete floor was marked as if heavy boxes had been dragged over it. The three bedrooms were crowded with beds, bunks, a crib—even a mattress on the floor. With the exception of the two in the first bedroom, the mattresses were merely stuffed and tufted, but they were misshapen, stained, and torn. Rips in the fabric showed ravelling holes in the stuffing. There were the marks of fire on the concrete of the patio, and a few large concrete blocks that might have made a fireplace. The sink was grey. After a half-hour of increasingly feverish prowling and exploring, while Farquharson took the many keys and tried every lock on every piece of furniture—and found scarcely any that could be made to work—Joan burst out of the house, hiccupping with suppressed hysterics, and when Farquharson caught up to her she was saying, "I never saw anything, any-where, so completely *dirty*! Horrible! It's got to be scrubbed, completely, with ammonia, with lye: everywhere! And every cushion and mattress thrown out. I wouldn't let Jamie even on to the patio! (Jamie was outside, driving the car: Farquharson could see Stanley guarding the horn ring and saying, in his unresonant bass, "Drive, Jamie, drive!")

"Elias can clean it up. It's only dust and smudge."

"It's *everything*! The place is horrible." She pulled away from him, as if she was never going to be able to make him understand. "Filth," she said.

He found her face to face with Elias in the kitchen. Elias was looking proud, and waiting. Jacob was arranging the purchases in the pantry, on a shelf. "Every wall in the house," Joan was saying. "With ammonia in the water. And the kitchen floor. With am-monia, every shelf."

"I am a steward, madam." A low, unbelieving voice.

"This is an emergency," she said. "We simply can't move in. We're paying hotel rates—we've got to move *in* here!" She collected herself. "Elias," she said, "please work quickly."

"You, my love," Farquharson said, "are getting out of here to take a rest, before you throw fits."

He put Jamie on his knee, left Joan the back seat to be enraged in, and took her to the Ormfords'. She sat in the divided living room, not even guarding Jamie against the cliff, and Ormford applied reason, gin and lemon, consolation, and apologies for his wife's absence. "Well, we can certainly do something about the mattresses," he said at length. "What's your man's name?" (He was walking to the door. Farquharson told him.)

"Stanley!"

"Sir?"

"You know the furniture clerk, Mr. Akinkugbe? Take your masters to him, now, after I gg-give them a note, will you? Where's the typewriter?" he said, coming back in, and then, "Oh, *you've* got it. All right." He wrote, crouching over a shelf, "Dear Mr. Akinkugbe. The mattresses and cushions in Prof. Farquharson's house at No. 1 Jaja seem to have become unusable owing to the combined efforts of age, tears, unsanitation, and abuse. Please arrange for their replacement as soon as possible, as the Farquharsons have a small child and would fear for his health if they were to place him on any of the mattresses within that house. Mrs. Farquharson says 'cushions also'. I agree. Please give this your most urgent consideration. L. G. Ormford, English. P.S.: the Farquharsons need only 3 beds and a crib." "I'd bb-better put 'L.G.O.' after that, I suppose," he added. "Now drink that up and come bb-back for more after you've been there. Your steward will manage at least as well as any other steward."

They went around the campus from one end to the other, and found Akinkugbe in a sort of small barn, loaded like a baggage car, with a big desk in the middle. It was raining again. Akinkugbe was a small square man with a pencil-line Mongol moustache; he looked alert, vanquished, and like the one male teacher

Farquharson had ever had in public school. "Indeed," he said, after having read the letter slowly. "This is very difficult for me, sir, you must understand that."

Demure, ruthless fencing. Farquharson supposed he had to do it. Given the necessity, he knew, he could do it with both glee and truth. Whether it would get him anywhere was another matter—and he enjoyed that, too. He depicted the intransigent impracticability of the mattresses; he enlarged upon their holes, their fluff, their stains, their possible sometime virtue. There were also the sofa cushions.

"I guess I shouldn't enjoy his outrage," he thought. "When, for the new mattresses?"

"But it has not been made clear to me, sir, that you *need* new mattresses!"

In the end Farquharson had at least the promise of the mattresses, and went back to the car reasonably content and somewhat tired.

"Cushions?" Joan said.

"We lost that round so far."

"So you gg-got the mattresses out of him?" Ormford said, rubbing his hands. "That calls for another drink. *Michael!*"

"We haven't got them yet."

"Oh, Akinkugbe always surrenders once he begins to. The masters would like a gin and lemon each. So would I."

So they had half an hour of watching Ormford play with Jamie on the patio, and drove back, down Sankore past the Baloguns', past the gate to the Vice-Chancellor's and along the long straight street between the science departments and the playing field, to the Clinic across the road from their own driveway, and the Language Laboratory, like a diminutive factory, on *their* side of the road, and at the entrance to *their* home.

Joan found Elias in the kitchen. She said, "Have you scrubbed the floor?"

"The boy shall sweep the rooms all well, madam. Madam need not fear."

64

And Farquharson heard her say, "That isn't point, Elias. I want the floor *scrubbed*. It's unclean; it should be the first thing done."

Farquharson let the door close behind him. Jamie, held carefully away from contamination, looked about him with grave approbation and bewilderment. Suddenly with the closed door they were in silence and underwater light from blue louvred windows. The house had been used into a state of dust and grime, certainly. But "dirt"? With the brown-and-green dress, and all that authority? There remained the mattresses, of course, and Akinkugbe flustering in his baggage car. (Quarrelling was fun sometimes.)

The door was open. His wife's feet came quickly after him. "I don't know what he's done," she said, "Farq, I don't think he's doing *anything*. He keeps saying he's a steward. I told him he *has* to scrub the floor. It doesn't seem to *mean* anything . . ."

"Madam?" the young voice said.

"Sweep *all* the rooms out, Jacob. And under all the beds. Mrs. Ormford warned me," she said as they started to leave, "that they never go under the beds."

"I can have visions of you going a long way off," he said, lightly, perhaps amusedly, "saying 'they'." He put his hand on her back.

"Well, don't let me go alone. Anyway, they are 'they'. Have you got any other quick expressions?"

"Master?" Elias said. "The key?"

"Well, we haven't got anything in here," Farquharson thought. "Why not?"

"Give me one key," he said, "to get in by."

"Yes, master."

But Stanley wasn't allowed to call him "master".

"We have to finish tomorrow," Farquharson said, "so we can get our things in. Don't forget the floors, will you?"

"Do I have to be unkind?" he thought. Obviously, Elias was going to wince or be proud or hang his head.

"I'm going to look at them *very* carefully," Joan said.

"I know full well what I am supposed to do, madam. I am a steward. I am trained."

"Aren't we a little hard on him?" Farquharson said.

"Well, I have to be hard on him, the way he's starting out. If he won't do the work he'll have to go, that's all. That's what Peg says and I agree. Anyway, it *is* dirty. Now, you're *not* going to tell me it isn't."

What had he thought in the hall? Dust, discoloration? "No," he said, "I'm not." So that was that: it *was* dirty.

Rain wept tranquilly, all about them. The insects passed into inaudibility, whether they shut up or not. Farquharson, hunched on his side facing the window, dreamed, rather horribly, that Elias was trying to find him, saying "Master!" and carrying a shiny shoebox streaked with dust. And he, Farquharson, in full view, wearing his shorts, was trying to hide. The image seemed to hold itself, unmoving, for a long time.

6

BUT the kitchen wasn't scrubbed. They found Jacob polishing furniture until the wood looked oiled, but the kitchen floor had been swept, and that was all. It had all its stains still on it, and as it was after nine in the morning and the servants had been there since six, Joan coldly and methodically lost her temper and made a speech, and Elias hung his head and stood with a cloth powerless in his hand, the hand moving, with crawling slowness, back and forth. Jacob hid and worked.

They went to the bank. They shopped for basic food, long-term supplies. They had a beer, lunch, rest; packed. The servants asked again whether they were going to move.

When they got back to Number One Jaja, late in the afternoon, the mattresses had been turned over, Jacob was waiting on the patio, and Elias was in the kitchen, holding a soft cloth in his hand, his face drawn; he might not have moved. The floor was dry, and stained. They toured the house without saying a word to him.

When they came back to the living room Elias was standing on the patio. He said, "I say good night to you, Madam," and walked away, dignified.

"What's wrong?" Joan said. "*What's wrong?*" Then, "We've got to go down to the Ormfords'. Now."

Farquharson tried to make it light. He said to the Ormfords, "The suppliants return." And fortunately Peg took charge, and turned rising hysteria into a programme of operations. Ormford took the Farquharson males down to where they could put their backs against a big tree, and having got them out of earshot, set

67

Jamie running games to play and tried to pull Farquharson's mind out of the house, as if he were fishing for him. There was this big boy with the silly nose, and he, Lawrence George Ormford, specialist in the modern novel, liked him. But friendships were a bad idea in the tropics. He was going to have to resort to mere hospitality.

They found the Ormfords' Michael in consultation with the women.

"Michael will have two men at the house tomorrow for us. They'll clean the whole place for us."

"Elias?"

"What do you think?"

At the Flats Farquharson ripped his hand away from the screen door and let it crash. "Can you come back tonight, Stanley," he said, "and take me to where Elias lives?"

"Sir? Shall you be dismissing him from your employment?"

The formality jarred him. "I want to talk to him," he said. "Don't tell him. Just come for me."

"Good night, sir."

"Not yet," he said. "Ó d'àbọ̀."

"I have to fire him, don't I?" he said to his wife. And yes, he had to.

Twilight dissolved rapidly in the air, like ink in water. The strident shimmering of white noise in the air began and grew, and in the full night fell away, out of the mind. He felt as if he manned, passively, all the controls of sense. It didn't give him an appetite for eating, but he ate. And he put Jamie to bed, and sang to him and lay beside the crib, staring into the black ceiling, into the underside of the cover of his dream's shoebox. "Stanley's here," Jean said. "Now be firm," she said when he was on his feet. "And quick. I don't want to sit here waiting for you."

It hadn't rained: there weren't clouds. They drove into the night, and Farquharson kept his eyes where the headlights hit the road. He wanted to explain to Stanley about sanitation and

68

immunities, but the words were only in his head. "I don't want to do this," he said. "But he's had two days to do that floor, and he hasn't even tried to. Okay, maybe we're foolish to think it was necessary, but we do think so. He *knows* that. Can you hear a bad conscience, Stanley? I don't know why I ought to have one." Stanley, he supposed, listened to him.

"Do you know Elias?" Farquharson said. "Stanley, is he a friend?"

"Mr. Okpata send for us to come to the master. I meet him that day."

Out Farquharson's window, on the left (he still felt strange being a passenger on that side), there was the empty cattle market. Not fully empty: he could see the shape of three beasts, close to the road, and a man in white. And in the other ear, as if through Stanley's window, there were human sounds.

He got out onto the grey road, at the edge of a shanty town like a prolonged flat stage set, suggesting rank after shambled rank of the same thing behind. Oil lamps and little fires made glowing hollow reddish spheres of light. Without looking at him Stanley led Farquharson between two houses, dodging from side to side over a glinting narrow track of drainage.

The slum *was* a stage set. The second rank of houses was much more open, and then they started to lift, and were on a long hillside with only a few far buildings, under a sky with sets of big stars opening in it. They walked with the noise of their feet on earth. (Farquharson had bought new sandals in the Kingsway, just like Ormford's.)

"This is his brother's house."

There was a woodpile, and then a big white building which he never really saw (he wasn't trying to see it). Stanley spoke to a boy. Then Elias came, wearing the same clothes.

It should have been clean, quick, fast; he should have asked for the keys, given Elias a full month's pay and had it over with, even with a witness. This he knew. But it was impossible to do it in any way well at all. One of them pulled the others out of the house and over to the woodpile: it might have been Farquharson, he wasn't sure. They got there, somehow. Elias said, "Master, I beg you, in the name of God!" and Farquharson had no answer. They were lost in a huge night, halfway up the hill. "I have debts, master. Master, I will do my best. Please, master, you must not do this thing to my children." Which answered *that* question.

"Elias," he said, "we have. We argued about this for a long time. Oh look," he burst out, "do you think I *want* to do this? *I* have a child. I take your job away, for his sake. I may be cruel, but I am one of two people who have made up our mind. And even if you could change *me*"—and then he stopped, suddenly, as if his disloyalty (to Joan?) had shaped itself as a fourth person"—it will still be the same. Something's over, Elias," he said. "Just bring me my keys, and I've got all your money for you."

"I could have done that worse," he said to Stanley, when there were just the two of them. "Maybe I ought to take lessons in how to. I don't know if you're ashamed of me," he added, "but *I* am."

"Sir, you do as you wish." It should have been judgement, Farquharson thought; in the motionless air it sounded like consolation.

Elias came with the keys. They rang, making a tiny high festive noise. Farquharson took the envelope out of his shirt pocket and unfolded it, uncomfortable suddenly because it had been sitting over his heart. (The keys in his tight shorts jammed against his leg.) "Ten pounds, Elias, five and five."

"Master knows that I can now have no work?"

"Master doesn't know. You have the same letters."

"And does the master have a letter for me?" He was separating the ten one-pound notes, slowly, as if they burned him, while Stanley lit a match in the still air and let the light shine.

"No letter," Farquharson said. "I can't do that."

Possibly that at least touched Elias Ateghie's pride. He said, "I have a wife and children." So at the moment where his charity should have begun, Farquharson said, "So have I."

"You have *one* child."

"I did have two. Do you think I want this one to become sick,

70

ever? In the filth and the infection of that house, as you left it, ever?"

"I have heard you, master," Elias said, bending forward as if his stomach hurt. "If you please, go now."

They picked their way back to the barrier of sick huddled houses, and the road. Farquharson looked up, before he lost sight of the hill: Elias was probably still there, in that muddle of dignity and desperation from which there was no way out. He couldn't think how he would have got back into the house.

"How old is Elias?" he said, when the car closed around him.

"Sir, I hope he is twenty-seven."

"And I'm thirty-seven. And I can treat a man like that. Take me home, Stanley." He turned as the car started. "No. Where do *you* live?"

"Sir, let me take you to your lady."

Farquharson said, "Yes."

"Well," he said, when they were moving slowly past the airport—Stanley was giving him time—"I guess I'm not a virgin any more, am I?"

"Sir, he did not work well for you."

So Farquharson let his anger take him and shouted for a minute, and then said, "And it was our fault how it happened." He subsided. "And that's the end of that."

He felt drained, sick, sorry for himself, ashamed. "Next time," he thought, "next time, it'll be done."

"If Elias doesn't get a job before his money goes," he said, "will you send him to me?" And he knew Stanley wouldn't, and that the act was indeed past and final. "It's late," he said. "Drive yourself home and bring the car back in the morning."

And Joan hadn't been there to do it, he thought. Therefore she was still innocent, and dangerous, and didn't know it.

"I did it," he said, "but I don't want to talk about it."

Michael sent over two helpers, while Farquharson, with Stanley, went around arranging to borrow pots, dishes, and bedding until their own stuff should arrive. He felt somehow that

Stanley was watching him, guarding him, so he had to say, "Well, did you use the car last night?"

"Sir?" Stanley said, lifting a big pot of crockery into the boot. Farquharson hefted a huge cast-iron frying pan, and decided not to ask again.

Carcasses of meat were tumbled out on to a metal floor behind them. He saw a woman buying bread, bought two loaves, and sent Stanley back to Joan while he walked to the office alone and sat with his cards.

He needed to be in business for himself.

"Literature as *re*definition; frame-story; *débat*; marriage group; Franklin's Tale. *Servaunt in love, and lord in mariage . . .*"

"Is the Professor in?"

He saw a big homely black man with large teeth, gentle eyes, and a high slanting forehead.

"Yes?" he said, and all his sorrow about Elias couldn't make his voice sound warm.

"My name is Mr. Q. Adebọwale; I am in the Professor's class. I should like to ask the Professor what he means to do."

"I mean to talk, I think," he said, feeling his head blank. "I don't know what about. I fly by radar sometimes."

"The Professor understands," Adebọwale said, "that we do not seek to be entertained, but to learn from the Professor?"

"I never taught here before," he said, and grinned because of course he had authority. "I can't have a reputation, why not wait for it? Adebọwale: 'Honour-has-come-back-to-the-house', right?"

The man nodded. "With what do we begin, sir?"

"Words. Seriously, the English language." And as the other looked bewildered, and not pleased, he said, "How old are you?"

And now the man was humble. "Thirty-four."

"Don't worry, Mr. Adebọwale, I can make it worth your time. Just don't expect it to be what you expected it to be."

"I do not fully understand the Professor."

Farquharson leaned back in his chair with his arms crossed, knowing how the shape of the arm muscle would stand out upon his forearm. " 'You think that out of this nettle danger we pluck this flower, safety.' "

"Is it *Henry IV*, sir?"

"Reverse the terms. Pluck danger out of this nettle, safety. Because that's what you're here to do." The man rose. "The Franklin's Tale!" Farquharson called out after him.

"Hello," said a girl at the door. "I'm introducing myself. Are you Professor Farquharson?"

"The one and only."

"Now, I'm Sylvia Levinsohn," she said. "I'm in your department. These are—now tell me if I haven't pronounced them right —Mrs. Victoria N-won-kwo (this is Oscar's wife, isn't she beautiful?), and Miss N-wa-la O-ka-gbu-e, and you probably saw *her* name on the office, too. And do like her, because I do. Mrs. Nwonkwo's in Graduate History, isn't it? And this, behind all of us is—aren't you Canadian?—a fellow citizen, Miss Gail Johnston from Toronto. We're the women here." Since he had to follow them, he turned and locked his door.

"Well, I ought to know Miss Johnston," he said. "I taught her once. Hello, Gail." He put out his hand.

She took it. "Hello, sir."

"Not now," he said. "You'll have to call me 'Farquharson' like everybody. I thought you went in for the theatre, though."

"That's why I'm here."

They walked over the bridge, the two Nigerians behind them.

"I'm not fond of recognizing old acquaintances overseas," she said. "Do you mind?"

He bought a book of flimsy paper tickets from the tea attendant and sat with the four women, feeling irresistibly like a show. Nwala Okagbue was plain and pleasant in the long narrow dress that seemed to be the younger women's uniform; Victoria Nwonkwo was quite simply beautiful, fine-boned and exquisite as Nefertiti. Miss Levinsohn might look brash and robust; Gail Johnston faded. But then, as he remembered her, Gail Johnston had always faded; a mousy-haired hurt spinster-look, made worse by neatness. At least here she wasn't neat: her hair straggling with the humid air, her complexion pallid and uneven (flesh colour again, he thought, remembering how he had sought out the shades of colour on his forearm), but if she still seemed to lack authority, she must have learned how to laugh somewhere in the last eight years.

"Don't measure me, Former Professor Farquharson," she said. "Pretend that we're both new."

So he talked to Victoria Nwonkwo and was delighted with her.

"Come and look," Joan said. "By tomorrow we're going to have a house!"

The new mattresses had come. Half of the beds had disappeared. "Stanley's been playing with Jamie all over everywhere. But I had to make Jacob babysit. The other two weren't getting along with him. Wrong tribe, I guess."

Let her be pleased, he thought, let her like it. *He* had earned his right to like it, and at a price.

"I've got an old student here," he said. "Someone from before your time." And he knew he hadn't meant to tell her.

The next day was a holiday. But not at the Farquharsons', where three perspiring men worked and an invigorated white madam kept coming to see how they were doing. In the afternoon they went to the Club and were introduced to a lot of women. Farquharson decided to swim and had the embarrassment of getting into the shower in front of Mr. John Cord, who wanted racial precedence, so Farquharson took his irritation to the pool and enjoyed the smooth-glove sliding of the water over his back. "Welcome to the *oyibo*'s dream world," Cord said.

"Well, we're *both* here," Farquharson thought, and pushed deep into the pool so he could drive to the surface and shoot, dolphin-like and liberated, into the air, up to his navel, down into a splash, and up spluttering. "I suppose," he thought, casting his chlorine-smeared gaze across the pool to where his wife was, "I ought to wear those glasses all the time."

So he ploughed across the pool, recklessly flailing water, and heaved himself over the edge to drip in benediction down on Joan, Mrs. Ormford, and a redhead who turned out to be Mrs. Charlie Spanier-Dodd, who taught household economics in a teacher-training school. Farquharson excused himself to go back and put himself together, and John Cord pounced on him, aggressive in a white shirt, and said, "I was impolite to you. I apologize," while Farquharson stood dripping in the ineffective protection of a hand towel.

Jamie sat in his underwear in the shallow children's wading pool, utterly contented just to make little splashes and look at them.

Farquharson saw Gail Johnston at the far end of the curved room, talking with speed and seriousness to the stricken profile of a man with a straight nose and a black brush cut. He wasn't put out, he thought, to find a former student. He merely hoped that they wouldn't particularly have to be friends. Students from his bachelor days walked behind a closed door. And yet when she didn't know he was looking at her, he thought, she had a different face. Neither gentle nor tough: the face of a woman who knew how to listen. He found himself looking hard at the man beside her.

"You," Jamie said, in a high meditating voice at bedtime, "me, Far'" (that was his father's name), "Stanley" (pronounced "Tanyi" in an extraordinary nasal), "Elias, go to *house*."

"No, not Elias," his father said. "Elias isn't working for us now."

"You, me, Elias, Stanley, Mommy, go, to, *house*."

Farquharson could think of nothing better to do with the words than to make a lullaby out of them.

And on Saturday, the second of October, as classes started, Farquharson put his family and all his belongings into the car, and, raising thanks for timetables, put them all into their new house, cleaned from end to end now and with fully three houseboys in it,

75

and went off to a hundred and twenty people and the Great Vowel Shift.

And to one flat, demanding baritone voice that said: "It is impossible to hear the Professor from the back corners of this room."

PART TWO

7

ROUTINE. With blessed suddenness all the compartments put themselves together into the liberty of a divided, organized life where he could take his own dimensions and move. Farquharson liked timetables; they freed the mind. Mornings till one: tutorials in a survey course, Shakespeare, practical criticism, poetry. Afternoons: collapse, siesta, drive, shop, beer at the Club. He thought, comfortably, that if he had come ninety degrees around the world to do good on this timetable, there was somebody somewhere who had his priorities in the wrong order. But he was here, with Chaucer, *Rasselas*, the Metaphysicals, Blake, Shakespeare, and with a set of obstreperous classes coming, *on time*, and that was quite enough. Meanwhile Joan made a regular morning trip to the Kingsway, and in the evenings they could go out and hunt for things to see. They took just one week to cut themselves a shallow, and complete, way of life.

(Just before they left the Catering Flats, Jack Okpata, in white trousers and robe, with yellow embroidery, came full of shock to have Elias reinstated, failed in anger, and went away misused, his honour gone.)

The sofa cushions, bare and stained, still made Joan nervous. She dismissed the older of her two temporary men. She said, "I'm going to keep the kitchen for myself, after that last one. I've got Jamie to think about." Besides, after watching Peg Ormford, she was afraid a good steward wouldn't leave her with enough to do, and monotony waited only until the day after they moved in to show itself: the Sunday lagged.

But the house was a good house. Even with nothing in it but

borrowed pots and cooking spoons and a two-burner stove, the kitchen was a good kitchen, a stripped-down version of a kitchen in a magazine: sinks, no hot water, many counters, a lot of shelving. The electric outlets were in the pantry, a kitchen table in the garage. Godwin, the retained houseboy, said, "For ironing, madam," and on his own authority took Farquharson's and Jamie's shirts through a little passage past the pantry into the garage, shut the door behind himself, and ironed them, and Joan said, "Did you ever *see* such beautiful work done on a tabletop?"

The living room looked gaunt, with curtainless windows, bare cushions, and an empty bookcase, but the dining room was comfortably complete with a smallish table and six chairs, a fixed sideboard in the room divider, and a baby refrigerator (which had had to be scrubbed three times and set out in the sunlight to bake). The bedrooms had bare blankets, bare light-bulbs, and wastes of space. The bathroom was snug, small, and green, dwarfed by the geyser tank. Throughout the house the floors were red concrete, waxed to provide red feet and knees for Jamie, and red sheets and sofa cushions finally. Also there were louvred windows throughout the house, and some of them stuck.

Oddly, the approach to the house was from the back, past the open garage and the unpainted grey quarters where Stanley was now living alone and masterful. The house did face a street, across a long sloping lawn, but a high fence cut them apart from it, and though El-Kanemi Road was in fact their legal address it became mentally invisible, and so did most of the garden near it. But there was a path between the edge of their property and the end of Kuti Hall, and the students swarmed on that from time to time.

Farquharson exploring on the Wednesday with Jamie, found a tunnel-like path leading out of his driveway and followed it to a long house huddled in trees, and the voice of Oscar Nwonkwo, shouting from the garage. So he finished his exploration in a cool, dim living room with a bottle of beer, watching Victoria Nwonkwo, still easily the most exquisite woman he had ever looked at, complaining with earthy and direct enthusiasm about the servants.

Stanley drove for them in the mornings and afternoons. In the evenings, Farquharson said, unless there was reason, *he* would drive. The houseboys worked from early morning till after lunch, then disappeared towards the servants' village to come back before suppertime and stay deep into the darkness to clean up after the meal. They weren't sure what perversity made them put Stanley next to them—but when they had stopped to say to each other on Saturday, "Who lives where?" they hadn't even had to discuss it. Farquharson wanted Stanley, and Joan didn't want two very young and squabbling men next door to the patio. "Madam," Jacob said, standing at attention and not looking at her, "I no live with Ibo!"

Nevertheless he had to. Godwin ironed much better, but Jacob had priority, and besides, Joan thought Jacob was rather forlorn and funny, and she didn't care for Godwin much. If there were hostilities in the Abadina house, Joan didn't want to hear about them. Stanley, who seemed to have the great advantage of being just one person, brought a friend with a truck and a good bed. Then the friend and the truck said goodbye, and Stanley sat on his concrete stoop, smoking his one cigarette a day, looking like an Old Testament lord, one of Noah's sons, say, after the Flood, with a world, if he wanted it, and all the leisure not to have it.

Meanwhile certain of the Onyeamas' servants came to claim their jobs and were in no slight anger when the honour of their position wasn't recognized. One girl came, seductive, petty, and aloof, to claim "Madam's bitter-leaf".

"Jacob, what is bitter-leaf?" Joan asked.

"Is like spinach, Madam."

"Then *you* take it," she said, and sent the girl away.

Then the Farquharsons made the Ormfords come to dinner, and covered the table with a spaghetti and Yugoslavian wine, and the houseboys, without uniforms, served as if at an armed truce while Peg told Joan how to do salad, and where to go for meat, and went into the kitchen to check how the servants were doing

81

things, and Ormford was relaxed and drank his wine and babbled, and Farquharson felt contented to be among these women, and wondered what had pulled Gail Johnston to Africa, and what she had found to be tragic about here, and thought to ask Ormford and decided it would be better not to, and Joan felt as awkward as an adolescent, and quite temperish before it was all over.

"Where in the world did you get the pineapple?" Farquharson said when they had gone to bed, and she felt he was criticizing her and wouldn't tell him that she had bought it from a girl at the door.

They had placed their beds in the middle of the far, wide wall, as if the room were a stage set. There hadn't been love made there yet: Joan said she was exhausted, it was hot; Farquharson never tried too hard. There wasn't, after all, he reasoned sometimes in the bathroom, all that much he got from it; liking and conscientious attempts weren't exactly love and ecstasy. But then ecstasy was a thing he didn't know much about. So he cleaned his teeth, using an ice-cold bottle of boiled water, and hosed his urine noisily into the very middle of the toilet (there was *that* much aggression in him, he thought, at least!), feeling himself stilled to the fact that most of the time his masculinity was a kind of standing at ease. At odd intervals, though not yet in Africa, he had simplified attention by some straightforward masturbation. Joan had her own ideas about that and, he suspected, didn't even mind. "Poor kid," he thought, she couldn't help it if she hurt; after all, he *was* big. Nothing ever removed that pleasure from a man, even if it made trouble for him.

He had used to whisper to her that he was married to a bedful of dynamite: all he had to do was ram the plunger once and she'd blow up, but that was before it had got fixed in her nerve ends that pain followed orgasm immediately, unless he pulled out. Nobody was proud of that quick trigger now, and it had ended her helping him. He was on his own, and sometimes he was half-soft and futile. It was only just believable that he had had children from her, and that she had wanted them. Oh well, he had a wife he liked; they both loved Jamie. All things had costs.—He thought

82

to wonder why he should be going over that all again, and decided it was probably just as well not to know.

"If the Professor please. We have made the point during two lectures now that the Professor is not being sufficiently audible. In addition, it has been a matter of concern to us that the course of the Professor's lectures is not clear, nor that it has a relevance to the matter of this section of the course. We should like to submit to the Professor that one hour of History of English Language is procured to the First Year regularly by Mr. Cord and to request humbly of him why he is speaking on it here, when it would seem apparent by the Detailed Syllabuses that these hours are for our education upon the books of the famous authors upon whom we are examined."

He thought some said "Hush!" The room rustled. He couldn't tell who was annoyed, or what anyone was thinking, but for warfare on his own ground, it didn't matter. He could enjoy this, and was sure his face showed it.

"I can *not* apologize," he started clarioning, "for the acoustics of this room. As for the exam . . ." He grinned and then as hard as he could belted out a five-minute manifesto for the unpredictability of a liberal education. He hadn't given it for several years, and it was fun to remember it. "Anyway," he finished, "Mr. Cord knows I'm doing this." He wasn't pleased at this instinct for authority, but it made an end.

In the corridor outside, after the class, he watched Mr. Adebọwale worry, but he was surrounded by young men and ladies who wanted to inquire of the Professor what they should do with what the Professor meant. He decided to have it out in Adebọwale's tutorial at twelve, but instead he was held to a long exploration of why they should study language change, during which he tried to separate eight people beside him from their aura of rigidly insubordinate compliance.

"Come on," he said, after the houseboys went, "let's see how far Ibadan goes."

So they drove past the edge of Ibadan, in a threatening, oppressive night, following the railway. They thought they were in the country, and then the road curved past crowded busy houses above an undulating wall. Then dark and country, glimpses of lights to the left, as if the car were beyond the border but orbiting; then, suddenly, stridently bright, a working plastics factory. And finally a wide sprawling nightclub hotel looking forbiddingly silent and furtive, and calling itself the Lafia. "Did you note the mileage?" he said, but they had both forgotten to. They came back into a sudden pelting exuberant overwhelming rainfall, and had to wait for about ten minutes at the railway crossing until they saw, moving very slowly, a tremendous headlight lancing the rain, then wheels, and a black moving wall, and finally the wet road again. "Golly!" Farquharson said, fumbling to start the car.

(Once, he remembered, he had been looking into a window, and there was somebody behind him, looking over his shoulder, or somebody floating in the air, almost malignantly passive, staring over him—and then he realized that both were transparent and overlaid, that there was a second reflecting glass, tilted forward and askew, and that the intent foreign guardian, unfriendly, handsome, and who so suddenly met his eye, was him.)

Visions of power. This time a train. Cars honked behind him. Fortunately, they could get into the house through the back of the garage.

"All right," he said to his class at eight o'clock, "in the first place, what is literature anyway, and why should we talk about it?"
Silence.
"Well?" he said. "Why should it matter what we say?"
Sullen, obedient faces. "Literature," one said, "is when you have poems, or plays and stories." He could see the words written down.

They went to do their weekend shopping at the Kingsway. As they flashed past the airport there was a black hump beside the road, and when they came back they saw it was a dead steer, with

84

its neck slashed open (the slash pale and bright), lying like a clay model on a brown stain on the road. Joan said it was horrible; Farquharson, with Jamie on his knee (singing comfortably and pressing his head into his father's chest), didn't commit his emotions to anything more than a small shock. Stanley steered slowly around it, looked alert, and didn't explain.

At the Club, Farquharson saw Gail Johnston playing tennis with the man with the sad profile. It was funny about unattractive people, he thought, that their bodies could blaze sometimes in movement, when they forgot about them. A skinny spinster too much in the heat; a girl, he remembered, who never knew what to do with men and always did it wrong. As an undergraduate she had been a walking reproach that other people had managed to learn how to live. He'd had to hound her essay out of her. He remembered her as if in a rage at what other people did. At least, he thought, she didn't look complacent, now that he guessed she had some man around. She went into the air after the ball as if every part of her was as exultant as it seemed spare. Farquharson went into the pool, thinking how a housewife might bring a cobweb down with just such a sweep.

Ormford bobbed briefly into a chair as Farquharson stood temporarily dripping beside his wife. "Did you say anything to these people about our little election?" he said, placidly picking up Peg's drink and taking a mouthful out of it. "Voting for your car's former owners' party—or against it. You know, it might be a very gg-good idea," he said, looking at Farquharson, "not to take that car out on Monday, or perhaps Tuesday, or possibly Wednesday. Thursday?" He savoured the possibility of eliminating the week, day by day. "In fact, I'm not gg-going to take *my* car out."

Joan said, "Seriously, are you expecting trouble?" looking momentarily, Farquharson thought, as if someone had thought of cheating her.

"Oh, they don't ever *expect* it," Ormford said; "it's just that they gg-*get* it, sometimes. After all, not even an African party can cook an election to its taste without h-having one."

Jamie fell over in the children's wading pool and howled, and Farquharson went over to pick him up.

"There's the NNDP," Gail said from behind him, "and the UPGA, which is the NCNC and the Action Group. The NNDP are the bad guys. Do you want any more?" She was looking sallow in a white bathing suit, with her hair caught by a rubber band. Farquharson was jolted slightly. "Dr. Bill Garnett," she introduced, "this is Professor Henry Farquharson."

The profile had a heavily weighted, lean face, not hollow or hard but filled out with pressure from behind, as if subject to the force of tears contained but only half congealed. The body was skinny and stiff. He had a child's dark-brown, extraordinarily clear and empty eyes. "Glad to meet you, Henry," he said.

"All right," Farquharson said, "what the hell is UPGA?"

"The United Progressive Grand Alliance."

Farquharson said, "Wow."

"The Action Group," Garnett said, "buddy-buddying to its dearest enemies of about three years ago. You'd think they'd use all their energy making up such big names, but the name's a sort of juju. It's a *source* of energy." He looked bleak.

"Well, is it an election *about* anything?"

Gail said, "Power, graft. Yoruba autonomy, as Akintọla sees it." She was holding Jamie's hands. "If Akintọla loses, then we'll have the south of the country allied against the North. The Federal Government's a Northern Government. It won't allow it."

"Is it a crisis, then?"

"The last election was a crisis!" Ormford said. "My gg-good Farquharson, they're all crises—they're *elections*. Of course, I suppose if you hh-have to h-have a h-hobby, you can think of them."

"I think you should definitely stay within the compound next week," he heard Peg Ormford say. "I'll send you my butcher—*he* can come and go all the time."

"But is it dangerous?" Joan said, looking, Farquharson thought, exactly as if she were about to remind him that he hadn't put the garbage out.

"Not if you don't get in the way," Ormford said. "Africans h-hate *Africans*."

"I've got a cracked rib and a bad ear that say otherwise," Dr. Garnett said, moving towards the pool, trying to get Gail away.

"You'd fight with anybody, Bill," Gail said. Farquharson thought she sounded comfortable, as if she were patting a good watchdog. He wondered what sort of a fight it had been, and what about.

"Well, hh-how are the students?" Ormford said, moving them away from the women.

Farquharson said, "Peremptory."

"So unlike," Ormford said, and Farquharson thought suddenly that it was a far from happy voice, "so utterly unlike the h-home life of Our Dear Queen." What was the humane European standard, Farquharson thought, but a thing to be failed from? No student could dream of attaining it without arousing a slight fear and some contempt. Comfortably for Ormford, he guessed, but badly for his conscience, few of them ever did.

Saturday they came to the Staff Store, and did a second heavy shopping. Joan had let herself be methodically convinced that there was going to be an emergency, and Farquharson was at least prepared not to disbelieve the possibility. They got tinned butter, dried soups, powdered milk, jams, more flour, many tinned vegetables. Farquharson said, "You're inventing hoarding."

"Never you mind. This is Africa."

Over supper he heard, "Godwin, this is *my* kitchen. *I* put things away in it where *I* want them to go. And Jacob, you take your directions from me."

Later, she said, "He told me how long Jacob took to make the beds. I can well believe it. But I'm not going to put up with this kind of jockeying for position. Somebody's going to find they've got to go!" She sat down.

"What if one of them heard you?"

She said, "I hope they both did."

Rain had come before supper, everything green-gold and black. Now there were stars. Farquharson walked down onto the grass, lured by the extraordinary clarity of the dark and the brilliance of a high moon just a few days from full. He ought to call Joan out, and let her soak up the trick vistas, the flat nearness of distant things, the suppressed sparkle, but he didn't. He felt as whole as a bubble in the air, tentative, and quite wonderful.

"Good evening, sir."

"I'm moon-watching, Stanley."

"Sir?"

Master and man, he thought. Uncommunicating, but it didn't matter.

"Sir, I wish for permission for my sister to move here to cook for me."

Somewhere beyond the fence were the Magellanic Clouds, but he didn't know the shapes of constellations. "Well, I guess that falls within the rules," he said.

"I thank you, sir."

"Do you have names for any of the stars?"

"No, sir."

"Neither do I."

"Sir, I have a brother who wishes to sell a tennis racquet."

"Tell him to bring it to me. To look at."

"Yes, sir. Sir, it is not like this, in your country?"

"No," he said, "it isn't."

So the man brought the tennis racquet, and the strings had the right tense bounce in them. He bought it, in the morning, after only a few minutes of haggling, picked up an opponent in the afternoon, and played a game. His opponent was an anaesthetist at the University College Hospital, but Farquharson didn't catch his name.

8

NOTHING happened on election day except his overload of
tutorials and an argument in the Senior Common Room: a Professor Pritchard from Newark was producing parallels to a
supposed Nigerian pattern, until it seemed nothing could be said
about anything that didn't dissolve into analogies. Oscar Nwonkwo said, "My friend. You have too many examples. Do they not
worry you?"

"Nothing, historically, is a surprise."

Oscar said, "Except to its victims," and put his coffee down.
"Say the government loses this election today—no reasoning
man can imagine them achieving a majority. So they must make
one, somehow. And then consider that the government has no
practical support whatsoever upon this campus," he grinned
fiercely, "except the Bursar, who we all know is powerful beyond
his job. Now they will invent a majority, they will enforce it. And
do you believe that this university campus will be safe? That they
will leave us alone? We know the truth. They must make a target
of us!"

"Mrs. Nwonkwo, do you believe him?" Balogun said, cosmo-
politan, above tribes.

She was sitting next to Farquharson, wearing a yellow up-and-
down. She said, "They will have to have won," calmly, as if for
the first time in that room there was a thing to fear, "and then
they will have to do what comes next. The Onyeamas may have
gone, but there are many active people here of the Opposition.
But I can't," she said, pushing her clasped hands forward, "*think*
like that."

Balogun said, "There are more who support the government than just the Bursar alone. I think Professor Pritchard forgets that parallels and statistics are only a historical aftermath. The event is random. And by the way, the Yoruba word for the assumption of power, which is *ìjọba*, is, in the most literal translation, the act of eating the king. A formality, granted, but still . . ."

Farquharson had a head-on clash with his third-year criticism class. Mrs. Onwujialiri, Miss Ngu, Miss Salami, Mr. Akinyẹle, told him slyly, or pedantically, that they understood the course; Mr. Babafẹmi Gbadebọ smiled like a fraternity brother. Yes, they knew what the course was: now would the Professor do it? No.

"So you write down your feelings," he said, "you verbalize abstract principles without the laws to back them up. *That* is scientific?"

Miss Ngu said, "Sir, we have not been taught that literature is science."

"Fine," he said. "Now you're going to be. After all, why should I teach you the course you already *know*?"

"It's an uphill fight!" he said to Ormford.
"Fun?"
"Sure it is. I like fights."

He played tennis with the anaesthetist. He liked the way things moved when he played tennis, especially the arm, adjusting in the air with the free wrist, thinking for itself, like a computer: trajectories, force, angles. Somehow the mind bathed in rest, comforted, and carried. Farquharson had three sports only, and they were all, he thought, mathematical: swimming underwater, tennis, and fencing (which he hadn't done for years). Something in him remembered the footwork between ballet and boxing, the eager mobility of the centre of gravity, but all that was left was that he did fencing salutes with the tennis racquet.

And that night they realized that they couldn't leave the compound. "Do as Ormford said," Joan said.

"Is not sure," Stanley said, "if there may be curfew, sir."

So they drove to the Gate, saw nothing but an empty road and came back, and then drove at random about the compound to keep moving, as if they had to discover how much space they still had. They saw their house from El-Kanemi, looking unimpressive. Then they found a dark straight road with a wide field to one side, over which the moon hung, menacing. It led them to a starkly modern school, where they had to turn around. Joan said, "That was the International School. I saw a sign."

"Then we have seen the International School By Night." With one use, the words had become a phrase.

They drove various looping trails. Perhaps ten houses were having a party. They saw white people in living rooms. White people themselves, they went home.

"Well, wisdom or no," Farquharson said, "I've got to go to the bank."

"But if it isn't safe?" she said.

"Suppose we're broke?"

"Don't you go alone."

He called, "Come on, Stanley, earn your pay!" And Joan was hurt because the insult was obviously friendly talk between men in a world she didn't touch.

Stanley looked zestful, as if he were doing something he might be punished for, and they went out to the highway and down the Bodija road to the bank. Nothing looked unusual.

Then about a hundred yards from the bank there was a barricade of round-shouldered gates across the road, and three policemen with guns. "Stop," Farquharson said, suddenly feeling that the word was necessary. Reluctantly, Stanley found the brake.

The barrier wasn't just across the road: all the way to the bank it ran tilting along the high ground on the other side of the ditch. Farquharson was a little startled to realize that, mostly, he was just annoyed. Stanley let the car inch forward.

"Stop, damn it," Farquharson said easily, then opened the door

91

and came forward to the barricade. He said, "May I walk through to go to there?" and pointed to the bank. It was a foolish thing to do, he thought, stupid but experimental, but before the police could answer him, another man came running up from about a hundred feet away, pointing and crying out, "Open! That is officer car!" The men parted the fence as fast as they could. Farquharson whirled around, pointed straight to Stanley's nose, and shouted, "You stay right there!"

Then he went around the fence, stumbling in the rough ground, keeping a good six feet from the metal. From instinct (of safety, he thought) he didn't turn around.

The barricade receded at the edge of the driveway to the bank. Then he looked at the long grey homely building on the other side of the road, with a sign like a blackboard under a protective roof: the offices of the Electoral Commission. For a minute he was scared; then for a minute he was angry. And then he thought, "These are Canadian emotions," and, almost laughing, went uphill to his money. He was placed in the line for the meticulous teller, and it took him almost three-quarters of an hour to get down the hill again.

The barrier was still open, as if he were wanted to come through. Stanley seemed to have gained about an inch and a half of authority around his chest. But he was in the car. Farquharson got gingerly in the other side and said, "Go home, and fast."

"Oh, I was worried sick," Joan said.

" 'Officer car'," Farquharson said. "Stanley, is a secretary to an assistant that important?"

"It is not Mr. Ọrẹsanya, sir," Stanley said, saluting them with the beer he had just been given. "Sir, they know Mr. Ọrẹsanya not in Nigeria now."

"All right, then. Who *is* in Nigeria? Who was that for?"

"It is for Akintọla, sir."

"The Premier?"

Stanley smiled as if for applause.

"Sometimes he use this car, sir. It is said."

"And he's NNDP and the NNDP are the bad guys."

Stanley was radiant. "Sir!" he said.

Farquharson turned to his wife, who was sitting on one of the stained cushions pushing her hair in place. "I," he said, making his eyes look wild, "have a car formerly used by the Premier of the Western Region!" He said, "Oh, my God," then had to laugh. "And they opened a roadblock to us. Stanley, what did he use the car for?"

"Sir?"

"Oh, never mind. I don't want it made too good. Joan, we're going to stay at home."

That night they drove out to look at the International School By Night.

"Did you tell somebody to read *The Anatomy of Criticism?*" Ormford said.

"Yes. There were two copies in the library: I put them on the reserve."

"Well, they're both gg-gone, and so is the one from here. I don't know if that means three people are reading it: I never h-*have* worked that out. Don't ever call a bb-book important. Sometimes we gg-get them back."

"Akinyẹle," Farquharson said, and explained: "Guessing. Possibly Mrs. Onwujialiri. Or Gbadebọ."

"Gb-gb-gb-adebọ did it last year," Ormford said, strangling completely on the Yoruba two-shaped consonant and for the first time Farquharson had ever noticed ruffled by the noise he made. "Bb-but they all could you, know. All of them. Oh yes."

Farquharson didn't tell him about his car. Obscurely, as if for his own defence, that was private.

"You're coming to dinner tomorrow night."

Farquharson said, "Are we? Good."

They parted, waiting for their cars. One of Farquharson's third-year students came up to talk to him. "I don't think you know my name yet," she said. "Mrs. Akinrinmade."

93

"Are there many married women here?" he said.

But she said, "My husband is with the government of the Western Region."

In a kind of embarrassment he looked out to the small domed mosque and a distant tumbling-up of dark and rich jungled hills.

"Does it seem beautiful?" she said. "You must see my husband's town of Idanre. It is a famous beauty spot. I have seen photographs," she said, "of many Chinese paintings. They are what Idanre is like. And we have a big, black, two-storey house."

"We haven't travelled yet," he said.

"No. You must wait until the emotions of this election have gone away."

"I had a roadblock opened for me yesterday."

"I wouldn't like that," she said. "It's better to be stopped." But she didn't ask him why. She was a sombre woman. Farquharson thought her likeable. But it seemed that he had taken his position in Nigerian politics from Gail, or from Victoria Nwonkwo as she sat being reasonable about fear and violence. The government of the West was corrupt and tyrannous: Mrs. Akinrinmade was on the wrong side.

He watched her face when WP2471 came by to pick him up, but if the car meant anything, she didn't show it.

"Has anybody won?" he said to his Shakespeare tutorial.

"The government has won," Mr. Enem said. He was a sober, thinly handsome, trustable person. Farquharson had him in the poetry tutorial too, and after two classes was convinced that this one was one of the comforting bright spots and was glad of him. "It will have to be up to the people now. UPGA claims sixty-two seats of ninety-four; the government has taken seventy-one. How have those thirty-nine seats been taken, sir? We are going to have a demonstration tomorrow. Will the Professor join us?"

"I only riot," he explained, "for the Canadian Liberals."

"May we speak of Shakespeare?" Mrs. Onwujialiri said.

But at the Club there wasn't much talk about the election or any aftermath. Grace Spanier-Dodd appeared, and was full of politics, but the election became involved with her husband's steward and soon they were talking about servants and Joan told them about Elias and the kitchen floor. Farquharson was playing tennis with somebody Joan didn't know, and she could imagine how he looked, and so she caught Jamie, who was pottering about the playground, talking to himself, and led him off. Farquharson played tennis, Joan thought, the way he danced, with every kind of enthusiasm and private grace, but without accuracy. He was an easy man to defeat, but that seemed to have nothing to do with whatever it was he was enjoying.

Grace joined her at the bench. "Those women!" she said. "They say you do your own cooking. Very wise. Doesn't he look nice?" she, added sitting down and frankly admiring another woman's husband.

"I've never understood," she said, watching as the game finished, "why the best men should have to go around looking innocent," and Joan felt the blood thunder into her face without any reason except possibly that her husband might have heard. But when he came up Grace asked him if he'd heard that the Eastern Nigerian Radio had made a fiery broadcast about the victory of the Opposition in the West.

"They've swapped notes with Adegbenro, obviously," the anaesthetist said.

"Akintọla isn't going to like it," Grace said. "Will you believe trouble now?"

"The Sardauna isn't going to like it. That's what we really mean."

But there was trouble at home, of a more immediate kind: Godwin, full of cocksure deference and a list of Jacob's deficiencies—also, with the vegetables prepared for dinner, and a cut pineapple. Jacob hovered about five feet away, aggrieved and waspish.

"In the first place," Joan said, "I didn't want anything cut up, Godwin. We're going *out* for dinner!" And Farquharson withdrew Jamie and took him to give him a bath, out of earshot. He was sitting at one end of the tub trying to dodge the hot-water pipe, and leaning forward to Jamie, who was standing at the other end, between his ankles, sinking a plastic soap dish, when Joan hammered on the door, burst in, was embarrassed to see her husband naked with his son, and then sat down on the toilet seat with a vicious sigh and said, "Stanley is making too much noise, did the Madam notice it? Jacob was fifteen minutes late coming back from Abadina, did the Madam know? Farq, you've got to fire him!"

The water swirled at his knees. "Now?"

"Oh, what does it matter if you drip? The damned floor's concrete!"

"Well, what do I fire him for?" he said, putting Jamie's hands on the side of the tub and then surging to his feet.

"Initiative," she said. "Enthusiasm." Her hands were shaking. "I never saw vegetables so beautifully cut up in my life. You saw the ironing." She had gone down on her knees beside the tub and was holding Jamie's hands. "He wants everyone to be in trouble. And I didn't tell you this. He took Jamie out for a walk and I didn't know they'd gone."

The legs came past her. She could have hugged him around the thighs, just as he was, wet, to make him do this.

"Where did he go with Jamie?"

"Just up to get the mail," she said, "I was afraid to tell you. We didn't know where he was."

"We," he thought. Jacob and the Madam. He caught the small towel around himself and strode wet-footed through his house. Stanley and his friends were drumming. "Godwin?" he said.

So it *was* easy the second time. Not quick, but easy. There was going to be no Jack Okpata coming in his finery to negotiate. Paid off, and gone. His wallet was in the top drawer of the sideboard: He opened it one-handed, and tried to tease bills out with his finger, and then went and sat on a chair and worked the towel across him like an apron—and all the while Godwin stood in the kitchen, by the counter, staring head-up into the wall. "Five

96

pounds," Farquharson said, counting them. It was enough. "And five shillings." The little purple banknote lay across the others. "*Godwin!*"

He thought suddenly that Godwin had a knife beside him.

Jacob stood watching, with the huge frying pan in his hands, as if quite hopelessly to defend himself.

"I can't be sorry, Godwin. There's only room for one boss in a house. That wasn't even a good try. Here's your money," he said. "Jacob, will you give it to him?"

Jacob, still holding the frying pan, took the bills and then had to put them beside the vegetables. It seemed a long time before Godwin picked them up.

"I'll give a letter to Michael," Farquharson said. "Don't come here for it."

After a while Jacob smiled, as if he could congratulate the master on a victory. "Ibo bad person," he said.

Farquharson got to his feet, holding the towel like a fig leaf. He said, "Pour me a beer, Jacob. And bring it to the bedroom."

("Elias on your hill," he thought, "this is what you've done to me.")

But when Jacob came in, Joan's face changed and became almost ugly. "One of us," she said when they were alone, "is going to stay in this house tonight. What if Godwin comes back and there's only Jacob and the baby?"

"You're imagining things!"

"Of course I am!"

"But he's my boss!"

"He isn't *my* boss."

"*She's* your friend, though."

"Go on," she said. "Nobody's a friend when you're only here for a year."

The result was that they sent Stanley with a message to the Ormfords. Mrs. Farquharson would go to dinner, then come home, then Farquharson would go by himself. Joan was inflexible. There was a power failure while she was gone. Farquharson lit a couple of the candles and put one of them in Jamie's room, and

97

then he stood over the crib with the other candle in his hand, thinking he was a homely man, a rather lonely man, and very proud. There was his son below him, tumbled into a cage of slats, baroque and rumpled, and he loved him. He was glad that he had stayed at home, and guarded him—but not so glad that he didn't also want to go and dress. So soon he was standing by a long mirror in the bedroom, rubbing deodorant into his armpits by candlelight, pulling his hair over his forehead to see if he should get it cut, carefully stepping into his pants and then working at the pressure-cooker discomfort of a tie, pinching the knot carefully. When his wife came home he was waiting with his suit coat. After all, he was in this country: he wanted to go to parties in it. He drove into the dark alone to find his first one.

"Lo, the gg-guardian," Ormford said.

They ate an elaborate moulded gelatine pudding, surrounded by fruit. He met the bearded man who ran the Clinic, and his wife, and Dr. Garnett, whom he had met already, and Gail Johnston with him, and then Edward Cronis and his wife, from the far end of the department. Cronis had thin blond hair and wore sunglasses. He kept trying to get Farquharson to admit to dedication and a portable passion for the undeveloped countries. He had taught in Beirut, Rhodesia, *and* Oregon, and he was only thirty-one. "Farquharson, how old are you?"

"Some academics," Dr. Garnett said, "aren't just migrant. They're refugee."

Mrs. Cronis was talking of Rhodesia, and Farquharson thought suddenly, "Damn it, the woman's a pedant!" and wondered how you could do that to the discomforts of your own liberal experience.

He was leaning against the edge of the stage-high patio. Gail stood over him and said, "Why didn't you tell your wife?"

"That's a superb phrase!" Ormford said.

Farquharson looked up into the stiff skirt hanging over him. He suspected that one of the doctors was also looking at them. The echo of a dismissed seamy love affair was almost tangible. So he just laughed, making the rollicking uncorrupted noise he could count on.

"I told her I had an old student here," he said.

"Not a female one."

"Come on, down with the conquests, Gail!" Dr. Garnett said behind them, and Farquharson looked up into the face of a threatened man, and then at a flatly provocative woman in pretty clothes.

"Word to the wise," Ormford said, perching on the patio later. "Keep away from the demonstration tomorrow, bb-because there *is* going to be one."

"Why? What happens?"

"Sometimes nothing. Once," he said, "they had to close the wh-whole university. But then that was about food in the h-halls, I think. And *this*—there's more NNDP inside this compound than the students think," he said. "Or than I think. This isn't a stupid gg-government. But they use stupid tools. And since it all spills out from Tower Court, I wouldn't go for your mail tomorrow afternoon. Or buy a book."

If he was within sprinting distance, Farquharson thought, he could look.

"Tell Joan it'll be a tiresome nuisance, having the air full of war whoops," Peg told him, when he was about to go. "Send her over for a long quiet tea."

Dr. Foley, thoroughly drunk and Irish, cried, "On to Bandage Day!" and went through the doorway as if the walls were full of electricity.

Dr. Garnett had gone to get his car. Farquharson said, "Are you happy, Gail?" speaking in an ordinary voice, even though their host was still behind them.

"Was I ever?" she said. "Yes. I am. I like it here." Then she said, more quietly, "I don't like the English making fun of my name sometimes."

"But why should they?"

"Because it's *the* name for a heroine in a lot of stupid women's fiction. English fiction. I don't read that kind of book."

99

(Ormford muttered behind them, as if to bother them, "My wife bb-buys them.")

"I should have known, of course," she said, "I always knew it was a name for a tin-eared glamour lover."

Farquharson studied her: a strong narrow woman who must have spent great parts of her life quite close to anger. He had always thought she had an irritating name, a sort of whining monosyllabic squawk that wanted to claim romance. It explained a lot about her, living not just with the name but with the people who gave it to her. He said, "You've got another name. I remember two initials."

She said, "Gail's me. It's the wives," she added. "Incidentally, I like the students."

He said, "I think I like Bill Garnett."

"*He* doesn't matter."

He wondered what Joan was going to say about the "student", but she was in the dark, wide awake. "Well, there was a Nigerian party!" she said. Then she seduced him.

He was in amazed delight, because she had done it very well. He rode her with an abandon that belonged to years ago, and in his love forgot her, and was himself. And he shouted like a cowboy when he came, and flung himself head down over her, straight on to ugly tears. Nothing else was going to be needed to turn Gail Johnston from a sometime student into a female who sat near him sometimes.

He pulled out of Joan and kissed her, delicately, dozens of times around the face, kissing up the tears, but not the anger, keeping himself back from that.

9

SECOND-YEAR practical criticism met at eight o'clock, and if they had their minds on a demonstration, it didn't show: they were interested in an examinable definition of poetry. The Senior Common Room was similarly for a while a closed area of its own concerns, talking academic gossip about African democracy, until John Cord, in a white *danşiki*, tried to persuade some of the Negro staff, African and West Indian, to join the students in the demonstration, and couldn't get anywhere. One man said, "I am not a student," and Oscar simply laughed at him. Balogun contrived to be in a discussion with two linguists by a window. Cord became desperate. Nwala Okagbue moved as if to be nice to him. "Man, you're *white*!" Cord said to the West Indian he was talking to, and the rest of the Common Room had to swing rapidly to work to head off unpleasantness.

Finally Cord, being eased out of the room by Miss Okagbue, swung out of her shepherding at the doorway and said, "I'm with the students. Are we going to see any of you there at the demonstration? Or are you only for the black man when you don't have to do something for him?"

"I wonder," one of the Africans said when he was gone, "what colour he thinks the government is?"

Victoria said, "He has no business being among those students. Professor Balogun, can't you stop him somehow?"

A big handsome white woman in a corner said, "I wish he'd remember which continent he's on."

"*Or* that he's got his back to the blackboard."

Oscar said, "Shall we send him to the Bursar?"

The white woman said, "You can't. He isn't in his office."

"*Will* the police try to come?" Farquharson said.

Balogun said, "I doubt it. They know they have no right here."

At lunch Farquharson said, "I'd like to look at that demonstration."

"I think we ought to go to Peg's. She wants us to."

He said the Ormfords were going to be tired of the Farquharsons in crisis.

She said, "You just don't want to go away from it."

Jacob appeared in the centre of the patio and bowed farewell to them.

"I want to understand these people," Farquharson said. "I have to teach them. What good's a demonstration to me if I don't see it?"

"And if it becomes a riot?"

"This is an Opposition house," he said, and grinned at her. "That means it's on the students' side. Onyeama's name is still on the sign up by the road. Granted," he added, "it's lying flat."

"Oh, you won't be serious!"

"Nor will I go flying ridiculously across the campus as a refugee."

"All right," she said. "*I* will."

So he told her more gently that if they supposed they had to have a fight, he supposed they had to, but could Jamie please stay where he was, because he was asleep.

"And you won't leave him?"

"No," he said. "I won't."

Stanley took her.

Farquharson slept on his back, like a baby with his hands by his head and his legs spread.

He woke to sounds. The demonstration was being noisy. He put on his shorts and sandals, and listened. Whatever the sound was, it was coming from more than just one place. He wondered if there was a counter-demonstration somewhere.

Jamie was taking his nap on a bed, not in his crib. Farquharson bent over and lifted one overhanging leg onto the mattress. He stuck a doorstopper under the living room door to keep the hallway open, because with the sounds coming in, he wasn't sure that he would be able to hear Jamie if he wanted anything. And then he settled down with a magazine on the bare couch and tried to read.

The air was hot, close, stale. Faintly, after a while, there was something unpleasant in it.

He had to see. The move was automatic. He knew that the car was back. "Stanley!" he called. "Will you sit in the house? I've got to go and look."

He knew what would happen. Stanley would come to the window, yawning, with his shirt open, and say, "Sir?" Farquharson saw the stir at the window, and, feeling like a boy, ran.

There was nothing happening on Jaja. He was halfway to Tower Court before there was much to see.

People, straggling in groups of three or four, running suddenly. Sullen groups standing. Then more noise, noises of wrath. He saw the entrance to Tower Court with nobody in it, and, as if to justify himself, stopped to ask for his mail, only there wasn't any. He turned to see somebody hustle a staggering John Cord around the corner with the blood streaming down his face: he knew it was Cord because of the clothes he wore. So he walked along the building, close to the wall, as if hidden there, and looked up the incoming lane of Oduduwa, towards the women's hall. There were grey uniforms and little helmets in patches everywhere, and big trucks.

A girl came running towards him. (He didn't know who she was.) She caught his shirt. "They're in the hall!" she said. "They're breaking everything!"

A boy gently detached her and led her into a group to wait. More people came running from the direction of the Arts Building. He caught the stink of tear gas. A voice next to him said about ten seconds of something venomous in African. Farquharson edged away. Behind him, three police came trotting through the opening from the courtyard. On the lawn under the

Vice-Chancellor's office, two men in khaki were rolling on the ground, fighting. Just taking advantage, Farquharson thought. His heart was going too fast.

He looked towards the theatre. There were people there too, now. He saw Mr. Adebọwale, moving at a heavy trot. Adebọwale detoured towards him, stopped as if at bay, called, "You should be at home, sir, please!" And a policeman from behind caught him and threw him over. Someone in what looked like a servant's uniform—and Farquharson could think of him only as a thug—stared like a lizard and kicked. Farquharson was helpless; he was white, and a professor. He turned his head in shame.

Fifty feet away, embedded in a small crowd, with his face peacefully alert, his head thrown back, there stood Stanley.

Incredibly, Farquharson's first reaction was that Stanley mustn't see him. He dodged for the passageway, and then, staring towards Kuti Hall, he saw two men, far off, clutch each other and run down Jaja. And nobody followed them.

What if Jamie was awake? Wandering through the house? Crying?

Farquharson couldn't run. Only when he was abreast of the entrance to the parking lot did his feet pick up speed. He had to get to Jamie; he didn't see the people. At last he ran.

There was nobody on Jaja: it stretched out like a stealthy tunnel beneath the trees. Nothing showed at the Clinic. Maybe they'd taken Cord somewhere else. At the head of his driveway he tripped over the Onyeamas' house sign.

He got up panting and ran—then he could hear Jamie crying. He saw himself bursting around the corner of the garage on to the patio, but that would be frightening. He went on his toes across the grass to the kitchen door. Then he was into the kitchen, silently, in a second, and (still, he thought, for Jamie), didn't let the door slam.

There were two thugs in the living room. The dining room chairs had been thrown around. Jamie was at the desk, holding on to Ormford's little Italian typewriter. One of the men tore it away and it went high into the air, held by the end of the roller, and smashed on to the concrete. Farquharson yelled.

Somehow he had the huge frying pan in his hand. He didn't even feel it.

The dining room was a morass of chairs: he went around them through the patio. The man who had smashed the typewriter came up as if sprinting, and the edge of the frying pan caught him against the side of the head and clubbed him out of the way. Farquharson didn't even look at him. There was the other man at the door, panicking, standing still, who could be driven into the bedrooms and trapped. Suddenly Farquharson was a hunter of men. "Get away from my boy," he said.

The man scrambled, flailing, over the chairs in the dining room. He fled into the kitchen, and over to the wrong door. Farquharson, with a barked shin, caught him in the closed garage, against the car. Shreds of light came from some gratings high in the wall. The door was on a spring, and closed. Cornered, the man fought back. Farquharson threw him down. The man's head hit against the bumper guard. Farquharson hauled him up by the shirt and laid him back against the boot of the car. And then— and he knew, lucidly, that this was what he meant to do—he lifted the hand with the frying pan (he still had it; he must have hit with it several times), and as the man tried to lift himself off the metal, with his head still dangling back, struck down, edge-on full force, on to the standing veins and the Adam's apple and the neckbone. The man bounced against the boot and then slid smoothly over the edge and into a huddle against Farquharson's legs. Farquharson moved, and the thing slumped like a sack on to the garage floor.

He pushed the door behind him open, so he could see. If he had done what he wanted, he had killed a man. His breath stung. Like a man at love, he'd been deaf. Suddenly his ears cleared. He ran to his son, through the dining room—and now he had to pick up the chairs to get to him. His knees were gone. He couldn't walk over the obstacles. But he could put his arms out to his son and pick him up. "Jamie, it's all right now," he said. "It's all right. I was here." Jamie rose into his arms as if he had no weight at all. Farquharson hugged him. "You're all right," he was saying. They were both crying. Farquharson went through the open doorway and stopped and kicked the wedge out.

"Where's your cuddle toy, Jamie?" he said. "Jamie, it's all right now. You just wait in your crib and I'll bring you milk."

Arms around a bruised neck, Jamie hugged him.

"Everything's all right now I'm here. Do you want milk?"

Large-eyed, rescued, spent, Jamie went down to the crib mattress like one of the men outside, and when Farquharson came back he was clutching a small white lamb stained red from floor wax, and he wouldn't move. Farquharson put the milk where Jamie could reach it and tiptoed out. He picked up three chairs before he could look at his first man in the living room.

He must have smashed his skull at the temple: the man was lying huddled on his right side, near a chair, and a bit of blood had come out of his nose. Farquharson couldn't see him breathe. He tried to find a pulse. But the man was a soft and still thing. He was in a servant's uniform. Maybe he was from the compound somewhere.

Nobody had gone by on the path at the end of Kuti Hall. Perhaps because of the demonstration there were no Hausamen, no vendors. Stanley wasn't back. But Stanley had been *ahead* of him up at the Administration Building.

Then the one thing to do was to get rid of these two men.

And yet he didn't. He had to wash the frying pan. Water foamed around it like the bottom of a fountain.

The Onyeamas' sign, thrown into the middle of the driveway. Political thugs? They broke the personal things, not the university furniture. They must have just arrived, and found Jamie, and not known what to do.

Suppose Victoria Nwonkwo came around the corner and there he was? Not that she wouldn't help him, but what a shame to have to know! He bundled the typewriter into the bottom desk drawer: it locked. He had been supposed to take that typewriter to the office anyway.

Then he saw a short sword sticking out of a chair cushion, something they called a matchet, and he couldn't think of anything to do with it but lay it on the desk. He put his coat over the tear. Somebody would surely find him. He had a dead man on his floor. He had to tell himself that he had given him time enough to come to life.

He had to wipe the man's nose, and the floor, with a paper handkerchief. If anybody came up to the patio, he would have no warning.

It was like trying to pick a dead mouse off the floor, sensitivity to all textures, and a sick little regretful nausea. He tried to pick the man up, and had to drag him by the feet, around the room divider, through the back of the dining room (pushing the chairs well in), as if he were on a stage. One of the arms trailed, and jammed at the armpit against the drinks refrigerator. Farquharson had to lift the hands across the stomach and hope they'd stay there.

A soft hissing noise over the rough kitchen floor. One of the arms got loose in the passage, and they stuck again. It made him remember that the door to the back yard wasn't locked, so he took a long step into the clear and then turned off the tap and dried the frying pan. There was a man's dead head behind him, on the passage floor. Now that he'd stopped pulling him, he could hardly make himself go back. He ought to wait until he was found, and then say "self-defence", or "my boy"—but what self-defence performed karate chops on a dazed man with a fourteen-and-a-half-inch frying pan?

The boot of the car wasn't very big; neither were the men. If he took out the spare tire, which needed to be replaced anyway, he could probably get them in. Getting the lid of the boot to close was frightening, but the resilient corpses were both dead. Farquharson locked the boot, and then heard Stanley's phonograph ("It is borrowed, sir") through the closed-down garage door. He closed the door to the passage; he closed the door from the kitchen, softly. He rearranged the dining room. He went down to the bathroom, to flush the tissues away. Jamie was wide awake, and staring. What he'd done, he'd done. There wasn't any threat left. But there wasn't any defence, either.

One matchet, in the living room.

"Are you home?"

What sort of a country was it where everybody's servants had open access to swords?

"I heard Jamie crying," Victoria said. "Like a good neighbour, I stayed away. Is he all right now?"

"He had a scare," Farquharson said, feeling stiff and stupid, and running at about three times his speed. "A dream."

She said, "Poor little boy."

"Most beautiful of beautiful women," he thought, "you couldn't have seen me, or you'd have come and helped me pull." "Excuse me a minute," he said, and called, "Stanley! I heard someone in your quarters when you were out."

"That was my brother, sir."

"I thought your sister was coming."

"Not yet, sir."

"Well, I don't want anyone in your place when you aren't there."

"He come after me in two minutes, sir."

They hadn't even seen each other; they had shouted through the black window. The "brother" must have heard, and got away, right then.

"Beer?" he said.

A dead invader's armpit had lodged against the drinks refrigerator. Without thinking of Victoria, he got a cloth and wiped the front and side of the thick door, and then went for glasses. He poured and spilled down the side.

"Are you all right, Henry?"

"Nobody calls me Henry. I'm always Farquharson."

"Henry," she corrected him. "You look dreadful."

"Sorry," he said, "Jamie upset me. He was so very scared and small."

"I suppose he heard the noises." He was (aware of the danger) almost sentimentally grateful for her poise. "Oscar said the police broke into the halls and caused a great amount of damage."

"It seemed so quiet here," he said, straining his words. "Rumbles and mumbles."

"Nevertheless," she said, smiling, "I don't think I recommend a matchet in the living room."

He shrugged. "I used to fence."

"When they come to *us*," she said, "they won't waste their time up there."

"You aren't as sure as you think," he thought, "but that was for *my* benefit."

He said, "May I bring Jamie out?"

It was odd, but somehow she was a necessary benediction. So he sat, playing host, with a child on his lap, pressed to his stomach, as if for a cure for nausea. Jamie's sleeping weight was supposed to tell him about heroism, and defence and honour. He was tempted to say, "I killed two men today."

"Were there others than the police?" he said at last. The beer would make him vomit, but he hadn't the courage to put it down.

"What I and all of us are going to want to know," she said, "is who let them in?"

"How am I going to get my wife home?" he thought. "If Stanley drives that car . . ."

And what was he going to do with his bodies? Where was he going to put them?

"He is a beautiful boy." She was gracious. She admired children. There wasn't anything he could say; he could feel the tears jump into his eyes.

It was necessary to bless Oscar Nwonkwo for his wife. "You are both homesick and worried," she said. "Please!" And then she left him.

When she was out of earshot he said, clearly, to himself, because somebody was going to have to say it, "I have put two men to death."

It was neither believable nor unbelievable. It had happened.

Stanley appeared again in the patio. Farquharson said, "That's it for today, Stanley."

"And the Madam?"

"I'll go for her."

So he sat, steadied, waiting to shake, trying to relive the fight, as if it had been any form of glory, and thinking that there was a curfew beyond the university gates. "Jacob?" he said. "I want you to"—he blanked, then said with a great effort—"put that matchet somewhere. I found it.'"

There was a honk and a scrunch of tyres. Ormford cried, "Hel-looo!"

And Farquharson thought that all sorts of people must have seen him up at the street.

"Anybody home? Ah, Farquharson, the Human Cradle," Ormford said, his habitual hesitation less than usual. "What a pretty sight. No, don't gg-give me a beer," he said. "You come to us. Peg has proclaimed dinner. I would have sent Nicodemus, but I don't think he would have found his way beyond the library. Joan says you're to send Jacob h-home."

Farquharson thought, "All things conspire."

"Jacob!" he said. "You can go back to Abadina. We're going out."

They closed the doors. Farquharson checked and locked everything. Ormford jiggled Jamie on his knee and gave Farquharson a full elaborate description of the character of the Bursar. Farquharson checked the garage door from outside. He didn't know what was supposed to happen to bodies in the tropics; he only knew it was supposed to happen soon. He was glad he didn't have to drive in daylight with the back of the car so weighed down.

Ormford drove a long way around, keeping away from the Vice-Chancellor's house. "Just in case," he said, while Farquharson hunted the roadside for a place to put his bodies, even thinking of rolling them into the bush at the edge of Ormford's lawn. But he was a professor, as well as a killer: Ormford wasn't a fitting person to leave bodies with. He carried Jamie into the man's house, suddenly afraid of what he would say.

But Jamie wanted only to sit on his father's knee. Farquharson ate one-handed, tried to be a cheering guest, and fed Jamie with thoughtful calm and without talking to him.

"Those two," Joan said, "get on so well sometimes, I'm just outside it."

Nor did *he* have to talk. Ormford (he blessed him) could always talk. There were no strangers about the house when they got back. He lullabied Jamie, got his wife to bed, managed not even to listen when she told him the things Peg had told her about Africans. Then Jamie called and said, solemnly, in his putting-together fashion, "Men come. Far' *hit.*"

"And it all came out all right, I was just in the yard. I chased them."

"Far' hit."

He said, "Not very hard."

"All gone?"

"All gone. Now you go to sleep," he said, firmly and with amusement. The amusement startled him, but it was as real as the hunting instincts.

"What was all *that* about?"

"Mm?" he said, coming back into their room, still dressed. "Nothing."

He wanted to sleep: he had to stay awake, listening. Finally, about three o'clock, he started the car (it sounded loud), took it without headlights up the drive, riding low behind, thought how this was going to look like an assignation, and drove slowly around the unguarded compound, here and there. He put the lights on, suddenly afraid to be without them. He went to the International School By Night, and the moon over its field was more menacing than ever, but he was too far away from where the men might have come. So he came back, out to Oduduwa—and then he knew what he could do.

Oduduwa was absolutely unlit, and it led only to the gate. There was curfew outside. Nobody was going to come this way. He let his lights go out and crept, in the clouded moonlight, to the road that went off into the houses on the other side. Here was the street with the wide, gentle ditches, where he had thought of the dead after Mrs. Kayọde's accident. (He should have asked Bill Garnett about Mrs. Kayọde, shouldn't he?)

The car was unlit except for the parking lights and, he supposed, the oval ornament in the grille. Big trees overhung him. He stopped in silence, waited, shut off the parking lights, got out into the close air, held his breath, crept to the boot. He wondered if rigor would have set the bodies, got his hand on to the head of one of them, and felt the hair and face. But when he shuddered and tugged, the body bumped on to the road, and he simply pushed it into the ditch, rolled it down, and let it go. The boot of his car was as clean as a car boot possibly could be: it had been all scrubbed out after he bought it, and it hadn't carried anything but groceries since. (They'd better put the groceries in the back seat, he thought, for a couple of days.) The second body seemed almost to slide into his hands. He eased it to the ground. Which one was this? There was a little moment of flat agony when he didn't know and couldn't know. It lay flat on the road. He thought he would touch its neck and learn. But he rolled it too down into the ditch, in a hurry, suddenly afraid to stay.

He had to close the boot quietly. He had to start the car. WP2471 didn't start quietly. It had coughed and sputtered for a minute in the garage. He thought it would do it here. So he started it with too much gas, and it revved and roared, not, at any rate, sounding at all like itself. And then he drove almost to the Club. He was afraid to turn around. He should have brought the typewriter; he could have put it in his office. But it would be a damned suspicious time to be seen with a broken typewriter.

He didn't want to cry for men he'd killed: what if he had to? He was still what he was, no matter if there was something latent. He hadn't asked for this. He was still Farquharson. He'd seen his one son threatened, and he'd killed. Then that was who he was. Whatever the country might be. No regrets, so long as he got away with it. And all regret.

Dozens of people on the compound wore sandals like his, if he'd left footprints. Ormford did, and of the same size.

No one else had seen those two men go to his house. No one had followed them.

He drove restlessly about. Up along Sankore there was a little half-house with a sign saying "Miss Gail Johnston". He went past twice. He could see Gail inside the window, if he craned his head. What he ought to do, at the end of such a day, would be to have love made to him. But he didn't. Anyway if Gail wasn't pretty, why should he have to think of her? His wife was pretty. He was spoiled. For faces.

Back at Number One Jaja he left the car on the lawn, found the living room doors unlocked, and locked them, with scraping, resonant sounds. He washed his hands. He was looking at a living body, with a shirt on, in the mirror of the medicine closet. He hadn't changed at all, except that his hair wasn't in order. The end of his nose was as round as ever.

So they had begun by putting tear gas into the telephone exchange. Then by fanning out to break up the residences. It was a concerted invasion, a thing planned. Casualties would be noticed. But if his two were servants, or university junior staff, was it going to be to anybody's interest to hush it up?

Joan was asleep. At least, she might have been. He lay awake all through the night, and she never spoke to him.

IO

"You were out last night,"she said, bringing him coffee.

"I was restless," he said. "I think that business upset me yesterday. Did you know they were clubbing people?" (Adebowale going down. It was odd to feel frightened, and to have a distaste for brutality.)

"Where did you go?"

"I just drove."

"Not past 1B Sankore."

"Yes," he said. "Twice." Then he looked at her and said ruefully, "Oh, dear. You know, I never liked her very much. You might build on that."

"Farq, don't go strange on me."

"Oh, come on, Pickle, I'm the same man as yesterday."

On the way to the Arts Building he said, "Stanley, I made a bad mistake yesterday. I thought you were in your house and I went up to look at things. Jamie got a real scare."

"My brother say you make him scared, sir," Stanley said. "He run away."

"Well, if Mrs. Farquharson hears about it, I'll never hear the end of it. So if you have to say anything, you were there." (He thought: Lie, lie, lie.)

"Yes, sir," Stanley said. "I was there."

"Sometimes," Farquharson said, "the men have to stick together."

"Whiche was the mooste fre, as thinketh yow?" He had to face a class. "Is it odd," he said, "that a story about love ends as a riddle

about the liberty of the human soul? What is *fredom*?" He wrote the word on the blackboard.

"I am trapped in the consequences of my acts, only to the extent that I do not know what those consequences are. Macbeth wishes that the assassination 'could trammel up the consequence,' remember? But of course it can't. And because Dorigen knows she cannot control the consequences of what she does, she spends a hundred lines of hysteria making certain she doesn't do any act that will have a consequence—and of course that doesn't work. Dorigen is not *fre* there."

"Tricky having to mention Macbeth," he thought.

The class moved smoothly. It was a sermon on freedom, almost a demonstration of the thing. This, he thought, was what he was here for.

"Is bad news, sir," Stanley said at noon. "There are two of the Maintenance Department. They find them dead at Obong. They are hit by car."

Incredulous escape was like a flat fist, pummelling his heart.

And Stanley drove him to the spot. "They are in the road, sir," he said. "Here, and here."

People crowded about his car, all speaking with panache and relish. He had to ask, like a master, "Where?"

One man ran and lay down on the road, like a child sleeping. Two boys raced for the second place. "Master! Master, look!"

Each flat on his back, on the other half of the road, feet to the oncoming traffic, knees raised and fallen. Farquharson shouted, "Which one of you?" Two of the women by his door began to make soothing speeches—he thought about the uncertainty of human knowledge—but he was too piqued by the locations to have anything more of conscience than fascination, and he got out and with a quizzical and benign look stood behind the boy's heads and said, "Which one of you?"

He was twenty-five, thirty feet away from his ditch.

An older man stood between the boys but four feet farther down the road. "In this place, sir. As the children show."

One of the boys suddenly jumped up, hit the other, and went to the right place. Everyone backed away. Farquharson muttered to himself, "Let's get this show on the road."

It was a convincing illustration of the aftermath of a hit-and-run. "In those very places?" he said. That seemed satisfactory. Was there room between them for a car to go? He didn't think he'd ask the question.

"And I," the old man said, "I find them, master." Farquharson had to hear a bravura tale of predawn twilight and a fast bicycle and a group of sleepers in the road, and when it was over, he dashed the man a shilling and threw threepence apiece to the boys.

Somehow, Farquharson thought, he had joined Africa. And he wondered who in the near-by houses had arranged the bodies. He said, "Take me to the mail, Stanley," and got a notice of an emergency meeting of the Association of University Teachers for the next Monday.

A. We the members and officials of the AUT, Ibadan Branch, 1. Deprecating the invasion of the privacy of the University of Ibadan by mobile units of the Nigeria Police Force; 2. Deprecating the considerable damage done by the aforesaid units to university-owned and private property; 3. And deprecating the wanton brutality of the self-same units to students and employees of the university;

B. Do call upon the Council and Senate of the University of Ibadan: (a) to seek legal redress for the aforementioned damages to property and brutal acts against persons and (b) to get assurance that this will not happen again.

Farquharson said, "Bully for them!"

His students had told him enough. Radios smashed, and typewriters (he understood how that happened!); people dragged out of bed and clubbed, girls hit. "They just drove in at the Gate," Sandy MacLachlan said in the Common Room. "Naturally. Who could stop them?"

"Nevertheless," Victoria said, "I believe they failed. Their purpose was obviously to provoke an incident."

Pritchard said, "And that wasn't one?"

"The students did nothing but look on or run away. They could have fought back. They were angry enough: we could have had people badly wounded, and the government would have swept in and closed the university, which must have been what they wanted. They didn't manage to get an excuse to do it. And they won't get a second chance."

And that, Farquharson thought as he looked across the square of couches into her face, was what warriors' wives were like. He wondered if the playboy husband had any idea of what he had.

The Club that afternoon was a mixture of gossip and outrage, a sort of owners' dismay. Farquharson thought there were a good many professional Africa-worriers about.

He began to cherish a vision of a master of a house, in bright pyjamas, lugging affronted bodies from *his* property. And at that point he stopped worrying for his own discovery, or even thinking of it, and dived triumphantly into the pool, raising a great splash. When he got back to his wife, dried and neat, she said, "Well, aren't you the happy one!"

The water in the pool was seven inches low. Somehow he associated that with the election.

That night there was still curfew, so they went to the International School By Night and looked at its open dining hall. And when Farquharson put WP2471 away and checked its tires as usual, he found a pitted sixpence on the floor that hadn't been there before. It was obviously fake. It must have bounced out of one of the men's pockets. He slid it into his own pants pocket and went to turn out the lights.

When they were waiting to go to bed, he heard an old train whistle. It was a desolate, lost, Canadian noise and it should have made him homesick, but he was in Africa, thirty-seven, male, vigorous, a happy murderer.

He slept the way Jamie slept. When Joan went to the bathroom in the middle of the night, she toured the empty house and looked at both of them. Jamie was going to be an embraceable, sensual male. Farquharson asleep had the small boy's enchanted innocence. It felt treasonous to decide that for her there wasn't much comfort in the adult combination.

"Jacob," she said, "what is a matchet doing coming around the corner of our house?"

Jacob went importantly out and brought a man to the window. "I come for my farm, madam," the man said, pointing to the garden behind the kitchen. He nodded. "Master."

"Madam," Jacob said, "is the Onyeamas' steward."

"Then he should have come before. I don't want strange men with matchets in my garden. This is *my* house. You can take what you can carry in one load," she said.

"But is *mine*, madam!"

"Surely by now," she said, "it is time that people knew that this is not the Onyeamas' house!" She put up her hand. "I will have *no* argument!"

"Golly," Farquharson said to her, "have *you* learned!"

"As if this was still the Onyeamas' house!" she said later. "Oh, damn them!"

It was Sunday afternoon, so they drove outside the compound. Farquharson decided that he didn't, after all, have very much to lose. Ibadan was a hot, restive city. Everybody seemed to be wearing his best clothes. Clean popinjay people mingled dignity, anger, conceit, and authority. The sun made the city clean. They went only on the streets they knew: the Ijebu Bye-Pass; the roads around the Kingsway; the detour back through Sabo past the Scala Theatre, where the Northern Moslems sat around in concrete yards in dirty white. Farquharson said, "Has anything changed?" but they couldn't know. "We might as well be at a movie," Joan said, "for all we can get into it."

Where were the images of dead men moved three times before they were found? If Ibadan was their city, Farquharson thought, then they weren't relevant. Little men in ill-tailored uniforms of pale khaki with sleeves that stuck out without relation to their arms, and long shorts that flapped. What life of honour or sex, he thought, for the shapes that had to dress up like that? He had to try to persuade himself, through them as agents, what to be suddenly dead would feel like, but he hadn't started yet. The brain wasn't willing to promote difficulty and blanked. The most that happened was that he felt divided into several indifferent parts. He had a survivor's instinct to make fun of that, without fuss. Being healthy helped.

All things conspired.

He and Joan cooked spaghetti for themselves. Farquharson had to stand over the stove, stirring sauce in the huge frying pan that the Catering Department lent them to kill burglars with. It was a meditative job; he had, under the circumstances, he thought, a good deal to meditate about. Composition of place, he thought, being professional. Point-by-point, sense-by-sense construction of an image to be a symbol for the subject of the meditation; the knobs on the stove pushed into the front of his legs and lower belly. There was a counterfeit sixpence in his pocket; not felt, guessed-at. Stanley's sister had arrived with two small children, one sickly. She was apparently scolding him; Stanley's subdued, thrusting answers came back from time to time. Jamie was making plastic animals pounce on each other on the patio. Composition of place for a meditation on wrath, or violent mortality, *"Man-slaughtre, and waast also of catel and of tyme."* He couldn't do it. People felt so important, over the finding of car-slaughtered bodies, it would have been a shame to tell them. So he guessed that between him and Joan there would be a wall.

Power at the arms' end: could it be ever regretted, once found? This was a man, too. Jamie hadn't been *this* valuable, before he had killed for him, had he?

The frying pan was all right. If he was at peace with the hands and arms, all there was for the tool was an interest, a speculative echo. The curiosity over the unimportant, like an aunt's souvenir teaspoon of Philadelphia, always with the same story of how she got it. *"That's the frying pan I killed the thugs with."* "I know, *you told me." "Well, can I help it if it only happened the one way?"*

They had a huge supper, and accompanied it with vodka and squash. "Oh, brother!" Farquharson thought in the night, perching on the edge of the patio and looking over to Stanley's single light bulb. "Am I glad I'm not a Catholic with a priest!"

Conscience was its own world.

Essays were due from one of the first-year tutorials on Chaucer. Opposition candidates, including Adegbenro, were in jail. Farquharson got a letter from the Catering Department across the road: "I should be most grateful if you would return the big kettle and frying pan loaned to you on the 29th ultimo, as they are needed for the use of the medical students at Ibarapa. Very sorry for the inconvenience." There was a notice on the board outside his office denying university responsibility for the appearance of the police at the demonstration. Farquharson took the kettle and the frying pan, triumphantly, to the Catering Department, borrowed a pen, and wrote a note. "Returned with thanks, one (1) kettle, one (1) frying pan. H. J. Farquharson." Smiting sun and muggy air slowed him on the short trip home. "You're a happy one," Dr. Garnett called from his Land-Rover beside the Clinic.

"Hi!" So he asked about Mrs. Kayọde.

"Oh, nobody liked her but the women. Say, what do you think of them arresting Adegbenro?"

And in the afternoon they got a letter to say that their belongings had landed and were going to be trucked up from Lagos. They rode to the International School By Night, for sentimental reasons. Farquharson also went past the Arts Building to see if the emergency meeting was taking place. They saw lights on, and then all went into the library to pick out books and watch two students on one side of the desk mercilessly browbeating the attendant on the other. Farquharson measured them carefully, knowing his strength, found them contemptible, then slapped his embossed senior staff library card on the counter and said, "Service, please."

Jamie held his hand.

Joan was aghast at the undemocratic treatment, and said so, outside.

Farquharson lay on the bed beside the crib, and sang softly, in the near-dark, his head on one side, looking between the slats.

The arrival of their goods was chaos. The Farquharsons, like the Onyeamas before them, considered their address to be 1 Jaja Avenue, whereas the official layout of the university called it 8 El-Kanemi Road. So by the time Farquharson got back from his next-to-the-last Chaucer lecture Joan had seen a truck go by three times, twice on Jaja and once beyond the fence on El-Kanemi, without stopping anywhere. But though she had taken one of Jamie's crayons and written "FARQUHARSON" on a paper, and pinned it up to a tree, and had sent Jacob with a note to the Estates Office or whoever he could find that would be responsible, she hadn't managed to make the truck stop on its third pass, and she had stuck in the Onyeamas' sign, so that *something* at least should say "1"—but she knew that wouldn't help, either. And then they saw the truck go down El-Kanemi again, and Farquharson sent Stanley to give chase. And so finally their crate was hurled to the ground beside their patio—with no need to break it open because it was now shaped like a rhombohedron. Their assorted boxes were hauled on to the patio, and Farquharson signed for them, wondering if they were insured.

They set up house. WP2471 was loaded with borrowed objects to return, and Joan set out to get them all back to their proper places, leaving her husband to put away the boxes and Jacob to remake the stripped beds. Farquharson took the demolished type-writer and covered it with a rubble of excelsior, in a box. All things conspired.

Pots, pans, dishtowels, sheets, blankets, toys.

Clothes, looking mouldy. "Jacob! Get these out on the line!"

Books: Milton, Shakespeare; two recipe boxes of lecture notes.

His great-aunt's braided rug appeared in the middle of the bedding and the books. "Dear soul," he thought. "She's dead." He lifted it through the litter to put it on the living room floor.

A young Hausaman came to the patio with a servant carrying a huge pale hamper. "I can sell you things, master. Carvings, leather, brass." The servant set the basket down.

"The hell with that," Farquharson said cheerfully. "Oh, come on, choose a better time."

"What better time than when the master is assembling his estate? Moonstones?" the Hausaman said, reaching into the opened basket. "Ivory fish." He drew out a dozen strings of rough green glass beads.

"Yes, and look," Farquharson said, and hauled out a skipping rope, a humming top, and a pull-toy.

"What you buy, master?"

"Look, you're on my patio and I've got work to do."

The man bridled. "Master."

Farquharson swooped to his feet with a load of blankets and left Jamie and his new-found toys among brass bracelets.

"Master?" The man held something up, and waited for him.

It was a necklace of malachite beads, the biggest almost an inch across. Farquharson couldn't help himself. He said, "Where did you get that?"

"Twenty pounds, master?"

Farquharson took it into his hand and let the beads roll down his forearm. There was nowhere, anywhere in the world, such a green as malachite. (The turn of the wrist suggested an arm to be raised, and struck down, violently.) But he knew that Victoria had a malachite ashtray. He'd put his beer bottle into it: a huge lump. She hadn't behaved as if it were valuable. "Nonsense," he said. "I wouldn't even give you three."

"For Madam?" the man said. "For the young man's mother?" And he sketched the shape of the necklace on his chest as if he had breasts, suggesting the ultimate voluptuousness of whoever should become the wearer of those beads. "You have to give me a serious price, master."

Farquharson said, "Three pounds ten."

He went back to his work. After a while he came back out to the patio and said, "You're still here."

"Master, fifteen pounds?"

"Four. And that's my last price."

"You have to be fair to a Hausaman when he comes, sir. He comes from a long way."

"Where this comes from they make ashtrays and doorstops out of it. For all I know they use it for hitting each other over the head with. Let me see it again."

It was put into his hands with deferential attention, but no respect.

"Oh, I do have to admit they're well made," he said, "if I wanted them."

He enjoyed this. This was the hunt of battle in a tourney of courtesy and insults, as he unpacked and took his time. Fifteen minutes later the Hausaman's things were all spread out in their newspapers. "Master," the man said. "Five pounds ten. Because I am the first to you in your house, master. I wish to make you content with your Hausaman, sir, even though it will lose me much money."

"Oh, very well then," Farquharson said. "I'll come up to four pounds ten."

"Master, you will destroy me!"

Farquharson said, "No more."

He set the table with the dishes. So what if they hadn't been washed yet! He hummed *Vissi d'arte*, made an arrangement of objects on the shelves, and turned only when the Hausaman came up to the open wall and with his head averted thrust the beads into his hand. And Farquharson said, "Four pounds ten," went and got the money, and paid it.

The servant (the slave, Farquharson thought him) took the basket back on his head. When they got to the corner of the garage the Hausaman looked back and called, strong and happy, "I come back, master!"

"I guess I got taken after all," Farquharson thought. But the beads were beautiful. He wanted them, and he had them.

So he swung them on his arm, put them high up in the

bookcase, unpacked their own black, comfortable frying pan, and hefted it.

He had a good week. He gave his first-year class such a lecture on Abelardian dialectic and the *débat*, and the educational process of dilemma and deadlock, "*Whiche was the mooste fre, as thinketh yow?*" and such an onslaught attack on the education of rote and answer that when he was done the room rocked with applause, and he was an honoured man, even if they weren't convinced. He was also surprised. It was just his final Chaucer lecture; he hadn't worked on it.

"You have attacked," Adebọwale said to him, "everything that we have been taught."

"Out of this nettle safety, remember?" Farquharson said.

And Friday the twenty-second, with the curfew over, they forsook the International School, and the cool air came fast.

II

EUPHORIA had to pass, Farquharson thought, sometime. But here were the streets, in the night, with the looming walls of the occasional high house crowding the road; here were the people, their colours obliterated for the shades of wood, rust, oil-lamp fires, and the surrounding dark. Voices were everywhere. Here and there were houses or barber-shops lit by lurid blue fluorescent lights, or sometimes a stark wild green, and here the continuous movement of the streets was invaded by this overpowerful dyed furnace glare. Men sat in barbers' chairs with incandescent blue shirts and purple skin. Outside, in the shadow, were the women with their little lamps. Farquharson thought, "I live here: I have to," and steered the car gently against the edges of the crowds, wishing that Joan drove.

A little man in floppy sleeves and floppy shorts stood in his headlights and peered towards them. "Well, don't just *sit* there," Joan said. "You can go six more feet."

After sunset, lightning now flared in huge tranquil sheets around the sky. Farquharson had no classes but tutorials for a few weeks. They found that if they didn't take baths at least twice a day they would stink. "It must be bacteria," Joan said. "You smell just like Jacob," she said. "I thought it was Negro, whatever they said."

"*Stanley* never smells."

"You do," she said, "like a cat in heat."

All things conspired. He said to Ormford, "It's too complicated to explain, but your typewriter got smashed," and then, surreptitiously, bought him one, and winced at the loss of money. The men from the Maintenance Department had been put away in the burying ground. He expostulated about *As You Like It* and the nature of expository prose, marked a discouraging series of essays, and wondered what, after all, Donne's eroticism had to do with the middle of West Africa. And Jeremy Fisher asked them to the promised party.

Joan wore the malachite beads.

Jim Fisher was a widower. That, on the compound, was the one main thing about him. His late wife, as he said when he had been challenged by sufficient drink and was standing in the dark on the lawn outside, "did the classic thing about childbirth. And don't tell me she shouldn't have come to Africa, because she did that in England. I was here." He pointed back into the night, presumably to some other flat. A dozen guests talked shop, and ate Nigerian hors-d'oeuvres like grainy fritters. Farquharson kept detouring back to the table and getting more.

"Are you going to try to be an African?" Fisher said.

Farquharson thought of his dead: he *was* one.

"None of the women can. Or they become white Yorubas."

There was a giggle in the dark. A thin girl ran barefoot around the corner of the lawn. Light from a car showed a short bright skirt, billowing with petticoats. Farquharson saw a thin mocking head, a little lewd mouth. As soon as the car went by the girl danced up to Fisher, long-legged, as if she were going to kiss him. Fisher said, "Go and help your uncle. You're a small bad woman. Go around."

She laughed and put out a hand as if to catch him below, before she ran away. If the move was supposed to be hidden by the dark, it wasn't. "Farquharson," Fisher said, staring straight into the dark, "do I have to explain that?"

Inside, Bernice Funmilayo, secretary to the Bursar, a bawdy-seeming, genteel, touchy, and dignified woman, played hostess for him. She had overseen all the food; she was telling Joan how it was made. Farquharson thought that he was standing on a lawn with a dilemma that at least wasn't his.

"My steward calls her his niece," Fisher broke out, suddenly turning his back on Farquharson. "I know for a fact she's not." He wondered whether Fisher had been finally caught, or whether he did this for everyone. "At least," he thought, "I only kill," and wondered, if his host had been looking at him, what *he* would have seen.

The hostess called now from the doorway, "Jeremy, come in!" She said, "The Nwonkwos are going."

Victoria said, "Goodnight, Jim," and gave him her hand to hold for a few seconds. Bernice Funmilayo smiled at her.

"She is the most beautiful of us all," she said to Joan, "and yet every woman likes her. Whereas I am not beautiful, and, oh my dear, I do have enemies." She linked her arm in Jim Fisher's and pulled him down on to a couch to sit. She said, "Let the servants wait on you." Farquharson was aware of a child's mocking face just outside the kitchen door.

"She was married," Oscar said the next day in his office, eyeing the door in case Cord should come. "Her husband hanged himself. Nobody knows why. I believe he was sexually impotent. He was certainly dishonest. Now anyone can have her. But her price is high—*she* chooses."

Fractions of lives, opening, like doors blocked, just so far. The gift of sight hadn't been administered to him with two killing blows two weeks ago. Maybe the wish to use it had.

Because he'd gotten away with it. Absolutely clear, clean, scot-free. He slept at night, in spite of the noises of African voices going nightly past the houses, shouting in the dark.

But he moved by day.

He got an invitation to the formal opening of the Students' Representative Council, sat on a hard seat on the aisle beside a tense young man who should have had red hair and been a *short* basketball player, and listened to young persons in gowns make speeches, it seemed endlessly, while the light faded and the faces became black holes. Again and again the single palm glimmered in a close-to-the-body gesture. Farquharson had borrowed a pencil and was noting the complaints on his invitation card. "Residences. Bad food. Examinations too emphasized." He asked the man beside him how many they wrote in three years and was answered, "Eight." He whispered back, "I had thirty-two in four." He wrote, "Oduduwa Lane not lit: bad for girls," and wondered if he ought to write down, "Good for murderers."

He tried to settle his hams in the very hard chair, and thought he was going to stick to the wood.

Somebody small, black, and gesticulating was making a well-enunciated roundabout speech advocating universal military service in the cause of a liberal education.

"Well," Charlie Spanier-Dodd said on the way out, "what did you think of it?"

"I never left home, except for the last. I just don't see what conscription has to do with education."

"I wonder how they'd work it," Charlie said, "to make you dash your way into the army, if you had to go, and they *had* to take you. I don't doubt they'd manage somehow." He wandered away brooding over it.

"I greet you, sir."

"Mr. Adebowale," he said. "I had an early supper: come home and talk for a while."

"The Professor honours me."

"Oh, come on. All we are is men."

They walked in step. It was an instinctively companionable thing. No wonder armies produced certain kinds of honour, Farquharson thought, if they marched. Adebowale made his apologies beside the theatre. He had indeed much work to do. If the Professor would pardon him?

Farquharson watched him go and then dawdled indecisively along the road behind him, where a Honda and a small station wagon stood behind the theatre.

A door shut, high over his head, and there were loose shoes with hard soles clattering down a long spiral staircase. He looked up. A few pieces of far lightning showed him an outline at the top.

There must be some rooms up there, at the very top, over the stage. He saw a white dress come down, one turn, and then another. Then he heard a dry rasping sound and Gail's voice swearing, and he said, "I know that voice!"

She looked over the railing to him. "Did you ever get the end of a bamboo leaf in your eye?"

"It's the sweet English heroine," he said, as her feet touched ground, "of the romantic books."

"I suppose I ought to come to your place," she said, "or you come to mine." She lifted up her Honda, steered it and pointed it to the road. "We don't have to do either of them."

"Your house, for half an hour."

She drove, he thought, badly, but then maybe his weight behind hampered her.

"In case you wondered what 'chalets' are in the brochure," she said, "they're this."

Half a house, joined end-on to another but with a wall of hedge between; a smallish living room full of huge square dull furniture, and piles of sketches, and magazines on and beside the furniture, as well as a partly completed model of a stage set on the table.

She said, "Everything's dusty. I guess my small-boy'd dust it if I gave him a chance. The cushions are grey anyway."

"We haven't covered ours yet. They haven't given us the right ones."

"Dump them in Akinkugbe's lap," she said. "Then he'll have to do something about you. Otherwise he won't. The basic technique around here is the ability to throw a tantrum. If you can do that, you're fine."

She gave him a glass of raw wine in a green 'cut-crystal' plastic glass, with bulging sides. "I live on a small budget," she said. "Sorry."

"And if I wondered why I was here," he thought, "I'd be a liar." Nevertheless, he did.

She took an elastic band up from behind the model and crammed her hair into a ponytail. "Elastics don't last worth a damn in this climate," she said. "No, believe me." She settled her hair, shook her head. "Now," she said, let me look at you."

"Better than what Peg's butcher brings around to the house, I hope?" he said. Then, as she stared, "Well, what am I? The innocent abroad?"

"I wouldn't say so. Oh, we all have our illusions. You were at the Opening of Parliament," she said, "tickling yourself with every overlap onto student clichés at home, and now here you are, being very alertly male and sure that the world is going to come out democratic as well as wondering what I want with you. Which is nothing."

"I'm glad I never had you in a classroom in this mood."

"Moods change," she said. So did her voice.

He became pricklingly conscious that he was married but that there was a (probably unmade) bed in the next room.

"Come on, Gail," he said, "you're beyond being a businessman's leisure. Look at me."

"I do," she said. "You could do quite well. However, your virtue's safe. I may have become dishevelled in the tropics, but I'm not morally sodden."

She looked down and moved a small pillar on the stage into another place.

"Gail," he said, "why are you here?"

She looked bitter. "I'm doing good. Why are we all here? This is Africa. I had to get a job teaching theatre design somewhere, didn't I? Do you know that nowhere in Nigeria can you buy the right nails for flats?" As if it were a small dance for advantage, they exchanged grievances about their students for a while. Farquharson felt half ashamed, and suspected she did too.

"You were supposed to stay for half an hour. I'll drive you home."

Somebody ought to do something for her, he thought.

"Now let us give you a drink," he said when she stopped at the head of his driveway, but he thought she winced at the "us", and maybe Dr. Garnett was still at the Clinic across the road. (Well, somebody *was* doing something for her, he thought.)

She turned the little machine away from him. And he wanted to look at the back of her dress and watch her move.

Joan asked him what the meeting was like, and he was suddenly weary that he was going to have to talk about that all over again. A gecko was hunting on the wall. "Look," he said. Joan liked geckos, she said. They were like cats. Intelligent black eyes in gentle faces, and they switched their tails, stalked, crouched, pounced. He made her a cocktail.

"I've had two baths since noon," she said. "It doesn't make any difference."

"Do I still smell?"

"Only of yourself," she said, and to his amazement laughed. "You can't help that."

"Then is it all right?" He was a man on a rising wave.

"Oh, honestly," she said, "who can manage to make love with the temperature like this?"

"I can"

She had to look away from him. She put the kettle on. She said, "I asked Jacob if he was getting on well at Abadina. He said, 'No, madam. I have no friends.' So I said, 'Why is that?' and he said, 'It is because of you, madam.'"

All right, he thought, we change the subject. "Why?"

"I didn't hire the Onyeamas' servants. Not some of them, *all* of them. They seem to think they have a right to their places, no matter who owns the house. I suppose they were half relatives. Anyhow, they've gone from Abadina; they've left deep feeling behind, and everybody around seems to be taking it out on Jacob. 'It is because of you, madam.' Huh!" she said.

He held out his hand. "Hate it?"

"Hate this part of it."

"Can't it be a game?"

"I try," she said.

"Look," he said, when they went to bed, "I'm not a celibate, even in the tropics. Please, I want to."

(And that, he thought, is for changing the subject on me.)

131

"Do you want *me*?" she said. She was putting on her night-gown, so she could take off her bra under it. Even in this weather, she wore a bra.

"Aren't we married? I haven't been in your bed since the night of the Ormford's party."

"Are you keeping score on me?"

"I don't know," he said, but he sounded oddly surer, and tough.

"I'm so hot, and sticky, and tired. Mr. Farquharson, I don't want to."

To have and to hold, he thought, throwing his shirt, shorts, socks, all on to the bathroom floor. "God damn it!" he said, as if with the back of his head to the door. "*Africans* reproduce!"

She said, "You think I'm not sorry for you." She had followed him into the bathroom. "You're wrong. You're very wrong. I hope you know *how* wrong some time."

He said, "We wear clothes for each other, don't we?"

"All right! I'm frigid for you!"

"Don't wake Jamie. Anyway, that's a complicated lie. Trouble is, we're here." He sighed. "Please, can I have my bath?"

"All right," she said, "I'll be ready for you."

"I won't take it that way." He looked away, into the toilet bowl. "I want desire."

So that night he slept naked. And she didn't tempt him.

The next day Farquharson followed Gail's advice, and he and Stanley carried fourteen cushions down the slope to the baggage-car barn doors of Akinkugbe's warehouse and announced that something else had better come back because those weren't going to. Half the effect was lost because Akinkugbe wasn't there. An agitated letter followed, and that night they had no place to sit, but on Tuesday the truck came with a load of men and cushions, and all that prevented Joan from going straight into Ibadan to pick out her material was the fact that WP2471 was in the Motor Transport Yard getting a new fan belt while Farquharson perched up on a high work table under some trees, reading Milton's Nativity Ode with half an eye and watching an orange-headed lizard jerk his head up and down in the sun—an image of male desolation, Farquharson noticed, as if for a lecture, which would be hard to beat. Grace Spanier-Dodd came to get petrol, and waved at him. On a reasoned theory of assistance, she called over, "Is everything all right?"

"Sure. Oh, Joan caught one of the garbage men selling our garbage again this morning."

"Tell him to sell it up by the road. You won't keep him from doing it, but you'll keep the flies away from the house." She turned back to her car. "Have you been to the cloth market?" she said then, "because you ought to. It's a sixteen-day market. In fact, ask your wife if she'd like to come on Saturday." And she looked pointedly at WP2471, looking innocuous and tan-brown, with its bonnet open. "We'll use my car. Tell her I'll drop over."

He thought that he ought to shout after her, "You're a feminist!"

"What," he said to the women in the Common Room, "is a sixteen-day market?"

"It's a wholesale market," Gail said, "that is, if you mean the cloth market. I used to go there, looking for stuff for costumes. But that wasn't a good idea. Now I stick to the downtown stores. You know," she said, "you can get anything in Ibadan, but everybody wears it all. I got a blue brocade once, two years ago, and damn it, if there weren't four *geles* and a sari of it in the audience at once."

"*Geles?*"

"Head scarves," she said, demonstrating how with her hands. "We had one of those family ceremonies where all the women dress the same. And then there was that Indian girl, too. *She* was embarrassed. It's hard to keep up the glamour of the stage when you can see a woman in the Kingsway with her hips in copper velvet.

"Anyhow, there's the cloth market," she said. "Buried inland on the other side of Ogunmola. It's *aṣo-oke* mostly, what they call up-country cloth, women in strips. It isn't glamorous. Trodden

133

ground between a batch of dirty houses with an open drain. Still, you could go there."

"Gail got up on the wrong side of the bed this morning," Sylvia said, as if possibly to apologize to the two Nigerian women.

When Farquharson got up to leave, Gail got up with him. Outside, in the passage behind the purple-flowered vine, she stopped and turned, looking ill in the dank light. "I've got to give the right side of the bed to *somebody*," she said.

A solid door barred the corridor. Farquharson felt marooned. There didn't seem to be any offhand or courteous answer, and he couldn't leave her.

So he held the door for her, and escorted her down to the steps at the entrance and even over to her Honda. "I guess you never philandered, did you?" she said. "No, I'm not inviting you. Do you mind if I say 'Men are brats' about three times over? Actually the word I want to use is 'shit!' Would you object?"

He said, "Give me a lift home."

"What?"

"Home."

He got off the seat beside his patio, feeling his teeth hum. Brand-new cushions, white as pharaonic linen, posed in every chair. "Be the first to sit on one," Farquharson said.

"Don't guess about me," she said. (Farquharson had waved Jacob off.) "If I make an indiscreet remark, it's because I want to."

"Dr. Garnett?"

"No, he's a nice sad man. Somebody else thought he was a fish to fry."

She was looking through the louvres out to the cactus and the sloping lawn.

"You aren't very happy, are you?" he said, a diagnostician, wondering about a beer.

"That's where you're wrong. I live here because it damn well suits me to. I'm an image. I don't have to be me: there doesn't even have to be a me to be."

"All things to all men," he murmured, pouring.

"*Some* things," she said, "to *some* men. I can preserve a virtue as well as the next one. Anyway, aren't you the one who ought to stand here saying 'I'm unhappy?'"

"No, not yet," he said.

"When it comes, will you let me know?"

So whatever was there had to be given, or it cumbered. He could see why Dr. Garnett would be around her. And she was moral still, pushing herself to be what wasn't her. One of those non-selves showed vividly lewd, like Jeremy Fisher's steward's niece, grabbing for the hanging disconnected rubbish in the dark. Farquharson felt a sudden slablike certainty that if he were to move she would reject him. He put his beer glass very gently to his face, and let an ice-cold trickle fill his mouth. He heard Jamie call, "Far' *here*!"

"We went to the Arts Building," Joan said, looking at the Honda.

12

"W H O were the founders of the Elizabethan vein of poetry?" Farquharson read, ball-point in hand. "What singing teachers were displayed as monuments in this undiscovered singing school? It is necessary first to consider the known biographies of these four men . . ."

Last night he had made love to Joan. They had both gone at it as if love were a substitute for worry about what would happen if it didn't work. It had been a sticky, unpleasant, scratchily unsatisfactory episode. Farquharson quit when Joan had had enough; not ungently, but still, he quit. And it had taken longer than usual. When she was washing herself he went out into the sealed-shut living room and sat, one buzzing hand on the fabric for the cushions. He felt cheerlessly undesolate, annoyed chiefly because he still had a hard on. She said, "Was it that bad?" and if he had had a toy car in his hand, he would have cracked it on to the concrete. This was one kind of fight he didn't intend to have. Or to lose.

He said, "I ought to take a bath."

"Don't be unfair."

He got to his feet, looking ungainly, as if he ached. She didn't want to look at him, with the pale hair at the base of his stomach, the thing still sticking up and the hairless ovals below dangling lopsided in their sac. She had never liked to look at that. He was a long way off, sorrowfully complete, full of himself: he couldn't help it. What was she supposed to do? she wondered; he *liked* what he was. ("I've got the worst parts of a boy and a man," she thought, "and that's what he wants to be.")

Why did she have to see him, carrying that forthright, solemnly

136

happy image of himself? Why couldn't she just want to look at and be pleased by the glands and shapes: that part of him? Love had to be blind, if it wanted to avoid distaste. Grown genitals were ugly; the only ones she ever really saw were Farquharson's.

"I can't help it," she said. "And it isn't fair of you to make me. That isn't love."

He went past her down the hall and ran the bath. Later he climbed out of the chill water, stood dripping in front of the toilet, looked down at himself, put a resigned hand to the thick shaft, and masturbated. A man had to have some daydream, but he couldn't choose one. The unchosen fantasy would be Joan, swarming over him, to take everything he ever wanted for her. The hand went on—not too fast—he had to slouch, and keep the other hand on the wall and his shins pressing against the porcelain. He mustn't let his thoughts go to her.

Other times, when he had splashed and mopped up and gone back to the bath again, he had cupped his balls in his hand, comforting them under water, thinking his sex at Joan wryly, warmly, in spite of her. This time he wondered if he would ever again come to her with his sex because it meant something.

"Spenser's *Epithalamion*," he read, "is a beautiful poem about the things that happen upon a marriage night. It is very long because there are many things happening which he has to write about."

They lay on their beds, side by side, for siesta. Joan read the *Sunday Times*, sitting up from time to time to fold it into a new shape. If there was enmity between them, it was curiously companionable. Given any empty party, they were quite likely to want to be talking to each other; if not friends exactly, Farquharson thought, at least parts of a sort of whole. He ought to be fond of her.

He was, of course, for what she was. But it occurred to him that that was a pretty unimportant sort of love.

"If the Professor please," Adebọwale said. "I think that this is

137

hard for us. The Professor knows what he is telling us, because he has grown with it." The big man with the sad eyes and the oddly wasted but full face held his hands on his notebook as if he were trying to keep them still. "We see only a theory of love, sir, but without the feeling. Sir, we can know only those things which the Professor teaches."

"And the Professor," Farquharson said, "can teach you only what you know. He can't teach you what sixteenth-century love feels to have. You learn by imagining book learning into emotion. So did they. You can't talk about any emotions unless you get patterns for them. The patterns aren't the emotions, but they're what you work with, and they're always foreign, and they always have to be learned. So you're on the right track." He grinned. "Besides, even the physical part has to be learned."

"Then are there no natural emotions, sir?"

Farquharson said, "I don't know."

Gail was at the Club, writing a letter outdoors in the shade.

"I'm having Nwala and her fiancé to dinner Tuesday," she said. "Would you care to come?"

"I think so. When can I let you know?"

"When you find out."

He went into the Staff Store: grey concrete, crowded shelves, tins of bean flour and melon seed, with unreasoning juxtapositions (and why so much Bombay duck?), and its sense of gutted luxury as of an island of survivors feeding on pâté de foie gras, tinned celery, lichees, loganberries, and beer—suddenly it offended him, and when he carried his few bits of party makings to the cashier with her insect-legs hairdo, meagre European dress, and bridling hauteur, he felt that he had to be angry, patronizing, or efficiently unpleasant, and he made an expatriate request to put what he'd bought into two bags.

A steward went by outside, looking partly like Elias Ateghie, partly like one of the men he'd killed.

"Master, you no buy from me?" A sorrowful, assured, triumphal, ingratiating rebuke from the vegetable man.

"*Ṣùgbọ̆n*," Farquharson said, wrestling to speak whatever Yoruba his book had handed him, "*èmi kò fẹ́ rà.*" (*But*, in his head, translating, he hoped, correctly, *I don't want to buy.*)

Well, *that* wasn't amends to Africa, whatever he did.

That evening Joan filled their living room with the Spanier-Dodds, the Eayrses, and the Ormfords.

Charlie talked about the old days, before the present compound; Grace kept a warning surveillance over how much Charlie might be drinking; Isobel Eayrs harked back to their meeting at the Baloguns'; Joan, in china-sharp makeup, presided, asking questions. Charlie erupted into a long scatological story, very badly told. Isobel praised the Nigerians. Charlie praised his steward and told a funny story about a party in the servants' quarters. Joan told again how Elias had stood for two days with a cloth in his hand; Charlie said that was damned unusual. Farquharson had to think that he had the story to end them all, and couldn't tell it, so he told, again, the story of how a clean brown 1961 Wolseley came to the barriers and had them thrown open for it—and wished he hadn't because they talked about the police invasion then, in detail: where everybody was, and how they'd known what was going on—"Farq stayed at home," Joan said, "and listened to it."

"You realize," Eayrs said, "that everybody's favourite Bursar, Mr. Sam Adeniyi Babatunde Majẹkodunmi, knew about the whole thing in advance!—and spent the entire sweet day at a politician's house in Jericho—Fagboye's, I think. Isobel saw him driving out the Gate, didn't you, dear? About nine-fifteen."

"No," she said. "After ten. I was coming back from the Kingsway."

"Is this evidence?" Farquharson said.

"He wasn't on the compound. Ask Bernice Funmilayọ, she's his secretary. He knew, and he didn't tell anyone. After all, *she* knows who phones him. I bet he set it up."

Isobel said, "You can lean on the police, you know, any way you want."

"Obviously," Eayrs said, "the university is leaning now. The government shouldn't have leaned at all, or it should have leaned with everything. There are, after all, more police than we saw that day. *My* hope is that we just don't fall over."

Farquharson said, "Is this a crisis, then?"

"No," Eayrs said. "It's just a damned unpleasantness."

Spanier-Dodd said, "Just the same, this used to be a happier place to live. My Yoruba don't smile and laugh the way they used to."

"The tribes?" Grace said, prompting him.

Eayrs said, "The politicians have made the tribes. There didn't use to be this kind of hatred and organization. God damn it, the tribal organizations were cultural. You try that now on the *Egbe Ọmọ Oduduwa!*"

"It all goes back, of course," Spanier-Dodd said, "to the census. That's when every major politician began to be afraid for the foundations of his power."

"Which census?" Peg said. "The '62 or the '63?"

"The '62. That's the one they suppressed." She was about to protest. He said, "No matter what it said. Population is power when you make constituencies. They all tried to rig it. I suppose they all found why they had to. So they did it a second time. Worse."

Joan said, "How do you rig a census? You just *count* people."

"There's a North American!" Eayrs said. "Honest, out of sheer lack of perception of the possibilities of fraud. Well, *something* put the population up from twenty-nine million to fifty-five million in ten years, and it wasn't natural reproduction, not at the rate *their* kids die."

Grace said, "The East was honest. They must have been. They lost ground."

"They may have been relatively less corrupt," Eayrs said. "That's all."

"UPGA boycotted the election. Now that must prove *some* principle!"

"Yes," Eayrs said, "it proves how weak they were. We might

140

have had a Southern coalition against the North but for them. I'm not sorry for them."

Ormford said, "You wouldn't have won."

"I'd put a bet on it."

"Africa has a very simple rule: the gg-government wins. It suits the Sardauna to have the country the way it is. Poor Bb-balewa!"

"Balewa has made his bed," Eayrs said.

Farquharson said, "Well, was the last election fought on the results of the census?" and when they looked at his ignorance, he felt he had to add, "What was it like?"

Ormford said, "The usual," and counted on his fingers: "Thugs, curfews, roadblocks, general violence—murders, of course. We were promised to go to Lagos for New Year's. We didn't gg-go."

An expatriate evening, Farquharson thought. They didn't live here.

He told Joan about Gail's invitation when they went to bed. She said, "Oh, I guess so," and he went over in the morning to the theatre with their acceptance. He had to climb the spiral stairs to find Gail to tell her. Then he had to wait on the high landing while she finished with a class inside.

When he went in Gail was at the far side of a bare room with a slanted ceiling, copying into a notebook what she had drawn upon a blackboard, Farquharson said, "Yes, we can come."

"That's good," she said. Then, "Do you want to see what we've got up here?"

There was a partitioned-off inner office in the back corner, and a locked door in the wall beyond it. Gail opened that and took him in among the costumes, in a larger room over the other half of the stage. A still-faced Nigerian woman bowed to them from a sewing machine. "This was for *The Taming of the Shrew*," Gail said, and pulled out a lavish and fantastical Elizabethan gown made in a strident combination of African cotton prints: two civilizations bashed against each other and both looked pretentious, ridiculous, and delightful.

141

"Excuse me," the woman on the sewing machine said. "I'm going now. Will you please lock the door?"

Gail said, "Yes, Mrs. Emenyi," without looking at her.

Soon they were in a welter of costumes. "Give me the blue one back," Gail said. "We've got to hang up some of these."

Costumes on hangers were pushed between others where they belonged. The conjoined slight muscle-work made them aware of each other as beings, things. Farquharson saw that she was plain, but that her face was hers, and that she moved well. She confined herself to being aware of the muscles in his arm, and his rather ugly, broad-fingered hands with the big joints.

"It'll be nice to have you come," she said. "I'll get the room dusted.

"Now let me show you my cubbyhole," she said. "That's where my *real* office is. See my name on the door?"

She was pleased, he thought, because she had her name on the door, the woman who did those impudent, somehow stolid and delightful costumes. He felt faintly sorry for her. They entered, and the door closed. They were almost in the dark, with the high drafting table behind them. Farquharson felt the corner of it in his back, and moved forward. Gail was by a dim, shadowy set of large pigeonholes with her back to him. "Gail?" he said. "Do you lock *all* the doors?"

But instead of answering she turned around and looked at what she could see of him, her face soft in the diffused light but still showing a kind of stiff and self-disliking anxiety.

"Come here," he said. "You've got to get that look off your face."

She said, "Show me how?" uncertainly, not hopefully; a kind of tentative daring.

Kissing her was an unexpectedly chastening, comfortable experience. Farquharson had put his hands on her shoulders, expecting something different, thinking, "We've been tempting each other since I walked into these rooms"; bending his head to her just to make a point of reference. It was how a man imagined the beginnings of adultery. (He had the right, he thought, to think of this.) She lifted her hands against his cheeks, held him, and held him off. Her mouth was still but not passive, faintly tense. He had to wait in such a kiss. Nothing she could have done about such an inept approach could have had more effect. Something outside him was presented to be known. The abrupt stirring of the flesh was just as much detached from him.

He said, "I don't make a habit of that."

She said, "For your wife's sake, I'm glad."

When Joan went to the cloth market she woke Farquharson so he would be sure she'd gone. It was only a little after five in the morning, misty outside, and very fresh and clean. It would be the perfect time of day, he thought, to make love to someone. He went in to look at Jamie, rumpled in sleep. Then he had the sealed living room to himself and made a noise with the doors opening them to the new air. He went to the refrigerator for a bottle of orange juice, shook it, and poured. The door to the garage was open. He went, glass in one hand (Ormford's Canadian style), to close it.

There was a hem of concrete around the car, with just enough room on the driver's side for the ironing table, a squeezed space unfit for a man to fight in, his killing ground—to smash a man's neck with a single blow, crush the larynx, collapse the throat, snap the vertebrae. Here was where he picked up the grey fake six-pence now in his pocket. The garage was a waiting place. He was going to have to remind himself, sometimes, to see whether he'd become something. Or could the man-killer's benediction be simply that *he* was alive, and in the early morning?

One of the tires was flat.

Joan was back before seven, carrying pale-brown cloth striped with grey. Farquharson had coffee for her.

"We didn't get cheated, Mr. Farquharson," Grace said. "Your wife has the right idea, but she's afraid she's going to hurt people's feelings. She got those for ten shillings apiece. I *think* she should have got them down to seven or eight."

Joan said the market was so crowded that she hadn't been able to notice anything, really. It was very African, and Grace knew an awful lot about it; maybe, she thought, too much.

(He thought he saw Gail's Honda at the Clinic. "Well, what do you know?" his mind said. "I kissed her!")

They drove to Agodi, going around the roadblock and the Secretariat buildings, and spent an afternoon roaming deserted suburban streets thickly arched with trees, or bare and exposed to fields and wide shoulders, with here and there patches of corn. They came out to a raw highway by two unfinished round concrete water tanks. Farquharson wondered again at how much traffic there was on all the major roads, and they turned back on a four-lane highway called Queen Elizabeth II Road, and had an argument about whether to go down an interesting road to painted apartment houses or to go straight past the hospital out of the Ọyọ road and home. Farquharson wanted to say, "It's *my* car," but Joan said that they were only riding on the spare tire and they had done quite enough for one day.

That night he left Joan alone and rode into Ibadan by himself, on the excuse of going to the office to work a dozen essays. One street curved under starlight, going downhill, with boarded shops and bare stalls, stripped and desolate except for one or two lit windows and a few street lamps. He left the car parked on a concrete shelf and walked past about five stores, as if like an adolescent to quarrel or commune with the empty places, talking into his head about the night and summing over like a catalogue the postures of mortality, that he might not be touched by them. Death and life, the ambitions of fornication and mortality, seen from the height of fifteen, sixteen years: too dim to mean much, too necessary not to work. Lust and love an odd methodical abstract, unconnected to the self-uprooting piece of admiration flaunting itself below under the constraint of underwear—and death, his death, a repeatable set of noble attitudes. Something over a fifth of a century away could distract any proper brooding in his head and re-enact itself, past Blake, past Johnson, conglobulated: Farquharson, as he was in high school, when he played basketball and had resolutions suggested to him by his gym teacher about living *clean*. Night-struck solitude wasn't adult meditation, but a luxury. The alternative, he thought, would have to be some Blakean or Johnsonian confessional. He sat in the car for a long time waiting to start it.

He drove too fast to get home, found Joan and Victoria being cosy neighbourhood wives, with crackers and fancy cheese and glasses of weak gin and squash, and so could at last feel guilty, but was instead sent over to have a beer with Oscar and one of his friends, and to listen to a new poem:

> This is my appointed land:
> This loveless habitation
> Budded into the complex forest—
> Even though by destiny I do not
> Live here, I do not
> Love here, I cannot
> Laugh here, and I cannot
> Leave.
> And this is a place of police.
> Who can I honour? the dyed expatriate,
> Bleeding as much as if he were white
> (Solidarity forever)? or rather
> The white
> Man
> (Note what I call him: *man*) who
> Hesitates,
> Procrastinates,
> Waiting despite beatings,
> And sees us?
> This is my appointed, and disappointing, land,
> And I was not born here.
> I remember Umauhia,
> And what men are,

And bid the phantoms of torment and defence be still,
For they are not for me.

"I don't expect you to scan it, Henry," Oscar said, watching him as an artist might. "This is simply my poem about the Invasion."

"To be published in the East, I presume?" Farquharson said, handing it back. "By the way, is the *oyibo* me?" (Fear in the loins.)

"My friend, you were there."

"*I* should like to have been there," the friend said, "to grovel, and to be made of words. Here." He laid the paper down beside him and started to drum on the wooden arm of the couch, chanting the words: "Or rather / The white / Man / (Note what I call him: / *man*) who—"

"Who," Farquharson said.

Oscar interrupted himself from the attention of listening, and raised his eyebrows.

Farquharson said, "Oscar, what is a man in Africa?"

Oscar reached out to the bookcase, and from a place where there were five copies of the same thing worried out a large flat two-coloured booklet with his finger. "These are my published poems," he said, while his friend still improvised. "And there is my answer. As a poet, you understand. 'I remember Umuahia,' " he broke in on the drumming, " 'and what men are!' "

The title of the book was *All That a Woman Loves*.

He opened the pages, leaned in a corner, read. There were curious limitations in the rhythm, as if the words weren't being heard:

> It is never true
> That I aspire to
> Take what I
> Love.
> The only aspiration
> Is to be able to
> Know what I have
> Taken and at least partly

Love it or
Her.
This is the lesson of a man.
And this is one
Thing that a woman
Loves.

It was entitled "Statement of a Theory of Defence".
When he got home, Victoria was leaving.
"I had a lovely time with her," Joan said. "I really did."

13

"ALL right," MacLachlan said, "so we're perfectly safe for the next few nights because there's a full moon and we can see them coming. What do you do next week?"

"Balewa will be here for Foundation Day," someone said. "You'll be choking under the Praetorian Guard."

Farquharson looked around the room, knowing its complexion now. Bohlender in Classics, having done the Praetorian Guard, would probably now use the *limes*. Pritchard was waiting for a chance to contradict. Balogun would perch at the side like a thick bird, delighting in the brief spectacle (he never stayed long). Jane Grant in History would sit solid as a lush statue and talk in a gentle ringing voice, solely for the purpose of making sense, and she would make so much sense that almost everybody would forget she was attractive: certainly the women would. Oscar Nwonkwo would mock the others by listening to them. Victoria would sit at one end of a sofa, Farquharson at the near corner of the next one. Like his wife he was uncomplicatedly fond of Victoria, innocent and unabashed. If she came in after he was there and sat down beside him, he felt pleased and easy, and they could talk about their children. Sometimes Oscar was with them, sometimes he wasn't; Farquharson suspected sometimes that he might become one of Oscar's trophies ("*Note what I call him: man*"), part of a testimonial collection.

"There is going to be trouble," Jane Grant said, "of some kind, somewhere. The temperature of the whole country is rising."

Pritchard sullenly said, "To what?"

"Simple violence," she said. "I agree with Sandy. We're going to have to defend ourselves. Politics and thuggery are companions now."

"I repeat," MacLachlan said, "*how are we guarded?*"

A miniature dehydrated woman in Linguistics, whose name Farquharson didn't know, said, "I'm *not* guarded, thank you, and I don't intend to be! There isn't a road in this country that I wouldn't drive on now—or a month from now."

"Oh, but you're Beth," Jane Grant said. "You aren't an enemy public institution."

"How many approaches to this compound are there?" MacLachlan said. "We have one guard on the front gate. Is he going to stop a load of thugs? Or a load of police breaking in on a fast lorry? Did he? Ridiculous!"

Pritchard said, almost sneering, "Border guards?"

"We have our back door to the University of Ifẹ, which is a government creature. Why shouldn't we guard ourselves? who else is interested?"

For another day MacLachlan filled the Senior Common Room with arguments of concern about the undefended university compound, and then he called a meeting, but Farquharson and Joan were going over to Gail Johnston's dinner. Curiously, the news of the meeting came typewritten or by word of mouth, not on the usual mimeographed sheet.

Nwala Okagbue's fiancé was a little man who tried to be completely European but couldn't keep down a kind of gaunt Ibo pride. Farquharson liked him from his first, almost Germanic, handshake. Joan didn't.

Bill Garnett was supposed to be the sixth. He didn't come. While they waited dinner, Nwala and John Akwuwkuma told Joan about the role of families in weddings, and Farquharson, permanently conscious that he had given this girl a kiss, followed Gail around the tiny house as she fidgeted about the late guest.

"It'll be spoiled," she said finally, after forty minutes. "Let's eat."

She gave them Nigerian recipes, as a North American would

make them, "a compromise on a compromise," she said, "but I don't have a cook. This is me, right or wrong." And she kept looking at the door. But she was a hostess born, Farquharson thought, even if she didn't want to be. Worry for the missing guest had to show, but only as honestly as it could without hurting anyone.

But they had finished their coffee when at last a car came up and Gail stared into the reflections over the table and said, "He's only got one headlight! That isn't like Bill, he's fussy."

And then Dr. Garnett came in with his head bandaged, and a bandage on his arm, and a bandage on his big toe, crowded against the sandal. "I was held up," he said. "Literally. At a roadblock, not ten miles from here."

He had been driving in the dusk. He had stopped, understood what was happening, and tried to get away. But they pulled him out of the car, hit him a couple of times, and took his money. He said, "I was a damn fool. I fought. I think I got a tire iron on my toe." He pointed: "I drove to the Clinic with it and the damn woman didn't want to help me dress it there. She said the place was closed."

"Never drive a Land-Rover," he said when they were leaving the house. "It's open."

"Well, you poor damn fish!" they heard Gail say as the door closed.

And Farquharson thought with astonishment that he wanted to go back in and hurt Garnett's toe.

Nwala said suddenly, "Come to our wedding. Come. You must come."

"Are you going to join the guards?" Joan said at home, and he said, "No."

"Suppose they did get onto the compound and come here, what would you do?"

So he said, "Well, I guess I'd have to take the frying pan and kill them," and was terrified. He hadn't meant to say that.

"Oh, you're no *use*!" she said. "Stop telling stories. What would you really do?"

Loving and not loving, judging, and not judging rightly. But if he wasn't going to be able to answer her, he'd have to go to bed and be thought a fool. "My dear sometime love," he thought, "I've guarded this house already too damn well. I guess I can't tell you that I couldn't trust you with knowing it." One day, somewhere, it was going to be a pleasure to tell somebody. Trouble was, would they believe him? There were times he wished he didn't look so much like a big kid.

"Look," he said, "I'm going to go to that meeting and see if there's anything left of it."

But the lights in the Senior Common Room were dark. He drove past and along Sankore to Gail's house. The Land-Rover was gone. He slipped out of his car, worried for a bit on the lawn, and went to the door.

"Well," she said, "what do *you* want?"

"The meeting was over. I don't know why I'm here," he said. "Can I be forgiven and come in?"

"What about your wife?"

"She'll go to bed." He pushed past her into the cleaned-up living room. "This guarding-of-the-campus business," he said. "Have they done that before?"

Something was agitating the big man, she thought. But she was tired after worrying for Garnett; she didn't want another restive something in her living room. She tried to make him talk, but he kept coming back to the vigilante guard, almost as if he was asking, should he go? and she didn't know what to make of him. He wasn't making sense, not as Professor Farquharson from Toronto who, she supposed, thought he knew her. And then, "Well, what if we had to use force? What if we had to kill somebody?"

"You're in a damn queer mood."

"Remember these two bodies up on Obong Road?" he said. "What if they'd been people who broke into a house and were killed?"

"Don't think there haven't been people thinking that," she

said. "They had Bill look at them, and *he* didn't think it was a car. But of course he wouldn't say so. So don't you."

"I don't have to. I mean, why should I? But what if they were?"

"You're in a funk!" she said. "You know, when I went to your lectures, I thought you were a big man."

He said, "I killed those men."

"Well, even if it's true," she said, "you don't tell *me*!" And then she heard him. He was standing, as if abandoned, under a light-bulb, and his hair was a neat dry halo, bright as sand. Steep shadows masked his face.

"You did *what*? And don't say it loudly. Sometimes there are people around this house."

"I'm King Midas's wife," he said, "I've got to tell somebody." He had to make words in place, laboriously, sound by sound. It seemed as if it took forever.

"It was heavy metal," he said again, after falling silent. He had kept his round teaching spectacles on for the evening; he had to take them off and dry his eyes by gouging at them with his forefingers. "The first time I didn't know. The second time I did."

"Well, I'm not going to tell on you," she said, "not even to Bill. Majẹkodunmi's an Akintọla stooge. If somebody murders an NNDP thug here, even a homegrown one, don't you think he'd open us to his party's vengeance? Look what he connived at so they could overawe the students."

Farquharson, drifting in his still, dangerous emotions, saw, fascinated, that in the crisis she had a university to defend. "If you want to read incitement to massacre," she said, "read the NNDP newspaper. If you've managed to kill a couple of them by acci-dent, don't come to *me* for tears. If the mobs they're trying to whip up did what they wanted, don't you think Oscar and little John'd be just as dead in a ditch as your two? What can I do to help?" she said. "Give you a big stiff drink?" But she saw he was looking past her. The bedroom door was open.

"No," she said, "not after just a single kiss. The Gails are good girls."

152

He sagged.

"You go home to your wife," she said.

"No," he said. "No. I'm on my own." It was weak, he thought, and wondered at how reduced he was, how uncertain about any kind of badness.

"Farquharson," she said, "I'm going to refuse to ask you what that means. I've got a person here. You even know who it is."

"Is he going to make love down onto you with a smashed toe?"

"I can do without diagrams of directions!"

"I'm sorry," he said. "It doesn't mean anything, and if it doesn't there shouldn't be a fuss about it. You don't have to forgive me or anything, Gail. It doesn't matter."

"If it was our time, we'd know it, right? Jamie isn't the only person you leave at home." She opened the door.

"I guess I ought to be glad," he said. "Well, if that's the case, I'm not."

"Oh well, mum's the word," she said. "Including the kitchenware."

He had to try to laugh. "The frying pan's gone away to Ibarapa."

"If they form the patrols," she said, "go out on them."

"Sir?" Stanley said, when he parked the car. "I have here visiting me Felicity Ezeanyagu, whose uncle is the steward for Mr. Fisher, and he says there was a meeting to make guards for the university. I wish to volunteer."

He saw the sly little face behind Stanley's open doorway.

"Mrs. Farquharson has to have a driver during the day."

"Sir, I know that it shall be my duty to drive every day."

"Where is your sister, Stanley?"

"Sir, she is away for a few days."

Farquharson looked into the black ground. "And am I supposed to put up with you fornicating in the back yard with children?" he muttered under his breath, he hoped only to himself.

"Sir?"

"I want you to send that girl home."

He was confronted with a flash of manhood. "Sir, she is in my house."

"Oh hell," he said. "Go ahead."

"About the guarding, sir?"

"Yes!"

"You look completely done in," Joan said. "You go to bed."

On Thursday Stanley was full of the adventure of sitting in the dark by the Fish Pond—like the statue of a faun, Farquharson was sure, peopling the dark with heroisms—and on Friday he was rather sleepy. But Farquharson, noting that the guest had gone, suspected another reason. On Friday the Faculty Board of Arts was supposed to meet, but Farquharson stayed away. He felt at arms' length from the students, did poor work in class, delivered the first two Johnson lectures as if he were reciting memory work, and had to endure Mr. Adebọwale's saying, firmly, "This is *not* as the Professor said before." Saturday he set Jacob to brush the mould and dust out of his doctor's gown. They now had a big red identity card for their car, and another gold-inked invitation to the Foundation Day Convocation, and in his pigeonhole on Saturday there was a long notice about security:

"The university's normal night security arrangements— patrolmen and watch nights—have now been strengthened by volunteer staff patrols." (Farquharson wondered what the normal arrangements were; he certainly hadn't seen anything on *his* night.) "Any untoward circumstances should be reported to that office.

"Thanks are given to all those who have volunteered and who are sacrificing many hours of sleep in the community's interest."

"Well, they got into the open," Farquharson said, "it's mimeographed. I wonder if Majẹkodunmi's on patrol?" He wondered if

Farquharson ought to be. "Where were you last night, Stanley?"

"Sir, by the Atiba Gate, and the children's school." Then Stanley got down on one knee and put out his hands to Jamie. "When you are big and go to school," he said, "I shall be guarding *you*."

Jamie said, "Up!"

Farquharson said, "My God!" and basked in pleasure.

"You want to be carried about?" Stanley said.

"Much of that," Joan said, "and I could really like this country."

"I guess I ought to be a vigilante."

"Oh, but you don't want to, surely."

MacLachlan was at the Club, in the bar. He seemed to have grown two inches and to have put on at least fifteen pounds. The woman he played tennis with was sitting beside him, enjoying him. "Now we're complete," he said. "We can cover any approach to the compound of any merit. They'll not get in."

"Covered everything?" Farquharson said.

"There's a few wee bush paths."

Instead of volunteering then, Farquharson reminded MacLachlan of the conquest of Quebec as something which showed what you could do with a good bush path, and went back to his wife less convinced than he had been that the compound was in fact safe. Dr. Garnett hobbled in with a cane and his foot in a shoe from which almost the whole top had been cut away. "Look at it!" he said. "It won't heal up." He held it up almost proudly. He said, "It looks *bad*." And suddenly *he* looked desolate.

Farquharson wondered whether Gail was going to stand by Bill or throw him out. But she sat him on a sofa, got him his beer, talked to him. Garnett wasn't spoiled, clearly, Farquharson thought after a long time, but he was a friend.

That night he volunteered. They gathered in groups in Tower Court, and the Estate Officer gave them their posts. "Where would you say Wolfe's Cove was, Farquharson?" MacLachlan said.

But he was set, with a young man from the Chemistry Department, to walk the long streets, at the western end of the compound. It didn't help that the young man was full of professional disgruntlements or that he should be elaborate about the futility of educating Africans. "They don't want to work in a lab," he said. "They want their *servants* to!" And Farquharson thought of Nwala's fiancé, when he saw Garnett's bandages, turning tense and grey but never stopping his courtesy, and he suddenly thought, "He was in chemistry!" and then thought of Jamie trusting Stanley with the great word of his loyalty, "Up!"

"And just how many of the patrollers," the young man said, "are African Senior Staff?"

Deep into the night they were relieved by a pair of servants, and Farquharson was glad to see the young chemist sprint aside and disappear. They were on Sankore, and Farquharson started to walk, alone, and with suddenly delighted breathing, towards home. "They shall not pass," he said aloud. "I shall preserve your chastity."

She was home. She was walking around, carrying books apparently from one place to another. Her hair was hauled back tight in a rubber band. And she wasn't wearing anything. ("Sometimes," she had said, "there are people around this house.")

He came around the corner of the hedge. True, he was in moonlight.

She was just walking around her rooms, doing heavy housework. He saw her look at the palms of her hands. The reorganization of a library, he thought, was a completely personal and eccentric job: nothing gave any warning, nobody could help you with it, and there wasn't any way to stop before you got the whole thing done. He decided she was dressed, practically, for the work in hand.

She had thin wide shoulders and pronounced shoulder blades. Her breasts were bigger than he had expected. It was hard to be sensual about them, seeing one of them bookending a spilling pile of books. Her chin in profile was tough and cramped. She had a comfortable belly. He thought he was going to be left to his imagination for anything more than a couple of inches below the navel, but she climbed up on to a chair and reached, and he thought of the medieval way of cataloguing a lady's beauty point by point, and knew, like truth, that for women of a certain kind that was the one right thing to do. "*With midel smale and wel ymake.*" Delicate shallow buttocks, lean silvery legs that moved. Not voluptuousness; serviceability. She turned on one knee to set down a load; he saw her like a sculpture, with a brown fig leaf, the gentle rustling apron of hair.

But of course his white face showed in the dark. She got down. He thought he ought to run. Instead he went to the door, and knocked.

"Yes?" he heard at the window, in a harsh voice.

"I saw your light on," he said quietly. "I've been on patrol." Anger would at least keep her within range, he thought. "Gail?"

"Come in and shut up," she said, and she twitched the door open.

"No, I don't apologize," he said when he saw her, and the door was shut. "It looked good, practical and useful. And it was fun to watch."

"And is it fun now?" His glance was resting against the bottom of her belly, as if his sight could nudge flesh aside, and he couldn't even help it. She said, "For a married man you get around."

It was a humdrum useful body, marked with book dust. "I know," she said, "you just want to put your tool in. Well, I've let you in the house."

He grinned at her. If he was going to be in a sudden state of silly contentment, he might just as well ride with it.

Everything about that face, Gail thought, she liked. "You want to fuck?"

He said, "Like that?"

"Is there any other way?"

"When are you going to get the books right?" he said.

The light went out.

She said, "There *are* curtains in the bedroom."

157

"What happened to Bill? You know, I didn't expect this."

"You haven't got it yet."

He heard curtains drawn.

A tiny pink lamp glowed on the end of the chest of drawers.

"All right," she said. "Show yourself."

He said, "I want to kiss you. Come here."

"Are you going to bother with love?"

"But you said we couldn't do this on one kiss. Well, I very much want to do it."

She stood in front of him, and without looking at more than her eyes, he put his hands on her shoulders and bent down. And again she put her hands on his face, and they were without any pressure, but there, knowledgeable. And when the kiss was three seconds old he felt his blood shunt below and begin to shove him up, easily, relentlessly, pulse by pulse. He had to let go with one hand and work the fingers down inside the waistband of his shorts to free himself, and then he felt her hands leave his face.

He half freed his mouth and said, "No," and then came back with pressure. And when he thought he was going to ache, or have to hinge his hips back from her, he let go and stepped away, and stood with the shorts wrinkled back from an ungainly jutting bump, and then stripped and let the machine stand in her sight because he was proud of it.

"All right," she said. "Now come here. I want to get my hands on you."

He played with her breasts, with her stomach, her hair: his fingers danced. She held him in both her hands, tightly, and didn't move. From sitting in a rather bunchy way in the middle of the bed, they slid into positions of rest with each one's head by the other's hips, and Farquharson played like a boy, and nuzzled her, and her legs spread. He pulled back, happy, to see what she was doing, and saw her tongue point and trace little lines against the underside of his prick. . .

He could drive; he could dawdle; he could do anything. He had her, surprised himself how good he was, moaning and yelping and saying quite surprising things, for a long time. She had come, and was cresting to come again, when he had to hold stiffly back, for a short while, and lifted himself on one arm to buffet and knead her breasts with the other hand. Her face got quite pink, with a dazed look, and then she went convulsively still and smiled and said, "Now you," and she got her fingers down against his prick, and, as he rode her, dug in.

His head might have come off.

But he didn't jerk, or thrash. Suddenly, he was as still as if he were a tree trunk coming to ecstasy, while the follow-up spasms pumped.

"Oh," she said, when his eyes opened and he came down on top of her. "Oh, it's a good thing I use the pill." And they both panted. "Wow!"

"And that," he said, "is what I haven't had for six years."

"Oh golly, can you do it!"

"I know I can. Your doctor with the bad toe had better watch out."

"Going to be in love?" she said.

He shook his head, tickling her ear. "Love," he said, "would be an extra."

A long while later she said, "You'd better go home now. You're going to need all the night to breathe. Oh, thank you very much. Very, very, very much."

He said, "You're welcome"—which was a proper thing to say—and then got dressed. There was a lot of night to breathe, and he needed every bit of it.

Joan was asleep and chilly; Jamie was mumbling. He pulled the sheets over both of them, and then went and sponged himself as he had the first night in Lagos.

PART THREE

14

November 14–28, 1965

RAPIDLY, in a few days, the myth developed that when the thugs came to the compound they would come in Land-Rovers, and Joan had a bad moment on Monday when she saw Dr. Garnett's Land-Rover by the Administration Building. Farquharson didn't commit himself to the Land-Rovers. He had other things to think of: the complexities of innocence and experience in Johnson's *Rasselas* and, in somewhat the same vein, Gail—two things to be done well for the plain joy of doing them.

He hadn't come to Gail on Sunday night; Garnett's Land-Rover was parked there when he went on patrol, and he hadn't wanted to be awkward, or drive her as the second-come man that night. But he was there on Monday, having caught up to her at the edge of the pool, their lips at the water's surface.

Joan was with her housewives' group. He had no intention, no interest, and no desire to feel guilty for her. He had given her a good weekend, and demanded nothing. If that was how he was going to have to treat her, he thought, she was going to bloom.

Gail waited for him in the dark, and at first he thought she wasn't there. But then he heard her whisper, so he undressed in the dark, without knowing how she was, and when she turned the light on him he was standing in the bedroom doorway, making the old small grooming gesture of the single downward tug on his genitals. "Straightening my tie," he said. And he tried not to have a hard on before she touched him, but he couldn't stop. They were carnal, ridiculous, and enjoyed themselves. But somehow they were in a tearing hurry, and it seemed only a minute until

163

Farquharson flooded her, and then afterwards they lay with Farquharson on his back and Gail on her elbow half on top of him, and he drew comfortable patterns on her breast with a lazy finger while she cradled his still almost-rigid organ in her hand, giving him every now and again a lazy tug. He pecked at her with a kiss and said in a pleased small way, "Ouch, it's dry," and in a few seconds he was stung with the coolish slipperiness of both their liquids, and her fingers soothed and smoothed him and he shunted his hips with content and let his head push back into the pillow. She said, proud, "You came big."

He read, sombrely, standing behind the lectern on the desk: "Of these wishes they had formed, they well knew that none could be obtained. They deliberated awhile what was to be done, and resolved, when the inundation should cease, to return to Abyssinia."

He took a long breath, and stared at the near faces. "To return. To the world of Innocence, to the enforced Earthly Paradise with its guards and cliffs, to the prolonged suffocating womb of the heirs who can never inherit. But while they were there before they had the ignorance and the ennui that were their 'Innocence'— and now they don't have them. Can they really go back? And what does it do to them if they can? 'If we cannot conquer, we may properly retreat.' That's Johnson too, remember. But you've got Blake's Thel also, the innocence of refusing to be born, because being born would subject you to Experience and loss of Innocence, and the ripping of the 'little curtain of flesh upon the bed of our desire.' I read that to you, and you know she shrieks and runs back—'unhindered, to the Vales of Har', and consequently is not born, does not live, has denied not only her own possibility, but the creating, tumultuous possibilities of the lovers —and what sort of Innocence is that? 'A conclusion,' he says, 'in which nothing is concluded,' because everything is set into limbo—all but the fact that they are what Experience has made them. And what that has made them, knowingly, soberly, maturely, is the creatures who go back to the blocked womb, and

164

curl up. No comment, no more than in the medieval *débat* '*Whiche was the leeste fre, as thinketh yow?*' "

He had the late shift that night, and was stationed down by the Zoo. Balewa was supposed to have arrived secretly in the afternoon: they had heard, mostly at a distance, sound-trucks and a helicopter. The guarding of the approaches that night seemed both considerably more important and considerably more futile than usual.

Stanley put their red identity card behind the windshield, but the car stayed at home. Farquharson and Joan walked to the convocation together. Then she went in alone. The procession assembled in the corridor to the Registrar's office, but the arrangements of the march left him near nobody he knew, and the accidents of a disorderly filing on to the platform put him in a row almost by himself. On each side backstage stood armed black soldiers with their sleeves rolled up. One of them stood by a huge two-foot fan that swung, blunderingly, side to side.

Farquharson had to lean forward and scratch behind him to keep a kink in the velvet of his hood from digging into his back. The official robes ahead of him were indigo damask, with gold braid. All the officials were there except the bursar, Majẹkodunmi. The faces of the audience below glimmered in a kind of glaring twilight. They were surrounded by police and army outside, in about three kinds of uniforms.

He tried to find Joan in the audience. Then he saw more guns at the back, in the doorways, and even on the wide curved balcony. Prime Minister Balewa sat directly in front of him, but all Farquharson could see was the back of his head, looking stonelike, under a stiff indigo mortarboard visibly too large for it. Candidates for honorary degrees were presented by a public orator standing at the edge of the proscenium—but Farquharson couldn't hear him because the echo from the balcony overlaid every word with a blanketing hallwide echo that didn't so much obliterate syllables as turn them into ear-dazzling gibberish. It was possible by great strain to sieve out of this something of what the speaker said, but the least let-up reduced the whole thing back to chaos, so that Farquharson got a lot of time to think—and then the pattering tumult of alien tongues got past again. The thinking didn't do much good; it was mostly about Gail and possibilities: after a while he was sitting there with a hard on, and with his prick trapped awkwardly at the wrong angle for what was happening to it. And of course that was when he saw Joan, close to Balewa's head, with a gun behind her.

He thought it was, in a small way, cruel to give even a wooden man a hat that made his head look so small. The Prime Minister looked, in profile, like a pinched tailor in a fairy tale, and his face was sad. Watching the Vice-Chancellor smile, Farquharson remembered that there was supposed to be some sort of hassle between him and the Minister of Education, and suddenly wished that the whole thing were over, so long as he could walk without sticking out, or hobbling as if everything had to pivot in the wrong place. He tumbled a pile of cloth from the gown upon his knees, and tried to manage things so he could look his age when he stood up.

Stanley and Jamie were waiting in the crowd outside, to get the gown. Farquharson shuffled his arms free, lifted Jamie high into the air as if he were going to throw him, then tucked him down onto his shoulder for a hug, and carried him home.

After lunch he got stickily out of his clothes and lay down, without his underwear (signalling, he supposed), wishing that the air could get all around him, and that it weren't so dull and hot. He had to gather his balls in his fingers and lift them up, to let the air under them. He slept as if he had been gassed or clubbed.

Joan looked over at him, and thought his sleeping nakedness was selfish. She made herself a long drink in the kitchen, touched it with gin, and sat reading the newspaper on the bed, with the corner of the chalky sheets falling across her husband's stomach.

That night there was a dance in Tower Court, and Jim Fisher and Mrs. Funmilayo descended on the Farquharsons in the middle of the afternoon, to find if they were going and to persuade them

166

if they weren't. Jeremy cried, "And to my place for a good drink first. All right?"

Mrs. Funmilayọ, Farquharson noticed, was as happy as an owner.

So about half the English Department gathered on the bare new lawn in front of Jim Fisher's flat and consumed hospitality, talking, with the men in shirtsleeves and the women in white-women's clothes, except for Nwala and Mrs. Funmilayọ, who were resplendent in up-and-downs of dull wine and brown chartreuse "If I wore those colours in this temperature," Peg Ormford said, "I'd look a ghost." (Farquharson thought he saw Felicity Ezeanyagu on the driveway behind the house.)

The air was slightly close, and when they came after their cocktails into the enclosed concrete of Tower Court, with its green and white boards slotted askew between their posts, and the hot sky overhead draped with bright fiery light-bulbs, Farquharson couldn't help feeling as if they had been put under some intense scrutiny from above; that all their greetings, conversations, and dancing (because he danced) were typical sequences for observation; and that if they had been anything else, there would have been more, and better, air to breathe. Charlie Spanier-Dodd played at recollections with a former, fattening, patronizing student; Grace beside him tried to be a housewife to the unknown status of the gentleman's dancing partner—Farquharson thought it was all unreal.

Some of his students said good evening: Babafẹmi Gbadebọ, still probably secure with his copy of *The Anatomy of Criticism*, was an effusive and political good-fellow in introducing him. Mrs. Akinrinmade stopped him and said, "Professor Farquharson, this is my husband." And he was once again urged to come and see Idanre and the old deserted village high on the rock.

"You cannot miss my house," the man said. "There are several Idanres on the same road. We are at the end. Look for a black house on the right-hand side of the road. A very large, black, two-storey house."

"You will feel," Mrs. Akinrinmade said, "as if you were

floating in the clouds and cowering in a chasm, and that is how you will know you are at our house."

"You make it sound like magic," Farquharson said.

"Sir, you may believe. It is."

Gail and Dr. Garnett were drinking at a round metal table. Garnett looked despairing, humiliated, yet somehow content. "And me a doctor," he said. "That damned toe won't heal. It just wants to fester and rot." Farquharson thought that at his most complacent, wallowing in the bathtub and seeing his prick break through the water, *he* might have looked like that. With his wife's permission he borrowed Gail for a dance and found that for him at least she wasn't a good dancer.

"I bet Origen looked at his balls the way Bill looks at that toe of his," she whispered fiercely, when they were in a corner briefly alone.

"Origen didn't have any."

She said, "That's what I mean."

"Well, not tonight," he said. "I've got the early morning guard."

Jeremy's party disintegrated; there was nothing, at last, to keep them from walking home with a flashlight. He saw a sign saying "Prof. & Mrs. H. J. Farquharson" in sharp black letters, with the number "1" of their imaginary address under it. "Hey, did that come today?"

"Yesterday. You didn't notice."

He fell asleep. When it was time for him to go on watch, she didn't wake him. Farquharson slept like a couple of half-empty sacks thrown on the bed.

The strings of lights dangled from the tower for several days. Farquharson collected his Johnson essays, hunted for improvements, found Adebọwale writing out only what he could find in books, took Joan to drink beer with the Nwonkwos, guarded at night, slept like lead in the afternoons, did his share of driving to the Kingsway (or rather, being a passenger), fucked venturously and to the limit of his delight with Gail whenever he could, made

168

Joan accept him a couple of times because he should (and was surprised to feel better with her), fought like a bad boy with his criticism classes, and was, capably (and the students liked him), a teacher in a country that hadn't yet managed to touch more than his eye and the muscles in his wrists and arms. He was increasingly fond of Victoria—which was all right because his wife was too— and liked Oscar in a mildly wary fashion, and liked the two of them without any reference to each other. He liked the spectacle in the Senior Common Room, liked swimming in the Club, liked his various abrupt inconclusive conversations with Stanley on the way to the bank and back, and did not like WP2471's seemingly permanent ability to get flat tires and not to feel like starting in the morning. ("I have to wind the car," as Stanley said.) He enjoyed, too, sitting in the dark beside the Fish Pond, or walking the long expectant roads at night, waiting to get to Gail's or, on one night, moving as steadily as a drunk, having gone first to Gail. Dr. Garnett's toe remained unhealing, and he brooded over it in the Clinic (Joan had to go twice and see him about an infection), and being enough of a recluse that he made his visits to Gail a schedule, he came less often, but Gail wouldn't make fun of him to Farquharson. And Farquharson would play tennis with his friend the anaesthetist, or he would watch for John Cord's appearances in the Club, the days when his black man's world left him suddenly alone, and he came to hide among the whites or to reclaim his territory, or whatever he came for when he would swim end to end in the pool, like a lithe sea beast among children. Africa was the place they all lived beside.

The students, he thought, were what he was here for, and he wasn't touching them. He couldn't follow their reactions, or be sure in advance how they were going to take anything he said. He couldn't play a class (as he could at home, sometimes) like an instrument; all he could do was talk and in tutorials try to goad them into argument, and try not to be pushed into lecturing within their prejudices. He thought that he understood that much, at least: the pressure to play safe and the temptation of memory.

"What do I offer them," he said to Ormford, "that they should take a risk? What kind of luxury is the freedom to be wrong, anyway?"

"Oh, resign yourself," Ormford said. "You can count on the fact that they'll learn wh-whatever you tell them to."

So he had to talk, plead, preach . . .

He could hear his colleagues' lectures through their doors sometimes. Cronis sounded incandescent (Farquharson could imagine him in his almost-black glasses, hurling his hands about), but when Farquharson listened, coming back from the library, he could hear only the dedication and the performance, and was embarrassed. Nwala Okagbue sounded sober, witty, and precise. Sandy MacLachlan declaimed by points, accurately, but Farquharson now knew that Sandy didn't believe Africans were educable. Jim Fisher sounded like a dull machine; he had no life at all. Farquharson hadn't listened to Cord, and his knowledge of what Sylvia Levinsohn did was confined to seeing her on the verandah outside his office, identifying cultures as hard as she could go. That she was determined to like Negroes didn't make her practice of liking them any less pleasure to her or to them.

He had never heard Ormford speaking to a class.

Oscar sounded like a learned undergraduate, speaking carefully. "They probably think *I* sound," Farquharson said to Joan, "like a prophet on the warpath"—and at least it was Joan he said it to, not Gail.

He began to read newspapers for a while, having enjoyed not having to. Rhodesia had declared independence; Balewa had announced that anyone who rebelled should be dealt with savagely. He read old news in the Club, over his silent beers with Joan, while Stanley played with Jamie over by the children's slide. "Anyone who rebels should be dealt with savagely." With a frying pan, with a set of thugs, by little professors crouching in the dark with empty hands. He wondered if, even allowing for fornication, the patrol was worth it.

He reached for a paper in the shelves and got one almost three weeks old. There was a little notice in the *Overseas News* that the

Nigerian playwright Wọle Ṣoyinka was in hospital in Ibadan after a two-day hunger strike and was to go on trial for stealing a tape and threatening violence in the offices of the Nigerian Broadcasting Company. He looked at the date, thinking that this ought to mean something, and wondered if he was insular not to have heard anybody talk of it.

The thought sent him plunging among the more recent newspapers. Two editors in Lagos had been arrested for sedition and false reports, having published stories that UPGA had won the election in the West. There were several stories of unrest by "party supporters". Lagos society photographs interrupted the text. He sat with the beer in his hand, looking out the open side of the room towards the pool. There was nothing in the English papers but a hypnotic preoccupation with Rhodesia and themselves. And here there was curfew still in scattered parts of the West, holdups on the roads, gossip, the *oyibos* swimming in their pool, housewives, servants—and Farquharson, maintaining a love affair. Open sunlight lay down upon the pool till the air shimmered. And Joan was reading a trade magazine, full of colour photographs.

"Well, if it's newspapers you want," Gail said that night, "this is my favourite." She picked up a paper trimmed with green and pointed to a photograph of happy people in a market place, going about their normal business. He said, "What's the point?"

"That for three days there was the body of an Ibo at Mọkọla, and for two of those days it didn't have a head, and that's what this picture's about, to show that it didn't happen. No 'party supporters' here. Have you picked up that lovely phrase yet? It means thugs. What worries me is that the violence waited till *after* the election. *That* happened while you three were staying home on the compound. Take a look at this editorial on Dike. They call him 'this Ibo person'. At the very least it's an incitement to tar and feathering. Or this." He hadn't time to read. "This is just general. You tell me what's beyond that but slaughter."

He read in scraps. After a while he felt a flush of anger in his face, and he didn't want to read. He said, "It sounds like the Nazis, talking about the Jews."

"Yes," she said, "they kill people. They *want* to. Don't you know that? *You're* a party supporter, Farquharson."

He was perched on the edge of the chair, with his feet tucked back and his legs spread. From where she sat on the floor she had a view up the leg of his shorts. "When are you going to go white native and leave off the underwear? I can't see your balls."

"Do women watch for things like that?"

"We get the presented view."

So for the rest of that evening they didn't talk about newspapers, political parties, or any people's hate.

It was illegal, in Ibadan, to buy or sell Opposition newspapers. It was illegal, in Ibadan, to listen to the Eastern Nigerian Radio. Curfews were still somewhere else. They could ride to town by night and see the sights. At the Mọkọla roundabout, the shuttered building of the NCNC, behind its small walled courtyard, still kept its house-sized neon sign on top. "ALWAYS VOTE," it said, "NCNC FOR UNITY, INDIVIDUAL LIBERTY, AND PROGRESSIVE GOVERN-MENT"—with each item in a different colour, and the party's rooster, in red neon, with only the tail working. Mr. Eyo Esua, chief electoral officer of the Western Region, had published his letter about "manifold election irregularities" and been repudiated by all his colleagues save one. The barricades in front of the electoral offices stayed up. Nothing in Ibadan looked, to visitors, any different; and Farquharson had taken a mistress on the university grounds, and hadn't yet assigned a failing mark on an essay.

Farquharson said to Joan, "This is a day off. Put up a lunch, we're going for a drive." So Stanley checked the spare tire, "wound" the car, and waited for them. And Joan put what she could think of into a basket with wet towels over it, and they got petrol into the Motor Transport Yard, and drove out the back gate north onto the Ọyọ road.

The road swung gently, cresting and sinking on long or short shallow slopes, between dishevelled walls of bush, jungly but dry, high, treed, seclusive, in ugly greens. Bananas and palms were always somewhere, with their dead leaves hanging brownly and always a new spike above. They passed rapidly through several long, close-built villages lining the road as if it were their aisle. He supposed they contained unified Yoruba, and wondered who in their midst they hated, and who were party supporters, and of which party, and what they did. They saw a few men drive a herd of black cattle beside the road, but in spite of that the feel of the road was North American. They were caught in the geometry of the automobile, he supposed. Suddenly the landscape changed.

Farquharson was used to the idea now that there were no vistas except the artificial ones, the perspectives of a road or the clearances of airport and compound, or all the massed city houses. And now, at the end of a long rise whose foot had been in the banana plants and the palms, they saw yards-high grass, scattered different trees, the kind of wide-open sky that squashed down on a flat country. And from there to Ọyọ they might have been in the American West.

The outskirts of Ọyọ were sun-baked suburbs, and they found a gas station like a country store. Farquharson went into it to buy soda pop. All the room needed was a pinball machine. The woman behind the counter was caring for her nails, with her hair in what looked like insect legs. "We're dying here!" Joan called, and so he went out to her.

They looked up a bleak wide street lined with stores, houses, parked cars, rising to they didn't know what; they didn't go that far. They found a place under one of the high trees, parked, ate and drank, plying Stanley as well as themselves with pop and sandwiches, and looked across the road to a big pale Italian-looking house hung about with filigree verandahs and parapet work, and at a Coca-Cola truck parked at an angle off the road. Men were eating out of enamel bowls under another tree, close to them. No one bothered them, no one stared into the car.

They drove back panting with heat, having, Farquharson believed, seen no real country. They stopped at a largish town in

173

the forest where there was a beautifully arcaded building he had noticed on the way out. The place was called Fiditi, and here at least there were people who watched them. The women crowded behind tables of drying peppers and giggled at him. Stanley got out of the car and waited, like a guard, on the edge of the ditch. Farquharson walked only a few yards, to be able to see the whole building between the corners of two houses, and he liked it. Earth walls, a heavy roof, a cupola, and a mud arcade, with fluted edges to the arches. "Well, now I'm here," he thought, "because they make things like that."

Stanley wanted him to go, feared for him somehow. Joan was holding Jamie firmly in the back seat, with the windows up. Farquarson looked at the women, smiled at them. He knew he was an ungainly big man with a silly nose, and his shoulders slanted. He thought that he wasn't wearing any underwear now under his shorts, and somehow the idea amused him, so he bowed to them and went away. "Okay, Stanley, home," he said. "Or rather into Ibadan. I want to buy a paper."

The next day two Action Group newspapers suspended publication because of debts.

On Sunday Joan wanted tomatoes, so Farquharson went by himself to Mọkọla, which was a set of stalls on a huge concrete platform, rigidly rectilinear, as became a Yoruba market. He saw a stack of tomatoes in one of the stalls right by the road, sprinted up the steps to buy them, was given a leaf to carry them by, and never got any further into the market than that, and didn't know where a headless body had lain not to be photographed. Pleasant people, pushy and nosy people, bickered around him, and he went back to the car with the child he'd bought the tomatoes from calling after him, "Master! Goodbye, master!"

15

IT was cold at night. When Farquharson got to Gail's, on the way home from patrol, he said, "It feels like fall."

"That's harmattan. You'll see the Africans coming out in wool sweaters now."

"I can tell you one thing, It makes a man want to copulate. I feel brand-new."

"Gentle vocabulary," she said, and sat down on the floor to look at him.

"Got a good view?" He moved his knee so she could see up his shorts.

"M-hm. They're hairless, aren't they? Is that uncommon? Bill's aren't."

He chuckled.

She said, "What is it?"

"I was going to say, 'Bill's balls aren't my business,' but it wouldn't come out right."

"No, but really." Her finger was poking at him.

"I don't know," he said. "I never took statistics."

"Balls to you too. Look, you're getting a hard on, just because I've got my finger there."

"Gail, you don't love me, do you? I mean, I hope not."

"No," she said. "You've got your wife. Go on, get into the bedroom, Henry. I just want to play with you. It's the wrong day anyway."

"Was that true about the Ibo in Mọkọla?" he said when he was waiting for her, watching his half-hard prick flop sideways against his bush. "I went there yesterday." He twitched a muscle for fun, and the shaft bobbed up and down. "I used to get a kick out of doing that when I was a kid," he said. "Look—three times."

"Well, we know why *I'm* here," she said, and put her hand on him. He stiffened and went hollow-stomached. "Now, why are *you*?" Her hands started brushing over him. "You aren't in love."

"I like you," he said. "Now, anyway." He lay relaxed, with his hands behind him. She had taken off her blouse.

"Now, anyway? That sounds like me." She had his prick between her fingers and was lightly jiggling the skin. "I mean, you didn't know I did this. It wasn't just cold-blooded fuck-her-for-a-holiday, was it?"

"Am I just a passenger tonight?"

"It's that time again. I've got to do something for you."

"Okay," he said, but he put a hand up to one of her breasts and moved it. "But let's not do any more trying to find why we started."

She bent, and her tongue touched him. Then she said, "Lie back and take it. This is for you."

He guessed that every man who hadn't had it happen wondered about this. Curiosity raised him on his elbows and tensed his neck, but only for a while. If this was an art, she was very good at it. He put his fingers down once to find what she was doing—but what she was doing was to make him forget, completely, about his will, his mind, or any of his desires but one, to make him (and only partly for the sake of looking at him) shunt, shift, moan, thrash his head, press his eyes closed and then open them blindly towards the light, and so get lost from any part of his personality except just what he was, and severed from any action that could bring him back to it. He didn't know how long she gripped and mouthed him, nor what she did. Whatever was happening was as private as a heart attack: ecstasy, and it didn't leave; agony, and it didn't hurt; power, and it broke finally, and spattered, hot and cold, all over his chest. She had her head raised and was looking over him, wondering, and almost gentle. He could just see her.

She had a towel to dry him; she wiped it over his chest, lightly. She went away and he lay dazed, and she came back with a washcloth. She said, "Roll over on your stomach," and he felt the cool damp washcloth on his neck, and then on his back, and on his rump and legs, down to the soles of his feet, and he lay like a man who had had contentment invented especially for him, and was afraid to lose it.

And Gail thought all night how whole and manoeuvrable he was, and how oddly patient his face looked when it got distorted, and how, no matter how much she might have obliterated a personality, he was nevertheless plainly and only Farquharson, and not a sort of male abstract foaming in applied rut—which was what she thought he would have been, which was what Bill Garnett was, who would only fuck on top, and couldn't do that now because of his toe, and consequently had to be taken in hand.

"Well, if she doesn't know there's something going on tonight," Gail said, commiserating, partly, with a wife, "she never will."

"You know, I said I wasn't in love," Farquharson said, and patted his balls. "We're going to have to watch it."

Father Christmas had come to the Kingsway. The store had fitted up a short square U of track and set up a couple of pastel landscapes and a gnome or two, and children (Jamie), and occasionally other people (Stanley), bought tickets to the train and rode around the walls to the toy department and a sweating blue-black Santa Claus. Jamie wanted to go around again, and Stanley looked so longingly at the train that Farquharson sent them around twice more, and stood watching with his arm on his wife's shoulder. "I've got to go into the Clinic this afternoon," she said. "That infection won't clear up."

"You and the Doc," he said. She shrugged her shoulders. He felt the muscle and bone lift under his hand and was suddenly aware that his wife, like himself, had cavities and circulation of the blood, and sex glands. He pressed her shoulder. Then he turned his back to fetch Jamie and carry him, African fashion on the hip, all the way to the main floor, while Jamie held on, African fashion, by his knees. And Farquharson wanted to take the boy and walk out with him into the Ibadan streets; proud, and alone.

The one-legged handsome beggar on his long pole said, "Master, after so long time, master?" and Farquharson said, "No," and grinned.

Grace Spanier-Dodd had decided that the Farquharsons were neglected. Therefore she had talked a friend into an evening invitation, so on the last night of the month they put on proper clothes and arrived—they realized almost at once—late. The host was English; the hostess was English; one of the guests was the Chief Accountant, and he was English; and they talked about amateur plays in the Arts Theatre, and of the time when the Chief Accountant and the hostess—clad, it appeared, only in their pyjamas—had some kind of rendezvous between their houses, because one got locked out and the other was trying to help. The host had come out in his dressing-gown, "squeaking, 'Does there seem to be something the matter?' as if the poor fool couldn't see us. You *are* a poor fool sometimes, *Professor* Larry Michaelson"; they had laughed for all the world as if they'd made a scandal (and whenever their host made a sentence with any kind of a long word in it, his wife would say, "Did you *hear* that rhetoric? Did you hear the *quality* of it?") and Farquharson had a vision of his two thugs battering their way suddenly into a Noel Coward play.

Obviously there were conventions to being an expatriate. All the weight of literary evidence made them conform, as if they had roles, not lives, and enjoyed them in proportion as they were outdated and second rate. Of course, they were all slightly drunk. Farquharson was tight himself before long, and listened unsteadily, his attention sharpening randomly into an obscure precision. He had been sealed to his hostess's various tales for over half an hour.

Then she said, "And when I think of what they're doing to each other in this country it makes my blood boil," and suddenly was talking of the trial of Wọle Ṣoyinka. "They did misuse him, you know," she said. "He was beaten. He made them fools. Of course, he knew the man who had the tape. He just swapped his own tape for the one they were going to broadcast, and instead of an election speech for the government they were putting out a diatribe against it, until they cut it off. Theft and violence! It ought to come to an end tomorrow. I'm going there."

She brooded, solemn and heavy, the stereotyped shallow woman of only a few moments back, and said, "We've been here twelve years. They're going to have a war. There'll be a coup or chaos, it just can't stay the way it is. Where am I going to go when this place goes? Consider it, Mr. Ferguson, this is the one real home I've got." She pointed to the host. "He wouldn't be viable in any other country. Would you, there, you with the rhetoric? Will you stay and fight when they kill us off? Or where'll you go? Do you see him," she said, "Mr. Ferguson?"

Farquharson said, "Farquharson."

That bothered her. "From Canada," she said. Then: "Welcome to Africa," and she put her face into her drink. Two minutes later she was being imperious and studiedly intoxicated to her steward.

She came into the Club the next day, walked straight up to Farquharson, said, "Judgement has been reserved, till December the twentieth," and walked away.

"Bitch!" Farquharson said. But he couldn't help seeing Mrs. Michaelson, sitting on her African cushion covers, holding a warm stale drink, staring out of the ingrown ritual of her *oyibo* compound, saying, "There's going to be a war. Where am I going to go?"

Charlie Spanier-Dodd came from the bar. "Last night," he said, "I was illuminated. Grace isn't happy with me. She was shining by the light of luminescent squash and righteousness." He sat down. "My steward wants to go back to the East. He's been with me sixteen years. Of course I wouldn't let him. So now Grace is mad at me in two ways. I tell her I simply don't believe in an uprising. No one could co-ordinate it."

"Then where are we going, if anywhere?"

"Nowhere. Rather untidily. It's possible some of the roads might not be good." He said, passionately, "I *know* these people!"

179

"That's the kind who get massacred," Joan said. " 'I *know* these people.' Farq, are we in danger? Do you think we ought to go home?"

"No," he said. "I mean no about going home. I don't know about the danger."

Something had happened to him the other night with Gail. "I have killed," he thought, "and I have let myself be manipulated to orgasm." (Those were the words that came.) "I *live* here." Like Mrs. Michaelson, where else was he to go? He had tried regret, but that was a dead emotion. In the moment of a killing he had taken the murder and wanted it. Being sucked off: was that such a horror? That too when it came, perhaps because he hadn't asked for it, he'd liked. Time wouldn't unmake either—why should he want it to? Or firing Elias when there wasn't a moon in the sky. God, he thought, how that had hurt. Judgement postponed, in this or any other court. "We've *been* in danger."

"I don't want to say anything," Joan said in their bedroom the next night, "because I don't want to sound like Mrs. Michaelson, but you're growing up."

"Poor Pickle!" He stood in his shorts, hesitant.

"No," she said. "I think I like it."

"Do you want me to make love to you?"

"Oh Farq," she said, looking at him as if she were staring at the end of his nose, "you don't have to!"

"Haven't I said that to you a lot of nights? How come the other way?"

"I don't know. You just looked as if you thought I needed it."

"What do I do to you?" he said, sitting on the edge of the bed. "No, seriously, you went for pricks—you went for mine, anyway. You didn't want to be a virgin, remember? You hurried me. I don't know how many guys get to de-virgin now, what with doctors and all, but I did. Who've you turned into?"

"I can't make love," she said. "I've got an infection. You'll disturb it."

"Disturb?"

"Well, you know how big you are. Sometimes you tear me. Only a little," she said, as if that too were a fault, "but with an infection . . ."

"What kind?" She was looking sullen. "Look, you can't blame my meat and then get all Victorian on me."

But she wouldn't tell him. After all, this was her body. She said, "Isn't it enough that it won't heal up?"

"No, it's not enough. But," he added, "it's all right, as you say. I don't have to."

He was going on patrol. There was a Land-Rover in Gail's driveway, and a light in the living room. There wasn't any sound. Without wanting to see people, or be jealous, or do anything but just sit down, he sat on the edge of the car, waited, breathing shallowly, and suffered a small heroic daydream of rescuing every neglected woman on the compound: Farquharson the Fulfilling, huge-pricked for the peace of all those beds. There wasn't any point in wondering why he was so bitterly hurt. He had loved to give himself to Joan, when she wanted him. No, he never lost his identity, never fused himself into an "our two souls therefore, which are one". He was only Farquharson, one self, liking. But it wasn't selfish to feast on yourself if you were available. He gave the other person greatly to feast, too. He could do that well. Wasn't that what a lover was?

A man was not a man in some cultures, he thought, until he had killed a man—the throat, lifting above the car trunk, just tense enough; the skin stretched over the Adam's apple, shifting as it moved, once, in the path of the iron, as the armed hand came down. Snapped vertebrae, cord, voice box crushed shapeless and askew: things that he'd meant to do. And then to slither down over the edge of the boot as if to beg for mercy. (He didn't have to turn against the act, because he didn't have to do it again.)

Maybe a man wasn't a lover (he *was* a man now, proved, by many systems, even his own) until he'd been once, by his own allowance, made into a thing with no will, harried to the limit of what he could take, just as an object. Maybe like the man inside with the hairy balls?

His body hugged itself, half shiver, half gaunt hunger. (He wished Garnett well.) The lover's obligation would be to do it all to his wife. But to make those passive, disciplined hands do things to him? They lay at her side unless she had to push him away. Such a proper field to till, he thought, to bear its children to its husband, and to hate guts and bleeding, and not to like hairs and smells. Oh, to be a lady and entertain other unacknowledged cunts seamlessly vacuum-sealed in plastic and sitting on the finished cushion covers, talking about their stewards. Well, their stewards had pricks and pubic hair and smelled. And so did their husbands. "That's the fun of it," he said to his feet, kicking off his sandals, "being the whole thing at once." If Joan farted when they made love, she was humiliated and had to stop. He wanted to give her a great big kiss and cheer her on. If they couldn't be the unified soul, let them be slapstick friends. She couldn't be either. She had a role, responsibilities, and liked him. Damn it, it wasn't enough.

He was hearing a few disjointed noises. Garnett, crying for the entry into his own mortality. That was all right; it was private. Nothing could break in, not even if he stood at the window and stared, instead of sitting on the man's Land-Rover with his head in the cool air, the comfortable sharp grit under his feet. " 'Any man's death diminishes me, because I am involved in mankind,' " he found himself quoting, fortunately for his ego at the end of the quotation. " 'Neither can we call this a begging of misery or a borrowing of misery.' " ("If any man is alive," he thought, "he is.") " 'As though we were not miserable enough of ourselves but must fetch in more from the next house, in taking upon us the misery of our neighbours. Truly it were an excusable covetousness if we did, for affliction is a treasure, and scarce any man hath enough of it.' "

"Peace in a land of swords and discords," he thought. "We sit in the dark and wait our turn."

But that wasn't what he was sitting there for, and before anyone in the house could find him or be troubled by him, he had gone away.

Friday night they ran out of toilet paper, and because they didn't know where to get any, Stanley drove them to Mọkọla and took Farquharson and Jamie across a drainage stream into a store like a wooden box, open on its side and full of crowded shelves. Stanley turned his head twice, then lifted out two thin white rolls. Farquharson had to put Jamie down to get his money out. Jamie held his father's bare leg and looked grave, and as if he had to have courage, and the girl who ran the store put the money in a box and then held a biscuit out to Jamie, saying, "You want?"

Stanley looked displeased and said, "*Kí l'o ńṣé?*"

"*Pa 'nu mọ!*" Stanley's face stiffened.

She said, "*mâa lọ!*"

Farquharson said, "What is it?" Stanley glowered and was about to bark.

"*Ọgá kékeré,*" the girl said, crouching in front of Jamie. "*O fẹ?*" And then she was delighted, because Jamie put his hand out for the cookie. Farquharson said, "*Adúpẹ,*" which as far as he knew meant *Thank you,* formally, gave the toilet paper to the glowering Stanley, and picked Jamie up again.

"We have a conflict between ethics and sanitation," he said when he got back to the car. "Jamie has been given a cookie. My vote is for ethics and to let him eat it."

"I ask her what she does," Stanley said, clearly to all of them. "She tell me to stop talk, and to go away."

"She called Jamie a little master," Farquharson said.

He handed the boy over the back of the seat into Joan's arms, and part of the cookie broke off against the ceiling light. Joan threw both pieces out the window. "I feel like a heel doing that," she said, "but that's how it has to be. No unwashed food, and no packages opened beside an open drain."

Jamie mourned, loudly.

Farquharson said, "I know. But how could I stop it? It was a present."

"I'm not taking any chances."

"Oh, of course you're right. I just wish you didn't have to be."

183

"All right, then. Oh, Jamie," she said, as she hugged him. "I'm awful sorry."

"Being sorry," Farquharson thought angrily: "that's nothing but what you have to do to get what you want." And he knew he wasn't fair to her.

They drove sedately homewards, nursing emotions and deciding to recover from them. They were past the hotel before they realized they were being followed by something with a great amount of shouting coming from it. Stanley hesitated, and then moved closer to the edge of the road. Farquharson twisted to look back into the headlights, and suddenly a little dark truck swept past them, its back crammed with men who were pounding on the metal panels and crying gleefully, "*Akíntọ́lá! Akíntọ́lá! Ọ̀rẹ́sányáaaa!*"

Stanley drew quietly off the road and turned his lights out. "*Akintọla,*" Farquharson said, making a muffled echo. "Well, they sounded happy. I guess somebody still likes him."

"Yes, sir."

"So Akintọla is in the car."

"Sir?"

"Well, *they* thought so."

"Stanley," Joan said, trying to be reasonable, "do we have to sit in the dark?"

"Put the lights on, Stanley," Farquharson said. "That's the safe thing, anyway." The car started, and he said, "Stanley, what did Akintọla use this car *for*?" Stanley accelerated.

Then a taxi came abreast of them, one of the usual Morris Minors, jammed with passengers. It began matching speeds, crowding them. The dim light showed Farquharson proud heads and damask caps. "Let them get by, Stanley," he said, but Stanley put his foot down and, half on the shoulder, began to race. The taxi moved slightly ahead of them, the faces got into the edge of the direct light, and Farquharson saw two heads turned towards him, both quite calm. Implacably, the taxi crowded them over. Stanley was at war.

"Stanley, stop," Farquharson said. "Stop now!"

With great reluctance, Stanley brought WP2471 to a jerking stop. The taxi slowed too for a moment and almost stopped, and then Farquharson jumped out of the car and the tail lights of the Morris Minor bounced over the railway tracks and sped away past the cattle market. "*Akíntọláaaa!*" Farquharson repeated softly, then folded himself back into his seat and closed the door. "I guess that's the other side. I wonder if they were roused by our friends in the pickup truck. I didn't like that."

Stanley was reaching into the glove compartment. He brought out the red identity card from the Foundation Day ceremonies and stuck it up. Then he said, "Sir, we go home Ifẹ."

At the other end of the cattle market there was a road branching off to the left. A few headlights caught and passed them, a few came glaring towards them, and then they got past the houses and made a quick turn into the dark.

"All right, Stanley," Farquharson said after a mile, "just what was this car used for?"

Nobody was following them. "Sir," Stanley said, partly turning his head, "this is a very delicate car." He waited. "Sir, we believe that when the Premier wish to see a lady, he use this car."

Farquharson shouted "*Akíntọlá!*" and reached his hand down to beat on the outside of the door. Then he said, "Good heaven's sakes above!" with satisfied inadequacy. "Let that man through! That is officer car!"

"It is good car, sir. And we afford to pay for it."

The road turned right at about two houses' worth of village, and after a while they were driving through the compound of the University of Ifẹ, which seemed at night a sparse and meagre version of their own. Then Stanley brought them on to a little stretch of almost homemade road, to the back gate of their own university, beside which stood a couple of guards, one of them young and white. Farquharson stuck his head out the window, but his red card was visible, and they were waved grandly on.

"I wonder if he did take this car to see his ladies," Farquharson said to Joan when he was getting ready to go on patrol. " 'This is a very delicate car.' I liked that."

"Hadn't you better sell it?"

"Do I look black?"

She said, "They knew you were white. It didn't matter, did it?"

He kissed her good night and said, "Just the same, I enjoyed that."

16

December 3–4, 1965

HE was on duty at the Atiba Gate, looking through its chicken wire at the empty Ọyọ road. Occasionally a big truck went by, down the middle of the road. Once one stopped and suddenly turned all its lights out. Farquharson was waiting with his fingers on the gate when he realized that the man had stopped only to make water beside the road.

A car caught him in its lights. A flat, very English voice said, "Professor Farquharson?"

He took his hands off the gate, alertly uneasy. "Here," he said.

"Your wife wants you to come home. I'm Ellis in Geology. I live next door at Number Six. We haven't met." Farquharson found himself shaking hands as he was getting into the car. The man was in pyjamas. "Is there another person on duty with you?" Farquharson nodded. Ellis called out, "I have to take Professor Farquharson away with me. His wife is ill!" and the car was moving.

"Sorry to alarm you, Farquharson," Ellis said, "but my wife is with her. We were in the garden, walking," he said. "We often do that. Fortunately she was able to come to one of the doors and let us in. My wife made her take some pain killer, and I came for you."

The road sped by. Farquharson sat as if every part of the seat had to be under pressure where it touched him, his head held very high. They drove right up against his patio. He almost tripped. He was rattled and full of dread and ready to shout at someone.

Joan was sitting on the edge of one of her sofa cushions, her legs very formal and stiff, her hands squeezing the little roll of padding, her breasts slumped over her stomach as if she had a soft backbone. Farquharson shouted, "What the hell's happened to you?" and the woman beside Joan stiffened and disliked him.

Ellis said, "We'll wait outside," and made his wife come with him, leaving Farquharson standing on the braided rug.

He said, "What is it, Joan?"

"Go in the bathroom."

He felt the sweat run down from his armpits, and put the door-stopper under the door, so they could be in the same stretch of room. He got to the bathroom and was staring around wondering what to look for; there was a pool of red in the toilet bowl. Joan said, "I didn't flush it," and he knew she must be terrified, because even to leave the lid of a toilet seat up was something she didn't like. She forced her eyes on him, as if to keep him from looking down again. "For a couple of days," she said, "it's been a sort of strawberry-juice colour." He saw her blush. "Oh God," he thought, the more venomously because at that moment he could believe he loved her, "why the hell did you ever have to have a body? You of all people!"

"Garnett made me give him a sample. It wasn't in it then."

She was walking with a hunched back past him, as if she were going to flush the toilet. "Cut it out," he said. "We need that! Now you go to bed."

She said, "It looks so horrible," but she let him send her out of the room, and he heard, "Now go to sleep, Jamie. Farq and Mummy just had a party."

The only bottle he could find in the kitchen that seemed right was a three-quarters empty bottle of pickled onions, so he turned them out into a refrigerator dish, sluiced the bottle in a vat of tepid boiled water cooling on the stove, and ran down to the bathroom as if he was going to have to stop his wife again, but she was standing in the doorway of their bedroom, looking at him as if to beg for help.

He plunged the bottle under the surface of the bloody urine, screwed the lid on with his hand, dripping washed, dried the bottle, dropped the towel on the floor. And then, with his wife watching, he flushed the toilet and set the lid down. "Now," he said, "I'm going to take this to Bill Garnett right away. I don't care what he's doing."

Stanley's house was dark. Farquharson got the car out, made a tremendous noise in the driveway with it, and left Joan with the Ellises.

Garnett lived two storeys above Jeremy Fisher; the fastest road there led past Gail Johnston's house. Farquharson slowed at the driveway without even meaning to. This wasn't one of Garnett's nights, was it?

Of course it was.

But feeling suddenly full of guilt he hurried on to the flats beyond the end of Saunders Road and with the bottle in his hand ran up the centre stairs to Garnett's and pounded the door, until some kind of sanity took him and he came back to see the Land-Rover in the driveway, where he should have seen it the first time.

"Who is it?" His name sputtered and hissed in the night. Then he heard her startlingly close, at the window: "What kind of a trick's this?"

"I've got to see Bill," he said. "Joan's damn near pissing pure blood. He's got to have a look at it."

His free hand was worrying at the door handle. "Let me in!" he said.

But the door wasn't locked. And before Gail could stop him he had got past the large furniture in the living room and had gone into the bedroom with the bottle in his hand and said, "Bill, look at that. What are we going to do?"

Bill was trying to do up his shirt across a black-matted chest. He sat on the edge of the bed, staring at Farquharson without surprise or distaste, with his legs together and a broad stub of penis sticking up past a scrotum that had been squeezed upwards by his thighs. Farquharson, as far as his panic let him, felt friendly towards him. He gave him the bottle and then watched his face.

"Take off the lampshade," Garnett said, and the glare went through the bottle as if it were a traffic light.

189

Garnett usually looked like a man dedicated to his own sorrow because it was the only thing he had. It was extraordinary to see his lean dry face pass through blankness and become a doctor's. He forgot about hiding; he hunched back on the bed and got his ankles under his shins, and then looked and thought.

"And she said to tell you it hurt so much she didn't want to straighten her back. She said it hurt like a migraine."

"Does she get migraines?"

"I never thought so."

"Then how does she know?" The voice was impersonal and interested. He kept tilting the bottle, holding it close to his eye.

"It isn't a pure sample," Farquharson said. "I had to get it out of the toilet."

"These damned modest women!" Automatically, he lifted his balls free of his thighs and let them drop. They were hairy, as advertised. Garnett said, "I guess I have to recognize your right of entry, Farquharson. Actually, it's news to me." Gail threw his shorts to him. "Dear Gail!" he said, but not to her. "I bet she doesn't know whether to be ashamed or proud of us."

She said, "I'm feeling stepped-on."

"Let's go and see your wife. If there were any justice, you ought to be able to finish what I've begun, but I guess some other time."

They drove off in convoy, leaving Gail to consider how unexpected men could be. She had been about to simplify things by having Farquharson alone; she was sure that after a few more nights she would have let Bill go his way. And now she was liking them both, with a kind of envy and jubilation. She would have had a long cool bath, only at her end of the compound there was hardly any water any more.

Farquharson thanked the Ellises.

"You shouldn't have gone out, you know, when she was sick."

"I'm going to take this across to the Clinic and look at it," Garnett said, coming out of the bedroom after a long time. (Farquharson had been kept out; Joan couldn't help being shy about him.) "There isn't anything more I can do tonight. She's got the tetracycline. You see, *I* can't put her into the hospital. Only Dr. Foley can." He hesitated. "I was going to say he might not want to, but I guess I can make all the fuss you need"—he was writing on a card—"ask to be referred to this doctor, will you? He's a Yoruba, and excellent. You know how to pronounce Yoruba *p*'s?"

"*Kpuh!* Right?"

"Dr. Lapipọ Popoọla. He's got rather a lot of them, and he's particular. Now don't let Sergeant Foley send you on to anyone else: I want your word on that."

They were out by the Land-Rover. Garnett turned and put his hand up to Farquharson's chin as if he had to steady his skull to see into his eyes, (and Farquharson realized with embarrassment how much taller than Garnett he was.) "I'm not going to ask questions about how you get to go to Gail," he said, hardly giving the words sound. "I don't have any attachment there, so I've got no rights. Your wife's a pretty woman. Just leave me some time, will you? And tell Joan to come first thing in the morning, and then park and shriek until the two of you get in to Foley. And leave your boy at home. But you've damned well got priority over V.D."

Farquharson sat on the edge of the bed. His wife was lying on her side under a smoothed sheet, a child turned middle-aged. She said, "You look so worried. I wish I could do something for you."

Husband and wife. He smiled into the dark, involuntarily, wondering what Gail must have thought.

Joan didn't want to leave Jamie behind when they went to the Clinic, so they went all together, asked to see Dr. Foley, and were told to wait. And then after a lot of waiting they were told to come back on Monday. At that Farquharson didn't have to pretend to stage a tantrum. He stormed to the desk with the rest of the room watching him, pulled Garnett's note out of the files where the clerk had put it, and shouted, "Urgent. It says Urgent. Now are you going to take me in?"

Victoria Nwonkwo came in with her oldest boy. "How long have you been here?" she said quietly to Joan.

"Almost an hour."

"Then put your head down and faint, and let me get to that narcissistic little man." Victoria and her son advanced. Joan did put her head down, but only because she had to cry. The beautiful clerk finally took the file and went out, his back held gently erect with disapproval.

"Well, now then, Mrs. Farquharson," a rough voice called, "*what* do you think is wrong with you?"

Joan closed the door behind her and left Farquharson in the waiting room.

After a long while Joan came to the door and said, "Farq! Come here." Farquharson scooped up Jamie and came in. She said, "He won't send me."

"As I told your wife, Mr. Farquharson," Dr. Foley said, "she must learn to avoid hysteria. I have no intention of sending people to a hospital just because they think they ought to go there." Farquharson saw a bearded sick martinet, ugly with integrity. "She is taking a prescription. She ought to go home and watch it work."

There was a cold, nasty quarrel. Jamie tried to hide his head on his father's chest. It became uncomfortably clear that Dr. Foley disliked Bill Garnett to the degree that he was almost afraid of him, and had therefore to maintain no confidence in his diagnoses. Suddenly he gulped medicine and drank water. "I won't be shouted at in my own Clinic, sir," he said. He opened the door. "Albert, send Dr. Garnett in." Bill Garnett came and seemed startled at what he could see in Joan. Dr. Foley looked at Farquharson's chin and said, "Please wait outside."

"Dr. Foley, I demand that you refer us to Dr. Popoọla." And the Farquharsons went back to the waiting room.

But whatever storm they had caused between Dr. Foley and his white assistant couldn't be heard outside the doors. After a while Garnett came out and said, "He's phoning now. Go over to the hospital: they'll be waiting for you."

192

"What was that all about?" Farquharson said.

"Never you mind. You just get out of here before it starts again."

Stanley drove them. They had to go round the road block at the Electoral Commission offices. The road up to the hospital was interrupted by a gang of workmen building a garden wall in the boulevard. A guard raised a yellow barrier to let them in, and they drove up a huge formal horseshoe-shaped drive. They were efficiently taken to a queerly dark and vacant elevator block, then along open galleries to a corridor that seemed to plunge into the middle of a wing, and so to a little room with a semi-private shower and a view to the Parliament buildings. Joan was looking miserable and stubborn, and a nurse came in with forms and told Farquharson to go and then, smiling with what seemed genuine pleasure, when he could come back. He took his wife in his arms and said, "Hell of a note."

"Go back to Jamie," she said.

He found Jamie and Stanley under the sheds of the parking lot, walking solemnly up and down. Jamie was crying, Stanley gently talking soothing matter-of-fact words about the roof and the posts.

So they went to the Kingsway, and he took Jamie on his hip up the escalators, took him twice around the train and once among the toys, and bought him something called a fairy castle, that came apart and went together again, like spools on spikes. Then he told Stanley to wheel Jamie among the groceries and bought a bottle of perfume for his wife and a bottle of vodka for himself—and wondered what a pitiful thing it was to buy perfume, and how afraid he was. So he bought some food, paid the flirtatious delicate cashier with the running eye, who was sweetly grave with Jamie, and then devoted ten sober minutes to buying Joan some books. When they were home he packed Joan a small suitcase and sent Stanley to deliver it, gave Jamie and himself their lunch, put Jamie down for his nap—unable to think, really. Stanley came to the patio and said, "You wish I stay with Jamie today, sir?"

"Yes, please. I'll call you when I go." He smiled, wanly. "This time I'll make sure you're here."

The nurse said, imperiously, "I will call you, sir," and made him wait outside. Garnett came and found him. "Well," he said, "you'll get to be all by yourself for about three nights. This is Dr. Popoọla."

Popoọla explained that Joan had an acute urinary infection, that she might have had a small one for some time ("Harmattan is dangerous, you do not know how much sweat you lose, you feel fresh and light"), and that rest, much drinking of liquids, and a stronger drug should clear things up. "Now you may go in and see her," he said, "and then you should go home."

Joan was sitting up on the high bed, looking pretty, with her books in front of her. They made the unreal conversation of hospital visiting hours, and then she said, "I don't want you to come and see me. I want you to give Jamie all your time."

He looked at her from the door. He didn't want to confess and he didn't want to be found out. He thought he couldn't trust her. And he thought then that this was a strange way to feel kindly, out of the middle of adultery with the alternate lover at his back. But whatever the feeling, this was the kindness he wanted to wish for her, the best he could do, and good. She saw him blank and handsome, thought that he wasn't worried, and said, with a slight edge of pique, "You can go now."

Ormford said, "I h-heard. Is it serious or not serious?"
"Not serious."
"Then will you come to dinner? This was all set up without you, so to speak. But Peg says we can fit you in. That's a sort of awkward nonhospitality," he said, "bb-but you're most welcome to it."

Farquharson opened a couple of cans for Jamie and sat beside him. Father and son were silent foreigners, playing with the fairy castle between the place mats. Where Jamie's mother was had been carefully explained, so Farquharson knew it was being remembered and thought about but wouldn't be talked about. Farquharson took time over Jamie's bath and bedding, sang to him, and slowly watched him sleep—then arranged with Jacob and Stanley how he was to be fetched if Jamie cried, and shut himself into the bedroom to get dressed. All Joan's possessions accused him of some kind of nasty, unimportant treachery. He was almost glad of it.

He wore a tie. He put on underwear. He told Stanley to drive him and go quickly back to the house, and spent the evening arguing about John Diefenbaker and Canadian politics with Ted Eayrs until good food and liquor sharpened the hunger for being alone, and he said that if Stanley came they were to say he'd walked home by way of Sankore Avenue and the Administration Building.

It was the sort of night in which a man walking alone drifts on air, with nothing in his head but the almost imperceptible meeting line of tree branches and sky. He missed Gail's house, hesitated, and continued walking. The library was dark; the Arts Building was dark; there was a single light in the passageway in the Administration Building. He stopped and looked down to where there were a few lights in Kuti Hall. Somewhere far away, faint panic started, as if he saw again his two men moving, in the dark now, by Jaja Avenue. He wanted to cry and run; he was silent and walked, foot after drifting foot, feeling his heart press his throat. He had to turn aside in front of the Arts Theatre and sit on a small wall, and put his hands together between his knees and squeeze them tight. The pain between his fingers, the cramping of his knuckles, had to become as much a condition of the quiet world as the night. Then he was breathing as if he had fucked long and unsatisfactorily. And he hadn't called out for regret or made any motion to have things undone: he was simply, as he stood up, what he had been by himself; the man under the skin, sensing, with minute electrical currents, infinitesimal chemical changes, in his own space and time, Henry John Farquharson, his buttocks printed with the irregularities of the stone.

"I sorry for the Madam, sir."

"Oh, she isn't very sick, just spectacular. That part's all right."

"Good night, sir."

Stanley with his car was courteous and obscurely flamboyant, like a misplaced cowboy; Stanley in his house was something Farquharson didn't know: young, but distant and still, lying as if in some office of honour, not waiting, but being present because he was expected to be. Farquharson scratched his lip with his thumb, as if he had to think, only there were no thoughts that came here. Finally he pushed himself away from the door frame and said good night.

Farquharson turned off the ceiling fan. Quiet stretched his ears and pocketed the last noises of the locks. He went into the kitchen and poured himself a foolish lonely cocktail: red vermouth and vodka, with one of the pickled onions in the bottom. Looking at its colour he felt carried, not back to last night but far away from it, to where he was in all ways alone, rattling in a closed house that had never been any different. He took the drink into the dining room, put it on the table, and unlocked one of the doors to go outside. He heard Gail and Bill say simultaneously, "We thought we'd find you."

He gave them more of the same drink, and they all sat at the edge of the patio, in a row. And first Garnett reassured him about his wife and then about the hospital, sounding grave, in the humourlessly pedantic but kind American manner. "And why with a wife like that," he said, in the same voice, "are you playing around?" His voice hummed with a bleak enthusiastic melancholy.

"Stanley's awake," Farquharson said.

"Then we'll go in."

"No," Gail said, softly.

"Oh come on, we've got to regularize this situation somehow."

And Farquharson said, "Why?"

"If only to keep out of each other's way without a timetable."

He had to laugh, a skittering whoop of delight, in which

196

Garnett suddenly joined and Gail did not. "Come on, come in," he said then and swept the other two in with him, snapping the lights on till they seemed to stand in daylight—and then he laughed again. "That doesn't answer what's wrong with your wife," Gail said, suddenly in a bad temper.

"Doesn't it?" he said. "Well, I guess that's too bad. That's *our* business."

"Christ," Garnett said, "I never knew any adulterer who was so much the happy copey married man as you are. When I think that when I was on the town I couldn't do any more with my wife than ask her for the morning paper or a divorce—you're *married*, Farquharson!"

"Do you want me to take Gail into bed," Farquharson said, "to prove I'm a free agent?" He pointed to the door.

"Don't *I* get some say?"

Bill said, "What do you think you've had?" and then sat down.

Gail said, "This was Bill's idea," and sat down by herself.

"Well, if you'll excuse me," Farquharson said, "I'll see if Jamie's still asleep." But Jamie looked almost elegiacally relaxed. The grown Jamie, as a spent, fond lover, might lie like that. Farquharson was stung by something between pity and exultation and went back to his guests, prepared to talk out the night with them or do whatever else might happen. He'd had his testimonial. The others were slumping in their chairs. "Sometime in the early morning," Farquharson thought, "they will go home."

Bill Garnett's toe was still festering under its bandages. He showed it to them. And finally Farquharson went to bed with the bemused triumph of a virgin after a particularly chancey party. They had at least taken the solitude out of the house. He made water and looked down at a small sharp vein snaking against his foreskin. He was glad for Joan to be cared for and to have herself to think about for a few days. The vein on top of his prick was a dull ropy ridge he could push with his thumb. When he went to bed he thought, "she should have wanted me". It wasn't very surprising to find himself, some while later, lying on his stomach

197

with a fist jammed into her pillow, his prick singing-hard and being rasped by the bedsheet at its tip. He had to roll over on his back with a flagpole sticking out of him. It lasted for a long time, signalling.

17

December 5–8, 1965

IN the morning he watched Jamie wake up, his great dark eyes open and unfocussing in his head, and thought that if it were possible to love anything more, a man would burst. It was Sunday, the day they were alone. He wasn't going to have to shave while Jacob stood over the bathtub pounding the clothes, but he couldn't think what to do with the long day. He said, "What do you do every morning with Mummy?" but Jamie played with his fairy castle, lifting the spools and discs of its towers, and its five conical roofs, and piling them on again, purposefully, with variations. He got stuck sometimes and asked for help. Their morning was huge and desolate.

In the afternoon, after he and Joan had asked how each other was, there didn't seem much to say. So he went to the Club and said, "Stanley, will you play with him?" And then stood at the bar with a beer while Jamie and Stanley played store with bits of concrete on the grass. (Once, Stanley had climbed the small flame tree to get seed cases for Jamie to play castanets with, until the unseen manageress ordered him off and he came to Farquharson and said, "That Madam say I get down.")

Farquharson saw Mrs. Michaelson and went out among the big chairs to talk to her. "You'd better make her get out of the hospital," she said. "Parliament has got to meet within two months of the election. That means by this weekend there's going to be nothing but roadblocks, curfews, and armed men. The danger is going to be acute for somebody—I *hope* the government. Did you know you can still buy an Opposition newspaper?" He hadn't known. "Go down the Bye-Pass towards Awọlọwọ's house. You can buy one every day. I let mine show in my car—they wouldn't touch a white. Did you know they killed one of the newsboys *on* the Bye-Pass? Of course, they're all thugs," she said. "Here." He looked at a grey newspaper that could suddenly cost a life to sell, diatribes and trumpetings of integrity on a page measled with random type faces. "Parliament is too near the hospital," Mrs. Michaelson said. "After all, there's no legal government, only a *de facto* one. Get her *home*, my dear."

Nobody came in the evening except Victoria, who sat down with a glass of squash and let him talk to her and then left him in an empty house, master of the reflections on the closed doors.

Gail didn't come.

Monday morning was full of classes, all in his office, and as he perched on the end of his desk before the first one, he thought: "Jamie is with Jacob and Stanley, they'll take care of him." And instead of drifting through the morning with a mind half distracted, be began firmly and had a good morning, even if it did have the Shakespeare tutorial with Mrs. Akinrinmade in it. *She* was all right; she was going to add learning to wealth, because the next step was Lagos, and her husband had money and the black two-storey house in Idanre. But the other women in that class were featureless, pretty girls, and the men were rebels who would never say anything that some teacher had not said, and one solemn boy from the villages whose memory would slip and lock. Farquharson fled from that class to the Senior Common Room most weeks: this day he fought them, and was so triumphant, if grim, at the end of the hour, that when he was asked over his coffee whether it was true that his wife was sick, he had almost to remind himself that he had one before he could pull himself out of his success and say, "No, not very".

Mrs. Akinrinmade was waiting for the next class in his office. She apologized, with the matter-of-fact self-abasement that so easily looked like insolence.

"Are you coming to Idanre?" she said. "Because I could get a place for you to stay, at Akurẹ. I'm afraid it would be easier to work through my husband than to write yourself. Unfortunately, you couldn't stay with us."

"Well, my wife's in hospital," he said. "The place is that good, is it?"

"Yes." Never since she first mentioned it had he questioned that he would go to Idanre. They did, after all, have to go somewhere, sometime. "When should we come?"

"It would be nice," she said, "if you could be there when we could greet you. If it could be just before the start of term."

He looked at the calendar. We'd have to be home on Tuesday. On the third of January?"

"I shall write my husband."

That afternoon when Farquharson went to the hospital (and to the Kingsway first for books), Stanley asked if he could take his cousin home. A straight-backed girl sat in the front seat without speaking until Stanley stopped at the top of Ekotedo Road and got out of the car with her. Then Farquharson heard coins slipped into the girl's hand, somewhere by the back fender, and had to look straight-faced out the window, not to embarrass Stanley, whose negotiations seemed to be taking a long time.

Joan said, "Tomorrow or Wednesday."
"Is it still bleeding?"
"Jamie all right?"
They had nothing to say. No, it hadn't bled since yesterday. She went out on to the verandah gallery to wave goodbye.

"Take me to 1B Sankore, Stanley," he said. "By the way, how much did she charge you?"

"Sir?" Then he turned his head and saw Farquharson looking mischievous. "Sir, she wish too much. Is not good agree for one price then ask for more."

"Well, I don't too much care to give a lift to a whore from my own back yard. Not in my car."

"WP2471, sir." Somehow that made them brothers, if uncommunicating.

"You're public," Gail said opening her door. "Well, come in, come in."

She was angry in her living room, among the white cushion covers. "I've just been to see my wife," he said, interrupting her. "Can you come to me," he said, "and can I make love to you tonight?"

"In *your* house?"

"Look," he said, "the students are becoming real. I've got to have some anchor." He shifted a tiny balsa tree. "That's a hell of a declaration of love, and you don't even have to take it that way."

She backed away to the far window. His face in the greenish light was so intense it was almost sick. She suddenly wanted to hold his ears and shake his head. She said, "You aren't supposed to love me."

"I've been giving myself," he said. "Haven't I? Look." He put down a tree. "I can't keep Jamie waiting in the car outside. Promise you'll come by ten o'clock." And there wasn't anything he was going to be able to do, he told himself, that could make that right.

"I won't promise."

When she was alone, she took up her glue to make another tree. But she found she had snapped a piece.

Farquharson cooked for himself and Jamie, ate, let Jacob wait on them and do the dishes, and sang Jamie to sleep after a bath—and after lying on his back and lifting Jamie high into the air while he arched his back, and flew, until Farquharson's long arms gave out and the aeronaut crashed blunderingly on to his chest. He was afraid, wondering whether Gail would come.

She parked her Honda at the Arts Theatre, and walked over. They talked in the living room, with the lights out and the doors closed to shine dead glass walls at visitors, and he didn't know what they said because he didn't really want to tell her anything. It was enough that he'd cried for help and she'd come, even if she didn't like him for it. Nevertheless, he made her let him come to her, and they made love in the unused bedroom on a sheet and with pillows that didn't belong to anybody because there were never any guests, and they fucked until finally, as she felt herself shimmering under him, he said in a controlled, ordinary voice, "I don't care," and he began to ride with his hips, to the full extent of his length, with force, and a little faster but without acceleration and without anything else moving, until it seemed impossible that he should go out and in one more time, and yet he did, sharper, harsher, but not faster, until there was something like a climaxless surge inside him and he hung very still, then slowly stroked her full length once more with a dying rod, and the heat flooded out. Only then, as if he had been touched by an electric charge, did he become galvanically disorganized and collapse on top of her. That was when he heard as if it had been said minutes ago and only just now recorded, "What don't you care?"

The second night Gail said, "I shouldn't be in love with you. That isn't even my style."

But that night she spent the whole night there, sleeping in his arms, or, as it got to be early morning, close against his side.

She woke him at a quarter to five and said, "Meet me at the Clinic. I'm going to take you to the cloth market."

So he went into his bedroom and ripped the clothes off the bed, bounced on it and rumpled it, and then made their bed as tightly as Jacob had made it up for show, looked in on Jamie, soaped and rinsed himself around the groin with cold water—and was *that* an effective way of waking!—combed his hair, transferred the counterfeit sixpence from one pocket to another, went to Stanley's house, and knocked on the shutter by the window. He left Stanley, in half his uniform, sitting on the living room desk, listening for the master's son.

Farquharson looked at Gail's Honda, said "No thanks" and made her get in his car.

They went down the Bodija road. The sky was whitening rapidly to sunrise. He was surprised to see men, in all sorts of garb, walking like people in accelerated silent movies. It should have been comic to fly past them on the road; it wasn't. They seemed obsessive.

At first Farquharson thought he was supposed to take the road to Adeoyọ with the new coloured flats and the huge overspreading trees, but Gail made him swing on to the other road of the fork where the brand-new daylight paled the earth walls and dusty ground, and showed him a potter's courtyard full of big blackened pots. Abruptly, they were at Ogunmọla.

Someone once had slashed a huge four-lane highway diagonally through the city. Farquharson had discovered it before at night, a pulsating midway hollowed down the middle, cresting at Mapo Hall and then, like a shallow roller coaster, swerving and spilling down, narrowing and becoming villagelike, until it died out flat and featureless at the Ijẹbu Bye-Pass beside a square blue nightclub. Ogunmọla in the morning gleamed wide and empty, or with long house numbers roughly lettered in black paint.

"Turn across from the gas station."

Suddenly he saw a traveller's palm sticking into the level sun: a huge flat green-gold fan, blazing against the colourless sky and the sandy monochrome of the buildings. They seemed to race towards an ensign of triumphant display. Farquharson felt so good at the sight of it that he grinned to keep it to himself. Gail guessed, and said, "Do you feel guilty now?" And he had a moment of fright when he realized that he had had to think for a part of a second to know what she was talking about.

They parked near an irregular intersection. Before they had even crossed the street they were holding hands.

The cloth market was jammed among small houses in wavering aisles between rectangles on the ground covered with bolts and bales of cloth, a guardian or two greeting and trafficking at every rectangle. A tan-brown striped cloth was suddenly stretched taut for showing. Gail stopped and lifted some of another pattern. "See the narrow width?" she said. "That's why the patterns break back and forth across the big pieces." Then she said, "Horrible stuff. I've had to unstitch whole pieces and sew them up again."

Now they were in a corridor between awninged stalls crowded against the houses. Cloths like bright tartans were held up. As he was passing one three-foot square, the woman at it reached out and touched him. "Ọgá?" she said. Farquharson shivered: the touch of the hand was almost immeasurably seductive. An adolescent boy appeared behind Gail, a self-appointed translator, guide, and chaperon, but Farquharson had his attention set on getting through the corridor without stepping into the drainage. They got into a kind of courtyard, the middle filled with a flat cloth-roofed shelter. Gail let him watch and see: this was his place, she had realized as they stepped into it, and not hers. It was odd, she thought, that she not only felt she could be wise around Farquharson, but that she had to be. She would have liked to design a costume for him for an elaborate play. She would have liked to lecture and know he was listening from the next room. "No, I don't love you, Farquharson," she thought, "but you're kind. Kind people need kindness; I guess that's what it's for." (But could it be tried with Bill?) She thought of putting everything she knew of stage work into an hour and hurling it at a class. She had the force, like tennis. Men, like work, belonged to her. She was still grateful for the twinned surprise.

Farquharson let go of her hand and gathered up a narrow, very thick, black-and-white checked cloth. The interpreter leaped, spoke. Farquharson said, "I can do this myself." Eventually, with Gail's help he got three of them for nineteen shillings, and walked away with the cloths under his arm and Gail's hand closing over his upper arm to keep him close to her. When they had squeezed back out and were in relatively open air, beside an *akara* seller, Farquharson rounded on their guide and ordered him off. "You no dash me, master?"

"*Kí l'o fẹ́?*" Farquharson shouted. "*Nkò fẹ́ k'o bá mi wá! O mãa lọ!*"

"*Ọgá!*"

"*Mo ti ṣe tán.*" Farquharson walked out from among the folded costumes and the people in crushed-velvet hats, quarrelling imperiously, and, pulling Gail behind him, got out between the trucks, dodged across the street, and stood looking down into a flat well between road and houses where a smaller, somehow stiffer crowd haggled among stocks of indigo cloth. Then he hugged her forearm and said, "Did we get away?"

"What *did* you say to him?"

"Well, I *hope* I said that I hadn't wanted him to come with us, and to get the hell out because I was finished, but maybe I said something else."

They strolled and watched, openly together, for a few more minutes. Then he said, "I've got to get home, Jamie'll be waking up."

"What's the cloth for?" she said, when they were moving.

"Joan wants some tablemats. I think she can cut these in half."

The traveller's palm looked dry and hard. Gail sat silently beside a man who thought he loved her. "Christ, do you have any conscience?" she said suddenly, "Tablemats, for your wife!"

"I'm sorry," he said, "I have to make her happy with the things that can make her happy."

"Your bed's dead. You couldn't be what you are with me if there were anything left. God, you know everything about it, and you're finding out for the first time!"

"Don't love me, Gail," he said, warning, frightened suddenly, "You said you wouldn't."

"You come in like some kind of glory—what am I supposed to do? Say 'Hi'? That market was *our* place!"

"She's Jamie's mother," he said. "There's a lot of things we've got, even if we've lost half of them. Maybe I get her back from the hospital today. You think I won't be glad to have her? What do I say? She fits my house. And no, that's not selfish."

"You should hear what it sounds like!"

"No. I'm going to rejoice. If I come in you, of course it's wonderful, as you say. Just riding beside you, I want to pull off all my clothes and swarm over you and goddamn *who* sees us. But you've got to remember she and I made Jamie, and we made the other one that died. I can't adulterate that."

"Lover," she said.

Roundabout and detour through the Western Region government buildings. Only a few slow people on the Bodija road.

He said, "I'm going to give you everything I can give you of me. But there's a whole part I can't. Most of the stuff in between's gone over to you of it's own free will already."

"Are you going to be torn apart?" she said, thinking suddenly and with a certain friendliness about Bill.

"No," Farquharson said, driving between Kongi and Bodija. "But I'm not in two places."

"Well, I gave you the cloth market and the street sellers, I guess I can be your mistress."

"Honestly," he said, "I'm not jealous of Bill."

"Well, maybe for your sake or for my sake," she said, "you'd better be."

"I will be," he said, and let her off at a quiet spot just before he turned on to his own road.

Jamie was waking up, looking worried. Farquharson picked him out of the crib and spun around, then put the two of them down on the bed and changed Jamie's clothes. Then they played. At about ten o'clock Ormford appeared suddenly. "They allowed your wife to make one phone call," he said. "She made it to me. To Peg, rather, who phoned me at the office after a certain amount of static. You're to bb-bring her h-home."

"Damn! I've got Poetry at eleven."

"In the local phrase, I shall gg-greet them for you." Farquharson thanked him. "Tell her I don't like her neighbourhood. Parliament on the weekend!"

Farquharson shouted, "Stanley! Okay, Jamie, let's go fetch Mummy home."

There seemed to be more guards at the barricade by the Electoral Commission. "Imagination," he thought, and realized that he wanted to see his wife so much that he felt quite shy and foolish. "And with my thighs peaceably asleep after last night," he thought. "Well, here I am."

Gail hadn't diminished. She had shaped a place in two days and left it empty. She could fill it again; it was like a mask: it waited for her. *Her* mask. He was on the road to fill up Joan's.

A little nurse said, "Goodbye, madam," and Farquharson took the suitcase and walked away. Jamie wouldn't hug her but sat on the seat between them, holding onto his father's leg. Farquharson's arm reached over Jamie's head to rest on his wife's shoulder. Her hair had been combed until it looked like a photograph again. Farquharson wanted to look at it, but didn't lift the back of his fingers against the curls. If they were meeting for the first time in a new world, then they were chaste. "Isn't there a store near here, Stanley?" she said. "I want to get some food."

But somehow as they moved in their kitchen, nobody touched anybody, and when they sat down they might as well have been eating tennis shoes for all the taste they got. Farquharson took the cloths out of the desk and gave them to her.

"You went to the cloth market."

"You wanted table mats. I figured you could get two out of each. There wasn't a fourth," he added.

"I'll work on them in the cool evenings."

They laughed. But the evenings *were* cool; they had forgotten that.

They went to siesta hand in hand, having watched Jamie crawl onto the bed that he used for naps, and lay side by side, each on his own mattress. Farquharson wanted to keep on holding hands, but their palms got too wet. And he wondered, not why he was uncomfortable but why he wasn't, why comfort and dread made a mixture so homely a man could go to sleep in it.

Suddenly Joan was angry. "Did you know they wanted me to fill in the name of my tribe on their damned forms?" she said. "I put 'White,' finally. I guess I shouldn't have. I'm glad to be out of there."

He said, "You're very pretty. It's nice to see you."

She put one of her hands on one of his. "That's good."

Then he said, "I haven't kissed you. Not once yet."

She let him take her to him, and gave him a friend's kiss. She didn't know whether he would take more or not, even if it was afternoon, or whether she was really as lonely as she felt because he didn't.

She was, of course, home again.

18

December 9-23, 1965

HEAVY mist in the mornings, almost fog, gave way to clear parching days and then came back at dawn. Water to the houses was now turned off two and three times a day, but Farquharson's spare water tank stayed in the garage till he lent it to Larry Ormford; he didn't need it. "Either we're very low and near the water tank," he said, "half of which is true, or we're on the straight line to the Vice-Chancellor's. I mean, you get *turned* off, don't you?"

"We most surely do." Ormford said, and snatched his glass away from Jamie, who was discovering beer. "And sometimes they forget to turn it on again. You should hear Peg on the telephone! 'Wh-why h-have we bb-been kept waiting for four hours, please?' Bb-but you can never understand the accent of the man at the other end."

"But why?" Joan said, hemming a place mat.

"Oh the pipe to the water tank is too small; it is full of bb-beasties, accretions, or eggs, seasonally. Or politics—did you h-hear about Akurẹ? They have a brand-new water system but the gg-government refuses to turn it on, because they vote the wrong way. Well, that story *is* true, but about our own I don't know." He had to defend his beer again. "Mind you, Jamie," he said, "bb-beer in the tropics is excellent for young children. But this is *mine.*"

The Nwonkwos were glad to have Joan back. They greeted her and made the Farquharsons come to dinner. "I think we four make the best team on the compound," Oscar said.

Joan was beautiful in company, Farquharson admitted that, with her make-up to get back the complexion that the tropics were taking from her, her eyes blue and Scotch, her hair perhaps a little rigid from being put up each night. She could be perfectly straightforward when a man admired her, as Oscar so flamboyantly and to his own amusement did. It was ridiculous to be homesick for Gail in a dusty room. Victoria was telling them how Nigerian girls put up their hair. "I don't envy you your skins," Victoria was saying, "because they never seem to grow old really well, and ours do. But oh, your hair! When I see those women who can just comb it and forget about it, I get so envious. Oscar," she said, "can have all the *négritude* he wants, but there are *some* drawbacks!"

"Do you know I had an appointment at the hospital for an X-ray," Joan said, "and I had to cancel it because Parliament was opening? I wasn't supposed to be able to drive past. They'd put a bullet through me."

"Well, in *our car*—" Farquharson began.

"I don't believe it!"

"There are roadblocks now," Oscar said. "Try your car at *them*."

Gail was at the Arts Theatre. Farquharson knew she was working late on costumes. He had seen her with yards of white corded satin and her hair caught in a shoelace.

"Can we go somewhere where there aren't roadblocks?" Joan said. "I'd love a ride. I've been so cramped up. And I've got both Stanley *and* Jacob in the house. They'll keep for hours."

"She's trying," Farquharson thought. "She's trying awfully hard."

"I'll see if our nurse is awake," Victoria said. Farquharson moved to the back window and saw her cross the garden between two light-bulbs. "Egypt was African, Oscar," he said. "And it's all there. My, she's beautiful!" Then he heard her voice come strident across the night, and they all laughed. Oscar said, "That nurse!"

"I'll get my car," Farquharson said. "I want to try it."

But there were no roadblocks between the university and the town, so Oscar took them deep into Ibadan to a nightclub whose entrance was a hole in a bare wall blazing with coloured light. They squeezed between people talking Yoruba and found themselves under a trellis, with their feet on concrete. The club was a walled court under a moon. Loud high-life musicians played in garish light in a kind of niche. Most of the light for the dancers seemed to come from their shirts. The floor was concrete. Part of it was raised as if a small building had been flattened off after the first few courses of concrete block. One couple danced there. The place seemed huge: hundreds of people could have been sitting in the dark, at the minute tables. Oscar signalled. They were given huge bottles of Star beer, and smallish glasses, and watched the people dance, as the stray light let them see. "We shall not be political," Oscar said, "and we shall not be intimidated by any government. Victoria!" he said. "Please?"

Farquharson thought nobody could dance on rough concrete. He was wrong. He remembered getting up in front of his wife in a Toronto hotel, beckoned onto the performing platform by a hula dancer; and was, for the first time in his memories of that display, embarrassed. Surely a person couldn't be so effortless and so tense at once, in the same thing. He saw Victoria bend her knees and move, waving, down to the floor, with Oscar following, mischief in his eyes. "She's got the right name," Farquharson said, "for some damned crazy reason." He mumbled, "Queen and empress, chaste and fair . . ."

"Don't be in love with her," Joan said. "She's unavailable. Besides, it's 'queen and *huntress* chaste and fair'."

"Shall we dance?" he said.

She was taken aback. "It's so loud. What do I do?"

"Come on, Pickle."

They were on the concrete, dancing whatever they could, in a North American way. And then they all drank beer. Farquharson said, "I've got a lot to learn." Oscar said, "Come, Joan, let me teach you," beckoning as if he were already dancing with her, and Joan joined him. And Victoria suddenly rapped her finger on the back of Farquharson's hand and said, "You have to be very nice to her," and then took him on to the floor to teach him.

Somehow he couldn't learn.

But they had a lovely evening. And then Farquharson said, "I wonder if there's a roadblock beyond the Atiba Gate," and they drove to look and found one suddenly in their headlights: a grey gate in the road, with soldiers who had a small fire. There was a big truck on the other side, stopped. The gate was closed. Farquharson crept forward. The men saw the brown car and its registration number.

The gate was opened. Nobody even spoke to them. The men's face, to Farquharson, seemed to be full of lewd delight.

Oscar said, "It worked. It worked! Henry, you have a jewel here."

But they weren't in the mood for the joke, and after a while they just stopped and sat. "Well, I guess that's been enough time," Joan said, giggling. "Shall we go home now?"

When they got to bed she said, "Welcome me home. I mean to try."

But it wasn't too successful. Neither of them was quite displeased, but he was slightly different, and she noticed; and she was trying to be, and didn't feel *he* noticed.

He was well into the last week of term; he stood beside Gail at the counter in the Senior Common Room, put down three penny tickets, set a sausage roll on her plate, and said, "Symbolic gift. *Faute de mieux.*"

Beth, the linguist, was behind them, waving her tickets.

"Are you still going everywhere around the countryside Beth?" one of the men said.

"Of course I am," she said. "The roads are safe."

"Not between here and Lagos."

"I was there yesterday."

("I haven't been able to come," Farquharson said, softly by the door, as if he weren't speaking to her. "I've been trying to make things right for her.")

"Beth, you are impossible. Gangs of political thugs barricade the main highway and raid villages, and you collect dialects!"

"Oh, but I've been in this country for so long, dear," she said. "Everybody knows my car."

"Please, Beth," Ted Eayrs said, pressing his hands together. "Keep away from Shagamu, keep away from Ijẹbu-Ode, keep away from the Lagos road!"

"May I go by Abẹokuta?"

"Beth, you're hopeless! I wish," Eayrs said suddenly, clapping his hands, "that when those Commonwealth prime ministers come to Lagos to talk Rhodesia they'd come into the sweet democratic hinterland and let them see what trouble *is*! Not that it'd do us much good. There you Americans sit," he said, pointing to Bohlender and Pritchard—and Cord, who was quiet in a corner —"probably cued for escape with bulletins from the CIA." He looked at Gail and Farquharson. "Has anybody heard from the High Commissioner's office lately? When the crunch comes," he said to the Americans, "we'll watch *you*."

"They've prohibited Christmas drumming in the streets," Jane Grant said. "They don't want gunfire under the drums. Or the excitement."

Gail said, "They've outlawed water pistols, too."

Farquharson said, "You can buy them in the Kingsway."

"Not guns, though; things like fluorescent eggs."

Eayrs said, "No drum, no squirt. What have you got there, Farquharson?"

"Just an odd-looking coin," he said. "Would that be counter-feit?"

"There are enough bogus shillings around. Here, let me see. You've been had," he said, handing it back. "Where'd you get it?"

"I found it on the garage floor." Sandy MacLachlan looked at him.

But the garage floor when they moved into the house had been swept clean. Violence was in more of the country than the roads, then. Garages, he thought, were the places where the roads hid. "Consider the country," Eayrs said, "where you can profitably counterfeit a sixpence, and ask yourself why 'party supporter' is a synonym for thug."

"You're gloomy, Ted."

"*Is* the government in control of the country, no matter what speeches Akintọla can make in his pet Parliament when he can get it to meet in fear and trembling for one part of an afternoon?" His arm swept out. " 'I *told* you you'd all be back!' And being voted for by the ancestral spirits of the Yoruba. There's a lot to be said for a tyranny that has that kind of joyous corruption in it, but oh my God." He put his head back to look at the ceiling. "Farquharson," he said, "What are *you* doing over Christmas?"

Farquharson felt that it was unfair to have all the eyes in the room on him. He said, "We've got an invitation to Idanre."

"Well, the roads east are all right still. I guess you'll make it."

Farquharson said, "Thank you."

"Don't be funny!" Farquharson was surprised how venomous Eayrs could sound if he was troubled.

He found Sandy MacLachlan in his office. "Farquharson, I want you on patrol Your wife's home now. The danger might be mounting."

"You know, it's odd how I don't believe that," Farquharson said.

"You've listened to Ormford too much. Or is it that the fall of the campus takes second place to the fall of a young lady?"

The blackboard said "Lord David Cecil: Pathos" until the words crawled in his eye.

"Mister," MacLachlan said, "that's your affair. Have all the fling you want. But now it's you who ought to be remembering the capture of Quebec." He said, "I'll leave you now. Beyond those gates—and you notice they're building a new one so that the trucks can't get in—is a government that knows it's got no right to be there. And on this compound are its most articulate enemies, *and* a fifth column Well, just because"—his voice dropped—"you dumped your garbage at the bottom of my garden, and I had to carry it into the middle of the road where it belonged, that doesn't say you're finished with this, Farquharson. But I'd put the coin away. There used to be a man in the Maintenance Department who had one of those. Do you want to sit down?"

Farquharson tried to start a sentence, but one wouldn't come.

"I had a lot to worry about that night," MacLachlan said, "as you can believe. I was down by the hedge. Well, I saw the car, and the little light behind the badge—well, you've got the only Wolseley on the compound and there was curfew outside. Farquharson, you look unwell."

Farquharson said, "Will you take me home?"

"I'll do better than that. I'll take you for a drive, lad."

Farquharson felt almost that he had to be led into the parking lot. MacLachlan had a big white Citroën. He put Farquharson into the front seat, whistled as he walked around, and drove with a silent passenger through the University of Ifẹ onto a red earth road that led them into a teak plantation, and there, between the narrow trunks of what seemed much more overgrown weeds than trees, he stopped the car and said to the man who felt like his prisoner, "Farquharson, I'm sorry for you. I had no right whatsoever to raise the subject."

"What'll you do about it?"

"Come, lad, there's nothing I *can* do without incriminating myself. And I've no taste for it. Were they in your house?"

Farquharson said, "Joan doesn't know. She was away."

"But was your wee boy there?" He saw Farquharson's face, and suddenly realized that he liked this man. MacLachlan had a good deal of savage in him; he was also a Scots sentimentalist. (The man's name was Farquharson, after all.) "Look, if a man breaks in and is killed it's all right," he said, but then he couldn't help himself. He burst out, "How did you do it? *Two!*"

But relief had suddenly made it all seem funny, and Farquharson sat in the passenger seat beside a red-dusted cliff of teak trees with huge shapeless leaves and laughed, as became a man, for a long time.

"Come on, you owe it to me!" MacLachlan was a big man

for wheedling. Then as a conscious gambit, he said, "I've got a mistress, too."

Farquharson got out at the Arts Building, then tucked his head back down to the window and said, casually, "Use a frying pan." MacLachlan wished he hadn't asked.

The last classes sped. Mr. Adebọwale asked if he might wish the Professor a merry Christmas, and Mrs. Akinrinmade said, "We shall expect you; we shall be most happy. Please do come."

Joan had to get a fresh prescription from the hospital clinic. She came back looking wild-eyed, saying that there had been a riot there, but Grace had said that they could get any drug they wanted at any drugstore, just by asking for it. So Joan said, "Farq, here's the name of it. Will you go and get it for me?"

Farquharson discovered then that nothing since he had come to Nigeria had made him feel as guilty as taking a bootleg prescription down the four or five steps at the back of the store to the prescription wicket and starting to stammer an explanation, as if all the ranks of toothpaste and worm medicine, insect repellant and shower caps were listening to him. And then he suddenly knew that he was in a state of complete delight, dodged the beggar in white on the front step as he came out, and said to Stanley, "Give me Jamie. I'm going to walk him up to the Kingsway."

They went hand in hand beside the moving cars. An immense woman in wrapper and *buba* stood in their way and smiled, and they had to go around her. After a while Farquharson said, "You want to be carried about?" They went into the Kingsway to buy a Nativity scene of small thorn carvings and pay two pounds for it. And Farquharson bought Joan a necklace. Then he saw a little carving of a man sitting with his back against a tree, reading a huge book about an inch and a quarter high, on which were written all the letters from A to H, his face strained with the most intense and desperate incomprehension. He was only a little semi-mass-produced tourists' toy, but some accident in the carving had made his brown face real, and funny. Farquharson had the girl put it in a box and set it on the shelf of the car, stuffed into a food bag. If he could ever give it to her, that was for Gail. He had bought silver jewellery from a Hausaman for Joan.

Saturday by near accident they ran into a children's party at the Club, and found *Peter and the Wolf* being mimed extravagantly, to piano music and a music-hall narrator. The Bird was Gail Johnston, fluttering long blue feathers of cloth from a pair of sticks.

"Well, look at you," Farquharson said afterwards, and Gail knelt in front of Jamie, fluttering her sticks, and said "Hi!" and Jamie was fearfully impressed and in a mad moment tried to chase her.

Farquharson had explained to Joan that they were going to Idanre and would stay at a catering rest house in Akure for two nights. "Well, if I'm all right inside," she said, then, "No. I will be. But let's take a practice run beforehand. Let's go to Ife."

Dr. Popoola said, "Travel by all means if the country will let you. Greet your husband for me."

"What is that?" she said to Jacob, pointing to where one of Stanley's sister's little children was standing beside a tree, with something around her neck on a string, like a bundle of hair or feathers. Jacob flounced visibly and said, "Madam, that is an ignorant belief!"

"By which," Joan said, "I guess he meant witch doctor's things. If that child is really sick she shouldn't be so near the house."

Mrs. Michaelson caught them at the Club and said, "They acquitted him! I was there! So there is at least *law* left. Did you know that fool of a husband of mine has driven to Lagos? *Driven!* Over *that* road? And Balewa wants to have a peace-keeping prime ministers' conference in *this* country! If they couldn't manipulate the evidence any better than that, they ought to be ashamed of themselves. Oh my, I am glad he's off."

"But are the roads dangerous?" Joan said.

"My dear, the roadblocks *may* be police. Even the *oyibo* have to ransom their way past some of them."

"What about Idanre?"

"Safe for whites, I should think. That isn't the government's country any more than parts of Ibadan are. Go to Akurẹ and ask them to turn on a water tap for you. For that matter, go around this compound in the morning and afternoon and ask for the same thing!" She veered away.

On the twenty-first a group of church leaders in Southern Nigeria called for an inquiry into the election in the Western Region: "The situation has become so critical," they said, "that the Federal Government cannot honourably remain silent."

On the twenty-second there was another army coup in Dahomey. The compound remained parochial.

The NCNC sign was still turned on, every night, at the Mọkọla roundabout. The tail of the rooster, without its body, made a cryptic squiggle. It was an advertisement for revolution now: "FOR UNITY, INDIVIDUAL LIBERTY, & PROGRESSIVE GOVERNMENT." UPGA had claimed sixty-two seats, sixty of them Action Group, if Farquharson had heard right. Two, therefore, NCNC. "FOR UNITY." Akintọla in Parliament, crowing, "I *told* you you'd all be back!" There was the sign. The warm night hung around it, and nobody looked at it. People said the government counted its votes for the Opposition, the Opposition's votes for it. That seemed a bit simple, somehow.

"Farq," Joan said at about nine o'clock, "I haven't been sleeping well. I bought some sleeping pills. I found you could. Would it be all right to have one?"

He hesitated.

"You take the box. I don't want it. And give me *one*. And I don't want to know where you put the box. I just want *one* sleeping pill, and some sleep."

"What's wrong?" he said.

"Oh, the country. I don't know. We don't seem the same any more. It's just that my brain gets going. I might as well have had flu last night." She smiled at him. "Is it okay?"

He liked her, really. He let her give him the box and gave her a capsule from it. And when she swallowed it she said, "Oh damn, I don't like pills and drugs," so he said, "Now there you are," and watched her put herself to bed.

"Now, don't fight the pill."

She said, "If you want to go out and visit anybody, you go and do it. It's an early night." He hesitated and she said, "I'd hear Jamie through any pill there ever was."

"Did you get Jacob and Stanley to come for Christmas dinner?"

"I asked them," he said.

"Good. . . . Oh, go out and visit somebody, I want to sleep!"

"She took a sleeping pill," he said to Gail.

"Oh, Farq, that's sad."

They did what they had done. Nothing was new; they were resuming places. He left soon afterwards, and then stood in his yard at home. He was looking almost straight up towards the Pleiades, trying to count them, but he was too tired, and however clear the air, his eyes blurred.

19

December 24–31, 1965

THEY had blue-and-white shelf paper to wrap presents in. Stanley borrowed WP2471 to bring a visitor home from his senior sister's house, counting on the car's reputation to get him through the roadblocks. They made a Christmas tree from the dead branch of a frangipani stuck in a pot and then hung it with bells and sunbursts made out of egg cartons and coloured cellophane straws and what Farquharson called "depraved icicles" of aluminium foil, while Jamie padded around being menacingly helpful. Farquharson said, "Maybe I ought to ask Stanley's sister for the baby's juju, and hang it on."

"But master," Joan said, "that would be an ignorant belief."

There were frozen turkeys in the Kingsway, but an eight-pound bird cost eight pounds, so they didn't have one. They put the Nativity figures up where Jamie couldn't reach them, and Joan got the place mats hemmed. A few Christmas cards had come across the Atlantic, and were in the bookcase.

Christmas Eve was a long, white-sunned day. Farquharson said, "Stanley, will you take us into town tonight? I want to be a passenger and see what Christmas Eve's like. Or are you busy?"

"Tonight is start of Ramadan, sir."

"Are you Moslem, Stanley?"

The car was at the patio at eight o'clock. Farquharson took Jamie on his knee.

For a moment it seemed as if Stanley was looking into his future through the windshield of the car; then whatever he may have been thinking about passed, and they started off.

Around the Kingsway, as usual, everything was deserted. The

rest of Ibadan that night was an eerie city. The streets were full of people, and the darkness was somehow thicker and sharper than usual. And people prayed, as if the shifting conversational mobs had had their feet enchanted, and could only bend, sway, and bow. Paved nooks in front of houses filled with men in pale clothing, and the sounds of prayer came in the window sometimes like waves, sometimes like a kind of pattering. Ibadan seemed to be trying to be an Arab city, in pockets, in the dark, as if against the presence of the scattered oil lamps. Women had been selling paper hats on the streets for days—they had been selling them in the hospital while Joan was there (she hadn't bought one)—and they saw a fierce swaggering young man with a yellow dunce hat hung about with streamers. It was as if the city were waiting for something, and bragging about itself while it waited, and at the same time its prayers seemed like anger and argument, its praying phalanxes not military but surreptitious and sly. They went slowly by the pink church, which was dark; they turned a corner by the blue Catholic church and could see that the yard in front had been strung with pennants, but these swung in blackness with highlights of plastic and no colours. The city was alive with a sort of furtive festivity. They saw a Santa Claus mask up on a wall inside a room, and a tree full of coloured lights in the Kingsway parking lot.

Farquharson was, as his wife's cliché had it, "not a religious man". (She was not a religious woman.) But he did have the states of Innocence and Experience for a theology—and with those, a lot of other things came, sometimes when he didn't want them. Still, he managed, even against Joan's orthodox indifference, to put the subject away, except for lectures, most of the time. One night's pilgrimage for evidence of conventional Christian occupation threatened to put it back again, and when they stopped to buy toilet paper at the little store in Mokola he bought a box of cookies, broke it open there and then, and gave Jamie two of them to eat in the store. It was hard to know what he ought to do about his dead.

"Now put your stocking here," he said to Jamie at home.

Jamie held up a little sock. "*This* mine," he said.

Farquharson came to Joan with the box of capsules and said, "Sleepers awake?"

"Am I a spoilsport?"

For half a moment, he thought he could love her easily.

She suddenly sharpened her face at him and said, "Are you up to something?" Oddly, she loved the look of gentle consternation on his face. If he had been on a movie screen she could have lost her heart to him. He had his round glasses on, and looked absurd. She had to fight the capsule to stay awake, but he was still in the living room. Feeling stiff-brained, she went to listen at the living room door. She heard a page turn, floppily. He was reading *Life*, or maybe her English *Vogue*.

At midnight Farquharson made up Jamie's stocking with a couple of imported apples, and a German chocolate dwarf, and one of the water pistols that looked like rocket ships—they had hardly any presents for each other. Somebody scratched at the door.

Gail said, "This is a merry Christmas for Jamie," giving him a big box wrapped in orange. "I didn't know anybody was up. I was going to leave it on the concrete." He put it in the room, but she didn't come in. "This is for you," she said, handing him a tiny package. You'll have to say you bought it."

"Can you wait?" he said, and got the little man and his tree out from the dashboard shelf of the car. Then he heard Joan say, "Who's there?"

There was a fortunate pot of water on the stove; he turned the heat on under it. "It's Gail," he called. "She brought something for Jamie: I was putting on the coffee."

Guilt, he thought.

He put the box on the garage runway. "Come on," he said, "let's all have coffee by the Christmas tree." The sky was as black as if the earth had never had a moon. They were rather formal. Farquharson couldn't help assessing the two women, each pedestalled, one on a pouf, one on a coffee table. He said, "We need a Wise Man's Star," and pointed to the leafless Christmas tree.

"Oh, I must go to bed," Joan said, trying to yawn.

"I'll see Gail up to the sign."

"Bring in the cups?"

When they got around the corner he scooped up the box from the concrete slope at the garage door and gave it to her. Then he put a foot on their sign to push it a half-inch further into the ground. "I feel uncomfortable," he said.

"Don't you want to see what you got? Open it."

He had to feel it: it was a big knobbed ring.

She said, "It's a little crystal ball."

"I *will* love you." He wanted to add, "That's an awful thing." He said, "Open yours at home. It isn't much."

She left him in the dark, not yet a traitor. He went down to his house with the ring squeezed into his palm, and hardly had the sense to get it into his pocket when he got there. Joan was washing cups. "Well, that was nice of her," she said, "whatever her reasons were."

So he showed her the counterfeit sixpence he had got his fingers on when the ring went loose into his pocket. "Funny thing," he said, "it really is a fake one."

Christmas was a clear, hot day. They opened their few presents. Jamie dragged a pull toy round and round the frangipani branch. Father Christmas was supposed to come around with presents that parents had left carefully labelled at the Club, but when he got to the Farquharson's he ran into a grim, raucous circle of dancing children, singing and drumming around a performer with a huge brown mask on—and Jamie had gone screaming into the house to get away. Father Christmas, white of face, perched in the back of a green pickup truck and called, "Master James Farquharson!"

The dancers, with the mask still among them, had scattered into the garden, waiting for their pennies. Jamie waited fearfully at the dining room table, holding onto a chair. Farquharson had to bring his present in. "Okay," he said, tossing a small handful of pennies and halfpennies (which nobody ever wanted). "Now go away!"

Father Christmas hoho'd away, bouncing in the back of his truck with a shoal of retreating children.

Fifteen minutes later there were more children and more masks. They went on all day. And when Farquharson took the car to see if he could get some petrol at the Motor Transport Yard (there had, after all, to be Moslems around as well as Christians), he met a group of about fifty men and women, all dressed in the same blue cloth, parading with dancing and hymns and hexagonal tambourines made with goatskin and bottlecaps. He had Gail's ring on his hand. The little knobs were ringed by dots, but the stone wasn't a crystal ball; it was a crystal bead, skewered by a little nail and half sunk into a pit. The ring was silver-pale, and he had taken a trip out of the house so he could put it on.

By mid-afternoon Jamie was almost hysterical with the masks, and they had to ask Stanley to guard the top of the driveway. The drumming up on the street remained, and Jamie tried to cover his ears and stood in the middle of the floor, crying without moving He had been good all the time his mother was in hospital; he had been good since she came back. Suddenly he clung to his father, and wouldn't let her near him. "Oh, God *damn* those drums!" Joan cried. "Those damned, *damned* children!"

Farquharson knelt on the concrete floor, holding Jamie to him, bewildered, sorry for his wife. Jamie's fears were out, and there mightn't be a thing to do about them. He carried him into his room, and lay down on the bed, on his back, with the heavy sobbing head in the hollow of his arm, and sang, and talked gently, and when Joan came in again, after she had gone to have her own cry, she found them asleep in the same position, Farquharson's wrist and forearm curled in to protect Jamie, the counterfeit sixpence pressed against the nail and joint of his index finger.

She had two chickens to stuff and cook; she tiptoed out.

Farquharson and Jamie slept almost the whole afternoon, so when Joan had stuffed both chickens and got everything ready for the candied sweet potatoes, and had set the table with the new mats and the right size of cut-plastic glasses for the cider, she sat down in the middle of the living room floor and played with Jamie's toys. Gail had given Jamie a wind-up German contraption of little cars and trains going around a mountain. Joan had worked it with him most of the morning, when he didn't have to go into hiding from the masks, and it was soothing now. She kept drinking liquids, following Dr. Popoọla's orders.

Farquharson came out tousled with sleep and brought her the malachite beads. She said, "I want my Christmas bracelets."

"You can have both." He put the burning-green beads over her head, then took the bracelets off the desk and held them out for her. When her hands came through, he held them. "Hello, Jamie's mother," he said.

Their guests came for dinner: Stanley and Jacob.

"This is as much work," Joan hissed in the kitchen, "as entertaining *students.*"

Jacob wore a pink plastic ring. Stanley gave Jamie a half dozen lollipops. They noticed Jacob and Stanley studying them before using their knives and forks—and if Stanley was a Moslem as he had claimed, that didn't keep him from eating heavily and drinking his full share of the cider, though he jumped up from the table a great many times to disappear outside for a moment and come back again. Joan asked, when they were at last alone, whether he had been praying or spitting out all the food, but Farquharson said he didn't think either one, and that the drinking had been real. Both servants smoked like diplomats, and it was the first time Jacob had kept his shoes on in the house. The Farquharsons were glad to have to wait on table. Then Stanley brought in a couple of small drums, and for Jamie's sake, they said, and to cheer him up about drums, they drummed for him, elaborately, with beaming faces and occasionally sombre and thoughtful ones, while Jamie listened, or occasionally hugged someone's leg—anyone's, but in proportion: he had to distribute trust. So Christmas ended, and left the Farquharsons with an evening full of the dishes and each other.

Joan had given him three shirts made out of African cotton, "because," she said, "you like the place". He now wore one of them, orange cloth covered with four-petalled flowers touching each other like a chequerboard. His head looked startlingly pale, sticking out of it. (The barber from the Catering Flats came every fortnight, and Farquharson sat under his trees and had his hairs yanked and nibbled at.)

They held hands that night in bed, for a little while.

One afternoon Christmas week he put on his ring, and went to Gail.

Before they went to Ifẹ he took Stanley into town to buy two tires and get a fresh hole in the spare repaired. He couldn't afford new tires; he had drifted steadily into next month's money. Nevertheless, they had their holiday. WP2471 took the road to Ifẹ on the morning of Wednesday, December the twenty-ninth; Stanley, in a clean uniform, driving them.

Just outside Ibadan they had to stop at a roadblock, but it was flagrantly military, not highwaymen, and in the middle of a stretch of road with wide pale green shoulders.

The Ifẹ road was straight, clean, serenely overhung by almost every kind of tree, and rough; going up and down into one vista after another, they could see as they bounced that the jungle was seamless beside the road. They saw very few cars but many buses, with mottoes over the windshield, usually in Yoruba ("Ọba bi Ọlọrun ko si," "Ọmọ na de"). They passed dark-brown villages jammed together as if they were part of a big city; they passed a large gaunt town where everything in the sun was rust-coloured, except for a red-and-white billboard advertising a health food. Several times they dipped out of the forest belt into the grassland and back again; in the open country red dust from the road covered everything beside it.

Suddenly at Ifẹ, shops and houses seemed to jam against the road, as if they had been funnelled towards it, and they went narrowly through a district of cloth sellers where the road was walled by box after open box lined with strident flat patterns and sour colours, queerly harmonious. They were almost sick with heat and the shaking of the car, and the patterns danced. But the road rose; and Stanley found the museum for them, and they stumbled up the steps, through the arched entrance and a court-yard, to the cool comfortable smallness of a single homely room studded with cases and cupboards, holding terracottas and lesser antiquities, and the Ifẹ bronzes. Domineering politicians' heads faced them on pedestals the moment they came in the door. A little terracotta king stood, humble and authoritative, in the back corner of a glass box. Joan whispered to Farquharson that she had to have a washroom, so he asked and they were ushered into a bright, large room full of partially assembled pottery, and to a doorway in the far corner where there was a single bare, very clean toilet. Joan used it, then Farquharson took Jamie in, as he had taken him twice into the bush already.

The Ifẹ bronzes turned out to be brass: arrogant, clean portraits, of uncomfortable men of power. Some were on plain wood pedestals, open to be touched. They were accustomed to dominat-ing and they dominated, even one whose head had been caved in on one side. They stared, hundreds of years old, commanding whatever were the marks of reverence to them when they were living. Farquharson realized he was contemplating the one with the broken head. (At a desk by the back door of the room an attendant assembled thorn carvings.)

"They're politicians," Farquharson said to Stanley. "Look at them." He moved among them, pointing. "Akintọla. This is the world we're living in. 'Natural rulers,' " he said. "It almost makes you believe in the word."

"They aren't Roman," Joan said. "I thought they might be."

"No. Fifteenth-century Renaissance. Good tyrant country." When they left the heads, he took the faces with him.

They went back to Ifẹ through the arch with its oversize eighteenth-century fanlight and a view of a stark grey church cresting a hill in front of them. Yet as they trudged back to their car, the African quality somehow fell away from the town; the level parking space, banked at the side, the trees, the layout of the turning road, the shape of walls and spaces suggested that, heat excepted, they had parked somewhere in the geography of an irregular New England town. The car was an oven.

They ate beside the road, then turned around to come home. But Farquharson had the map, and decided they should go back through a pair of towns called Ẹdẹ and Iwo, in case the road was better. It wasn't much, but the country was more open. Indeed Ẹdẹ, where the road ran through the town like an elevated ribbon, was a sprawling place surrounded by what seemed wide barren fields.

And Iwo was big, grey, and patriarchal, with a sort of abandoned modernity. All the little corners of the country were different from each other, but they were tired and wanted to get to their house. When they came back to the American-style suburbs of Ibadan, the uncompleted huge water tanks, the views to pink and green apartments perched on hillsides (and they had *not* passed a roadblock on the Iwo road), it was like coming home. Farquharson said, "*This* is Rome," and Joan knew what he meant. The bare arcaded buildings, the heaving hills, the people of a hundred languages, a dozen types, villas, tenements, the myriad tiny shops —a million people selling objects to one another.

They panted into the Kingsway, had two bottles of pop apiece, and alternately raced upstairs to the washroom. Their tires had held.

On New Year's Eve they ate a Catering Flats meal in the Club at about ten o'clock and then danced on concrete, with the big chairs moved somewhere else. The Nwonkwos were near them, back from the East and not talkative. At midnight somebody put on *Auld Lang Syne*. Then, stepping back and forth, with a few people almost stepping over the edge of the pool and not noticing, they sang the words and shouted "Happy New Year". And Farquharson kissed his wife.

They tried to dance as the Nwonkwos had taught them. They

watched other couples dance, some badly, some very well. They enjoyed themselves, rather as if they were out on a date for the first time and didn't know each other very well. And Bill Garnett, still with his shoe open at the toe but with a clean bandage, came over to them with Gail and said he couldn't dance and it wasn't fair and would somebody dance with her and let *him* sit down with a clean conscience, so Farquharson had to take her. "See those two?" Bill said, aiming a hand at an almost uncomfortably skilled couple who had caught all their eyes, a Nigerian woman and a skinny agile American from the Peace Corps. "She's a whore. Someone's going to scandalize tomorrow, do you mind?" Joan recklessly didn't mind, and then did.

Gail and Farquharson didn't feel it was right for them to dance. Gail said, "I wish you could wear the ring."

"I'm trying to find a way to, but I don't want to lie." He swung her about, and her heel caught on a climbing plant. He said, "What about the afternoons next term?"

For the last hour they could see Stanley watching them from beside the closed-up newsstand, looking at more than them, looking also at the dancing whore and the lean American who paid for her. Farquharson thought, "Of course: the cousin who asked one price and then tried to get another." He winked at his driver and danced his wife away into the dark.

When they got home Jacob was asleep on the floor across the living room doors: anyone trying to get to Jamie would have had to step on him. All of Jamie's plastic animals were on the table, arranged. Joan and Farquharson caught their breaths and stared at each other. On a small sheet of paper there was a lion on its side, dead, about two inches long. At three of the four corners of the paper sat or stood the other lion and two tigers, and all the other animals were in a double line that curved out on to the table and half around, like a violently stretched-open spiral, the big ones near the paper, the size steadily tapering off until the smallest were at the end of the lines. One line came to look at the death, and the other line went away: giraffe, ape, ostrich, wolf, polar bear, baby kangaroo, turtle, ibex, all of them. The lines ended and began at the corner of the paper. Noah's Ark, but without a boat, and with one line leaving. Nothing human. Only a dead lion, and watchers, patient, queuing even to go away. It was almost horrible. Jacob might have spent the whole night on it, and now he lay curled, like a slave, guarding the king's son. Farquharson wakened him, paid him, and told Stanley to drive him home, and not until the car was gone did he meet Joan on the other side of the table and, with the tableau between them, shudder and eliminate it with a single sweep of his arms. Pattering plastic animals shot out on to the floor. He sighed.

Then he said, "Happy New Year."

PART FOUR

20

THE roadblocks stayed. The Ormfords had gone to Jos; the Eayrses were in Lagos, having flown. The Farquharsons drove out of a lightly populated compound to go to visit the Akinrinmades at Idanre, taking Stanley with them to know a language in case of car trouble. The Nwonkwos had appeared at their door, grey with cold, to wish them safe travel. Now cars passed them going the other way, and after a while they began to feel that there were people in those cars who hated them: the sense was raw in their faces.

"What is it, Stanley?"

"Sir, I hope it is the car."

Within a mile it happened again—two cars in a row. Cold, hating eyes; there was no doubt.

"Those were Ibadan cars," Farquharson said.

"But they don't do this *in* Ibadan!" said Joan.

"We aren't in Ibadan. Oh well, if they can get freedom to hate out of the open road, I guess we can move on it."

But she said, "Open? Just where would we turn around?"

The width of two cars and a bit more, a few feet of earth on either side, and then the trees; no side-roads, shoulders, only once in a long while room to turn.

There was an oil truck on its side, straight across the road. Farquharson said, "Watch it. Roll up your window, Stanley." He had a tire iron on the floor of the back seat; he picked it up. "Here we go again," he muttered, and leaned out the window, with his hand free, feeling rather sick to discover that he wasn't going to be excited, that he had done this before.

But it was a real accident. There was nobody there. They crawled around; there was just room. When they got on the other side they could see the skid marks.

"Doesn't even seem much hurt," Farquharson said, as he peered back with the tire iron hanging pressed against the door. "I wonder what he saw. It's a straight road."

Later a car full of people honked at them and waved. "Jinx gone," he said. "We're out of the territory. WP2471 will now be ordinary."

They went to the Ifẹ museum. This time they dashed the guard a shilling for the toilet, and the kings and the politicians were their friends.

They went through hilly, lovely country and had lunch near a huge white tree. Nobody passed their car in enmity; hardly anybody passed it at all. Farquharson stretched luxuriously beside the car, and using the roof as a table poured squash for everyone, and put a little gin in it. They ate bland sandwiches.

Once they all got out and stretched by a white church on a bare hill. Half a dozen people greeted them without saying one word they understood—one of them lifted Jamie in the air, and hugged him—and then the Farquharsons got back in their car and friendliness sped them off. He looked for a sign and said, "Ẹrin-Ode. Remember that."

They came to Akurẹ through almost open country; there were fields to the left of the road. Then there was the same rusty town, but this time lined up on either side of a ruler-straight wide road as if the lots of a dozen Hollywood westerns had had their colour stripped away and then been laid out on the scale of a Parisian boulevard. Suddenly they liked Akurẹ: the extravagance was homely; the place seemed friendly. They had to ask directions, and while Farquharson listened, he looked across the road and saw a long grey-white church with slender windows and lines so good that it might have stood with photographs of Ravenna and not been shamed by them.

"Excuse me, what is that?"

"Is our cathedral, master."

They drove the rest of the long road feeling rather dazed. The road to the Catering Rest House was at the other end of town. "Rich Man's Row," Farquharson said, looking at the few big houses. Stanley brought them off the road to the front of a rather barren building, in which was a lobby and a dining room, harmattan dust and a calendar, and almost nothing else except a variety of doors onto a part-octagonal verandah. They signed a register and were conducted to a little separate house with a tiny living room full of huge wicker chairs, a bedroom beyond, and a small bathroom that looked as if it had been scalded out and then forgotten. Stanley promised that he could find quarters for himself. He said, "I have a brother, sir." The Farquharson's unpacked.

"I want to see the place today," Farquharson said. "There might be a store in it."

"Well, you can see it by yourself," Joan said, comfortably.

"Can I take Jamie with me?"

"Put him on a leash and run him." She was already half asleep on the chintz coverlet. He smiled and patted her.

He passed Stanley on the road and gave him a lift. Stanley went off into a lane—carrying, Farquharson wondered, how much of his yesterday's pay? (Up a pound a month, with two pounds for Christmas, because Farquharson wouldn't lend him five.) He said to Jamie, "I like him."

Up and down the long street. He saw an NCNC sign, rather like Ibadan's. "If it weren't for the bad pun," he said to Jamie, "I'd say that looked cocky." He talked to Jamie a lot now if they were alone; carefully, because some quality about him was going to understand those words. He looked at the cathedral again and saw that it wasn't finished yet, but though he wanted to get out of the car and go into it, he was shy. He found the store on the return. The sign said "Adebọwale", and he wondered, but the building was just the usual mud wall with a high-pitched rusty roof, slanting four ways. He had to remember that Adebọwale was probably a common name.

Inside, the store was half like any country store, half like a section of the Kingsway shrunk and jammed, and almost entirely European, with three shopping carts. The people were again friendly to him. Jamie was much fussed over. Then two big men darkened the doorway coming in. He heard, "Professor Farquharson! This is an honour, sir," and had only time to shake hands with Mr. Adebọwale, whether the name was common or not, before being introduced to "the other Canadian, sir, who once tried to teach me. This is Brother Patrick," and he was shaking hands with a tall, narrow redhead with an extraordinarily boyish face and a pair of questioning intelligent, almost old eyes that seemed to have seen about three things too many and so to have got stuck on the outskirts of wisdom. "We were just renewing friendship," Adebọwale said.

"Is this your store?"

"No sir. They are not even my family."

"Ọlatunji isn't from Akurẹ," Brother Patrick said. "His people are from Ilesha—you may have driven through it. He has come to see me, very kindly. But I had to go shopping. In fact, I must." He excused himself and went about gathering long armfuls of what looked like emergency supplies. "Well, 'Tunji," he called, "does that look like the fatted calf?"

"Professor Farquharson may not consider that I look exactly like a prodigal." Obviously the two men were friends.

Mr. Adebọwale looked normally as if his face had been honed down from too great a size, and was now alert and sorrowful. Today he looked comfortable and at rest.

Somehow before they got out of the store Farquharson had been invited to visit Brother Patrick's school. The next morning, when Stanley came to wait for them in the car, Brother Patrick and Mr. Adebọwale came too and filled up the tiny living room of their chalet, while Brother Patrick drew them a road map of how to get to Idanre and said that if they got back early he would be pleased if they could dine at the school with himself and some of the brothers, though Mr. Adebọwale would have gone by then.

They had eaten in the Rest House dining room once: they

didn't want to again. Just why that dull room with its four tables of Nigerians and one of whites should seem so heavily under corruption and tyranny, Farquharson didn't know: there was nothing essentially evil about people who ate with good manners and loud voices, and were dressed for cooler weather, or for the night-time, and whose women wore up-and-downs and head ties in the highest Nigerian fashion, but of fine European fabrics, and who ate their own food. But the waiters were craven; the pretensions of the silverware and the white cloths troubled the eye, and the room seemed to live in the attention of a large flat grey photograph of Akintọla. Farquharson had gone through the stew manfully with his eyes streaming from the fire in his mouth, but that had been the only pleasant part of eating there. So he was glad of an invitation, glad too that their breakfast was nothing but cornflakes and coffee.

They hopped into the car in the still-cool morning air; they had Brother Patrick's map and lunch, and followed the road south across a bright weedy landscape, and on into the high forest. Farquharson was sitting forwards, anticipating the black house where he could feel as if he were floating in the clouds, and cowering in a chasm, at the same time. He tried to remember what he had told Joan about Mrs. Akinrinmade, and whether the two women had met or not.

They went through several villages. He noticed the emblem of the Action Group—palm tree, AG and sprinkled dots—painted on several houses, hitched himself into a more attentive position, and wondered why a government man still lived in such Opposition territory—unless of course his wealth was here. "A very large, black, two-storey house," he remembered.

But they were out of the world of the reputation of WP2471: they hadn't had a flicker of attention that wasn't friendly since they had left Ifẹ. No highway trampled towards Idanre; they were on a little grey road. The sky glared.

In a temperate landscape, Farquharson thought, they would have seen the place coming for miles; here among the choking trees, even though they weren't large, they got no warning. Suddenly the hills were there. "The old village," Farquharson told Joan, "is apparently at the top of a great stone hill but nobody lives there." People turned in the roads and stared at them. Children called "*Oyíbó!*" Steadily the road sank, or the land rose: hills and stony sides lifted: black, polished, steadily higher, steadily more spectacular. Dust haze blurred distances. The road narrowed. By the time they had gone through the first village they were in a world of Chinese landscapes: vaulting tree-scattered rocks shouldering for attention (but with no softness for the eye—there had been no Chinese here to invent that), and the low human world cowering below, stuck among its own concerns, tiny and without Chinese dignity. The cry was up all over the road: "*Oyíbóoooo!*" Children ran, people stared.

The road threaded among giant boulders and shooting cliffs of rock, an uneven pass threatened by power. Farquharson was growing exultant. Joan said, "Farq, it's like Yosemite. Look at that!"

They went under a high smooth bulging cliff, and came into the last Idanre, wedged in a Y among its hills. Somehow the land they were on seemed to swell upwards for a while. The road climbed slightly. Stanley slowed. Children were walking quickly beside the car. "Climb, master? Guide, master? Master, dash me! *Oyíbóoo!*" An adolescent grabbed the window frame. "Take you to old village, master?"

He was going to ask where the Akinrinmade's house was, but he drew back from the clamouring avarice at the window and said, "For Pete's sake, Stanley, move!" The car jumped ahead. "As if you were in the clouds and a chasm at the same time. Look!" he shouted, "there it is!"

A big, black, two-storey house to the right of the road. He said, "Stanley, don't stop. Go past it. Stanley, don't stop!"

African Yosemite, Chinese painting solidified to gritty sculptural fact: yes, it was all there. A place to exult and be humble in, as a rich woman can among power and in the troughs of the whelming motionless waves of rock. But the house had no roof, and part of the walls had fallen in; all of the windows of the upper storey were broken at the top, the rest were holes. The house and a delivery van beside it had been burnt thoroughly. "Keep moving, Stanley."

Some of the children caught them. The car had to stop. Boys haggled and jostled to lead them up to Old Idanre. Nobody seemed to pay any attention to the black house.

"No," Farquharson said. But it did no good. "*Bẹẹ kọ́.* Please."

"Master!" a fat young man said, clutching his arm. "Why you come here?"

"*Oyìbó! Fún mi l'óhun!*"

Stanley said, "*Ẹ máa lọ.*"

Slowly, in the long run irresistibly, they got the car around the turn in the road and then, almost suddenly, their following fell away and let them go. Finally Stanley stopped.

"Farq," Joan said, "what happened to the house?"

"They burn it," Stanley said.

"But the Akinrinmades?"

Stanley said, "Perhaps they go."

"Why?" she said. Not frightened, Farquharson thought; insistent.

He said, "They were NNDP. I guess the government can't protect them any longer."

"Oh, don't say they *were*!"

"All right, they *are*. But they aren't here."

"Could you be wrong?"

"Not about that house." He repeated the description as the Akinrinmades had given it to him.

"No," she said, "you're right."

Stanley said, "I am sorry, sir."

"Go slowly back," he said. "I want to have a look."

Again they got stuck at the corner. This time the children let them alone, except to cry "*Oyìbóoo!*" and reach for money, but three women reached in the window and tried to touch Jamie's hair (Jamie shrank away).

"Come on, Stanley," Farquharson said under his breath. "Get us out of here, will you?"

Slowly they moved. Now they were on the same side of the road as the burned house—not that the road was much wider than one lane, but they felt proximity. Farquharson stared, he hoped, like a tourist. "Nobody there," he said.

"Farq, there's a parade!"

He looked. "No," he said, "they're singing. They're like that group at Christmas."

A close-formed band of people was coming towards them. Stanley said, "Sir, party supporters."

"Drive slowly."

They danced; they sang; they had a few palm leaves and a banner of white cloth inked with the emblem of the Action Group. He heard Stanley say "*Awo!*" to them in a sort of toneless, half-whispered cheer. "No," he heard Joan say, "don't ask them!" They were curiously, far from amicably, stared at. But the dance kept its way, and after a while they were alone.

They twisted among the boulders, climbed out of one Idanre into the broadening indifference of another. The mountains and valleys were eaten up by the jungle until they couldn't be seen even by looking back along a straight stretch of the grey, narrow road. "Get us out to the main highway by the first road possible," Farquharson said.

"All right," he said when they were there, and the black road swept past them, looking fraudulently like something out of the unmenaced temperate zone, "let's eat."

He took Jamie into the bush with him to make water. He used the tire iron as a matchet against a couple of tree branches, wondering if he'd still kept the knack. He supposed Mrs. Akinrinmade and her husband were alive, and one selfish part of him suddenly realized that he was disappointed at not having got into a real African two-storey house. He ate the sandwiches as if he were ravenous, and gave his squash and boiled water a heavy stiffening of gin.

21

January 5–15, 1966

THE day after lectures started, there was an attempt to have a state of emergency declared in the Western Region, because of "rioting, looting, arson, and indiscriminate killing on a large scale". The Senior Common Room rang with fascinated speculation of just how bad things were. Shagamu, on the Lagos–Ibadan road, was deserted, or the Shagamu market was a shambles. "You went to Ondo and Ilesha?" Jane Grant said to Farquharson. "My God." She said, "I went to Lagos, by Abẹokuta, but was still stopped. I had to pay, too, and I was glad to do it, believe me."

"The gangs loot whole villages, poor souls."

"There have been *no* houses burnt in Ibadan!"

"There have in other places. There are refugees in this country now."

"I left Lagos at seven this morning. I didn't have a *bit* of trouble."

Oscar said, "And people are killed in Ibadan, almost every day."

"And in proportion as the country falls apart," MacLachlan said, "the night-time patrol of this university dwindles."

"You can't drive into Ibadan now without being searched for guns."

Farquharson said, "I bet *I* could."

"Have you ever considered," Ormford said happily, "the riot potential of the junior staff of this university? Majẹkodunmi's clientele versus—not to embarrass the Vice-Chancellor—all the Ibo servants?" He added, "Poor Nicodemus!"

"Have you thought what Adegbenro and his people may do to

247

call the world's eyes on themselves with the Prime Ministers' Conference here?"

"I will give you a wager," Balogun said, "that nothing will happen till the conference is over."

"Done, Joseph! I put a bet on fire. Between now and next Wednesday somebody near Lagos is going to be doused with petrol and set on fire: either that or a whole street of houses."

"Do you realize," Jane Grant said, "that the army comes back from the Congo this weekend?"

"Food," Cord said suddenly, from where he was watching over by the window, keeping half an eye on the mosque. "Be on African wages and try to buy food. Prices are skyrocketing."

"That hits everybody. Political injury is on one side only."

Eayrs said, "The political murders on this compound were on the *other* side. Remember those two bodies on the Obong road last fall?"

MacLachlan said, "That's dangerous gossip. They were practically at my back door, remember."

Farquharson went to meet Mr. Abedǫwale's class with the sudden feeling that the sky might shift and let down the Bursar. Mr. Adebǫwale said that he had had a telephone call from Brother Patrick, and he was to let the Professor know that as far as could be discovered the Akinrinmades were alive at the time their house was burned. Farquharson said that wasn't necessarily reassuring. Then they talked about Brother Patrick and the teacher-training school, and the class that followed (Farquharson couldn't help this) was given almost entirely to Mr. Ọlatunji Adebǫwale, somewhere in the future to be a teaching brother at Akurẹ.

Farquharson told Joan that because of the Shakespeare lectures he was going to have to work afternoons and drop the guarding.

Gail rented an air conditioner, and Farquharson put his ring on and looked down to see himself sticking out between the flaps of a long-tailed shirt. Gail said, "You look like a hatrack with a dust cover."

"I'll catch my death of cold."

"Do you know I missed you?"

Firmly planted, he gave himself over to the pleasure of long slow control. She said, trembling, trying to keep her face from coming unstitched, because he seemed godlike and almost grave, "You're a mile away."

He bore slowly down, and then, as if with great force, withdrew. "No, I'm here," he said. "I'm just trying to know what this is like. Look." The broad flesh shaft was taut, like a bridge, between them. She reached her fingers to it.

"Easy," he said. "That's all there is. All of me just to push that." He twitched it, and she cried out a little.

He said, "I've got no conscience at all," and sank home, and lifted, making his whole body into a pump. "Watch out," he said. "I'm shimmering."

"Don't hold back."

"I'm not. I'm going to build till I blow up." His coxcomb had fallen away from his head and looked like a ravelled horn. "Keep looking at me," he said. "I feel as if I wasn't going to be real."

"Don't talk," she said.

But it was as if he had death at bay: he had to talk, calm reasonable words while his own round nose and smooth boy's lips became a flushed looming portrait. Then everything was still except his eyelashes. Her own passion had clubbed her and was sinking away again; suddenly she couldn't think what his was, and it almost frightened her. She felt his prick fill her and fade, and come back again, as if it got larger all the time. Then his mouth hung open, his head started to roll and twist. What was inside her was going with a runaway violence. She tried to catch it in her fingers, as if she had to brake it or slow it down, and her fingers were suddenly prisoned by the bones, wedged between her hairs and his, and he went into a disorganization as total as if a guillotine had been dropped upon him, made a thin screech as if his lungs couldn't be got to work, then stiffened, high in the air over her, simply fell on her; and what she saw on his face, in the fraction before she lost it, she couldn't have told anyone.

He was nuzzling in her ear, breathing with a complacent, humming noise. After a while she felt him start to laugh. And she loved him.

She was completely unprepared to, and terrified about what to do. He was squashing her, glued into her, and her fingers were trapped around him. Even his breathing squeezed her. She felt she couldn't get him out of or off her body even if she wanted to. But she didn't want to, and to her astonishment the mere decision that he was what she was going to love made her shake as if she were going to come yet again a second time, and she turned her head away. She couldn't try to squint at what she could see of him. She wanted just to feel him as a hot live weight all over her.

Finally he could draw away and roll beside her, but the last brush of the head of the long flesh coming out of her seemed to be more than he could take, and his breath hissed in. And then he was beside her, and she scrambled into his arms in the air-conditioned air.

She said, "I'm going to have to call you Henry. Please don't say you mind."

But he said, "Darling," and rolled almost on top of her, and his face pressed down onto her open mouth.

She held him below, hard.

"What happens to Bill's nights?" he said, when he was getting dressed. "Because I have to be part-time, love and all."

"Does it matter?" Then she said unexpectedly, "I feel so sorry for Joan."

He did up his fly. "Don't make me feel sorry for Bill, though."

She was delighted with him. "Am I a hoor?" she said happily.

"A friend. Look, he's a lonely guy," he said. "I guess I'd feel better if we both had responsibilities. I mean, he knew you first."

"You taught me," she said.

"Not this."

"No, well he didn't either."

She was starting to dress. He hugged her. "Gail, you have to be lonely. This is 'Our two souls therefore, which are *two*.'"

But he kept the ring on his finger until he was walking in the smiting sun back to the library, where he had left his car.

On Friday he said, "I've got a bet on a roadblock. Stanley, go round behind the hospital and drive down Queen's Road."

They ran into a line-up of cars being searched for weapons. As they settled into the line, he said, "I wish we had Oscar with us. Will you two bear witness if we get through without being looked at?"

Joan said, "This is playing for danger. I don't like it."

Stanley looked alert, content.

Cars were made to drive on to the shoulder, one by one. People on the far side of the road stood on a flight of steps cut into the hillside and, Farquharson supposed, made comments. The car ahead was waved into place, and they watched the beginning of an exact and total search, while the driver stood beside his car making wrathful comments about efficiency and pointing to his watch. Then one of the police looked at their car, seemed suddenly more alert, came to them, leaned down to the window and said, "You need not wait, sir."

"We can drive on?"

"Yes, sir, please."

"Okay, Stanley." The car eased forward. "We probably just made ten enemies," Farquharson said, "but we wouldn't have made one friend if we'd waited for it. Now are you both my witnesses?"

Oscar said, "If I'd been with you, they would have searched me to the skin, no doubt. What have you won?"

Farquharson said, "The right to take you to a nightclub."

So they went again, and Joan held her husband's hand at the table and wondered at how taut his arm was, even when he was relaxing. "When we get home," she whispered, "make love to me."

He managed to.

251

On Sunday Jamie wanted to mingle his animals with the fairy castle, and Farquharson was unwise enough to pretend that one of the pieces of the fairy castle was a rocket ship, so then he had to match colours and animals, while trying to eye the text of *Julius Caesar*, and show why turquoise was right for a lioness but purple was better, even if a little small, for the giraffe.

In the afternoon, feeling comfortably undersexed and wondering in blurry reminiscence what had made Joan so much more easy last night, Farquharson thought of guns and political murder upon the roads, and fell asleep in a formless repeated naming-over of their roadblocks: Electoral Office, Atiba Gate, Ifẹ Road, Ondo, Electoral Office—no, Queen Elizabeth II Road, Atiba Gate, Ifẹ, none on the Iwo road, Ondo, Ondo. He dreamed that Ondo had become one of Dunsany's doomed cities of marvel and humdrum, waiting for the gods.

When it was dark they went for a ride into Ibadan. Grace had filled them with items of rumour that her husband had brought back from Lagos: clamour in the markets, strict security precautions for the prime ministers, rival political gangs with matchets rioting in the suburbs. "The Opposition has to make a scene, of course."

Joan said, "Are you a fool to go out on the road, *in that car*?"

"I like this car."

She said, "Oh, you're as bad as Stanley," and indeed, Stanley was keen to see, under the protection of the Farquharsons and the car, anything that he could of danger.

So they went to Bodija, and around the hospital. Nothing looked different from any other Sunday night. The town was perhaps faintly quieter. They went home past the cattle market, with only a few people in it, under a fat, rising moon. And then the airport had lights in it. Suddenly Stanley went off the road, stopped, and put the lights out. "Akintọla," he said, pointing his hand out the window.

There were at least seven large cars going down the road, with headlights blazing. Farquharson thought he saw the last two of them come round the turn of the Bodija road, at the service station. One of them was a police car, with a bright-blue light on top. They saw a long Mercedes in the middle of the line, and the glint of rifles out the windows of the cars before and after it. Stanley said, "That is the Premier," proudly, as if a possession had got out.

The convoy swung recklessly past them, moving in their imagination with the sound of its tyres only, holding rigid speed as if the cars were all chained together. Seven sets of headlights cleaved the road. WP2471, brown, neat, and exposed, crouched by the pavement. The Farquharsons were left dazzled in a kind of robbed silence.

Stanley was smiling. "I think he come from Governor's House in Agodi, sir."

"Well, our car gets through Ibadan. I guess his can. I wonder if he recognized the licence plate. You can bet he saw us."

He wondered who drove the car when Akintola had taken his rumoured carnal pleasure—if he ever did. Somehow, since the road to Ifẹ, Farquharson didn't believe that story. The banging of the men on the panel truck made him believe; but not the taxi, not the waves of hate on the Ifẹ Road, not the assiduously brusque attention they got at Ibadan roadblocks. Those suggested knowledge of a hanger-on of power. But if this *was* that car, would Akintola have thought of it, going by like that? One of Akintola's creatures had creatures of his own, and two of those creatures Farquharson had killed. Suppose the man in the guarded car had known that? And that this was his car? "All right," Farquharson thought in the night, "then I am political."

"Come on, Stanley," he said, "before they all come back. Let's go home."

"Farquharson!" Eayrs called. "I won my bet. Not just one person. Three or four people burned alive at Ikorodu over the weekend. Petrol, just as I said. That's mighty close to Lagos."

"The feud," he said, lecturing, "in *Romeo and Juliet*, no matter

253

who may have begun it, belongs, as a feud, when the play begins, only to the servants. As the Prologue says, 'From ancient grudge break to *new* mutiny.' "

"And if only," Eayrs said, "our dear Lester Pearson would just take a drive in an ordinary car up the Ibadan road and learn a couple of facts about the sweet African democracies! Balewa's going to get away with it, you know. A beautiful diplomatic whitewash in the name of harmony and fatherly concern, and—you're a Middle English man sometimes, Farquharson—what's that word?"

"I'm not, really. '*Courtesye*'?"

"No. '*Gen-*' something."

"*Gentilesse.*"

"That's the word. In the name of *gentilesse*. Nobody's ever going to believe that there's one thing wrong here at all."

They went for a ride the next night, hoping, perhaps, to see the convoy of cars again, but all they saw, on quiet empty streets, were the gnarled yellowish trees looking like concrete in the headlights. If Ibadan was restless, it was quiet about it. "The Opposition's putting all its effort into Lagos," Charlie Spanier-Dodd said. But rumours of violence came in from all over: "Shagamu is empty," he said. "Absolutely deserted. I drove back yesterday."

The Commonwealth Conference was due to open. The prime ministers had arrived, under strict security. The cries were up that Balewa was trying to conceal the facts in Nigeria. The *Times* wrote: "*In the name of Nigeria that we all love so dearly, all the dirty linens should be kept aside in the next few days. We can bring them back for washing when we are alone.*"

Rioters blocked a highway into Lagos with a sheet of fire. Eleven people were killed in Ilesha. Brother Patrick phoned Adebọwale again to assure him that his family was all right, and to have him tell the Farquharsons that there was still no information about the Akinrinmades, except for an indefinable rumour that they had escaped into Dahomey, "but," he said, "they're probably just saying that because other people have. Tell him Akurẹ is all right. I think he liked Akurẹ."

Gail said, "Are you bothered by this?"

"No." He sounded surprised.

The Lagos Conference of Prime Ministers was held and evaporated. The newspapers were full of platitudes: "A very great success," Prime Minister Wilson said. The heat grew worse. Ibadan looked unchanged except for a slight quiet, a slight pre-occupation—and of course the roadblocks. They guessed at riot and trouble in Abẹokuta, Ijẹbu-Ode, deserted Shagamu, even Akintọla's Ogbomọshọ, but Ibadan was Ibadan, absorbing discord because discord was its normal state. The Farquharsons kept their evening rides to listen to the blaring phonographs on New Court Road. They knew that the Americans were meeting, spurred by officials, to discuss emergencies, but to be a Canadian in those few weeks was to be in limbo. They were reduced to doing daily head counts on the Americans in the Club, as Eayrs had said they would. "They ought to be making some arrangements, shouldn't they?" Joan said. But the silence from the High Commissioner's office in Lagos was complete. (The English seemed simply to assume safety.)

Dr. Garnett drove to Abẹokuta to fetch a member of the family of a dying servant, and they were set upon at a roadblock. Garnett said he was convinced he would have been killed, because he was fighting like a maniac, only a truckload of *other* party supporters came by, by accident, and they had had what he called a small war, under cover of which he crawled into his Land-Rover, found his passenger unconscious, and suddenly drove away. "And at that," he said, sitting in the Hospital on Friday afternoon, where Gail had taken Farquharson to see him, "somebody threw himself up on the back and I had to shake him off and drag him." He then drove, he said, "like the wind, all over the road," and for the last fifteen miles was sharing the front of the car with a dead body which kept falling over because, he said, "I had the insane idea I had to sit him up." His face and hair were stark white and black, and his hands shook. He said, "I never do heal up."

When Farquharson got back to the house he found a Hausaman on the patio, with all his goods spread out, and Joan shaking with anger in the living room, holding Jamie on the seat beside her.

"What's it all about?" he said.

She said, "He won't go away, and he laughs at me."

The man was sitting at the end of a line of carved heads as if he were one of them. Farquharson said, "Were you buying something?"

"One of the heads, but I don't want it!"

Jamie shrank away from her, but didn't try to get down.

Farquharson went on to the patio, squatted facing the heads and the Hausaman, and looked at them. "I am going to make you give me what I want," he thought. "And I am going to make you take just what I want to pay."

"Now," he said, and went to work.

After a long while Joan tried to stop him, but he went past her into the kitchen for a drink and then back out to the patio.

Every gambit, he thought, every ploy. He didn't really want anything that the man had; that was his strength. And he could take all day. Finally he stood with a brown head in his hand, and said, "Joan?"

"I don't want it!"

And Farquharson found that he was playing with her distaste to get the price down five shillings more.

"All right, You can, and I don't know how to. Do you have to use *me* to get your price down?"

"Look," he said, "nobody's going to upset you and get away with it."

"I *said* I didn't want it!"

"Christ," he said, "I come in shining armour to your rescue. And all you do is bitch at me."

"Jamie," he said at bedtime, "I love your mummy, but loving people still fight sometimes. Okay?"

"Well," he thought in the bathroom, "I've told my first lie to Jamie."

"Oh Lord," he thought in bed, "if it just *wants* to be love, instead of *being* love, doesn't it make mistakes?"

Saturday morning came clear and hot, and he had office work to do. He had Stanley take him to the Arts Building, and had been there for well over an hour when there was a knock on his door, and he let in a first-year student who wanted to negotiate an extension on an essay, and said, to start, "I have a complaint."

(This, Farquharson knew now, meant, "I've got a difficulty," but it always sounded like peremptory bad temper anyway.)

"Yes?"

Mr. Fakunle, who was heavy, looked, as always, unconvinced about anyone's good will but as if he had been sunk glowering into a state of obligation. "I have many works to do," he said. "This, in order of assignment, is the third. Therefore I feel that it should not be asked for by the Professor until the second has fallen due, which will not be until the twenty-sixth. At ten a.m."

"How much time do you want?"

"The Professor knows that it will then be necessary to study well for his assignment."

"I'm not going to give a ten-day extension, Mr. Fakunle."

"Does the Professor want good work from his students, or bad work?"

Stifling the remark that what the Professor wanted was work, Farquharson readied himself for haggling. Rule-of-thumb said that one started with quarter to a third of a Hausaman's demands, and never came up very much. He aimed for four days and was in the end content with five.

"This will be much work, sir."

Finally he was left alone to write his notes on *Caesar*: "Too many crises; continuous; repeating; what kind of Crisis? Is

257

Tragedy possible?" He underlined the last three words, wrote, "Logic of Tragedy: the single unified action. What if parts separated and fragmented? The unmade jigsaw."

Stanley came to the door. Farquharson looked at his clock; it was barely after ten. "Madam wish to see you in the car."

As Farquharson locked the door, Stanley said into the air beside him, not quite complacently, but with a certain pleased attention, "They shoot Akintọla, sir."

22

January 15, 1966

THE stairs in the Arts Building were in the bridge that joined the two halves of the building between the courtyards. Farquharson followed Stanley to them, then turned aside at the landing and went into the lavatory, ignoring the notice that the water was turned off, and, with the air moving through the pierced concrete of the wall, only faintly rank, listened to his sound and tried to bring a vague amazement into focus. He had to think: "I am here, this is real."

He did up the zipper carefully, leaned over the dry washbasin towards the mirror, and put his hand to his shirt pocket to put on his lecturing glasses. His dead man had drifted down as if he wanted to hug his judge about the legs. ("*They shoot Akintola, sir.*") He went out into the sunlight and across the courtyard to meet his wife.

A few people were standing around in little groups; Jack Okpata and Ogundele were having a whispered quarrel by the porter's lodge. Joan, with Jamie, was sitting very uprightly in the front seat.

She said, "Stanley says we can't go to the Kingsway." The grievance was as sharp as the light sweat-stink coming from Stanley, who was holding himself formally aloof. She said, "What are we going to do?" meaning, "What are *you* going to do?"

"Find out if it's true, for one."

Ogundele said, "I think you will find it true, Mrs. Farquharson. It's too much to hope for—no one would have invented it." He seemed afraid to be jubilant.

Farquharson looked down the street: there were three people

talking urgently beside another car. Back in the Arts Building there was a quarrel going on at the top of the steps. Abruptly, he went to it, leaving Joan alone. A young Yoruba in the Linguistics Department was saying with fervency and anger to Ogundele's secretary, "It can *not* be true!"

Farquharson said, "Why can't it?"

"Because it would not be allowed. It would not be possible."

But Mrs. Popoola said, "I told you my sister lives in the New Reservation and heard shots."

Jack Okpata bowed. "They have taken the Premier to the hospital. Therefore he must be alive."

"I haven't seen my husband today," Mrs. Popoola said, and Farquharson suddenly realized who her husband had to be, "but if that man is at the hospital, he is *not* alive. And if he is at the hospital, surely they will *show* him!"

"Farquharson!" his wife called. "Come here!"

Her eyes were smarting with vexation. She saw a pale, big stranger foolishly pleased with violence, as if Stanley were his kid brother, and felt hopelessly distant from him and annoyed with him. "We've got to plan," she said. "If there is an emergency, we've got to plan. Stanley," she said, "will you take us to the Staff Store before everyone else gets there?"

Farquharson, in the back seat, caught himself thinking how practical and unlovely survivors were, and then told himself he was being grossly unfair to her.

The store had been rebuilding itself and was now bright and air conditioned, with a new door. The ground outside was strewn with cars; boys were readying empty boxes. Inside, where the store had the cramped, distracted festivity of a cocktail party, Joan moved as if on a programme, sending Farquharson on scouting missions. Rice, macaroni, cheese (in tins), tinned butter, a tinned ham, a tinned chicken, flour. "And I," Farquharson announced, "am going to drink my way through this," and put three bottles into the cart: gin, red vermouth, vodka. A radio on top of one of the shelves blared music. They met extraordinary numbers of convivial strangers. One pointed to the radio, and shouted over *The Moldau*: "Not a grain of news!" Farquharson saw a man stand in front of a frozen-meat box holding a wrapped mass of sausages, visibly speculating how many power failures there had been lately. Finally he looked up, laid the meat reverently back, saw Farquharson, and said, "No. Some things not even a coup makes possible."

"A coup?"

"Well, we have to hope so, don't we?"

Joan said, "I brought all our money."

They got into the line-up just ahead of Gail. She said, "I'm buying for Bill."

The manager watched, looking as if he had just been wakened up. Farquharson wondered what his politics were. "All I can say is," a man said, "it had better be true, with all the dough we're spending on it."

"Nineteen pounds," Farquharson said, waving the long bill. "You know, we're going to look silly if that man's alive."

He was balancing the box against his raised leg while Joan got the door open for him. "Guard that," he said to Gail, pointing to his other box.

Peg Ormford was at the foot of the steps. "Oh, you don't have to do *that*," she said.

Farquharson said, "Does anyone know what happened?" It was odd, he thought, how monumental he felt with his shoulders and back counterbalancing the box.

She said, "There was a pitched battle around his house from two to four in the morning. Jennifer Bradshaw and her husband sat up and listened to the shots."

"Stanley!" Farquharson called.

Stanley took the box. "Hold it, we've got another," Farquharson said, and went back up the stairs, almost getting hit as the door burst open. Gail faced him with a small box of her own.

The people in the store pushed back and forth. He bent to his box, saying, "We all know, and nobody knows. Why doesn't it feel like a crisis? All these people." He straightened. "Is he dead or isn't he?"

Gail said, "Henry, can I want you today?" The doors lashed shut behind them.

"How can I promise?" he said. "We're going to be the rest of the day unpacking food."

It was almost noon. There were huddles of happy people all over the centre of the compound. The expatriates at the store had been exhilarated almost dutifully, as outsiders should be; the people on Park Lane, and by the Administration Building, were celebrants.

"Master!" It was the elderly steward who had shown him how the dead bodies lay. "Master, this is a great day for Nigeria!"

He called, "How was the body this time?"

(Joan said, "Farq!" "It's okay," he said, "I know him.")

"Master, they make him kneel." He knelt. "They make him pray." He clasped his hands and stretched up his head. Then he touched his hands against his throat and threw them outwards, forward. "They say the blood go five feet!" He got to his feet, miming the holding of a man's head.

Farquharson grinned and got out. He said, "They shot him."

"No, master, no."

People by the mail counter stood with mimeographed pages in their hands. He came back to the car reading one, then handed it to Joan, silently. Then he remembered about Stanley, but she wouldn't let him read it to her.

University of Ibadan. Today's Events.

It is reported on reliable authority that the army has taken over in Nigeria. The Federal and Eastern Nigeria Cabinets are under arrest, the premiers of Northern and Western Nigeria have been killed, and telephone communication between the main centres is cut.

Ibadan appears to be quiet and there is no threat to the university, but it is obviously advisable for everyone to remain on the campus as far as possible.

Further bulletins will be issued if necessary.

When they were in their kitchen he said, "Stanley can't read: did you have to make it show?"

"Help me to put away the food."

But instead he went through the path to the Nwonkwos' and asked Victoria, "Does anybody *know* anything?"

She said, "There were a lot of people in this region who supported Akintola. So I wonder what *they* will do."

"I wish we could *know*. I've been told he was beheaded, I've been told there was a two-hour battle."

"What are you hunting for, Henry?" she said. "The right rumour?"

He went back to lunch, and found a whole box of tins left for him to put away. Joan looked self-exiled into a kind of holy irritation; he wanted to go to her, put his hands on her shoulders, and draw her to him, and he wanted just as much to tell her about himself, about the frying pan and Gail. Therefore he could do neither. "Where's Jamie?"

"Playing with Jacob. Sometimes I can't stand Jacob, lurking around without saying anything."

"What's wrong?" he said.

"Murder and revolution," she said to the stove, "and he says 'What's wrong?' "

"I should have said something, shouldn't I?" he said to Gail. "I shouldn't just have gone out to look for Jamie. Damn it, she needed me! She was mad at my country."

All the blinds but one were drawn as if there were no one home. They were sitting on the white-cushioned chairs, naked. His arms alternated between resting between his legs as if he wanted to hide himself, and being crossed on his chest as if he wanted to display himself. "It's ridiculous to be so much not in need of her," he said.

Gail saw he was looking at her breasts. He looked so boyish and unsure she was sorry for him, so she let her knees fall a few inches apart, then spread them to let him see the cleft. He stretched his hands above his head to yawn, made an abrupt pelvic thrust, and slid a few inches forward on the cushion. His equipment flopped, and remained soft.

"Do you want a drink?" she said.

They worked beside each other in the kitchen, squeezing lemons, trying to get ice cubes loose with no water in the taps, enjoying the way they moved around each other in the tiny kitchen, their skin touching. Then Farquharson brushed her teasing fingers away from his bush and said, "Listen, what's that?"

A raucous murmur, not a chant, getting nearer. It was on the road.

Without agreement, as if they had been told to, they put their drinks on the meat safe and went to the front window of the living room. Farquharson said, "Up!" and the blind went up. They heard, "*Awo! Awo!*"

Suddenly, in the gap of the driveway, they saw the students appear, faces unashamed, mouths open, eyes alert. They were waving pieces of palm trees; some of them with scraps of fronds, jerking their hands in the air as if they were masturbating. One of them had a branch of flame tree. He saw Adebọwale go by with palm leaves in both hands, crying "Awolọwọ is our prime minister!" and for a moment thought that the big man must have looked right at him. It was a march of triumph around the bounds of the campus, he supposed. He put his hand down to give the old little tug to his genitals. His car was advertising its new master much as it might have done its old. He felt Gail's hand grope behind her and like a little animal hunting for comfort take hold of him, the fingers curving around his balls and warming them. She was afraid. With the pressure of her hand, so was he. Savages danced on a university compound, exulting over a death. Except for Adebọwale, he hadn't recognized anyone. They were all in old clothes as if their apparel had been suddenly made crude and poor, because the spirits were. And he saw the old steward again, kneeling in the middle of Park Lane, to have his head cut off.

"*Awo! Awo!*"

Her hand held him. His prick pushed up against the angle of her thumb, a hot other self. She didn't stroke or jiggle it until the last capering undergraduate had gone by, yelling with his palm branch. Finally the air moved with a cold rumour of noise, and they were breathing through their mouths, dry-throated.

"Our drinks," he said. "Let me go."

So he had to warm her, seduce her, make her relax, do for her what she had done for him, open a piece of time with nothing in it but the signals of the nerves and the surrender to them, carry his mouth, his tongue, his breath, his murmuring of love, all over her, nuzzling between her thighs, with his tongue out and playing, clamping spread lips on to her breast while a vacuum grew in his mouth, and not until she was sighing and her face was blurring out of its lines did he plunge down, and use himself as if he were even bigger than he was, until she was in a kind of hysteria of ecstasy. Farquharson stayed extraordinarily rational, compassionate, learning more about knightly service that he had imagined possible. And then he couldn't help her. He lost himself. He had to go on and end. Spirit, fresh-clothed with flesh, stung everywhere, and couldn't live that way. Reason remained.

Man and mistress were one flesh. Two souls. The army and the rioters had the circumambient roads. There was a child somewhere. He was asleep with nightmare, frightening the woman he had fallen out of. She had to lift herself, somehow, up from the humming dead bottom of the world to send him on his way, but he slept even when she got the water out of the rusting tank and bathed what she had to of him. It was frightening to be so alone. "Please, Henry," she said, "wake up!"

"Oh, poor Joan!" she thought, "if they come to the house drumming and shouting and the child's there!"

She got the ice cubes melting, and rubbed them on to his stomach, he woke, gasping and scared, and had to be told why. And then he raced the car, charged down his driveway, and saw Joan, with Jamie at her shoulder, standing under the trees and cheering the marchers on El-Kanemi Road, beyond the fence. Jamie was waving a flower, his face puffed.

"Where the God-damned hell were you?" she said to him.

"I'm sorry," Farquharson said, "I didn't think." He put out his hands.

Joan turned so that Jamie was held away from him. The parade on the road beyond the fence seemed to roar *"Awo!"* at them, or possibly it was the blood in his ears. Joan shouted "Hurray!" but only loudly enough for Jamie to understand her. Farquharson was in no mood for dilemmas of conscience: he watched the parade. The marchers were untired. Perhaps the shouting had stabilized.

"They came along Jaja too," Joan said. "That's when we decided to cheer. We were right near the road." The parade passed. Joan's arms held Jamie. He would have to act.

"Stanley!" he called.

"*He* isn't here!"

But Stanley was in his doorway. "Sir?"

"Take us to the Club ... Joan," he said, "can you bring the money? It's in our room."

So she said, "Aren't you the clever one?" and put Jamie into Stanley's hands. And went in. Farquharson found her in the bedroom clutching the wallet, her face so white he was for a moment afraid of her. She saw a selfish, lazy man, too big to help because what they were afraid of wouldn't bother him. "All right," he said, "why were you near the road?"

"Because he went up to the road to chase them away, just like you did at Christmas. And he ran away from me! He was *so* scared ... I got him right," she said, and suddenly seemed to realize that she was holding all that was left of their money, because she threw it on to the bed. "I got him believing it was a parade we had to cheer. And you come home and try to take him out of my arms!" She said, "I *earned* that hug. Where were you?"

He said, "I was in the library. I didn't hear."

And it had become a solid joy to lie.

He escorted her to the car and put Jamie between them so he could choose the lap he wanted, but Jamie sat without either of them, his hands down tight against the seat. He went away with Stanley then because he was brave and had to, and Farquharson and Joan stood on the grass outside the Club and had their fight out, saying nothing that either of them could remember five sentences after it was spoken. They ended hand in hand, simply

266

because they had to have hold of someone then wondered, in a moment of agreement that they didn't recognize what sort of a country they were in. The day of revolution had the bartender at the bar, the swimmers in the pool, the gossip about food and health and the way the school was run. The Americans were there. Farquharson suddenly realized that Joan was about to forgive him at least for not having been at the house, if not for anything he'd said, and that he didn't want her to. "I wasn't there and you were," he said, putting a hand on her arm. "And you did a damn good job."

"I thought you must have fallen asleep."

Gail brought Garnett that evening, when the Nwonkwos were in the Farquharsons' living room. He was bandaged and looked sick. Oscar got out of the chair where he had been sprawling, and almost as if Bill was blind guided him into it and made him put his feet up (finally, Farquharson noticed, he was wearing a closed shoe). Gail said, "We came because we had news"—and she said it to Joan, as if Joan had the right to the explanation.

"They've got him in the hospital," Bill said. "Akintola. They showed him to a few people. Well, his head's still on."

"Shot?"

"Oh God, yes. But now there's a rumour's all over everywhere that he was full of drugs."

Gail said, "Didn't they say one of his friends died of drugs? Who was it? A woman?"

Bill said, "His friend."

"His inspiration!" Oscar said. "His impetus!"

Bill said, "As I understood, his *raison d'être* at least for rumour. Anyway, she died." He added, "Rumour also made *her* an addict. I never believed that."

"No, no, my friend," Oscar said, leaning forward. "She was in UCH for months, mad, driven mad by fear! She caught the fear from her great friend. Akintola was a man of fear."

"People guess how much he could have recovered from her death," Bill said, staring blank-eyed ahead of him. "It doesn't matter. She was forty-odd. I met her once. She probably died quite naturally and with no drugs in her except what the doctors gave her. It doesn't matter. He's been well and thoroughly shot, and he's gone up on show. Anyway, what we came to say was that they've taken Balewa to Calabar, apparently for some sort of negotiations with Awolọwọ. Anyway, he's alive." It was as if he felt that now he had to stand up and go.

"Rumour at the hospital?" Farquharson said, to be kind to him.

"Some of us were through to the hospital in Lagos. They haven't got *Balewa*'s body."

Suddenly there was no problem of how to make a social evening, and they had a free-for-all on danger, compounds, and the organization of rumour—and a renewed set-to on "the innocent Muse of Tyranny", as Oscar called her, while Bill with almost fanatic vigour said no, she was not an addict; no, she had not committed suicide; no, she had not gone mad incognito, but yes, she must have been afraid. Yes, they must all of them have been afraid.

Oscar scribbled at the desk, then held a piece of paper far in front of him and started to read:

> The innocent Muse of Tyranny
> Maddens inside the lace
> Of the hospital walls,
> With the serum of what she has inspired
> Drugging her arteries.
> We who live carry the Muse to her grave with festivities.
> Tyranny can look only to itself now—

"You don't give up, do you?" Bill interrupted, pulling back his feet and talking in a voice raw with enmity. Oscar didn't look abashed, but he put his poem away, slowly.

"Anyway," Gail said, "it's a damned bad poem, Oscar."

"It's what Victoria said," Farquharson said, "hunting for the *right* rumour."

It was necessary, eventually, to send people home and go to

bed. "I still can't understand," Joan said, "how you could have left us alone this afternoon the way you did."

He said, "I bet it's the aftermath of every revolution that wives scold husbands in their beds for having gotten taken up by it."

So at last she laughed, and Farquharson, up on one elbow to look at her, rolled over on to his back and spread his arms up across the pillow until his nails hit the headboard.

"Good night in the Year One," he said.

23

January 16–21, 1966

RUMOUR and radio broadcasts consolidated, it almost seemed casually, what might have happened. The Prime Minister was missing; the Minister of Finance was missing, kidnapped from his house, probably killed; nothing particular seemed to have happened in the East, or the Mid-West. The Premier of the North might have been burned alive in his house. "Rebels" had staged the coup; "loyalists" had taken over. The new government abolished the Republic on Sunday, and by Tuesday the Supreme Commander was saying to reporters, "We shall not censor the news: we shall censor *you*!" or, on another matter: "I know nothing of laws. I shall give orders, and they will be obeyed."

Meanwhile fall mixed with spring: black leaves covered the ground, and half the trees had their branches stuck with small pastel flowers. Farquharson felt unhooked from time.

The government was sending to rescue kidnapped Balewa in Calabar: Akintọla, it was said, had been planning a coup with the Sardauna (Farquharson must have faced Akintọla, with WP2471, just as he was on his way to that meeting)—and this meeting had been to plan a coup to crush the Ibos, only it was discovered. Farquharson found that rationalized rumour was the basis of the language of dissertations. Oscar Nwonkwo looked wonderfully jaunty and yet afraid. More and more he announced that he had friends in Lagos, friends in the army, friends who would tell him what happened, but it seemed he didn't hear from them.

The "loyalist" army had taken Ibadan by noon on Saturday. Farquharson was going to drive into town on Sunday, with the excuse of finding one of the drugstores open, but truckloads of

Moslems were coming out of Sabo and going north—crammed with silent standing men and a few mattresses standing on end—so he stopped at the unfinished gate and turned around again.

The army was outside the campus. Across the road from the university entrance was a small market. In the sparse shrubbery beyond he could see the sky shining from windshields, and dark-green doorposts and roofs.

On Monday, after two hours of distracted tutorials, marked mainly by ordinariness, Farquharson went into the Shakespeare class, exulting in the coincidence that would have him talking about *Julius Caesar*, to find written on the blackboard, very neatly, "January 16, 1966: the *real* Independence Day". And the class seemed to be looking at him to see what he would make of it.

"I can't know the truth," he said, after reading it twice. "I suspect that I'm in the wrong sort of country for knowing it, for me. But I know *that's* wrong. Independent of what, yourselves?" He put the Shakespeare on the desk, and smoothed his notes on to the lectern. "Cry havoc!" he shouted, "and let slip the dogs of—peace?" He straightened. "Where is Mrs. Akinrinmade? Why isn't she here? I've seen her burnt house—are you independent of her? I suppose I saw some of you going around this campus on Saturday. You weren't recognizable. Are you independent of yourselves? We have the illusion countries *are*, you know. But say I killed someone, and got away with it. Sometimes people do —am I free now? I'm the person *now* who did that *then*. I may have left over passions. They limit me, they tug for a different balance than the one I want to assume. Well, what if a country has its past on its conscience? Or not on its conscience but merely there, past causes still having effects? What is it independent of? Other countries? In a very genuine sense it always was. And to the extent that it wasn't, that it got a momentum and forms, it's still got them. You're not all that independent if your military coups are dependent on Sandhurst training."

"What is the Professor trying to say?" Mr. Enem asked.

Farquharson said, "I don't know." He ruffled his pages, trying to start the lecture. "Euphoria ought to be able to fade into mere

271

well-being. But it doesn't, usually. It puts its demands too high."
He sighed.

"Perhaps the hardest thing to reconcile yourself to in *Julius Caesar* is that it puts what you normally expect in Act Five into the middle of Act Three."

Halfway through the lecture, somebody got up and erased the board.

University of Ibadan. Information Bulletin.
Everyone will by now have heard the main news about changes in Nigeria's constitution and government as given by the NBC.

Ibadan city is reported to be relatively quiet after yesterday's sporadic burning of houses. The main stores and banks opened as usual, but large areas outside the business section are said to be obstructed by roadblocks and it is certainly advisable to avoid the town if possible. Although everything so far seems to indicate a return to normal conditions, nothing should be taken for granted.

Further trouble cannot be ruled out.

"Nice note about Akintola," Eayrs said, as they stood reading beside the mail desk. "That it was unintended—they didn't mean to kill him."

"Well," Farquharson said, "if he did get out on the steps of his house and harangue that they couldn't arrest him and then shot one of them—well, you don't need to mean to kill a man. You just do it."

"They mowed him down!" Eayrs said. "Trouble is, I heard that tale about the Sardauna, too."

"I think it makes more sense with Akintola."

"You shouldn't judge immediate history by artistry. That's what rumour's all about. Anyway, *as* a literary critic, you ought to know what's wrong with that story. It's just O'Neill's Emperor Jones again. The silver bullet. I like to think he was in bed, with the mattress taking the thuds." He looked sideways. "So should you, with your car."

"Ted!" Isobel Eayrs called, driving up in their car with the children hanging out the windows, looking proud. She was sputtering with amusement. "We've had to evacuate the school!

"Something about a holy war coming down out of the North," she said, "of all the ridiculous things! But the army's taken over the school. You should have seen Lady Jane being heroic to rescue the children, and we were taking them all home anyway. So they've called school off for tomorrow, on the theory that a holy war will only take one Tuesday, I suppose. Hi, Mr. Farquharson!"

Eayrs said, "I think the *jihad* would be Baptists from Ogbomosho, don't you? Akintola's homefolks? Followers? What is it the man said?" he said, waving the bulletin. " 'Further trouble cannot be ruled out'?"

They went away, waving their hands.

"Apparently they burned things here last night," he said to Joan, and gave her the bulletin.

"And I'll bet you want to see them."

"Yes, I think I do."

He decided not to tell her about the holy war from the North, but she heard about it anyway late in the afternoon, from Victoria, who was almost hugging herself with delight over the idea. "But they're so unfair to Lady Jane," she said. "It was the Army she was trying to chase away from the school, not the children."

"It's extraordinary what rumour is," Farquharson said. "In that little time!" He dropped a piece of pickled walnut into a cocktail of his own devising and said, "Where do you suppose Balewa is?"

Victoria shrugged. "I don't think you'll find that anybody is worried about that. What significance can he have? His master's dead."

So they went into Ibadan Tuesday morning, to shop and see. The city seemed normal enough, perhaps slightly underpopulated. All the reconstituted milk products had disappeared from the

Kingsway. They went down the Ijẹbu Bye-Pass. For weeks, it seemed, they had gone only as far as the jog by the cemetery and the first of the Opposition newsboy thugs, where they could buy a paper.

It was a huge, modern, modernly commercial street, its buildings thrust wide away from the road. Flats here were mansions, and off to one side there was a close-built suburb more North American and city-like than anything else in Ibadan. They drove bending streets, saw garages, verandahs, ordinary people, came back to the Bye-Pass, and then saw a huge green house like a low, long apartment building, with thin red concrete window frames; a vivid house, burned, with all the windows cracked, and many brown and black goats or sheep feeding in the weeds beside it. "Which are they, Stanley," Farquharson said, "sheep or goats?"

"I do not know, sir."

"Primitive forms," he said to Joan. "I never thought separating sheep from goats was a real difficulty."

Jamie liked the goats.

Then they passed a toast-brown apartment mansion, also burned, but apparently on the upstairs only. Farquharson got out to walk nearer, and a passer-by warned him to get back and go away. Farquharson said, "It's public. It can be seen."

"This not your house, sir, to be glad of."

"I don't rejoice. I observe."

"You must rejoice, or hate, sir."

"And which do you do?"

The man said, "It cannot matter to you."

The dull-blue nightclub at the end of Ogunmọla was also burned. It showed like an antique ruin—massive mud walls and holes—and also like something cheap out of a midway, sun-faded blue and purple-pink. The name was untouched. "Modupe Club": the "I-Thank-You Club". Somehow that said a good deal more than the houses did.

Ogunmọla in its narrow domestic end was a normal street. No signs of trouble. They went uphill. There were two Mercedes trucks linked by a tow, both burnt, and on the one, around the wheels, strange ribs and sunbursts of curved shining metal where the tires had been burnt away and had released these springing skeletons of themselves. It was incongruous, Farquharson thought, that the only revolting thing visible after coup, looting, mobs, perhaps minor killing should be the corpses of a set of truck tires. The traveller's palm near the turn-off to the cloth market looked cheaply showy. So they went home. The army, presumably, was around the school, guarding them from a Tuesday holy war. They had to read the paper at the Club; they hadn't been able to get one in town. All the parties were proclaiming loyalty and enthusiasm about the new regime.

The information bulletins were still coming out from the office of the acting Vice-Chancellor, but they were becoming chatty.

Today Ibadan city appears to have returned pretty much to normal. Markets are operating, and the streets quiet but busy. Buses and taxis are plying as usual. The Lagos road is still to be avoided if possible, though two professors managed to get through from Ikeja by car yesterday without difficulty. Ibadan Airport had a busy day.

Wednesday the school opened again, without the army, and Victoria came over in celebration to tell them so at breakfast. "No holy war," she said, "even on a Tuesday. No invasion of Akintọla's survivors. So that's that."

Information Bulletin: There is little to add to yesterday's bulletin. No less than three daily newspapers reached me in time for my breakfast this morning.
Opera: The Ibadan Operatic Society's production of *Die Fledermaus* will open as scheduled in the Arts Theatre.
General situation: This is still by no means completely clear.

This was the last of the bulletins. Balewa was still missing; nobody seemed to be interested. Eayrs summed it up as "Hohum!

We seem to have mislaid the Prime Minister," and nobody in the Senior Common Room troubled even to smile at him. By now Okotie-Eboh's body had been reported found, and dug up, at least twice, so presumably the great hated Finance Minister *was* dead.

Jacob confessed, on Friday, when asked how he had been—and for this Joan, for the first time, really and unreservedly liked him— that on the night of the seventeenth and eighteenth, when Monday became Tuesday, and Tuesday was set for the invasion from the North, he had sat up all night, unable to go to sleep, "because of fear, madam," and had cut up yams for occupation and because the deed gave him a knife. That was when he confessed that he wanted to join the army, "when Master and Madam go from here," and then he smiled.

They drove into town that day just in time to have to stop outside the airport while five trucks of soldiers drove out from the parking lot. "Is Fajuyi," Stanley said. "He have press conference." The last of the trucks had an army band in it. The sun was so harsh the air was white, and when they got into town they found more soldiers in trucks, and in the streets, patrolling, and with leafy camouflage stuck around their helmets. Their uniforms were green anyway, but Farquharson couldn't understand what green camouflage was supposed to do in a city of almost uniform black-brown, rust, cream, and white. And dark red: across from Dugbẹ Market, there was a jeepload of men in ordinary ragged clothes, with blood running down their heads in patches, as if for a movie scene. They went quickly past. There were many happy faces beside the streets; stray truckloads of soldiers went along the Ọyọ road as if they were a liberating army, moving amid cheers— only there were no cheers. The people were happy, but nobody cheered.

There was milk in the Kingsway again, and whipping cream, but no sour cream yet. Farquharson had been letting his imagination play with the idea of Akintọla haranguing the soldiers from his steps in a white *agbada*, making a speech of pride in the night like an old phonograph, taking out a tiny pistol and firing it at one of the soldiers in the dark and then being clubbed back dead and slack by the instant thudding return of many bullets. He wasn't normally that kind of imaginative man, but the reality that some-how had to back this followed him, even to the white cardboard tetrahedrons full of reconstituted milk, or to the lovely imperious girl with the bad eye at the checkout counter, who now greeted Jamie as if he were a small honoured happy prince.

And he thought of the blue flashing light of the police car, the multiple headlights of a charging convoy of cars, the meeting or the not-meeting of two men in the dark, across the single, pos-sibly unread licence number, the two rumoured mythical users of WP2471. He wished he knew how the man had died. It wasn't enough to have all the frank rejoicing in the streets, to sense so early, so thoroughly, that the whole country was on honeymoon, that it was a charmed time when nothing could happen, nothing could go wrong except that the old politicians were going to have to cough up their graft and profits. Government was dead: what was going to be let live was a lovely amalgam of anarchy and authority. After all, the post office went on working all through the coup; the water didn't go off, not in Ibadan; the electricity kept up, as much as it ever did; they would take Joan to the hos-pital in the afternoon, to see Popoola again, and the hospital was there, the checkups continued. Farquharson guessed at a random dogged orderliness as acute as England's, swung the box of groceries high onto his shoulder, and strode out of the store with Jamie, trotting fast, held by his other hand.

The white-coated doorman held the outside door for him, and he nearly knocked against the boy with the tray of wrist watches. The sun was like waves of heat coming off a black frying pan ready to sear meat. The one-legged beggar with the royal face and the big hopping pole wasn't there. But the beggar sitting at the very foot of the stairs was a patiently wicked philosopher with distorted limbs. Farquharson, head up, almost walked on an outthrust, glazed leg, and when the beggar cried, "Master, where you go?" didn't apologize.

There were people; there was Farquharson. *They* had killed for their peace and rescue now; so had he. After euphoria came the flatfooted pleasures of breath, walking, teaching, standing in a parking lot waiting for your wife and driver, and elaborating deaths: the right rumour, artistic considerations for the immediacy of history, wondering not what the bullets felt like but, he thought unmorbidly, what would the dead thing be? Nobody was going to pay attention to WP2471 now, as a symbolic car—they *didn't*, anyway—yet it was now that the brown car linked its users. He felt oddly elegiac, day after day, about Akintọla. "Let him be a bad guy," he thought. "*Tyranny is dead*, like the banners of the Lagos students." But the words out of the newspaper, in Parliament, stuck in his head: "I *told* you you'd all be back!" the delight, the enthusiasm, the fun of having got joyous open corruption to work so superbly for them. He hadn't of course heard Akintọla say that, but he felt he had, off the print on the page. It was odd that it stuck in his head on the same terms as one thing he *had* heard: Lee Harvey Oswald in the police station before he was killed, bobbing towards a television camera as he was being led away and in a soft, sullen, surprised voice, saying, "A policeman *hit* me."

His eyes were blinking in the sun. All right, he thought, he was in Africa. He was here. And he didn't know what here was. He was a tourist with a heavy hand. "I have a complaint," he thought, echoing his students. Stanley took the box from him, because he was just standing there. So Farquharson picked Jamie up, and carried him on his hip down to the car.

Joan insisted on going alone to the hospital in the afternoon. Farquharson played at home with Jamie. And then, because he was really alone, he put on Gail's ring to watch the light in the round crystal bead, and to see the soft, almost unreal shimmer of the gin-coloured silver.

When Joan came back she said angrily, "Now there are going to be a lot of jokes that I was under arrest!" and sat down in a chair, looking as if she ought to be wearing a hat and gloves. Farquharson said, "What?"

"Oh, Garnett was having himself looked at. I swear he spends

278

more time as a patient than as a doctor. So he was over at Dr. Popoola's, I don't know why. You know how you wait on a batch of benches on that sort of verandah thing? Well, there were five policemen there. With guns. They all came up at once. It was just that one of them was sick, and the others didn't have anything to do now that they aren't beating up on people and bullying for the government. Only Garnett had to come up and say the Farquharsons broke too many laws away from their houses and he was glad to see the police had caught up with me. I could have murdered him!"

He thought, "The ring's on my hand still!" and got it into his pocket, and tried to work it off with his thumb, but finally had to put his left hand over his pocket also to use its middle finger, with the right hand's thumb, to shove the ring off—and then there wasn't room in the pocket for it to fall clear of his finger. She said, "What *are* you doing? Playing Tristram Shandy?"

"Itching."

And at last the ring fell off.

"Well, pay attention to me. He got everybody on those benches looking at me wondering what I'd done. And the worst of it all was they had their police car down below, by the rail of the driveway, and do you know what it was? It was a pale-green delivery truck with red roses on it. On the back doors. I saw them get into it. Oh, Farq, I didn't like it!"

But he didn't say, "Oh, Pickle," and be nice. He shouted, "*Why?*"

She said, "They're as corrupt as anybody can be!" and then sniffed.

"Bill was just making a joke."

"Sure, you defend him! Oh, I know," she added, tired of the whole thing. "But it isn't a joke to have Africans looking at you."

"Well, I don't know what to say. Have you lost all the sense of humour you ever had?"

"Oh," she said, "I think you're *happy* they had a revolution!"

"So is everybody we know," he said, trying to be gentle with her.

"I'm not!"

He had to take her to the Club, and have supper with her, and spend the night with her.

24

ALWAYS, if there were cattle on the road, they were moving south to the cattle market, driven by thin men in white, from somewhere in the North. Saturday, the week after the coup, Farquharson and Stanley saw a herd of fifty cattle beside the road near the airport, being driven north. *"General situation,"* Farquharson thought, *"this is still by no means completely clear."*

"We seem," he said, coming into the house and putting the *Times* on the dining room table beside his wife, "to have found the Prime Minister."

"Victoria told me," she said. "It was on the radio."

"How could he be just freshly dead," Ormford said, "and Okotie-Eboh a week gone and hh-higher than Cocoa H-house and the two of them left side by side? Refrigeration, my dear Farquharson. Morgues."

"But he was formally dressed. And leaned against a tree. Okotie-Eboh was just thrown into the ditch. And he wasn't marked."

"Bb-bullets all over him, among the worms."

"No. I mean Balewa."

"Poor Farquharson," Ormford said. "I could have wished you to have h-had a quieter year."

"But why was he dead? What would be the point of killing him?"

"I'm not among those who regarded him as nothing bb-but the Sardauna's puppet."

"All right," Farquharson protested. "Have him a prime mover.

But could anything be more embarrassing to this government than to have what's happened? 'Ho-hum, we seem to have lost the Prime Minister!' *Oh no, we haven't!* They must have carted him round with them not knowing what to do with him. And people have been digging up Okotie-Eboh in so many places that they finally had to leave the real Okotie-Eboh where somebody'd notice him. Maybe they even dug him up and went off hunting for a good place."

"And they h-had Bb-balewa with them."

"Right. He's an old man. He'd be sick from the stench anyway, wouldn't he? They probably opened the back of the truck, and he thought they were going to kill him and just took off lickety-split into the bush and had a heart attack, white robe and all. Maybe they even propped him up against a tree to get his wind back, and he died on them. The paper said there wasn't a mark on him, and he *was* brand-new."

Ormford looked away from the bar. He said, "You've gg-got your mind made up."

"That's the only combination of the stories that makes any sense." He was supposed to be at the Arts Building, working. Gail wasn't home. "God, think of the embarrassment!"

Ormford said, "You came to the right country."

"Yes, I know. It's ridiculous. And in the right year."

Ramadan ended on Monday. So did the period of mourning. They saw people walking along Jaja to go to the zoo, dressed as if for parties and ceremonies: brand-new *agbadas*, up-and-downs, and the little girls in party dresses as abandoned to lace as if they had been on a Venetian quayside. Joan came back from a morning drive dazzled with the sight of a whole city in new clothes, but Farquharson had work to do, even on a holiday: preparations for Shakespeare. Suddenly he felt that the unreality of those classrooms was so great that nothing from outside would affect or alter anything. He contemplated Mr. Fakunle, who could ride joyously with the rumour of Akintola's death and walk into his office full of legalisms to demand an extension on an essay, without a quiver of the other communicating itself anywhere. Why should it? What was real in class? A striving teacher? Joan told him all about the clothes in Ibadan at lunch, so he went in to see for himself and took Gail with him, while Joan slept. (Some of the tallest of the bare trees were budding new leaves.) "Come on," he said, parking at the Kingsway. "Let's look at fashions."

He stared along a bare broiling street.

She said, "You didn't notice the signs that said to buy for a long weekend?" She was delighted with him.

"No," he said.

"Let me drive you. We'll cruise."

They went back to the car, and Farquharson, feeling ridiculous, had to be extravagantly gallant in holding the door for her. They owned, temporarily, a kind of raw delight in something that might have been their own silliness, and Farquharson's ears were flushed. For a moment, as he got into the car, they were so acutely aware of where the other was, and how the least shift of movement was made, they felt that the car might have been made of glass, they had to move so delicately. Yet the air burned on their faces and arms like metal. Farquharson tucked himself into the hot shade. "Where do you know," he said, "where a man and a woman can make love in the open air?"

"Nowhere in Africa."

He panted and said, "I agree."

Nevertheless she took him around by many back ways, and there weren't as many people showing themselves off as he thought there should have been, and they went past a reconstituted milk factory, and lavish houses, and went this way and that, until they finally found themselves in what seemed huge open fields. Suddenly she brought the car to a stop at the edge of a small bunch of trees. "I haven't the least notion where we are," she said.

He said, "Don't stop. We'll broil."

So they continued on the little grey road as if it might lead them somewhere, passed several soldiers, one of whom looked hard at them, and finally drove out the front gate of an army camp, *the* army camp, creeping, suddenly aware, past all sorts of No Admission signs. Farquharson craned his head. "Holy cow!" he said. "Where did we get into that?"

Then they were both afraid. The fence might have been guns aimed at them. The road ahead pointed to the big unfinished hotel (so they knew where they were now), and it too was a thing watching and being watched. They, and their landscape, suddenly huddled in a military dictatorship. "I'm going to have to look that one up on the map," he said. "I don't want to do *that* twice!" Then, "Was there any barbed wire?"

They drove to the familiar road. "They wouldn't do anything efficient, you know," she said.

They went back by way of the Ifẹ campus. "Goodbye, spy," she said, and then with an echo of fright, partly for Joan, "Be careful, Henry."

"And there goes another great story, that I'm never going to be able to tell," he thought. The Day I Gate-Crashed an Army Camp in the Middle of a Military Revolution and No One Saw Me."

Joan said, "Well, did you see a *lot* of fashions?"

They went to the Club. "Oh, all the little white faces," he said as they got out of the car. "Damn!" It was completely unfair, he thought, that he should have arrived at the Club in a raging temper; unfair, particularly, to Jamie, who alone hadn't earned it.

"What's wrong with you?"

"People are dead."

"Well, granted," she said, "it *was* mean of them to put him in a mortarboard too big for him."

Sympathy, he decided at the bottom of the swimming pool, was a useless, interfering, and degrading privileged tourist's quality.

Grace Spanier-Dodd and Mrs. Michaelson had taken over Joan. In relief, Farquharson went to the playground to play games with Jamie (while Stanley crouched in the grass and watched them). Slowly, with discipline so tight it hurt almost like a stomach ache, he fought himself back to temper and calm, and only when he thought he'd done so went into the dressing room and then into the swimming pool, where he made his declaration against sympathy and came up to the surface again. He swam a few more times and then with a resurgence of irritation climbed out and got dressed.

The women were looking at cloth and jewellery in the lounge. Someone had just taken over the end of the room selling tourist things. Shimmering fabrics were folded on a sort of sideboard, beside a Ghanaian stool. Farquharson went and got a beer.

But he was a man who loved pretty things, and so it wasn't long before the new little shop folded into a corner drew him to its ornaments and cloths, and with his glass in his hand, as Orm-ford had imagined a Canadian would roam about, he leaned and looked, and thought of the pressures of the people at the cloth market, and their anxious bullying, so that what he looked at here was only part of a toy: only silver and stones, and satins dyed gold and green as if they were rough cottons steeped in indigo. There were also rings.

Joan was spreading out something dyed in a burnished yellow background to sunbursts of white. Farquharson looked at big, knobbly silver jewellery, the hand in his pocket juggling his two talismans of metal.

There wasn't a ring like Gail's, but there was a big one of grey-ish metal clutching what looked like a piece of amber. He almost took it, then his fingers disturbing a tray found a ring with a rough piece of malachite, and his hand closed on it. Joan said, "Farq, have you got some money?" so he put the ring down, guiltily, and went over to give her the wallet, keeping a few pounds for himself from it. While she bought golden cloth, he bought the malachite ring. This one, he thought, was for Gail. And now he could wear his own.

"Grace is going to take me to a dressmaker," Joan said. "Oh, I could really be happy if there were a lot of this!"

She held the gold and white satin against herself and spun about, dancing in her own African house while her own servant was cutting and washing vegetables in her own kitchen. So Farquharson put out his little finger with the crystal bead and said, "Look what *I* got!"

Mutual exclamations, he thought; hypocrisy, and nothing to be ashamed about. Jamie said, "Far' give Mummy so pretty dress!"

Farquharson went to the cloth market, to breathe, to see, to walk jostled among Africans. He wanted next to bring Jamie here, among these drab, clamorous people reaching for him. He stood in the middle of the more open part, not taller than everyone, just big and white and visible. An *akara* seller stepped beside him. He watched someone give her a piece of money for a few of the small golden doughballs, so he did the same. The ring on his little finger shone like a globe of water, and he stood with his left hand cupped against his shirt, fishing the peppery *akara* out of the space with the other hand. It tasted of crayfish and oil. "You like, master?"

"Yes," he said. "I do." His shirt was going to be oil-stained. At his feet cloth rigid as plywood lay coiled like belts.

He flung a crazy salute at the traveller's palm when he was going home.

Grace insisted he come with them to the dressmaker's. There was a gas station across the road, chickens in the front yard. They had to step over a ditch trickling with black-green water. Inside was a cool, wide, stained hall, and a doorway into a small bright room full of sewing children, with pieces of dresses and blouses hanging on the walls above them. "Ah, Mrs. Spanier-Dodd!" the dressmaker called. "A moment, please!"

Deftly, fiercely, she showed a child how to do something. Then she was introduced (Grace trying very hard to be her equal), led them deeper into the hall, said, "Mind my husband's motor-cycle, Mr. Farquharson," and took them into what must have been her bedroom, where she sat down and gave them pattern books. Farquharson tried not to notice that Joan, feeling dust on the floor under her feet, was rapidly throwing her delight away. Mrs. Ezeokoli studied the cloth, said, "Can you get another piece?" Joan shook her head.

Joan was turning, undecided, between two pages of the pattern book. Mrs. Ezeokoli turned the page decisively and said, "There!" She added, "I couldn't remember exactly where it was, but this is obviously what we're after." Obviously, it was.

She said, "Let me measure you."

Farquharson moved out into the sun among the chickens. Grace was waiting in her car. "You aren't a very close couple, are you, Mr. Farquharson?" she said. "I suppose nobody is out here."

"I don't know what to say to that."

She gestured towards the drains and chickens. "You should do more of this sort of thing for her. Women aren't as easily at home here as men are. Certainly not as you are."

"Does it show?" He was suddenly so angry that he had to turn away from her.

"In every bone and muscle. Canadians love Nigeria. Is your wife an American? Because they don't."

"No," he said.

"I see."

High trees arched over the road, making it into a green nave. New blocks of flats with walls of fading turquoise and maroon crowded against the shade. Road construction spread mounds and gashes of black-red earth. Two women, with stained blue wrappers and bundles on their heads, quarrelled. By what right was this beautiful and by what justice was he constrained to be fond of it? Joan appeared, questioning Mrs. Ezeokoli's skill, and was reassured. They continued onto the Kingsway, with Grace explaining how one could get anything in Dugbẹ Market.

Farquharson felt curiously compelled to consider Ibadan a quiet city. He was going to get out and walk in those streets sometime with Jamie—if he could just find the street.

And Grace found it for him. "If you want cloth," she said to

Joan, "real African cloth the way the English women don't ever wear it, go down Lebanon Street."

A teacher's life, he thought, as a teacher, was disconnected names—Miss Ogoruvwe, Miss Ogedengbe sulking and censorious; Mr. Fakunle of the extension; Mr. Lewis, who wore Western suits; Mr. Olusanya, who dismissed subtleties and qualifications as lies and was thus insatiable; 'Tunji Adebọwale—the struggle was to find the real people in the names. And then the names swam into the personalities of classes. He loved teaching, or whatever it was he did when he was in a classroom: preaching, questioning, lecturing, whatever name it had. He took up a position (by the window, in the Shakespeare lectures) with his shoulders against a thick concrete upright, and his hands, palm upwards and spread fingers taut, reaching down in front of him as if to drag the subject up on strings, from where it was stuck against the floor; and then he was who he was, and talked. He measured his success by silence: he would say, "They were listening to me."

Whether they were learning from him he hesitated, even at home, to judge too closely. He marked essays to see whether they were learning from themselves. If they told him about Innocence and Experience he might be quite apt to fail them.

Adebọwale was telling him about *Wuthering Heights*. And about Storm and Calm, which he had certainly got out of books. And about Yang and Yin, which might have come from the lecturer (who *had* taught that? Nwala Okagbue?) and then about Innocence and Experience, which inevitably had come out of Farquharson—and he was having a subtle, rather delighted time overlaying them, awkwardly. Farquharson wrote, "Good. Cranky and bothersome, but good." Every time he marked anything he had to look up the marking schedule: it was so different from his own that he could never feel where he was. He wrote in his book, "67", and on the essay with a red ballpoint and in large letters, "B-plus".

And in the third year there was Mr. Enem, still willing to be convinced, still trustable; Mr. Gbadebo, still smiling and presumably still in possession of *The Anatomy of Criticism*. And Mrs. Akinrinmade was not there. The burned house was sometimes one wall of any classroom.

Meanwhile the Senior Common Room, released from politics, shared gossip of the various Moslem countries that might or might not have rushed to the revenge of the Sardauna but hadn't done so, and he could see Gail sit with Victoria, listening to Americans talk shop. Or he could stand at the window and look down across the mosque and the lawn, and watch men slashing a new red road to replace Sankore (which was going to be cut apart by the extension of the library). Well, he walked to Gail's across the grass of the playing field now sometimes. Sometimes he really *was* in the library. He wore the ring all day, fornicated with happiness, never fell in love, but liked her, sometimes a great deal. They made love often, with abandon, with care, with control, by whim, any way they wanted to.

Bill befriended both of them—almost, it seemed, anew, as if he hadn't liked them much before, but now did. They found it rather touching. Bill let Gail make love with him too; he wasn't jealous. Farquharson always shook hands with him when they met. Meanwhile, Joan went through a small crisis in the house and made Jacob find her an ironing girl. Why she never seemed to guess about Gail, Farquharson didn't know. He might have thought it enough that she didn't; it wasn't. But it was all she gave him. On the whole they were safe: who was watching from windows at two o'clock in the afternoon if a man walked somewhere, with the heat coming out of the shadows as if tree branches or leaves were the coils of an electric fire? Gail ran a bathtub for him, before the water went off, so he could plunge in it and be cooled before coming to her to give her whatever he was that day.

He went to the Club with Joan; he had lunch with her; he slept in bed and sat through the evenings with newspapers and little talk, all with Joan; aspects of some kind of protection for her. He had to give himself to her also at night sometimes: it was a reasonable duty; he performed it reasonably. Even leftover love for her was fading out as the dresses she had bought from Canada were fading in the sun, every time they were washed. There was his son's mother, but to think that she was, was a deliberate act. Oddly, he was a better lover to her: she was beginning to want him more. If anything should have touched his conscience, he thought, that should have. Only how? He was more her husband, in the terms she seemed to want, than he had been. They talked; they planned; they invited people; they went out. Every day they were alone at the Club when he wasn't swimming or playing his one game of tennis a week with the anaesthetist. At the bar, in the chairs, or beside the pool they were man and wife, partners, recognizing each other's tastes, necessary to each other unless someone should ask them how, apart from Jamie, they even knew each other. They both liked to look at the store. (Farquharson turned his ring around.)

They went to *Die Fledermaus*, enjoyed its view of a Strauss Vienna racially mixed (including an Indian) with a Yoruba Frosch, wearing a curtain as an *agbada* to be comfortable while talking to the audience—and said to each other, "Now! we've been to the theatre," and brought Bill Garnett and Gail home for a drink afterwards. Joan wore her gold dress. Mrs. Ezeokoli's sewing school, or whatever it was, had made it beautifully. She also put on the malachite beads.

"I've got a ring of that," Gail said. "It's beautiful stuff." And Farquharson felt her eyes searching for him, and put his hand on the desk, showing his crystal bead. Garnett watched the three of them.

Jamie woke, and cried, and had to be brought in for comfort, so he sat on his father's knee and took all the people in, with large eyes, fighting against sleep. After a while he was a little huddled lump, slowly drooping forward. Farquharson shunted him so he could sleep in comfort, and still sat there with him. Gail saw a drink in one hand, the adulterer's ring on his finger (hers, in imitation, at home), the boy on his knee, sleeping against his body, and so much like him; and she recognized, as if it didn't matter, that she would have to love him while she had him.

Garnett's hand was on her shoulder. He said, "Don't we have to go?"

Joan said, "Farq, walk them to the road. I'll put Jamie down."

Up at the road Bill kicked the sign that said "Prof. & Mrs. H. J. Farquharson," and below, "1". "I wonder if this country's got you," he said, "or have you just got yourself? You're too successful. I ought to be afraid for you. You've got it all."

Farquharson said, "None of it'll last," and sounded happy.

Garnett said, "Kiss each other good night, I guess," and turned his face.

Gail said, "If he says do it, do it."

Farquharson held her for a long, distant kiss. Garnett kept his head away. Then he went off into the night, back to the theatre, with Gail beside him. When they got to where there was light Farquharson could see that they were holding hands.

He must have sat on the bed by Jamie's crib for about fifteen minutes, looking through the slats, almost helpless to go to bed, meditating upon his anchor.

And Joan got out of her new yellow dress, and called him.

Jamie mumbled, deep in his sleep.

Farquharson went naked to his bed, and lay there—so successful, as Bill said, that there was no woman near who could just roll over and, so simply, love him. He lay like a map, a country, within the borders of his body. Garnett was the man in love.

25

January 30–February 8, 1966

THEY read in the paper that the Government had turned on the water in Akurẹ, and that the display of party flags, symbols, and slogans was absolutely prohibited. WP2471 celebrated its release from legend by a physical collapse: the steering failed. It had to be hauled off by a mechanic friend of Stanley's. Farquharson wanted to celebrate an idea by walking down Lebanon Street, but he couldn't get into town. Stanley didn't appear for supper, and late at night, when Farquharson went into the garden and found Stanley's sister there, he still hadn't come. He arrived at breakfast, dazed but exhilarated, and gave Farquharson a typewriter-sized piece of lined blue paper, written all over: "Work done on Car WP2471, 31.1.66," it said, and counted points:

(1) Both side suspension dismalte. ("Dismantled", he supposed it meant.)

(2) Pivot and king pin overhauled, news metal bushes remered and fitted. ("I will remer it tomorrow," he thought. "I wonder . . .")

(3) All suspension rubbers-bushes replaced.

(4) four worn out nut—(steering nuts), replace suspension shackle bushes replaced. (He began to wonder at the counting and started to keep track by hitting his fingers against the tabletop.)

(5) Complete steering removed and

(6) overhauled. All damaged parts replaced, steering worms replaced,

(7) steering gears replaced,

(8) steering ball bearings replaced,

(9) all parts checked and done.

(10) Wheel alignment done. Work start on 31.1.66 at 9 a.m. and finished on 1.2.66 at 6.25 a.m. Total bill £8.12.0.

"All that?" Farquharson said, having long since run out of fingers.

Stanley heaved the sort of huge sigh that might have come from complete sexual satisfaction, or from the truth, and said, "Yes, sir."

"Okay, take me to the bank in it."

He got the money and was served just slowly enough that he could savour the immobilized anguish of the people in the line next to him, and the almost contented meticulous agony of the man inside. "What am I to do with this?" he heard, as if it was a happy, light voice. "You have not signed on the right line."

The mechanic's house was well up on a hillside overlooking the Ọyọ road. The man was leaning over his railing, wearing a rich covering cloth with a roll of fabric around his waist. He greeted them like royalty, took his money, discussed the car, expressed concern about some parts of it but also about Farquharson's having to be the owner of it, controlled a couple of small children who were around his feet, congratulated Farquharson on having such a driver as Stanley working for him, and having conducted as much of an audience as he wanted, let them go.

"Is good mechanic, sir," Stanley said. "Very good."

"He kept you working, didn't he?"

"All the night, sir."

"Well, all you have to do today is drive us to the Kingsway and back."

"Sir, I have business."

"After we get back. Oh, by the way, it's payday."

Stanley smiled as if to a friend and said, "*Yes, sir!*"

For some reason, Joan became very bossy in the Kingsway and Farquharson quarrelled with her.

They rode home in silence; sulked, it seemed, during lunch; and then Farquharson stripped and lay down, and Jamie climbed up on the bed beside him. Harmattan was over: no more fresh wind;

the air was gummy. A fruit seller came to the house and they yelled at her to go away. Farquharson had to go down the hall into the dining room to order her off, and then, since he had put on his shorts to go to the door—not to save the fruit girl from embarrassment, but to keep her from having grounds for comparison—he thought he might as well get in the car and go somewhere.

Jamie said, "I want drive!"

If it was too hot to go to his mistress, he supposed he could make the wind blow his son. His bare back stuck to the plastic seat cover. They went almost up to Fiditi, and back again. Jamie, sitting alone, talked grave politic conversation, as far as he was able to. "Talk about trees," he said, and then, "Talk about Mummy now."

When they had come, Farquharson thought, Jamie had had only a few set phrases, and the passion to make patterns out of them. "Talk about toys," he said now.

"What about toys?"

"Talk about animals."

"Well," Farquharson said, suddenly remembering Jacob's New Year's Eve tableau, "what do I say about them?"

"Animals *jump*!"

"Ah, but you *make* them jump."

But points were being established. "Animals *sleep*."

"Animals," Farquharson suggested, "wake up again?"

"Animals hit people."

"Sometimes." Cocoa trees flashed by the window.

"People hit people." Then Jamie looked at Farquharson as if not too sure of this. "Far' hit," he went on, his eyes widening a little. "Man go to sleep?"

"No," Farquharson said, "the man got up and went away. How'd you ever get to talk so much?"

"Talk about Far'."

"Okay." He drove. "I am a big man, and I love your mummy." It was the needed small untruth.

But Jamie said, "Far' pee."

"You're in a remembering mood!"

"Far' carry me?"

"Up?" He slackened speed. "Not when I'm driving."

But in fact he did need to make water, so he got out of the car with Jamie on his hip, went into the bush and put Jamie down. Jamie watched with solemn pride. Then they went back again.

"Want to try to swim?" he said.

So when they went to the Club, he took him into the deep pool. Joan didn't like this; she was afraid of water. Just because it was all right for Farquharson . . .

He held Jamie carefully, floated him, made him put his hands on the edge of the trough, gave him a few minutes' lesson. Jamie got water on his hair, none in his eyes (by luck), loved it, and then said "Up!" and Farquharson lifted him into the hands of John Cord who had been standing at the edge of the pool, arrogant in a white world, envying him parenthood.

"I'll take him," Joan said, and did, and Farquharson said, just loud enough that she could hear, "John, I apologize."

The NCNC neon sign hadn't been lit for nights. Now it came down. Now there were posters everywhere, in Yoruba, with round photographs of Ironsi and Fajuyi, and the large headline, "IJOBA AMULUTORO". (Ì, low tone, he thought, prefix to make a noun a verb, to make a process into a state; je to eat; ò, low tone, I suppose, prefix making the one to whom something is done; ba, mid tone, to hide or be hidden. Ìje-òba: the act of eating the hidden one. The assumption of power, as Balogun had said last fall. "I bet it's a long time since there was a hidden òba in Nigeria," Farquharson said, "that is, if the word ever did mean that." He knew the dangers of an amateur's profound games-playing with another language: this was for himself only. The word meant what the word was used for: a takeover. An òba was a big man outside the Kingsway, with a fly whisk, being curtsied to by an old labourer with a load on his head.)

The poster was on every fence, on walls, even on Cocoa House. That, Farquharson found, shook him. Nothing had been pasted on

Cocoa House before. Indeed, there was a new age: IJOBA
AMULUTORO. "Amulutoro", he supposed, was "Military".

So the trees were in flower, the burnt cars were gone from
Ogunmola, the Russians made a soft landing on the moon and sent
back photographs. WP2471 with its new steering could in no way
be made to start only a day later; despite "winding" they had to
get a new second-hand battery, and a guarantee: "Sir, these
Battery under Guarantee for Six months and if There is any
wrong with it, it should be returned At once. Thanks."

Farquharson had had to write home to the college for help:
they had been sent five hundred dollars. He supposed he ought to
be worried about his money, but didn't want to be. But here was
another subject for minor quarrels. Prices were going up. She
said, "We lead normal lives, which is what we came for. You
know I never squander money."

"If we need cloth we buy cloth, if we need drink we buy drink.
And food. And gas. And a car. And servants. We do need them.
Why have we got an ironing girl?"

Joan said, "She does good work." He was being warned off.

"And you?"

"I can go teach in the children's school, can't I? They need
teachers."

He said, "Damn car costs money." Why did he have to push
her? He wanted her at home.

"The school does need teachers," Victoria said. "But then, they
always do. I really don't think she ought to."

He said, "*You* tell her."

Joan gave the idea up till the next crisis.

The former Deputy-Premier of the West withdrew from politics with a public flourish on Saturday. "Of all the marvellous
gestures!" Ormford said in the Club. "As if anybody cared!"

"Consider the poor man," Victoria said in the Farquharsons'
living room. "Politics has renounced *him*."

But it hadn't quite. He was detained, with about ten others,
the next day, taking some of the edge off the joke. "This is

296

not,"Victoria said indignantly, "the way one behaves to one's clowns."

Farquharson was at Gail's on Monday, tired and somewhat distressed, cooling in the bathtub while she watched. He said, "I don't have everything. I wish Bill hadn't said that."

"I'm fond of you," she said, "I've got no right to be."

"Have I got a right to be here?" he said, then sat up suddenly and put his elbows on his knees. The water surged.

"What is it?"

"I was thinking. We were over for dinner at Nwala's. She and John Akwukwuma are very relieved because it's all over with. They're safe, and the Ibos are going to be all right. Oscar and a friend are going to bring out another book of his poems to celebrate." His skin felt dank. "Nwala said they were really worried for a while."

"Well?" she said, looking at his hunched smooth shoulders and the green water against his spine. "Do you think they should be?" If she reached into the water, and put two fingers against the small of his back, and drew tiny lines with them, she could make him shiver and forget oncoming history.

"Why? The state of Innocence is where you think you have what you believe you have, and therefore have it. I have you. Thesis by Farquharson. John Akwukwuma has a safe country. Innocence isn't always wrong." He stood up. "Dry me?"

She put the towel to his chest, rubbed, and said suddenly, "Are you good in class?"

"Am I good in bed? It's the same man."

" 'Come hither, love, and I will read to thee A lecture, Love, in Love's philosophy.' " She had the towel at his hips, pressing against him.

Suddenly his face felt tight. "Just get up on the bed and fuck for me," he said. "I want to come in."

She had to be gentle and busy with him; hold him. He said, "I've got my dead men on my mind. Haven't I outlived them?"

She had to work him to keep him hard and happy; fondness

297

could do it, or could supply techniques. Finally he sighed as if he were slipping into a hollow of rest, and she gripped her hands against his buttocks and held him forced into her, as if hoping out of plain love to come, because she hadn't yet. But he was too spent to help her: Bill, she thought, was going to have to make it up.

Then she was in his arms and crying.

"That crazy fool's in love with you," Farquharson said, "with every one of his unhealed wounds."

"He won't ever marry anyone."

"He was married once, wasn't he?" He drew back to look at her, then put a thumb on her nipple and wiggled it.

"He divorced her and she died. He says he's had it both ways and he isn't going to have any more of it."

He laughed. He said, "Do you lie in bed with him, talking about me?"

"We do."

"I'm glad you came to my house those two times," he said, "to lie with me. Do you mind the Elizabethan phrase? It's better than 'sleep with me'. You keep us both awake." He sat up as if he had to, and looked down at her. She was a strange, plain girl. He said, "You do, you know."

"I used to be desperate to have a man," she said, stretching out below him, "but not to give him anything. You remember what I was like over that business of Ted and Bruce. Now I've got two men loving me, or at least as good as. 'Everyman,'" she said suddenly, reaching up to him, as he had to her, to put her thumb against his left nipple, near the heart (his big chest stretched them out, but his nipples were smooth with pressure and had soft flesh under them), "'God give you Time and Space.'" She patted him. "Also, you'd better go home now."

"I wish I could *sleep* with you sometimes," he said, getting up.

"Don't ask too much."

"I never have. When I think of it, I've made a habit of not asking. And yet if you don't ask for it, and do get it—it's almost as if you lost the right to it." He spread out his hands, making a show, he thought, of looking foolish, and said, "Oh well, *Thaes ofereode: thisses swa maeg.*"

"I ought to remember that?"

He said, "*I* didn't teach you. It means, 'That went by, this also may.' Whatever 'that' was."

"Please don't let 'that' be your marriage," she said.

There was nothing to do but tip her a small bow and say "Thank you." He put on his few clothes and walked into the furnace of the afternoon.

Lebanon Street wasn't unfamiliar territory: every day they came to the Kingsway they drove along a small half block of it. And he had come to Lebanon Street the night he parked his car and walked in the dark, trying to be sixteen years old. So when he drove to the Kingsway on Tuesday with Joan and said, "Let me off here; how long'll you be?" he knew where he was.

Just at the top of the street, the road curved gently over the shallow crest of the hill under a gaunt line of palms. The street they shot upwards from was an ugly one: searing blacktop, concrete terraces joined by cumbrous steps, dull painted walls of concrete and rammed earth, rusting roofs, wooden stalls crammed with cloth turning the terraces into stage sets, and the permanent jammed traffic line of dusted cars, most of them black—and then the dull people. Cloth was rectangular.

It was the lingering illusion of department stores, he realized, that made this odd. Cloth there was wound around a mannequin, rolled, or tumbled glamorously on a countertop. To find it rigidly flat, folded as if to make huge tiles, made it into different stuff. The stores were built of bricks of cloth—and it was hard to imagine the designs draped. His African shirts at home, being saved for Toronto, didn't help.

He started at the top, moving into each of the stage sets in turn, a little shyly, looking at what there was, as if he had to crane his neck or hold his body slightly on a lean; as if he didn't belong there and so mustn't let himself become part of things, but still

299

might watch: cottons or shiny tartan brocades. "Master, you want?"

If there was a Frog Princess in a fairy tale, he thought, she must have touched the Prince like that: a little, cold, delicate hand, with the back of the fingers wrinkled and the palm gentle. Sometimes, he thought, the senses shudder simply because they want to.

He cried, "I'm doing nothing but looking!" and made, without meaning to, such an expansive holiday sound that they all smiled at him, and two or three of them said, "Master, look here! Look here!" So he turned, looked, almost, as his feet moved, danced. They were such little women!

"Ọgá! Wá!"

("Wá sí mi!" to Jamie, in the living room, in Toronto, so long ago. "O fẹ́ bá mi wá?") He ought to have Jamie with him.

So he drifted, like a chip on water, down a stream of eddies and backwaters and sharp little surprising currents. Always there were voices and hands; always there was himself, there. Here there were purple butterflies; there there were fishes like Victoria's, but in the dragged-open spiral of Jacob's animals on the tabletop. The street sank lower; he sank with it, always on the one side, looking sometimes across the road, as if the other side were real. Finally he came drifting against a cross-street, and a set of tables on the other side, bright with head-tie cloths, and he found he was looking at the side of WP2471.

Joan said, "We had to wait for you. I knew you wouldn't get back to the parking lot. Can we go home now?"

"Did you buy, sir?" Stanley said.

Farquharson said, but to Joan, "I can see millions of shirts and dresses."

She said, "I don't want to wear them. The women don't here, do they?"

"I could wear one of those robes," he said. "Agbadas."

"With your pale head? Better take us home, Stanley, before Professor Farquharson turns into an ọba."

300

He thought, "Yes, Mrs. Michaelson.'

The street was a dance. If he left it, it was only to come back again. "Jamie," he said, "I'm going to bring you here next."

And his wife said, "No, you aren't," as if she had to reason with him.

26

February 14–15, 1965

FARQUHARSON shaved in the bathroom, bellowing *Vissi d'arte* for the first time in weeks. It was St. Valentine's Day; it was his wedding anniversary. It was also Monday, and the third of three lectures on *Othello* ("Negro, nigger, blackface, Pulcinello, 'A Bloody Farce' "), and he had gone on Saturday and bought material for Joan, for himself, and gone to Stanley's tailor in Mokola and said, "I want an *agbada*," and stood like a happy fool while they measured him. "Master, buy? Ọ̀gá! Wá! Oyíbó!" "How much a yard?" Consultation. Mutter: "Ṣílẹ̀ mẹ́tàdílógún abọ̀." Farquharson: "Ṣílẹ̀ mẹ́wà." Ultimate reconciliation at twelve-and-six. Further contemplation and regretful, firm departure. "Ọ̀gà! ṣílẹ̀ méjìlã." Riposte: "Ṣílẹ̀ mọ̀kanlã abọ̀." Collapse and victory: eleven-and-six the yard. Three yards, like a silk plaid of dark and silver grey, sparkling with geometrical fantasies of blue and green. Then he went into a store and got eight yards of something like shattered Paisley with huge borders in royal blue, and he ordered bright-yellow embroidery at the neck for it in the afternoon. He felt silly to be pleased, pleased also to have been safely silly.

"Do we get a present?" Joan said at breakfast, and he gave her the cloth. She thanked him—but she didn't go to the dress-maker's, so the glinting cloth stayed wrapped in its piece of sixteen-year-old newspaper.

"What is Shakespeare doing? Making a tragic hero out of a buffoon in blackface? It's a way of putting it. There isn't much tragic or dignified about a burnt-cork face with white skin under

302

it. Think of a Negro playing Hamlet under the same conditions, with his face covered with white chalk. The cuckold husband is a farce figure—Pulcinello played in a black half mask. But not like the mask of an Egungun dancer, because you can see the skin."

It was a month tomorrow since the coup.

"You," Joan said, "are going to have rest for once. Lie down."

He almost said aloud, "Do you think I'd fuck my mistress on my wedding anniversary?" but instead he caught a look at himself in the mirror, lay down, and slept. A young silver ring pressed into the pillow by his head. Joan thought about weddings in general and lay beside him.

It was as if a dream were trying to form and couldn't do it. He woke after more than two hours, feeling his mouth thick and hot. Some dread or attentiveness, something incommunicable, woke up with him. It was as if he knew who he was, and yet had had nothing to wake up from. Going into the bathroom was an attempt to create himself. So he stepped into water as stale and close as air, got out and dried himself, tugged at his genitals, and with that was home again; Farquharson, seven years very much married, ready to take on an evening with his wife. "*Vissi d'amore . . .*" They had steaks from the Moor Plantation for supper. "That was an abundant memory," he said when he got through.

Farquharson sang lullabies, "sad-songs" as Jamie called them, but Jamie was gratefully wide awake and wanted to be hugged. Joan said, "How you two love each other!" She might have been glad of it; Farquharson wasn't sure. "There's Mummy," he said. "What do you say to Mummy?"

"Good night!" Then to Farquharson, very precisely, "Put me to bed."

"Gosh, he's growing up!" Farquharson said outside the room.

"Well, I talk to him all day. So do the servants. He's *spoken* to."

If a door had closed, he would have been on the outside. He went into the kitchen, made them both drinks, and made her sit down and have one.

Then Stanley drove them to the Lafia Hotel. Jacob would babysit. They went up carpeted stairs with a mirror at the halfway landing where they could see themselves: Farquharson tall, sandy-pale, slant-shouldered, in a fawn-coloured suit buttoned by two buttons, and a hot tie pinched in a tiny knot till his collar buckled, with his rubber-ball nose and the long squared chin gouged as if for a dimple that hadn't fully happened; Joan in her white-and-yellow with the tie-dyed sunbursts and the malachite beads, her face precise as porcelain and too pale, her hair curled—black, shining, short—as if she were in a photograph. "Happy anniversary," he said, wishing she were someone else, and thus having to honour and respect her, and to be very fond of her.

The nightclub upstairs was called the Gangan. It was a faithful reproduction, probably, of what it ought to be: an ill-lit bar, with mirrored bottles and skyscraper stools; a dining room beyond, fading into a tiny dance floor; a band on a platform, under the huge fluorescent head and shoulders of a drummer in ecstasy. Apart from a table of six, they were the only people. They had a candle on a tiny table and faced each other past it, after they had first perched towering at the bar and been given easily the worst Martini Farquharson had ever had. They surveyed each other sidelong in the mirror. Farquharson gnawed at a hard olive. Joan, after one nip, left hers.

They had a menu at the table. Joan said, "But we ate steak."

"It's almost ten o'clock, and I'm hungry."

The menu called for scampi, so they ordered wine and scampi. It was suddenly unexpectedly comfortable to talk about themselves in Africa, so they did, as if they had been other people, and the place nothing but what it was. When the scampi came, Farquharson said one word of delight, "Venice!" and went luxuriously through the plateful in a series of small bites. They were as good as the Martinis had been bad, and, with pink wine, established the night on a basis of meticulous self-satisfaction and content.

The people across the room were a young couple and what seemed to be the parents of each of them. Joan guessed they were celebrating an engagement and, faced with a choice of being

304

sentimental or clinical, was sentimental. Either approach, Farquharson thought, would do for a country you didn't like too much. She said, "They look sweet."

Well, it was their wedding anniversary. He guessed they too had looked sweet once. He raised his glass. "Seven years?"

The abandoned fluorescent giant drummer had had the end wall all to himself. Now the band came back. Farquharson's blood jumped to dance, but before he could creep one foot to touch Joan's ankle, the young couple got up and took the few yards of dance floor entirely for their own, and Farquharson, frankly shoving his chair aside so that his long legs were parallel to the table, looked at them. They were young; they were sedate, seductive, thorough. He thought that Victoria was a better dancer but that these had an audience. He almost laughed when the man's *agbada* slid down his arm and had to be hooked high up in the air on his thumb, and draped again, while the attention to his partner and to the parents never varied. The girl moved like a three-dimensional S. The parents had a lot of fun.

"Now would you have done that for me," Joan said, "when you married me? In front of all our families and your great-aunt?"

"We didn't have the whole set. I don't know: Your father would have had a fit. Aunt Jenny would have loved it."

After a while one of the sets of parents got up and danced. The woman was huge, mounded with cloth; she looked magnificent. Then there were two couples, the same two, with the partners switched, and the young man, alert and self-content, dancing with the big elder woman—duty that had nothing to do with his not enjoying himself. Dance by yourself, Farquharson thought, but as a partner: all attention, and synchronization, but everyone was alone. It came to him that what he was in Africa was a dancing man. He said, "Try?" and they went out, hoping to be unnoticed at the edge of the other party. But the others left the floor, whether out of courtesy or not, and gave them all the room they couldn't use and didn't want. Farquharson felt the hula sneaking up on him, and Joan, though she tried, was too conspicuous to do well at anything that Oscar had tried to teach her, and in the end they had to dance in each other's arms for a long time, remembering who they had been, possibly, not saying much. The band was loud.

After a while another white couple came in. The engagement party came back to the floor and then left, exposing the room suddenly to white pretence being watched only by black waiters. And because sentiment and remembering and being under obligation to each other for whatever amount of a good time they were having were suddenly stiff and almost tiring routines inside the head, they had to find a way to come home out of their anniversary without either telling the other that they both knew why they were going. It helped, for this, to have been married for seven years. Stopping at the mirror on the landing going down, they saw the same faces and bodies in clothes that had gone up the stairs, only there was carpet and a view of the railing between them.

They had to make love: it was their anniversary, and seven years (and more than a few days) before, they had made love with economy, enthusiasm, inexperience, fun, and wonder as to whether there were more there. There hadn't been more there, except for a misshapen daughter whom her mother had called Evelyn before she was born, and then a boy whom his father named James John and meant to be loyal to. The bedded amateurs took fire, and died. They celebrated their anniversary by preparing to copulate because it was straight in their way and they would have felt silly not to.

She was so long in the bathroom getting ready that he knew she was having trouble fitting in the diaphragm again (sometimes she did), and since there wasn't much love in the act, there wasn't much amusement either. She made a brave try not to be bad-tempered when she came out; she suddenly, almost against her own intention, liked the big naked man—and he came to her as he should, and almost as if he wanted to, so much "almost-as-if" that he nearly fooled her, but didn't, so she felt like a prostitute, as he kissed her and lay over her—and as the big prick went deep into her, and gouged her, and moved, making its own man's time (as if she had to be pleased quickly), she thought that she might have been kept from contempt of what he did—and to her—only if there had been another man there.

He caught the absence, the dead inattention, the dislike. He had to be good for her. It was as if he were trying to bring life to her. He had to seduce her to wanting him, while he was still shunting and moving in her and over her, and he couldn't do it. Even when he had come (and he came, he thought, ungenerously), he still had to try. Everything she could master and make plain said finally, "It's all right," and he could get off her and guess what happened to her.

Fucking, dancing, the long evening, should have left him spent (and whether Joan slept or not he didn't even turn in his mind to notice), but he took the dull lukewarm heat of the night— and the air that almost had to be brushed away from his face to get a fresh breath out of it—and lay numbly awake, grainily attentive to every bit of it. Wherever his body lay, a flat unseemly discomfort of pressure worked in towards the bone, as if the skin prickled and had in some part (but not in self-knowledge), gone to sleep. His balls weighed and were uncomfortable; he could feel sweat on his stomach, stealing uncooling into the air. Obviously the sense of being alive came when you didn't want it to, and far from kindly, or comfortably: the fallen citadel, grinding away to make dissolution work for it—like everything else, rotting uphill to stay functional. (It was possible to go and see Akintọla's house, they said—Stanley certainly said, insisted that it was a fine thing to see.) *"But at my back I always hear Time's winged chariots,"* only he didn't, really. Didn't one have to feel being dead, at least as often if as indirectly (unpleasantly?) as one felt alive, to be dead? "Now I lay me down to sleep, at any rate to try to sleep, I pray the Lord my soul to keep, and to at least *tell* me about it?" Time sneaked a night against him. His wife breathed steadily; unaware, possibly awake. What she would be, it seemed, she was. He had to imagine her.

The extinction of sleep was unimagined, and a continuation;

307

the same indetectable temperature and air held his soul in, if he had one; held him down. Not fourfold Eden, out of the Blake lectures, if he gave them; nor the threefold state of Innocence, "expanded and released desire"; not Generation, the state of Experience, the double life, but Ulro, one-dimension, "single vision and Newton's sleep". Not awake, not *not* awake or he wouldn't have had the presentments of the language, without sound or time, and not attentive, except to the blocked unmaking of himself. If it was a dream, it failed. He faded in it, neither fixed nor random, steadily nearing nothing: rushing towards it, in time to his fading out, as if the last monad's knowledge was that he had to reach it.

He must have made it. There was no break to hideous, unending consciousness. He couldn't breathe, and he had to keep trying to, and he wrenched himself over in bed, stark awake from eternity, so afraid that he could only make uncouth noises and flop his hot dead arm across his wife, and then with the one arm that served clutch her to him, rolling onto the crack between the beds, with little noises of sobbing, as if he had to hold hard onto another life or he would be dead again.

"What is it, Farq?" She was afraid of him.

He clung to her. She could be the wrong person later. "Hold me," he said.

She said, "Whatever happened?" holding on, as she had been told, with wooden arms.

He finally could say he didn't know. "I didn't dream. I just wasn't." A man couldn't remember if there hadn't been anything. . .

Oddly, with the last warming ripples of fear, he simply rolled onto his side and lowered himself into sleep, neatly, comfortably, and within a few seconds. She covered him. Not even in his panic, not even holding her, when he had just come to life, had he said he loved her.

Stanley, when asked, was full of praise for the idea of going to Akintọla's house. It wasn't clear why the government had opened the house, but Farquharson was assured the house was open and that it was a very interesting sight. Joan said, "Oh, to be a ghoul!" but he said, "This is the world we're in. We're going to go." Death needed more than a frying pan and a panic in the night: it needed a place to have happened in, signs. This was his own made country—didn't he have to have his wife and son look at it?

They went. They turned corners in a rich suburb until Farquharson lost all track of what direction they were facing in; Stanley might have decided to make a maze. And then they turned up a short straight street with a high fence wired at the top, and so many cars parked in it that it might have been a parking lot. The locked gateway opened between in-curving pieces of a stone wall, one of which had a door in it. Farquharson went up and watched, leaving the others in the car. If anyone noticed the car, he refrained from staring. The intermittent legend of WP2471 was gone.

Around the house there was no shade. A pale driveway led between curbs to a large, plain, ugly house set sideways to the lot, with upstairs balconies, and a box of concrete grillework before the door, with a room above it. A soldier seemed to be coming to let in a small group of people, so Farquharson signalled to Joan and then had to run and fetch her, and she said, "Not Jamie: no!" So Stanley was philosophical, and they went away from the car hearing, "Drive, Jamie, drive! Turn now."

A man called "*Oyíbó!*" and gestured to them to run before the gate closed, and so they ran and got inside, past a soldier who seemed almost implacably inattentive. The gate locked. They were on the driveway. He made sure to walk beside her.

Somehow they had both expected a palace. Even seeing through the gate, Farquharson had expected a huge house, worthy of the corruption that had made it. It was just another moderately big house in an Ibadan suburb: heavy, and rather blank, with slightly eccentric colour. Windows, of course, were broken; it seemed as if every pane on the façade was raggedly split between a sort of blind dirty-grey and black. The upstairs balcony on the left had concrete railings; in places they were shot away to the reinforcing metal. Random bullet craters had bounced out of the walls in circles, all of the same size. Around the balcony most of the holes overlapped. French doors opened onto the balcony, and there was no glass in them except for a few bits stuck in corners. "Then if he harangued them at all," Farquharson said to Joan, "it was from up there."

They went up to the front door. The concrete grillework was painted a peach colour; the sheltering box glowed with pink shadow. They looked into a semicircular entrance hall almost filled by curving stairs. The floor was thick with glass. She said, "It's such a *cramped* house! You'd have thought he could have done better."

"Maybe it was defensible."

He turned around. Someone had written on the inside of the plain front wall of the box, in quick black lettering: "*Rest in Hell, Akintola.*"

They went around the house. It needed paint. But all the walls now, and the outbuildings, were covered with the black letters, saying, "*Rest in Hell,*" "*Burn,*" and probably vicious statements in Yoruba that Farquharson couldn't read. At the back were the palm tree, "AG" and scattered dots of the Action Group. He wondered that the new Government, forbidding political displays, hadn't blacked it out. Joan said she guessed the soldiers who were here felt differently.

The place was desolate, cheap, and raped. What it was necessary to see, they had seen. They went back to the gate, Farquharson hanging behind, and were passed out through a small guardhouse. Then they had to wait while democracy sent Stanley to look around for himself. "Well, Jamie," Farquharson said, "one day you're going to say that you didn't at any rate see *this.*"

He wondered where he would have been, if he'd been there when the soldiers came, the murderer of two men already. Where did Experience put you when it came to the thing again? Fornication obviously made adultery easier. He couldn't think, now, if at home, of fucking only for Joan, only for obligation, kindness, and because he wanted to. He had fired Elias. If he had to, he could fire Stanley, though it was hard, here in a piece of shade, to think of a reason to. Experience was of what one *did* do; what one *might* do was always a matter of the state of Innocence, not recoverable at any point because not, until any decision at that point, ever lost. Then the decision to refrain was as much a fall into Experience as the decision not to. And the question for the class was whether, where, or how paradox became paralysis. It certainly wasn't much help to a decision about the moral reformability of murderers.

On their way back they took detours for the fun of them and were stuck in a police-halted line near the clock tower. Farquharson saw letters on the back window of a little car in front, perhaps decals. They said, "*Say Folly*". He wondered, going home, what he would have put on his own car.

"Did you notice," Joan said, "that there were women selling oranges outside that house?" He said he hadn't. "Well, you see what you want to. They were doing a roaring business."

He decided about the inscription on his car. One of the wooden buses said over its windshield, "*Ọmọ nâ dé*". This he had figured out to mean, "*This Kid Gets There*". (It was better than "*God's Time Is Best*" or "*No King Is God*".)

"*Ọmọ nâ dé*": *Child* (emphasized) *arrives.*

Child (emphasized) ate in a dining room through which he had chased one man to kill him and dragged another. Child (emphasized) kept in his pocket a dead man's sixpence. Child (emphasized) moved between his wife in the kitchen and his mistress in the living room, carrying beer at night, and a tray of things to eat. Child (emphasized) taught. Taught well. The third year was smoothing under him, like proper velvet. (He had spoken to the head of the department about Adebọwale.) Pitched battles with the criticism classes were becoming rituals of discovery. He went out to the tailor's to get the blue *agbada*, and he didn't know how to drape the sleeves, or what to do with all that cloth when he sat down. Joan told him he couldn't wear it if anybody came, so he went over to Victoria's and asked her if he looked a fool. "You look Yoruba," she said, "and really quite silly, and handsome."

311

He was too incongruous, he decided, not to let them give him a beer, and he had to listen to tales of the coup in Lagos by men who wanted to be thought to have had to do with it, and who tried to ignore his embarrassing attire, until he left. Victoria said in his ear, at the bottom of the verandah stairs, "I think it's a splendid colour. Wear it a long time. And don't worry about showing off in it, that's what it's meant for."

Ọmọ nâ dé. All things conspired. Gail let him fill her; the students lent him their minds. The killer's hands were good. They gave him a country. The dream of extinction did not come back.

PART FIVE

27

THE heat climbed. One day Joan was dizzy with it and sent Farquharson to the Moor Plantation to buy their meat. The sharp pink, white-boned carcasses were tossed around and cut apart with quick knives, in shade among busy peering women. Everything had a clean, happy air, and the walls shoved in. It was as if suddenly he had cut his men, and seen them, and he remembered the slash in the throat of the dead steer by the airport. Bodies were unexpectedly brighter than he had thought. He went home with a dread of what they did, but still with an appetite. Truth freed a man in odd, grotesque, happy ways, but he would leave Joan to do any further shopping there.

Farquharson was used now to having his back oily with sweat and to forgetting about thermometers, because heat wasn't degrees but enclosure and oppression; the air seemed parched and sodden at the same time. Anything wet—spills on the floor, clothes on the line—dried almost instantly, but a man lived somehow under a plating of his own sweat. He walked to Gail's in the afternoons (fewer afternoons, and sometimes not to couple and gasp but to lie on a bed in a chilly room while thin fingers smoothed and comforted him with a dampish towel), and the path around the playing field took him past yellow alamanders and hedge plants dry and hot as sticks. Strangely, it was almost worse in shade than in the sun. Sometimes it felt as if his head could burst; his short hair, skinned above his temples and the back of his neck, prickled like pins, and his coxcomb, cut shorter now than it had ever been, fell down and stuck up and trapped dead heat against his skull. He would reach her door with his

315

eyes swimming with too-strong tears, and a brain stupid and obsessive about nagging accidental things. Sometimes he came in with his shirt-tails flapping in hope for wind. "I suppose people know about us," he said, shut into the bedroom, with suddenly cold air cutting across the upturned small of his back.

"What if they do?"

"Well, there's Joan," he said. "How's Bill?"

They were laughing naked in each other's arms, and it was easy to be a husband to her.

Bill worked, healed of his various injuries; more sad-faced, but less set on the tragedy of being Bill Garnett. Being Bill Garnett was becoming interesting, for a while; to be part of a three-cornered fucking pattern where nobody resented anybody and the rivals were increasingly necessary friends reassured him. Like the others, he rather wished he could like the fourth with whom they so often were, drinking beer or one of Farquharson's peculiar experimental cocktails, but Joan had not only decided not to like Farq's Africa; she was becoming, he sensed, semihysterical about it in an almost deliberate fashion—and she wasn't letting her husband see. He took to calling at the Farquharsons'—partly, he said, because she had been his patient briefly, partly just to keep an eye on her. Usually she was waiting for her husband to come home for lunch. Sometimes, when he knew where Farquharson was, he came in the afternoons.

Joan didn't like him either, particularly, but he gave her a person to complain to and he listened to her talk about how Jacob had to be told what to do ("I have to steer him," she said, "like a vacuum cleaner!") and about prices, unpunctuality, lack of cleanness, pushiness, Hausamen, petty miserable dishonesty, unlikeableness, how Farquharson didn't see any of it and liked it if he did, how there weren't really any friends but expatriates patronizing them on one side, and Africans condescending towards them on the other, "but not ever asking you in", isolating them in special occasions here and there. And how Farquharson loved the place, and couldn't tell her why, and didn't even try to share whatever it was he felt.

Bill bowed to each self-exasperating outburst, sympathetically (clinically) tried to steer it, quiet it, neutralize it; behaved to it, in fact, almost as if he were the husband of it—which was what he owed to the other body of the mortal rival, he supposed. He couldn't know what Farquharson was giving Gail beyond sperm and motion; whatever it was, Garnett was released from having to produce it, so if that were true, as divorced dead wives were true, then questionless he loved Farquharson as he might love air or the sustaining ground, or the fellow soldier present to absorb the bullet, and might when the time came injure him out of the need to have something to do with love. Possibly he was doing the injury now, wearying a wife's complaint, detouring it from its true healthful target.

So he played with Jamie to keep *him* from hearing his mother's anguish, and beat down the desire to walk in on Farquharson and Gail, and so share content and comfort. The doctor in him mapped what he thought and knew, and gave verdicts that denied innocence, and diagnoses that denied hope, so he made his endurance out of what he could, and had no intention of calling it honour. He had had a dead man in the front seat of his Land-Rover; he distrusted the Nigerian honeymoon, and waited for violence on the compound between Ibo and Yoruba, swearing to anyone that it was going to come.

Farquharson carried Jamie down Lebanon Street. The women reached as if to fondle his arm, or the child; Jamie looked back large-eyed, and seemed to establish wary possible liking, distance, and dignity. Farquharson said, "What do you think Mummy would like?"

"Here is very nice," a woman said.

He held Jamie close to the stacks of cloth, waiting for him to touch a bright-red stuff close to him, but Jamie, after a long time of studying what was within his short arm's reach (and not looking, Farquharson noticed, at what he couldn't reach), put his hand out

317

to a checked material of yellow, turquoise, and yellow-green. "You want that one?"

Farquharson signalled the woman to spread it out, and, huge in her wrapped hips, she did, beckoning to a little girl to hold up the other end. Farquharson and Jamie looked at a swag of curiously self-defeating colours. What hadn't shown, folded up, was a scattered repeat of a bright-red rooster. He haggled the material to ten shillings the yard, paid two pounds, strode back to his car, very whole and pleased, and took Jamie to the dressmaker's. Sitting in her room, with Jamie on the thick arm of the chair, his feet kicking against his father's legs, Farquharson went from page to page of the pattern books looking for the right happy dress, and finally said, "That, or that?" flipping a quarter inch of huge pages from one side to the other to let Jamie see two dresses. This time Farquharson wasn't going to guess which one he'd pick.

Jamie said, "That one."

"That one" was a stark evening dress, almost featurelessly plain. It wasn't either of the dresses Farquharson had put up for choice. "Not this one?" he said. Jamie said, "That one," so that one it was.

Mrs. Ezeokoli was enthusiastic. They left her jotting notes in a notebook under Mrs. Farquharson's measurements and met Bill Garnett in their house, going home.

"What did you do?" Joan said.

He said, "You'll see."

"Farquharson," Bill said from his Land-Rover in the shade, where Farquharson had accompanied him, "does a married person have a private life?"

There was a president's coup in Uganda; Azikiwe was booted from his position as chancellor of the university in Enugu; Kwame Nkrumah went to Hanoi, and there was an almost hilarious coup in Ghana. The former politicians of the Eastern Region were at last arrested, and clouds piled up, futilely, every afternoon, towering. The second term moved, contentedly overactive, into its last month. Somewhere on the campus, Farquharson thought, there must be some kind of speculation. Mrs. Michaelson was almost effusively friendly when she saw him. "I wish that woman wouldn't act as if I were up for grabs," he said, and then wondered whether he should have. He was mired deep in what he called to Joan "the care and feeding of tragedy": spending hours on *Macbeth*. "Logic," he thought, "and what people do . . ."

"Okay," he said. "Tragedy is the downfall of a 'big man'. That leaves 'greatness' aside. Other things enlarge, then. You get the so-called 'high mimetic'—verse, insight, doom—everything to scale *except*"—he paused—"cause and effect, time and space, *other people.*

"But cause and effect clarifies. You get a form that insists on a single cause and a visible single chain of effects to the end; hence inevitability, catharsis, for the *effects*—especially at the end—and our old friend the tragic flaw, fault, at the beginning. And as there isn't any chance, or even possibility, of making a logic machine moral except as honest logic may be moral, the tragic flaw isn't morally measureable, *as the flaw*, though it can have any degree of moral value *as itself*. 'Given X, Y follows, and will produce Z.' What is X? *Anything.*

"The fuss has been about tragic flaw. It *should* have been about the logic. Flaws one can run into everywhere: they are, by definition, the ordinary item out of the tale. Life has them everywhere. But where does life have the logic?" He put his fingers on his chest. "I live, say. I have some reasonable collection of qualities any one of which could be a tragic flaw—but if I come to a downfall out of them, the chances are all but one out of a hundred thousand that whatever the dénouement—and it's incurably open— it's going to result from the operation of all the flaws at random, in random shifts, with lardings of accident, and with everybody who can impinge on me operating the same way. Unity of action, apart from the fact that it's all me, you aren't going to find. You couldn't find. Or could you?"

He had them; someone was driving a herd of cows on the road outside, and the students didn't stir, or turn.

"Is this why 'high mimetic' is a contradiction in terms? Why it has such tension? Maybe it's a shame to devalue a literary construct by trying to pretend a real life into a tragic one, but we've just been through the sort of thing that makes Shakespeare tragedies. Downfalls and deaths of big men: you can pretty well take your choice." He had rehearsed this.

"I have a story," he said, "(as Sir Philip Sidney might say) of a man, enthusiastically devout, brilliantly exuberant with words, a gleaming tyrant quite out of his own control. A man resoundingly cynical and yet naïve; a man who let his country turn into a chaos of murder and burnings, riot and thuggery, and so fell, in a reaction of puritanical righteousness and murder, which was only his own pattern made bigger and striking deeper. Is this the logic: going around the world like Cinderella's shoe, hunting who it can fit? The tragic flaw as a *gestalt*, a complex molecular whole, not a single quality?

"How do I put it? 'Cheer up, Farquharson, maybe you can be a tragic hero after all'?" They dutifully laughed at him. "Question," he said.

"If it is Akíntọlá," Mr. Enem said.

"Did I name a name?"

"Sir, no one will defend him now. The point is to use a real person. Let us have the name."

"All right," Farquharson said. "Samuel Ladipọ Akíntọlá."

"Fine. I am of the other party. But what you say, sir, is gossip."

"If I concede that?"

"Then you are *not* testing the possibility of tragic action against a fact. The Professor will forgive me if I say that his model is a fiction."

"Yes, but the real person is always a creature of the rumours by which we know him. I'm suggesting that this is what we have to know. The *right* rumour." He leaned forward. "Suppose I used myself, having to face the limitation that though I may come to the appropriate end, I haven't yet—and if I had the nerve to construct for you *my* set of similar qualities, and as truly as I know how, that would also be gossip, and a fiction, and you would still be left wondering over the corpse of Farquharson, in whatever way it came to show up, whether I had the logic, or it had me, or whether it was all fiction. We're all tragic heroes if we can be total enough in our definition of flaw. Say that all flaw is a complexity grasped all at once, like a defining flavour. Tragedy as a form simplifies a taste to a single dominating ingredient. All scientific laws are gross oversimplifications. And they are laws. Tragedy is, perhaps, a law. All laws are fictions. Fictions are things made. Any attempt to understand ourselves works by making a model and studying it."

"May one ask the Professor what in his life or in ours could make one into a tragic protagonist?"

Farquharson said, "Cause and effect. I want to Be Who I Am." His voice dropped. "No details." There was a little scattering of paper sounds. A muted reaction, something unusual, he thought, in an African class. "And please don't go thinking," he finished, joking, "that the reason I wouldn't have tragic flaw as a moral is that I was using myself as a possible example!"

"Nevertheless, sir," Mr. Enem said, coming up to him afterwards, "isn't your last point one that any literary critic would have to make? The ego cannot think of tragedy as the consequence of a moral defect if it is bound also to think of tragedy as a thing that could happen *to* the ego?"

Farquharson had to gather up his books under a stare that felt like judgement. "Actually, it's original sin," he said. "See the Book of Job." And he got away.

"I wish," he thought mildly, "I hadn't killed myself off today. It isn't the right weather for it."

He told Gail about it in the afternoon. "Murdering Maintenance men," he said, "isn't a condition of personality, which is maybe where the whole thing breaks down. I don't know a condition of personality *for* it, except that for the couple of seconds it took to do, I was able to want to do it. I guess I was palming bad goods on them: I'd make a pretty inadequate protagonist. Stone cold dead in the market, through gratuitous happenstance."

The weather changed. The mocking clouds out of which rain failed to fall gave way on the eighth of March to a sudden wind, almost out of the east, and with its coming it was as if the lights went out. The wind was beyond the treetops at first: they didn't move. Suddenly they stirred, and the wind lowered and hit the ground, making a noise like sails cracking. Farquharson was watching from the garden, awestruck. He might have been looking up through fast, very clear water at the underside of dirty foam shaping to the waves and going faster than they were. "Farq! Come in!" Joan shouted, and he ran, and hardly got into the house to slam the windows before the wind blasted down onto the concrete, solid with rain, and drenched Joan and Jacob as they were getting the big patio doors closed.

Lightning struck. Jamie hid face down on the sofa, his head in a pillow. Farquharson saw him and ran, just as the power went off and let the brown, vicious stormlight take over the house.

When Joan turned from the doors, soaked, to see them, Farquharson had the boy held to his chest and was sitting with his head bent over, shielding him, being as absolutely as he could be the wall of parental flesh against death and fear. She had nothing to do but change to dry clothes by touch in the unlit bedroom, with wet luridness filtering the storm shadow at the windows.

Afterwards, they had candles and a cold supper, with all the doors thrown open so they could gather in great scooping breaths of the washed wind. Farquharson's ring shone like a soft star, but his fingers were swollen with heat and sweat.

Suddenly Joan announced that next term she was going to teach. She waited till bright noon, when Farquharson came home with tickets to a Ṣoyinka play, and told him after lunch that she was going to see the head mistress first thing on Monday morning. "There's a woman in the kindergarten going away, and damn it, I *have* taught kindergarten!"

"And Jamie?"

"I'll take him with me."

"And my lunch?" he said.

"School ends at twelve-thirty, you end at one." She burst out: "What the hell sort of a remark is that?"

"I don't want to see Jamie shushed down in a class of five-year-olds."

"Farquharson!" she said. "*I'll* be the teacher!"

"Quite. You're his mother."

Jamie had eaten and was dead asleep in an airless room. They were, in effect, alone with their marriage except for Jacob in the kitchen.

"It's all right for you to enjoy yourself," she said. "*I* can't? I enjoy teaching children. They also have to have someone."

"So does this house."

"When you're not in it?"

He thought about it, or seemed to (actually, his head was locked), and finally said, "Even when I am."

"I suppose it ought to reassure me, that you're possessive," she said.

But there was no end to arguments where all people could do was listen to facts and shape their own hurt to answer back.

She said, leaving the table, "*You* go out and work," and taking the trouble to sound wistful rather than vindictive, she made him sorry for her.

"All right," he said. "If I'm possessive, I won't be."

"I'm possessive," he said to Gail. "That makes her know she's wanted. Oh God, I don't want her beginning to guess!"

This was what conscience came to? A prickly annoyance that you couldn't always have your own way or butter both sides of the bread and set it down unsmeared? Gail said, when they'd made love, "Suppose she did find out?"

"You only write to the Advice-to-the-Lovelorn when you've made up your mind what to do."

"Well, you're *not* selfish!"

"Why not?" he said. "You have to have a self to give it. Don't kid yourself," he said, "I guard me. Apart from Jamie that's the only thing I do guard. I'm content to take very little, that's why what I get seems so much. But I'm bad at gratitude."

"Thank God for that," she said. "Gratitude's an awful thing. Poor Bill's got gratitude."

He said, "You give me comfort." Then he stopped talking and in a few minutes was as neatly asleep as his son, something no love could catch up to. So that was what Christ was doing, Gail thought, in becoming flesh: arranging that there should be love from somewhere for people who were as complete in themselves as Henry Farquharson. And yet she knew that a good wife could learn to hold him, and, in his words, make him content. She thought it would be a brave thing to do—because there would be no lack of reward, and, having tiptoed into the un-air-conditioned furnace of her living room, had, she supposed, to be grateful (whether gratitude was bad or not) that she wasn't the woman who had to do it. Besides, she had seen Garnett out at the road. "Don't trespass," she called, opening the door. "Come in."

He said, "Isn't he here?"

"He's asleep."

He came in. The door closed. He said, "What'll you ever do with both of us?"

She got him into the kitchen.

"Nobody's permanent," she said, "but I know when *he* ends. End of the school year. June. The man goes home."

"Am I the favoured one?" For something to do, she was making him a sandwich.

She said, "Nobody's favoured. You'll *last* longer."

"Poor Henry Farquharson."

"He should have had a wife."

Farquharson slept, alone, blown on by the air conditioning, dreamless, with his bones cushioned in the slack breathing muscles, and the tough heart squeezing blood in jolts. There was the sound of a car, a ticking clock, voices on the road, and a bird, going on and on, with a single pure demanding note like a radio time signal, on and on and on.

28

March 12–20, 1966

JOAN didn't get the kindergarten job. Someone was ahead of her. But she did have an interview with the headmistress, whom no one on the compound called anything but Lady Jane, "and she asked me if I had come to see their Sports Day!" she said. "Why should I? To teach kindergarten? But that was all she would talk about! Did you know that the running races are always won by Nigerian children?"

She wasn't petulant, he decided; she was just angry at herself. She had believed about something in Africa, and shouldn't have. Everything, even the meat from the Moor Plantation, had gone the same way.

So he said, "May I take you to a nightclub again?"

"Yes, but not that one out in the open. I want the European one."

So never mind the essays on *Macbeth*, he thought, and for one day never mind Gail. He had to be a married man.

Lying on his back, the tepid sweat trickling out of his armpits, he hunted for an occasion for the evening, some reason to have a nightclub. Then he remembered how Pooh and Piglet went around to wish everybody a Happy Thursday, put his clothes on, and got the car.

"Fisher!" he called. "Rise from slumber and can you go to a nightclub with us? It's the fourteenth of March! Well, if you have to invent an occasion," he said, "why not a simple one?"

"That's a pleasantly fine idea." Fisher's face clouded. He said, "Mrs. Funmilayọ?" uncertainly. "We've had a fight."

"Then make it up—we'll celebrate *that*."

He left Fisher, glanced towards Bill's balcony and then thought,

"No," and went to the Nwonkwos', found himself standing on the verandah doorstep, facing a silent house full of windows with African life behind them, and not wanting to disturb anyone, perched on the end of the railing until there should be a voice. A child cried. He heard Victoria soothing someone sharply, then a pause, and then the sound of slippers on concrete, and she was coming through the closed verandah towards him, in a dressing gown, her face delicate, soft, and sourly wise. She said, "Henry, how long have you been here?" mockingly severe. Then she sat on the railing with the space of the steps between them and said, "Now then, why have you come?"

So he explained about the fourteenth of March, and then he felt awkward, because this was Victoria. "Jeremy says they've quarrelled, and I don't know whether they'll come or not."

"Have you asked Dr. Garnett and Gail?"

"I wasn't going to. Is something wrong, Victoria?"

"No, of course not," she said. "I've had a quarrel with the whole Clinic over a misdiagnosis of one of the children. I don't know which I don't want more: Dr. Garnett defending Dr. Foley or attacking him. I've had an exceedingly sick child, thanks to them." She said, "Oh, it's all right now. That wasn't Ogbu you heard, that was Nneji."

"Well, will you come with us?"

"Let me tell you," she said, "when I can wake Oscar."

They were six at the Gangan, three and three, white and black. And they could forget it was the fourteenth because Mrs. Funmilayọ was there, and Oscar was flirting with Joan, and Farquharson could dance with Victoria with all the room he needed for his mistakes, and discuss Joan with her when the band was loud enough.

"Remember," she said carefully, "you've had more happen to you."

"Come now," Mrs. Funmilayọ said, almost at the end of the evening, "I must have one dance with Mr. Farquharson. He has made me come here."

Farquharson had his hands in the air as if he were going to leave finger marks on plate glass. He felt as if he were dancing sideways, not to come too near, as if there was a copyright on her and he didn't have it. "Jeremy says you didn't know we had a quarrel," she said. "I thought everyone on the compound knew. Thank you for making us give it up, for the time being, at least."

Farquharson wondered what the quarrel had been about: the steward's niece? Or perhaps (remembering Oscar) *her* infidelities? So he said stray gallantries. They were dancing to make fun of each other by the time they stopped. And Fisher was jealous of him.

They had to go.

Joan said, "*You* enjoyed yourself."

Farquharson said, "You did, too."

Three cars spurted down the same road, severing from each other.

"Why didn't you ask Gail and Bill?"

"The point is," he said, "did you have any sort of a good time?"

"Yes," she said, "I did."

He thought, "All right, she was tired." He looked in the mirror in the bathroom and accused himself of manufacturing discontent for no reason that would do him good—in short, of doing what she did—but what he really wanted to think was, "I gave her a day, I put a day on this. For what I got out of it I might have had a different day." Of course, he had had fun even with her—and they had eaten scampi—but now with this familiar stranger in the mirror who looked as if his Adam's apple had been smoothed by force into his neck and as if he ought already to be doing tomorrow's shaving (shining fawn-red stubble) there wasn't any fun: here he was, with a toothbrush and dancing loins, turned away again. He put his hands up as if he were going to dance with Mrs. Funmilayọ, and watched his reflection mock contentment and then assume it. "To the sufficient," he muttered across the first sting of toothpaste and the interference of the brush in his mouth, "all things suffice."

327

Only they didn't, really.

It should have been enough to go into Jamie's room and look at what he protected, laughed at, and without fear loved. In the end he fell asleep on the bed beside the crib. That he was missing from an unslept-in bed gave Joan real fear in the morning; she wasn't reassured to find him almost unwakable, worn out by dreams, with flushed face and a foot trailing onto the floor.

Stanley took WP2471 out of the garage, and when it bounced once at the foot of the garage ramp there was a noise, and one corner of the car slumped over a broken spring. Stanley's mechanic friend was in the Mid-West. His substitute bullied Stanley, and, because Farquharson was too hot to bargain as he should, charged too much, occasioning much bad feeling and stalking from the patio to the garage and back. ("How far?" Farquharson thought. "Fifteen feet? Too short for a processional or any sort of dignity; one might as well try to force respect and honest dealing out of a home in a cuckoo clock.") His temper didn't improve when the resprung car failed to start and his guaranteed battery was found crusted with eruptions of acid. Stanley was sent with a note to rent a battery from the Motor Transport Department, and then with another note to the giver of the six month guarantee to get another battery. Farquharson had been going to go to Mrs. Ezeokoli's to get Jamie's dress; he ended in the Club.

Gail called, "Hi!"

He went to the bar beside her. "Sorry," he said. "I've just had a bad two days."

She ruffled his hair, almost, she thought, as if she were a man, needing to express comradeship without involvement, and said, "Go on and take your wife a drink."

Jamie and Stanley were parading around on the lawn below the swimming pool. Farquharson could see people turning to look at them. He took Joan her drink. She was looking carefully into a case of rings. "I've been looking for another one here like yours," she said, "but the girl doesn't remember."

"Good heavens!" he said. "What would you want two for?"

He wasn't afraid; he was, remotely as if there had been an explosion on the radio with the sound turned almost off, horrified.

And he couldn't go to see Gail, even in the evening. She was involved with the Ṣoyinka play; her house was dark and didn't even have Bill's Land-Rover in the driveway (her Honda was at the theatre). He remembered her coming down the spiral staircase and being rude to him. He had to say to himself, "I do not feel lost," and he was so childish in his mind about it that he climbed all the way up to the dead air at the top with sounds of a play below him, and with nothing to think about except that he had only one more Shakespeare lecture, one body, and one mind, and that he couldn't see the stars.

To get the guarantee on the battery to work took another irate note, and another day on which Stanley took the car for himself and finally came back with a battery, a look of triumph, and, still in his hand though mauled, the guarantee. His face was running sweat. Farquharson sat him in the living room and made him drink a beer, and Stanley, carefully drinking, said, "I do two things today, sir. Sir, I am engaged to marry."

A few more mouthfuls. "Sir, I ask permission that she live here."

"And your sister?"

"She gc to live outside the Gate, sir. At the market."

"Oh hell yes, sure," he said, envious. "Somebody's love life has to be openly corrupt. May I wish God's blessing for you?"

"We thank you, sir." Then he gestured to WP2471. "Sir, it is by this car, before New Year, that I first bring her to Ibadan. Is it in your mind, sir?"

Farquharson put his hand on Stanley's shoulder, then cuffed him lightly, as if the gesture were part of a piece of thought. "Greet her for me," he said.

The Ṣoyinka play was about political dictatorship in modern African countries, specifically an imaginary and entirely Yoruba state. Farquharson couldn't quite figure out what he thought of it. A still-powerful ọba clashed with a robotlike modern dictator named Kongi. On the dictator's side were a coven of advertising men; on the ọba's a memorably quarter-witted servant, such as no white author would have dared to write. ("My God!" Ormford said to them at intermission, finding them under a palm tree. "Did you see? Nicodemus!") There was a pair of modern lovers in the middle—and the plot was presumably whether Ọba Danlọla was or was not going to perform the harvest ritual and thus submit to or legitimize Kongi's government. Then there was dancing, the stage full of girls and people—undergraduates, a lot of them—with nothing but drums, and an old bugle with four notes, extraordinarily filling the air with the illusion that this was music.

When it was all over, the heroine had left a decapitated head to be unveiled in front of the dictator instead of the first yam of the harvest, and the stage emptied—except for Kongi, ranting into the sound effects. Then the lights went down, and up, and there was the empty stage, and the head. The programme said, "III. Hangover. Kongi Square," but nothing happened. It took the audience about three minutes to realize that nothing was going to happen, that the play was over. "III, Hangover" might be themselves, but was probably just as easily something unresolved on stage—and in either case they weren't going to find out about it by staying there. So there was hardly any applause, and no curtain calls, and the audience, balked, went out. Gail was waiting, and said, "Well?" But there didn't seem to be anything to say.

"One thing about tragedy," he said to his class next day, "is that there is an end. What is wrong with *Kongi's Harvest* is that it takes the action to the breakdown point where nobody can imagine what any end would be, and so there isn't one. If it were possible to provide an end for *Kongi*, it would be because one had been provided by the world in which *Kongi* was written, and in that case it wouldn't have been necessary to write the play. Where that takes you, I don't know. Maybe I'd better be a coward and finish Shakespeare." And to his sorrow, that was what they wanted him to do—even though two of the dancers from *Kongi* were sitting in the class.

No solution, no way to depose the rational hysteria that takes over from the sanity of sensuality and comfort. He regretted a good play lost.

Still, he could end his Shakespeare with a good deal of bite and passion, doing *Coriolanus* and demonstrating the devastating neutrality of the ultimate political play, and where tragedy ended in a self-divided state of citizens. It didn't hurt to have *Kongi's Harvest* on the side, in the consciousness of something over half the people in the room.

He was going to wind up to a peroration and a finish, but there was a small commotion among the pretty women in the third row. Someone giggled. Farquharson let his voice lift into a question. They flustered, and something dropped.

Loops of magnetic tape were coiled across the girls' skirts so that they didn't dare stand up. With a sort of triumphant embarrassment (and pleasure), a small battery-driven tape recorder was lifted up. The tape must have been spilling slowly for a long time. They were suddenly all trying to get it wound again. Farquharson put his hands behind him, heaved himself on to the desk, and made his great happy laugh. "And I thought you were all listening so well!"

It was one form of communion in which a course could end. Everybody crowded around, offered condolences and suitable observations, grinned and laughed with him. Farquharson leaned to the girls and said, "I don't know if you meant it, but this is a great compliment." They might have been at a stand-up party. Finally, the tape was wound. The embarrassed possessor looked at him.

"Go on," he said. "I have to hear me!"

So his voice came back. The machine ran slow. A ponderous overbass pontificated tinnily.

He said, "No, I am *not* offended."

He started to laugh again during the tutorial, to Mr. Adebọwale's bewilderment. Mr. Adebọwale was at that point trying to frame a question about one of the bleaker parts of Joyce's *Dubliners*.

("Sir," Miss Ogoruvwe said, "would you discuss for us the ways in which O'Casey indicates his concept of the value of patriotism in *The Plough and the Stars*, Act One?"

"I have never before," he said to Gail, "heard anybody ask a verbatim examination question as if it were a real question. God, what preliterate rote learning and fundamentalism have to answer for!"

Or, as Farquharson said on the occasion of the question: "No.")

But Mr. Adebọwale was a student, and a thinking man. "This at least," Farquharson thought, "I have helped do."

He said to Ormford, "What is the third term?"

"Nothing really, a sort of hh-holding operation."

He would have a haircut. He wanted to move into the holidays with no plans to go anywhere. He was tired. He wanted just to enjoy the vacuum of a country now without politics, a happy world where the rules were known and injustice was being done only to the popular villains of the old order. He was waiting for his thirty-eighth birthday at the end of March.

The barber appeared on Friday. They had forgotten about him. Farquharson came sleepily to order him away and the man went. Farquharson's wallet was on one of the little tables in the living room; he had come in from the Kingsway and emptied his pockets. When they got up from their siesta it wasn't there.

"Eighteen pounds," Joan said. "You just leave out eighteen pounds. And I suppose all our papers."

He said, "Not much that matters here." It was a poor excuse, but he didn't want blame. He wanted silence in which to get used to theft.

Joan said, "Did Stanley take it?"

"He's honourable."

"Jacob?"

"The barber? What about your ironing girl?"

"She never comes in the house."

He said, "Don't be so angry at me!"

"*Why* don't you want to think of it?"

By that time they had been quarrelling for a half-hour. And had searched the house. Then Jamie stopped them. He said, "Far' and Mummy, always mad." And Farquharson bellowed, "Stanley!" And they were off to the Club again.

He crouched beside Stanley on the grass, looking pale and big, and told him about the wallet.

"Sorry," Stanley said. Like the woman on Lebanon Street who had said "Sorry" to him when he stubbed his toe.

But he didn't ask questions. They were able to crouch above the grass, allies in a loss, friends; Stanley making an earnest face, sharing sympathy and nothing else.

"Well," he said, walking dry-suited to where Joan sat beside the pool, and knowing that there were at least three women (not Joan) appreciating him as he moved, possibly because there was gossip now, "it wasn't Stanley."

"Oh, have your barber!" she said. "We won't get it back."

Joan told Jacob. Farquharson, listening to her, thought, "You know, that's cruel!" Then they went off to other things. Farquharson played with Jamie and ransacked his memory for the contents of the wallet, and Joan changed her clothes. And then they missed Jacob. Joan called "Jacob!" and then angrily, very angrily, "Jacob!"

They found him in the pantry, behind the door. They could have pushed his arms and legs into any position they wanted to. Even Joan, sure in a flash that he had taken their money, had to comfort him. She named the barber. Farquharson wondered suddenly if the barber hadn't had the power to force Jacob to steal for him, and wished that unhappy sick emergencies wouldn't blow up without warning. They had to lead Jacob into the kitchen. Joan was trying to say that it wasn't the money that bothered them, they weren't upset, but there were a few minor necessary papers, and who knew, maybe they had mislaid the wallet and

333

would he go and look for it? Then she sent him into the bedroom hallway and closed the door on him.

"What are you doing?" he said.

"Letting him put it back."

"He didn't take it." He felt foolish.

She might not have heard him. "I'm not going to break in a new servant now," she said, "even if he does steal. There just won't be anything he *can* steal from now on!"

Farquharson said, "You're frightening when you're like that."

And in the morning Jacob appeared from having put the wash into the bathtub and bowed in front of them, holding something out.

Farquharson's wallet, with the papers in it.

Farquharson took it. He said, "Thank you, Jacob," then called after him, "we never thought you took it, you know." But Jacob didn't listen. He went back to the bathtub, the steaming water, and the wash.

"What's in it?" Joan said, when she could.

"No money."

"I don't mind theft," she said, "but that's impudence."

"I don't think he has the money."

"Where did he find the wallet?"

"He says in the dirty clothes. He didn't find it last night, notice. I'll bet he had to go and get it."

"Then he knew who took it."

"Where it had gone," Farquharson said, "and I don't want to know more than that."

"Don't let anything change," Joan said, but things did change. They let Stanley have the car to take his sister to the market. He was alone for a day, and then friends took him away and brought him back in a taxi exuberantly drunk, as if he walked on balls of air. Joan wanted to visit Peg Ormford; Farquharson wanted to stay at home. Total intoxicated enchantment veered into their living room and offered to drive Madam anywhere she wanted, and Joan went. Farquharson, incandescent with a kind of bad delight, let her.

It was only a few minutes before Ormford was at the door saying, "Crisis. Your wife sacked the driver and is now sitting in our living room absolutely fledged with tears and you've gg-got a car to bring hh-home. H-hello, young man."

Jamie liked Mr. Ormford.

"He seems to have driven her almost off the road in every direction at top speed. I h-had to make sure he went away. My, he was drunk! Wh-why did she ever gg-get in the car with him?"

Farquharson gathered Jamie onto his knee. They passed Stanley sitting on the end of a culvert in the ditch, staring. Farquharson said, "Stop."

He left Jamie with Ormford.

"Madam say I have to go. I have no job."

Farquharson sat on the culvert beside him, and pulled a piece of grass. "You're as drunk as an owl," he said.

A dead voice, despairing: "Sir?"

"What can I say?" he said. "If she fired you, you *are* fired. I say what the Madam says." He added, "A party because you were engaged?"

"Sir?"

Farquharson thought of saying, "And now I know you didn't take our eighteen pounds!" He said, "Stanley, I want to hire you to be my driver, on a month's probation. Now go home and sleep it off. And for everybody's sake, move your young lady in soon."

Hope couldn't believe him. "Sir?"

"You heard me."

"Yes, sir. Thank you, sir!" Stanley was on his feet too, then staggered and sat down again.

And Farquharson said, "*You*'re lucky. Now I have to go and tell my wife about this."

And he thought there was nothing like loyalty to make a man a traitor.

29

March 21–30, 1966

IT rained now, evenings, gently on the whole. The days began in mist, cleared and brightened, were cloudless till the afternoon, then built up cloud on top of cloud in a huge high sky, until it seemed to Farquharson as if the earth were suddenly a bigger planet. Some nights there were sky-shattering thunderstorms. Sometimes then, for days on end, the rain held off. They would go out on the roads at night after the rains cleared and drive with the tires singing (and usually take in the International School By Night.) The rain was often warm; it was pleasurable to get wet in it. Sometimes the flying ants came, witless armoured biplanes, and they had to go around the house closing everything, or take to roads where the things were a snowstorm in everybody's headlights.

They began their vacation with everyone having fevers and laryngitis, and a bad temper. Farquharson couldn't even go to Gail's for most of the first week, and Joan got drenched in one cloudburst and was caught in such a spasm of teeth-chattering that Farquharson had to dry her roughly from head to foot, give her a brandy and hot water, and wrap her in the coat she had brought to wear in case London was cold. She sat in it all evening, shivering, and he was as sympathetic as he could manage to be, but it was funny, and she couldn't see it.

They were still sick at the end of the week, when Nwala Okagbue and John Akwukwuma were going to get married, and they had to send a letter of apology and say they couldn't come.

Jacob crept miserably around the house for days, knowing, Joan was sure, how rightly he was suspected; knowing Farquharson was sure, how he had been trapped by some power into serving theft, but, whatever was the truth, doing poorer work. If they had revenge, Farquharson thought, it was that they had to make him start every morning now by cutting the burgeoning crinkled grass outside.

Farquharson came out of the laryngitis, almost a week after the end of term, feeling rather lost. Joan said, "You were working on a book once—isn't this the time?" and he didn't know whether she meant well or not. Undoubtedly he might have to do a book some day, if only to show he could, but not here—not that Innocence and Experience weren't getting, as he thought, a workout. The states, when a man made only an indifferent job of being in either one, were easy enough to write about—he had a reasonably good thesis under him, how many years ago?—but when a man seemed to be operating full time in caricatures of both of them, it didn't seem the time to be passing judgements about literature, or the history of ideas. So he played with Jamie, lovingly, and yet with his mind half absent. They wound the tiny German cars and sent them around Gail's now somewhat dented metal mountain.

When he decided he wasn't going to be contagious at close quarters he went to Gail's (on a backwater now, with the street closed just beyond it), and found the Land-Rover in the yard. Bill stood in the doorway and said, "Hi, Henry, join me."

He walked back into the house. "Gail's in Dakar—there's a Festival of the Negro Arts. I came here to co-opt the perishables out of her refrigerator. That's a thing we do for each other." He added, "I'm late doing it."

Farquharson said, "She never told me."

"Oh, we found out the same hard way," Garnett said, "I spent the night here."

"With that out in the front yard?" Farquharson pointed to the Land-Rover.

"It's usually here, for all the good it does me. And don't for Pete's sake be jealous. It'd be a waste of time." He was loading a basket. "You know, if I had any sense," he said. "I'd refugee. I give this place two months."

337

It was going to be necessary, Bill thought, to cheer the rival, and this day, however much he might honour him, he could wish he'd never heard of him. This stripping of the refrigerator was a sort of melancholy, after-the-dead job, much like cleaning his ex-wife's apartment after the car crash. "If you think I might marry her," he said, "and you're in the way somehow, that isn't how it's going to be."

"When'll she be back?"

"Oh, the long days of chastity! I contemplate Nigerians, but I'm of the wrong build to please them. Don't take me seriously."

"Are you in love?"

Bill was worried for him. "*She*'ll take care of that if she ever has to. Look, do you feel the need to be in love?" He stopped to dig a finger into his shorts and scratch. "You just present yourself. Oh, it's grand luck, but everybody can have some of it." He pointed to where Blake's *Glad Day* had been Scotch-taped to the wall above a calendar. "There's you," he said.

"Where are you?"

"Oh, I'm a cultured doctor. Waiting to have love put to me so I can get petulant. But if I'm alone at night," he said, "I can't sleep. The late Mrs. Garnett doesn't allow for divorce, I guess. I'm not bad for Gail, you know, quite good. But we're of a kind." Garnett took the last thing out of the refrigerator and kicked the door shut (it fell open slowly). "*If* she is in love, then it's with you, not me. Not to be crude, you carry a hell of an advantage in your pants, not to mention that you are who you are—whatever that is. Neither of us can figure it out, even when we talk about you. God damn that refrigerator." He went back and kicked it again. "Damn thing's full of cockroaches, anyway."

Bill walked out with the basket, drew Farquharson after him, pulled a key out of his shirt pocket, and said, "Lock the door. Come on," he said. "I'll give you a man's drink," and drove him to his apartment and kept him there. With the air like hot glue they were supposed to sit between open windows and confess, as if they were undergraduates. They ended by discussing the government of hospitals and universities.

338

Garnett drove him back to his car. When Farquharson was standing beside the Land-Rover, ready to say goodbye, Garnett said, "Do you remember the night you came in with your wife's sample?" Farquharson nodded. "What did you think of me?"

"I had things on my mind. Thanks for the drink."

"No, you don't get away," and Bill reached out and caught him about the forearm. Farquharson looked down at the yellow pressure marks under the nails. "Look, I'm not going to marry her, I don't even mind joint occupancy. But *you*," he said, then: "I don't understand."

Farquharson said flatly, "What?"

Garnett dropped his arm. "The *Glad Day*," he said, "how you didn't lose it. Which means what the hell *are* you? You've got a bad marriage with a kid in it, you must be about five years older than I am. God, I haven't been innocent to enjoy things since I was about nineteen! What are you?"

"Thirty-eight the day after tomorrow."

"Congratulations. So you can walk in on me with my feeble little prick up in the air and not even be embarrassed by me." He reached for the gear shift. "I wish I could be locked into my skin the way you are. You must be contented right clean down into the bone marrow, just to be."

Farquharson nursed his forearm. "I woke up the other night so scared of death you wouldn't believe it."

"Join the club. Isn't that what fucking's all about? Only I bet you went right back to sleep."

Farquharson said, "*Somebody* went back to sleep," and got into the car to leave both of them wondering what was trying to get said.

Joan said, "And was she home?"

"What? No, I've been at Bill's. I've had three whiskeys. Gail's in Dakar."

So that, he thought, was what *that* tasted like. Joan came into the bedroom with him. She said, "Do you want to make love?"

He said, "Not in the middle of the day."

339

She "gave herself" to him in the night. Somehow he didn't want to look at her.

"Oh," he said, "it's the weather, dammit!"

"All right," she said, "it's the weather. I won't ask again."

"*I'm* the one who used to ask!"

"Yes," she said. "Well, I'm the one who did tonight. Believe it or not," she said, "I do sometimes want you."

"Christ!" he muttered into the sheets. "Glad day!"

He woke early in the morning tingling with an idea: if tomorrow was his birthday, he was going to get himself a present. He reached for his round startled glasses. To get to Jamie's room dressed and unshaven took only a few seconds.

Jamie was singing, languorously, full of peace and mischief. Farquharson got him into the bathroom, oversaw a dazed and accurate making of water. He wrote: "Jamie and I have gone to the cloth market, see you when you wake up." Then he woke Stanley and rode triumphant through the predawn, a man and his son, and the man's friend and servant, here with the cantankerous crazy slovenly city of his imagination. He had worn his *agbada* during his days of laryngitis, tangling in its sheets of cloth. Now he walked to the bell-and-bark sounds of haggling and greeting, with Jamie on his hip and Stanley behind them, a handsome uncertain guardian, brown as a black cat. Women clustered about them: Farquharson lifted Jamie high on his arm, to be seen as much as to see, and to make it his market.

Stanley helped a man unfold a piece of sand-coloured *aṣo-oke* and hold it up to view. Jamie shook his head. Farquharson said, "Ọkùnrin nâ kó fẹ́ ẹ," pointing to the boy: *The man doesn't like it.*

"Ah! Sorry."

So cloth was held up for Jamie to inspect. The game was on. They had to go from stand to stand, while people tried to win Jamie's approbation. "For Mummy?" Jamie said, in the middle of looking at a piece of brick-red cloth.

"For me."

340

"Crazy little kid," Farquharson thought, "so much beyond himself."

Jamie said, "This for Far'," and held his hand out to the brick-red.

Something like an animal was fumbling into his right-hand pocket.

He had never met a pickpocket. He had always thought his reaction would be a kind of sexually affronted rage. He said in an amused, almost kind voice, "Please take your hand out of my pocket."

The hand turned stiff, then jerked free. The wallet still weighed against his hip. Farquharson saw a young man back almost into Stanley's hands, then butt his way into the crowd. Stanley stood outraged.

So Farquharson set Jamie between his knees, with one arm around him, and settled down to the pleasurable job of getting his money's worth, and if possible, considerably more. During the bargaining the woman gave Jamie a piece of *akara* out of her bowl, while his father was doing as much of a strategic retreat as a man could do, squatted on the ground and being bumped into by passing people. Jamie nibbled, looked dubious, and thrust the ball up to Farquharson's mouth. "You eat!" he said.

With the dough ball up to his lips, and the market woman looking at them both with a look of arrogant commiseration, Farquharson opened his mouth, took a solid bite, said, when he could, "*Adúpé*," and added, gesturing to the cloth, "*Póùn kan*," but failed in the long run to get it for a pound and had to settle, since his legs were blood-starved, for twenty-four shillings for the two pieces and the *akara* ball.

He stood up to deal out the money and get blood down to his feet again. Stanley said, "Farq, that young man watch you."

Farquharson took out a pound note and four shillings, paid the woman formally, accepted the tightly folded cloth, and used the pause to consider what it must take for a Nigerian servant to use his employer's nickname. He was both pleased and wary. It was an important moment and mustn't be let hang.

341

He lifted Jamie into Stanley's hands. "Your turn."

They went through the market now with Farquharson as the guard behind. New sunlight hardened on the rust-coloured roofs and walls. Somewhere behind him was a young man in a pair of white shorts and a white shirt with a monogram (he wondered whose), but he had his fist in his pocket over the wallet, so that there wasn't any harm here for him. Stanley stepped out onto the blacktop road. "Sir," he said, "I wish to fight that man that want to rob you."

His name had come and gone; he was sorry.

"He follow us, sir."

"He didn't get anything, Stanley. He's inept!"

Longing for battle and sacrifice flared as duty forbade either of them, so both men were happy. "Stanley, what's your fiancée's name?"

"Celina, sir."

So he told them to wait, and before they could say anything he had turned back into the crowd again. He had seen one lovely cloth, teal blue and soft yellow in wide stripes. But he knew better than to be in a hurry, or anxious, gave the process all of the businesslike ceremony it had to have, got the piece for thirty shillings, wrapped like a big limp fish, dashed off through the crowd, came face to face with the pickpocket, said, "Oh, for heaven's sakes!" and went past him, utterly delighted. He sprinted out to the road, tucked himself into the car, took an apprehensive Jamie onto his knee, and put the cloth, still wrapped, beside Stanley. "Where does Celina live?"

"She come today, sir."

"Well, that's a present for her. Now, don't you look at it. That's for her."

"Our thanks to you, sir, please. I tell her, 'this from Farq'.'"

There, it was done. Farquharson added, "And Mrs. Farq."

"Yes, sir. You tell me so."

"Take me to your tailor, Stanley."

He was measured for a jacket of the brick-red in the tiny front tailor's room of the shop of Mǫkǫla, knowing that Stanley and

342

Jamie were in the car, far out at the road, sneaking looks at the new cloth. He could have sung out loud. He mumbled his scrap of *Vissi d'arte* and went home in triumph.

Joan said, "I got your note." Nothing, Farquharson thought, could accommodate that kind of dislike. She said, "I hope you had a *good* time."

"I bought Stanley a wedding present, for his fiancée. She'll probably come and thank you for it. Will you remember that it was your idea?"

"And if it wasn't?"

He tucked his chin in, to look down at her. "Shouldn't it have been?"

"I don't see why," she said. "He was drunk and fired."

"I hired him back."

"So that answers everything!"

He said, "Yes." Thank God Jamie was still outside. "Why are you so mad?" he said.

"You wouldn't care. You don't pay any mind to me."

"What have you got around your neck, then?"

She put her hands on the malachite. "Things," she said. "Presents. Stuff *you* wanted to buy."

It was too much. He said, "Go to hell."

Five minutes later he was wondering what sort of a fight it could possibly be when the two of them were helping each other, not saying anything to the point, not openly declaring one thing about why they were wrong, but uprooting together the pieces of a marriage, sometimes as if they had their hands on the same plant and it would need two to pull, because one couldn't. All that was the matter was that she was a woman alone in her skin, as he was a man. He could invade in love, rejoice in two skyrocketing human beings. She could be invaded, burned: that was all. It was hardly right that this sort of thing could come to a spread-eagling in a locked bedroom, with a stranger-man hot and urgent on top of her, but this was the only thing Farquharson could think of to get her to stop, to prove, if not fondness, that they were Jamie's father and Jamie's mother.

343

It was easy to fuck when all one had to do was kick down one's shorts.

She didn't fight him, even when he made her put her hand on his prick and tightened the muscles as if to educate her that this was what babies came from and would she honour it, please? She hadn't been glad when the first died, even when there had never been any hope of life, and the year was a miracle; she hadn't been glad when the second was born. Nevertheless Jamie was *her* son. If there were certain things necessary to keep him, and with a father, then she might as well have the fact of doing them: it wouldn't have to outrage her. She wouldn't have to fight down the exasperated, violent nerves or the pain. That would be all settled.

She tried to do the one thing she had to do to prove difference: she put her mouth on him. But he dodged, pulled her into the right place, pushed her down. She reached for his head, to hold that anyway.

He was rough. He rolled onto her. Suddenly she would have jammed her legs together, but he was between them. And he nailed that whole great thing in, and held it.

And she could take it. And she could close around it. And she could hold.

She would not, she thought, make an orgasm—fake one or have one. But he came, gracelessly, suddenly, with his mouth open, while she was clamping him. So she was stung, and came, and was not silent. She would not meet his eyes, and then did, and he could not have been more blank. "Did we have to wait till now," he thought, and put words in his head, lest he should say this, "to be compatible?"

He pulled himself out like a cork, and stood at the end of the bed, glistening and dead, looking at her.

"I want to go into town by myself," she said. "I want to buy you a birthday present."

"*The figurehead*," he sang, "*was a hoor in bed. And the mast an upright penis!*"

344

Jamie was asleep, but a man had to be brave and sing in his bath, when he had just committed adultery.

"A practical demonstration," he thought, "of what I could have had for years. I'd rather have her screech and glare and order me out. At least that's her."

Drying himself off, he wondered. He had taken particular care to wash his genitals. That, he supposed, said everything. Who would be Joan's lover and teach her things? Garnett, because he was her doctor? He supposed one Henry Farquharson might be mad as hell if it happened. An excuse to take Jamie, with justice, and go away. He was afraid. He mustn't believe in that. She was *his* mistress, by demonstration. And she hadn't learned any of it; she'd made it up.

A spent man does too much to ask himself for pity. He tugged at his genitals. "Why?" he thought. "To face the world." That decided, he could put clothes on.

He said in the living room, "Long live me," and took a glass of pineapple squash with a big belt of vodka.

He made Jamie's animals into a zoo, with towers of the fairy castle. They played on the floor, defensive men, listening hollowly for WP2471 to bring a mother with it.

She took the whole afternoon.

30

March 31–April 11, 1966

FARQUHARSON sometimes called his birthday a prelude to April Fool's Day, but it was an epilogue. Husband and wife lived quietly, and there was a single present, a brown-and-gold shirt, cut like a tabard with sides. He wore it when they went to the Club to reserve a table for the evening. They didn't discuss why they didn't want anything more ambitious; they agreed wordlessly, as exhausted people might, then had their afternoon beer. Jamie looked as if he was measuring them to see what had happened— and then they went out for dinner, into rain, and were waited on by the waiter from the Catering Flats who had wanted Elias's job. Farquharson would have been reluctant to remember him if it hadn't been his birthday. They extended their dinner as long as they could. The waiter asked if they remembered their servant Elias and knew what had happened to him. (Farquharson looked at a dish of chopped fruit and remembered the slope of the hill and the sound of his house keys changing hands in the dark.)

Elias had had other jobs. It seemed he was dismissed from one house because he stood for three hours in front of the sink, "with the cloth in his hand, sir," and didn't move.

"He was sick man," their waiter said, "very sick man. Nobody see him now."

"I should say he was," Bill said, when Farquharson asked him the next day. "We had him at the Abadina Clinic. Cancer of the stomach, aged twenty-seven. I forgot he was yours, or I would have told you. We had to send him home to die. They sent for me

346

then, I don't know why. There was a whole bottle of pain killer, almost the whole prescription. I don't think anybody gave it to him."

"When?"

"A couple of days ago. I guess your waiter didn't want to tell you that. It would have spoiled your party."

They had been caught in the lounge, and at the bar, with nothing to do but dance to a radio among strangers, or stare out into the multiplying overwhelming rain, the sheets of water gliding in from the entry, broken and overturning steadily into the swimming pool. "Very sick man, master."

"Well," Joan said, "it mayn't make you feel any better, but he couldn't have worked, could he?"

He was thirty-eight. He had danced. Joan in her new role considered that it was necessary for a man on his birthday to make love. Farquharson couldn't see why he shouldn't, because if there were sin there, it had been done.

"Stanley!"

"Sir?"

"Elias. Dr. Garnett told me he died."

"Sir, this is Celina."

A plain, rather delighted girl. She made embarrassed thanks for the cloth. "What about Elias, Stanley?"

"Sir, his wife cook him bad food, they say, for a long time. He die."

"And where is his wife?"

"She go back to Mid-West, sir."

A man uses much formality, Farquharson thought bleakly, in the presence of his beloved.

"Sir, he have bad pains. But he have three jobs, sir, after he leave you. You may be of good conscience, sir, after you tell him to go. You have not been his enemy."

"Cancer of the stomach," he said to Joan. "A man dies in agony, and all his friends say that his wife poisoned him."

She said, "This is *your* country."

And indeed it was sad if a man's wife could be his enemy.

The pool was muddy for days. The Club servants attacked it
with long-handled rakes and baskets, quite as if they had been the
villagers in the tale of the Three Sillies, trying to get the moon out
of the pond. Then someone put in a little asphalt dike across the
entrance path, so they had that to trip over.

Farquharson tried to take Joan to Lebanon Street. She had been
there, she said, to buy him shirt material. Only in the first store, at
the top of the street, where there was polite help, was she content
at all. She shopped there (since, she said, she had to), and got a
length of something almost ostentatiously not African-looking:
bronze and black, with yellow Chinese dragons.

Jamie trotted all over the store, touching everything in his
range gently, saying, "So *many* shirt!"

But by the time they were halfway down the road, Farquharson knew she couldn't see the point of it, so he stepped out into
the street with Jamie, dodging traffic, and signalled back up the
slope for Stanley to bring the car.

For the rest of the vacation Farquharson was like a man ob-
sessed, unable to settle or to get anything out of his restlessness.
And then, because he had to, he went to Elias's brother's house,
using the woodpile to remember which it was, knocked, and had
to speak to a large man who looked like Adebọwale but was, he
said, Elias's senior brother. Farquharson explained that he had
employed Elias for a short time in September, and had had to
dismiss him, but had just heard he was dead and wanted to say he
was sorry. He had not known he was sick.

"But sir, it would not have mattered. He could not work for
you."

"No," Farquharson said, feebly, "I know. I still would have had
to let him go. But he *couldn't* work. I suppose that's what I want to
say I'm sorry about."

"And you have said it, sir. We have to know that you mean it."

There was no reparation in apology, no being forgiven for a

deed not done. It was as if some kind word could have eliminated the man in the garage, and because the word didn't exist everyone had to say others, and it didn't matter. Could they have got Elias to a doctor in time? With cancer that he was going to die of six months later? "Joan," he thought, almost with hatred, "adjusting to Nigeria!"

Oh, it was unfair: what had *he* done?

Adjusted to Nigeria. Fired people without mercy. Given no charity (that at least was *not* adjusting to Nigeria!). Lain with an immoral woman. Killed twice for fear and certainty, with the muscles liking what they had to do. Up with the tough man's arm and the fourteen-and-a-half inch frying pan and the death at the end of it, tangible as the real dreams are. What was he to do? Walk in a strange city, sunburnt? Take an almost-three-year-old to a university zoo? (He was going to do that on Thursday.)

"Love somebody?" he thought. "Man is in love, and loves what vanishes: What more is there to say?" Poem of Yeats at the tail end of the last term. What was he doing, being sick not to have loved Elias? Not to have loved the Maintenance man, breaking the typewriter in his living room? Or being strung tense over how he had loved Jamie at that moment, because of all their mortalities? Or because he had to value himself so much, because of being stung so with the same mortality, then and since? Wasn't that what made him a lover? *Moriturus me saluto.* Aftermath of a birthday. He was the same old Farquharson; nothing was answered.

There was no rain all week. He breathed sodden, stale air, as if in a room with the windows sealed up with tape. If he refugeed to the Arts Building the trees in the courtyard were full of riotous purple flowers. Friday was Good Friday. He drove himself all week, doing nothing and being everywhere. Joan and Jamie had to be kind to him, because they didn't understand who he was.

"I want," he said on Friday, and couldn't finish the sentence because he couldn't think what to attach it to.

So Joan called Stanley and told him to take them all for a long ride, please—and the fact that Stanley and Celina were romping on the grass behind the house, out of sight of all but the kitchen, didn't please her. It was a not very chastened Stanley who got into the car with his shirt open.

Whether he was out to punish her or simply to obey her, she didn't understand. He drove them, moderately as usual, towards Ibadan, and once in it he seemed to shake the paved roads out of his consciousness and find one collection of ruts and holes after another. They drove past garbage middens like green ruined hills dotted with tiny goats. They passed stenches. They passed radios turned to full volume, playing Bach because it was Good Friday. The plangent mathematical stateliness of Christian mourning came blasting from rust-roofed houses, from transistors in people's hands, from stalls full of cheap twinkling plastic (not run by Christians), and from the affronted wealthy houses that stood leaping up from among the shacks as if on tiptoe. Organ music, with a brave set of trumpets. Nothing else was broadcast. Good Friday was a Christian feast.

Farquharson came out of his restlessness to be delighted. Joan, who didn't like music, knew better, she told herself, than to make fun of Christian religious music dutifully crashing over a pagan town—but she didn't know enough not to let show that she *wasn't* making fun of it. (And Farquharson hadn't taken Jamie to the Zoo this week, and he'd promised to. To have a grievance against her husband for anything not done about Jamie was so new she was afraid of it.)

Saturday noon he stumbled on the patio and could hardly see to get into the house, and Joan had to force salt pills and water into him, and sponge him, and go and get fruit juice for him. He couldn't make his mind think. He felt seasick, cheated, vengefully sorry for himself, and as if he were caught in a queer kind of incontinent despair. Joan said, "You've got heat prostration," and couldn't make him go to sleep.

She left him sprawled naked and dull-witted. She came back three quarters of an hour later to sponge him again. He had rolled over on his face, long and collapsed, woodenly asleep, with a red mark on one of his buttocks ripe for scratching. It would be wrong to say that she was taken by love of her husband as she sat down to brush his skin with the damp washcloth. She told herself as much. She wasn't very fond of him sometimes, and as a wife not maternally fond of him at any time. Here with a purple washcloth she was only a willing servant, but at least she *was* willing. She wondered if she got credit for that.

And then he rolled over, hardly awake, to present his front with complacency, and a lover's happy shunting of the hips, as if to tease her with a nudging memory of something nicely done that there could be a pleasant, impotent thought of having done again. And then his eyes were looking at her. And suddenly he sat up on his elbows, straining his stomach and neck muscles, and she met his face, and then after a long time he lay back, and after a still longer time said, almost inaudibly and in a croaking voice, "Oh, my God," and rolled over away from her.

When he came to see her finally she was sitting on the toilet seat, still holding the tepid washcloth. There hadn't really been tears to make; she had shaped the noises but hadn't been able to make anything come of them. There wasn't anything he could say, because she hadn't spoken to him. What face told face couldn't be explained, pardoned, or left alone. Liking to be honest naked, he would have liked not to confess but to say some words: not, at least, just to stand over her and look at her. He hadn't dreamed, daydream or sleeping, about Gail or about making love, he hadn't been aware of thought. He had just moved, to receive the cool cloth. He had done only, what he needed to.

Urine was tickling scratchily inside his root. He finally gestured to the seat. She had to leave him alone. He didn't want to make a noise with his water, so he sat down, and stayed, hunched over, tucking himself in with one hand and resting a dry and dirty-feeling forehead on the other, until anxiety ran out with the draining urine. He flushed the toilet and sat in a whirling draught and the illusion of a cool spray of water. He would have to take his cue from her. Still, he did finally have to come out of the bathroom, and put his clothes on.

351

Joan didn't know why she had been so certain. A man rolls over on a bed, turns his stomach to the ceiling, and waits.

To have felt sorry for him, even for a moment, undermined her pride. And no, she didn't like him. And no, she couldn't, now or at any time, bring herself to say it. What he had done, he was going to have to continue doing. She wasn't going to help him. She should have known, anyway, a long time ago. Shouldn't some of her friends have told her?

He came into the kitchen and waited for her.

Joan had read too many columns of women's advice in the newspapers. She made herself smile at him, and asked him nothing. And didn't let him ask anything. She said, "We're having lamb chops." Then she made herself say, "I hope you can eat."

"Thanks," he said, "but I'm better now. Are prices really getting bad?" Then: "Want to go to church tomorrow?"

"No," she said.

"Nor me. The more Christian I feel the less I ever want to go under one of those roofs again."

"Oh," she said, "you're *Christian*."

He said, "I run a danger of it."

Supper; an evening; no rain. Joan read newspapers, Farquharson thumbed over a *Vogue* pattern book. He was wondering what could be done with the Chinese lions, and what was going to be done with Farquharson, when the woman for his deeds of fucking got back from Dakar. There was at least this satisfaction, he thought: he was going to be full up for her. Surely, he thought ("Oh God, virgin sensitivity!"), surely at least Mrs. Farquharson wouldn't want to stretch out for *him*! (He had brought the dress Mrs. Ezeokoli had made out of Jamie's strange material. Joan hadn't tried it on.)

He was staring at her, covertly, across the room. What was guilt? You had to have an answer for that before you knew who had it.

"Poor Joan," he thought, "I am very, very sorry, except for one thing, that I ever married you."

In much the same way, she threw looks at him. They caught each other eye to eye and were embarrassed. There was no way to avoid sitting the evening out. All they lacked of motionless slapstick, Farquharson thought, was the desire to laugh. He put the pattern book on his wife's knee. "That one."

"Oh, do you think so?"

She looked at it, holding the magazine away from her.

"Think of it," he said. "I'm going to go to bed."

He had written, in firm pencil, in the margin, "Hi, Mrs. Farquharson."

She wondered if she was supposed to be angry at a child.

They took a drive Easter afternoon and ran into a procession: the Church of the Cherubim and Seraphim, drumming and singing, half-dancing as they walked, dressed in enthusiastic finery, good manners, and joy. Joan avoided being sarcastic. "The discovery of adultery," Farquharson thought, comfortable in his brown-and-gold birthday shirt, "had its advantages." They went to Ogunmọla. Farquharson promised himself that one day he would get out of the car and walk the whole length of Ogunmọla by himself, greeting people and having insults shouted, being nothing but a hot white man in shorts, pottering about little stores. Some day. Some day to buy a cylindrical brocade hat, put on his *agbada* and walk, wearing things, foolishly conspicuous.

Another Easter procession toiled up the hill. There was just enough room in the lane that they could pass them. Stanley slowed the car. They glided past the paraders like spectators, and they discovered that the parade hated them.

For a short while it was like being on the Ifẹ road after the New Year, but then they realized that this was different, not necessarily more casual but with a good deal more bad temper. (WP2471, suddenly in its old erotic character, crept past the godly.) Yellow-whited eyes condemned them, raked them with dislike. No gay colours for this parade: blacks and browns, furious white shirts, dullness and anger. Far ahead, two banners showed nameless backs.

No happy drums. "If Jesus Christ is risen today," Farquharson said, "he'd better keep out of the way of this lot!" The marchers toiled sullen and interfered-with up the hill. Farquharson looked back, finally, at banners that were either high Anglican or Catholic, and said, "Hallelujah!"

Jamie played at processions in the afternoon, carrying a long stick on which Farquharson had fitted a piece of typewriter paper with the words "Holy Holy Holy" in three colours of crayon and with no blasphemous intent: those were simply Jamie's words, the right thing for him to march with.

After supper, because it hadn't rained and the air was stifling, Farquharson took his family out into the steep dusk and around the suburbs, with all the windows open, scooping air. Finally he brought them homewards past the bank and along the Bodija road (trying to remember if he'd noticed when the barricade had come down from around the offices of the Electoral Commission). It was almost dark. They were on a long straight dip with a gas station at the bottom, its sign full of hard white light. He could see little lights then, moving on the far shallow slope, beside the road. He thought, "It's a procession at night," and gently, courteously, slowed the car and stopped it. And then like any African driver he turned the lights out. "Parade," he said.

The empty air carried a low moving sound. They waited in the dark to be passed unseen. Farquharson put his head down on the steering wheel.

"Farquharson," Joan said, waiting until they were quite near (Jamie on her knee), "those are cows."

Not many candle flames then, but the light from the gas station twinkling off the unsteady horns. Farquharson's head came up with a jerk, and he would have been angry at somebody if the cattle hadn't been so purposeful, passing like a ghost army, random and ugly, walking to their butchery in a night that wasn't cool enough.

It was easier to let them all go by and look at them than to start the car.

"Holy, holy, holy," he said at last.

354

Jamie said, "So many cows. Thank you for cows, Far'."

"You're welcome, sir. Shall we go home? Mummy with amusement, Jamie with delight, and Daddy with egg all over his face?"

"What do I say?" Joan said, "Holy Cow?"

He held up a finger in front of her in their bedroom, and said, comforted, and as if it was an accusation, "You laughed at me."

Uncertainly, she said his name.

"Don't forget," he said, "I had sunstroke only yesterday."

He helped her undo her dress.

What was she to believe? That was he any different? "He isn't," she said to herself, "not a particle!"

She tossed, unable to disturb him because their mattresses didn't touch. In over thirty hours she hadn't once pictured what Farquharson might have done with a mistress that he didn't do with her.

It rained Monday, and at the height of the downpour Victoria came pelting onto the patio and emerged dripping into the dining room. "I couldn't stay in that house one more minute!" she said. "But finally Oscar came. This morning," she said before they could get in a word, "the nurse-girl ran away to Ghana with my silver teaspoons, and this afternoon I sacked the steward. Ohh!" she said, raising her hands, "I'm almost glad. I hate having all these *little people* around! The Westernization of Nigeria!" Her head jerked imperiously. "She took the spoons! We might as well be living in Oxford!"

"May I offer you a towel?" Farquharson said.

"Oh, I should love that. And tea?"

She was furious, a lady amused at both herself and them. The Farquharsons were suddenly released to be happy and civilized. Then the patio bloomed with headlights, and Bill and Gail were dripping at the window, making faces at them.

Victoria gave them her towel, apologizing for its being wet. Bill said, "She needs a drink and kindness. She says Dakar was busy."

355

Farquharson came into a room in which everybody was on his feet, even Victoria.

"Drinks," he said, giving them to Bill to hold. "And kindness." And he kissed Gail's cheek plainly, with only a tiny sound. "Welcome from Dakar," he said.

31

April 11–May 3, 1966

"ARENʼT you going to kiss me, Henry?" Victoria said, "and say, 'Welcome from the release from servants'?"

So he kissed her too, in almost the same way. Bill held the drinks.

"Or me?" Joan said.

He said, solemnly, "Welcome from a parade of cows."

He would have kissed her on the lips, but she turned her head. He was afraid suddenly, rejected, angry at her. So he said, "Won't everybody sit down?" and they made a society for a while and learned about a festival in Dakar to which everybody had worn superb clothes.

Farquharson walked Victoria home. She winked at her husband and then said, "Thank you for the kiss, Henry."

Oscar shouted, "What?"

Victoria laughed and ran into the house, leaving Farquharson on the edge of the rain.

Bill and Gail were going, too.

"Why did you do that?" Gail said, standing beside her seat while Bill tried to get the engine started.

He said, "You mean I shouldn't have?" patted her, and went back to the house grinning.

"Had fun?" Joan said.

Gail, looking back as Bill sent the Land-Rover into the sodden darkness beyond the garage, caught a fraction of a glimpse of Farquharson bear-hugging his black-haired wife.

Joan was muffled against his wrinkled shirt front and the hard big self behind it that she could feel breathing. When he

357

let her go she said, "Why are we both happy, now she's back?"

They didn't want to make love, but suddenly there they both were, full of the knowledge of adultery, necking on the living room couch. Joan wondered when it was all over and they had made apologetic faces at each other and Farquharson had made them a nightcap cocktail, what had happened to a half-weekend of well-cultivated moral shock. She raised her glass.

"To Nigeria," she said. "And I want to go home, now."

Stanley and Celina were still idyllic beside the house. Celina received visitors every morning: young men skidding down the driveway on motorcycles; girls in pairs or alone. The record player returned. Celina was a girlish and triumphant matriarch-to-be, and Stanley's world bent to her, enclosed her, centred on the stove where she worked, the doorstep where she sat, and the back lawn of the house where by unspoken treaty with the Farquharsons they chased and caught each other. "Kids!" Farquharson said.

Joan thought of her own session on the couch, and was nostalgic and critical enough not to make any comment.

Wednesday morning when term started, there was a baleful female presence standing on the patio. "Jacob!" Farquharson called. "The ironing!"

Florence, the ironing girl, was somebody Farquharson hardly ever saw, except to pay her twelve-and-six a week on Saturdays. She had been produced by Jacob and had hardly been hired before Jacob took a sulky dislike to her and said she was a bad person. There was thus a feud between them about who should carry the laundry to and from the garage, as Florence was not permitted in the house and the door to the garage was locked when she was there. Florence, clearly, would steal if she could, Joan said, and Farquharson didn't want to argue with her. Florence *would* steal, he thought, brazenly and like a hawk. Joan guarded her world by making shopping lists on the dining room table.

Jacob appeared with a rough pile of clothes. Florence waited, her hands by her sides, until he came near enough. Once, in a power failure, she had been seen walking away from the house, muttering that someone had played a trick on her. Farquharson wondered whose family was bending Jacob to its will and maneouvring through him for a job with a salary of a dollar and eighty-seven and a half cents a week. He had to remember that he was in a country where somebody thought he could make a profit by faking sixpences.

He was sitting in his office wondering what Ormford was going to do with the last term of Shakespeare, and what he was going to have to start talking about at nine, and why he felt, for now, so much like a happy cushion for both his women, when the door opened and somebody came into the outer part of his office and apparently waited for him. He looked up at "Lord David Cecil: Pathos," still on the stub of blackboard beside his desk, made some sort of decision in his head about the habits of the African student who would use your office as a waiting room for a class that wouldn't begin for another twenty minutes, and went back to looking out on the deserted tennis courts, suddenly unreasonably bleak. Whoever was in the outer room was just sitting too.

"I suppose whoever it is doesn't know I'm here," he thought. Usually they looked in and stared before they went to their seats.

He considered the folly of coming to convey any one civilization to another. But at least if there was guilt as well as futility, it belonged as much to the people who made gas stations and sold football coupons and put up signboards for beer with a white man's Negro waitress smiling hugely into a camera, as to someone who came to teach in a Canadian style what England regarded as a necessity. He had heard the tiny drumming of a ballpoint pen; incuriously, then, he heard the door close. He waited to think of Shakespeare. Finally he got up to see if he had fresh chalk, and found a note:

"I called to see you," it read. "I am sorry I didn't find you in. I will try to come back at noon. (Mrs.) Olubisi Akinrinmade."

The black gutted house and the barely dancing parade went across the back of his eyes, with the glinting horns of the cattle on the Bodija road.

Brother Patrick hadn't phoned Mr. Adebọwale. Surely he would have if he had had news. "(Mrs.) Olubisi Akinrinmade." What was her husband's name?

The class assembled for a professor who couldn't think very well. Tribes, parties, politics, noises in the Senior Common Room that the regime wasn't getting anywhere, that it couldn't make up its mind—how long a holiday had he had, two and a half months? He wondered how belated he was in knowing that the honeymoon was over. All former politicians, except a very few, were safe and rich. The Akinrinmades were back.

"Is the Professor going to meet his class today?" a voice said.

Mrs. Akinrinmade said "Professor Farquharson," tenderly, like a woman.

"You are alive."

"My husband is in Dahomey. He says he will not come home as long as this government remains in power. But someone must see to our property."

He said, "I saw your house."

"Yes. I have seen it. Well," she said, "the Yoruba have run. Next time it will be the Ibo. I shall enjoy the next time."

"Next time?" he said.

"Those who take the sword," Mrs. Akinrinmade said, "will perish by the sword. And when we burn the Ibo house, it will be with the Ibo people inside."

"But your house was burnt by Yoruba."

"Who rules this country?" she said. "Were Ibo officers killed? Were Ibo politicians killed? Were they even arrested as anything more than a show?"

Was he glad that the Akinrinmades were alive? They were slipping into the kind of quarrel out of which enemies come. "How long do you think Nigeria will put up with the Ibo?" she said. "In the government, in the army, in the civil service? How

360

long are we going to put up with an Ibo Vice-Chancellor in a Yoruba university?"

He said, "This is a *Federal* university."

"It is in *Ibadan*! You will see," she said, shaking her finger. "They will try to oust the Bursar here, because he is a Yoruba. But they will fail. Oh, how they will fail!"

"Oh come," he said, "they should have ousted him last October, when he let the police in."

"You have chosen your side, Professor Farquharson."

With two blows of a frying pan. "No," he said. "I worried about you for three months. Please don't make me wish I hadn't, that's all."

She said, "I understand. It's natural you should have Ibo friends. There aren't any Yoruba on the English Department of Ibadan. But believe me, Professor Farquharson, the time will come when there will be no Ibo in the North, and then none even in the Mid-West, and they will all be driven back into their own place, and then this Nigeria—which they in large part invented, as an idea, I will admit that—then this Nigeria will begin to be all right. Whether you want it or not. And even whether *I* want it or not. They are preparing their own destruction, and we shall give it to them." She might have been explaining a point to an obtuse servant: her voice was soft, implacable, very womanly.

"What sort of thing is this to say?" said a voice in the doorway. Farquharson recognized one of his Ibo women students in the doorway. (*That* was who had asked him if he was going to meet the class!) Mrs. Akinrinmade didn't know who it was. She said, "You have a class?"

"Yes."

"I must see Professor Ormford, to find what I am to do. After all," she said, "I missed the whole second term. I find also," she said, "that they have given my room to some Ibo person." And she walked past the student in the doorway as if she were sixty-five years old, and a grandmother of power. Farquharson realized that he preferred her as someone lost in the commotions of civil disorder.

"Who was that person, sir?" the student asked.

"Her house was burned last January. I don't think she lost her money. Her husband was NNDP." That dismissed Mrs. Akinrinmade, and whatever happened when she saw Ormford, she didn't come back to Farquharson's classes, nor did Ormford say anything about her to him. But then they didn't see the Ormfords much these days.

Farquharson didn't mention Mrs. Akinrinmade at home, except to say that she was apparently back. That she had given him a function in a civil war, he thought, was *his* business.

He met Mrs. Funmilayo at the Club. She thanked him for the evening at the nightclub, "but I'm afraid it didn't work," she said. "We're separate now. You probably know why."

"That's too bad," he said to Joan. "Fisher and Mrs. Funmilayo broke up." Where was Gail? he thought.

Not only did Stanley and Celina have visitors; Florence the ironing girl had visitors in the garage. And Joan began a campaign of driving them away. Usually the intruders went, mocking them en route, "as for Pete's sake why shouldn't they?" Farquharson said.

"Then why," Joan said to one group of three who had just assured her that never, of course, would they ever trespass on Madam's property, "are you in my garage?"

She should have laughed at it, Farquharson thought; it was funny. But laughter now failed near Joan. Her husband was as resilient and comfortable as a good pillow. He had been found out for a while, and then he had been made free. So he was very nice to her. She wanted to lose her temper all the time. "Florence," she said "you *must not* have any visitors while you are doing the ironing. Now you are a bad girl!"

Farquharson said, "Either you're a white Rhodesian or you're in the middle of the nineteenth century!"

"And where do you suppose this whole place is?"

"WP2471 belongs solely and only to the twentieth century. Make no mistake."

Another Thursday. Adebọwale, at twelve o'clock, worrying about European folk tale patterns in *Lear*. He said, "Why two and one?"

"There's at least one story where it's three and one."

"We often have the stories of the twins," Adebọwale said. "Or of the one bad and the one good. But why should you have the *two* bad and the one good, almost all the time?"

"Rhythm?" Farquharson said. "Stories are worldwide but the rhythm in which they're told is local? I don't know. Why *should* it be three?"

Adebọwale said, "The Trinity?" Farquharson's heart leaped.

"We'd better say 'two *x* and one *y*' rather than 'two bad and one good', hadn't we?"

"But is not the Trinity," Adebọwale said, "simultaneous?"

"Only in eternity. Historically it's State A, State B, then a third state emerging from an amalgam of the first two. Not exactly thesis, antithesis, synthesis, but something close to it. Of course, Hegelian dialectic comes out of a Christian system. Maybe there's a Trinity because we had a sense of threes. Civilizations with a sense of twos go Manichaean. Or yang and yin. You can't square *Wuthering Heights* with a Trinity. Body, brain, and spirit," he added on a new tack, "or body, mind, and soul. Marvell's Garden. Trinity too. A sophistication. The original is self and non-self, the other. Lear and the fool, perhaps; not Lear and the three daughters."

He was almost certain that Adebọwale was tracking his cadenza; he meant him to. Adebọwale said, "*Lear* is not a Christian play, sir."

"But at the heart of the play two triads hold the stage at once. Three madmen, and at least two of the three daughters, projected on the stage in the form of—I'm sorry about this—*three-legged* stools."

"If the Professor please," Miss Oguruvwe said, "will we be questioned upon this on the examination?"

"The kingdom is a unity," Adebọwale said. Farquharson's rejoiced: Adebọwale was ignoring both the interruption and the examination. "Lear wants to make the kingdom a trinity. And because he fails, the kingdom becomes dual and is torn apart."

"What is the good of a third term," Farquharson thought, "if you can't be irresponsible?") "So Cordelia is Ibo," he said. "Goneril is Hausa, say. Regan is, I regret to say, Yoruba." (He was still smarting from Mrs. Akinrinmade.) "Lear is the British government. Heaven knows the senility and the egoism are all right."

"If you please, sir, what has this to do with literature?"

"Oh," he said, "you work it out."

One good class, he thought, out of a dozen dreary ones.

"They're going to have to think sometime," he said to Oscar, "why not here?"

Afternoon rain cleared the air. The nights began to freshen. Farquharson set class essays for Adebọwale's first-year group and got ten essays, of which nine were identical, idea by idea, and almost phrase by phrase. The tenth was Adebọwale's. Irresponsibility was bearing fruit.

"The *Lear* of Shakespeare," he read, "according to Charles Lamb, cannot be acted. One must first ask why the *Lear* of Shakespeare should be acted now, for we are not Shakespeare's audience. Nor can Charles Lamb, one might add, be in any audience in which *we* might sit. Perhaps if one were to consider the 'unactable play' in relation to a Nigerian performance, the problem would be clarified, since many problems are clarified by the act of imagining them in an extreme case ..."

Farquharson thanked God, and said, "We did it, he's on his own."

There remained the problem of what to do with nine spontaneously identical essays, repeating notion for notion and almost word for word Sylvia Levinsohn's lecture on "*Lear* and the Theatre of the mind".

Jacob appeared at the house in a state of subdued enchantment.

"Madam," he said. "Florence is wicked girl. The police come to take her away. She cut her friend with a knife, madam."

"Laugh that one off," Joan said to Farquharson. "Knives!"

"We knew in January that this was a violent country. Mrs. Akinrinmade wants to burn down houses, with people in them."

"That was politics. Now *I've* got to get an ironing girl."

"And if *that* direct eye to the main point isn't African," he said, "what is?"

"Why do you want to make me an African?" she said.

"Because *I* am!"

"Oh no you're not! You're Milquetoast with a tennis racquet and a nice way with kids. And maybe a roving eye, maybe *that's* African! What's your African quality," she said, "violence?"

"Just the same," he said, "if another delegation comes to see us, we haven't fired her."

The delegation did come: four men, including, to Farquharson's slight shock, Elias's senior brother, and his own janitor from the Arts Building. That at least explained how Jacob had been obligated to bring Florence to the Madam. Diplomacy and representations took place on the patio, largely with Farquharson. "This inconvenience will surely be of brief duration, sir." He might have been buying something. Madam had to receive their gratitude for her consideration. Joan never managed to find out what had happened by the cattle market till the delegation had gone. "They fight over a man!" Jacob said, primly shocked, radiating, Farquharson supposed, if one could believe it, virginity.

"Oh hell," he said, "what Florence does on her own time is her business!"

"Thank you. And what was all that about violence and you being African? I thought you kept your violence to the dance floor, and, if you'll forgive me, bed."

If it weren't for Jamie, he thought, he would have to send her home.

365

He had his afternoons. Long, slow, lovely tumblings-around with Gail, when they did anything. She sponged him again, defiantly; she made caresses for him. He had the ease and calm of a thrown ball at the top of its flight.

"Are you going to stay here?" he said.

"Theatre's a big thing here. Oh, teach them how to build a set, and that means working with their hands, but, well, you saw *Kongi*. Maybe it was only a half-born play, but it was a real one. Where am I to go? Broadway? England? *Canada*, for heaven's sake? I've got a job." She put her head on his chest. "I'm sorry," she said. "I do lose you—there's no way around that." He let her find a position to be comfortable in. "Unless," she said, "you stayed here."

"I can't think how to manage it," he said. "Anyway, there's Jamie."

"He needs me," he said after a long nuzzling kiss. "Otherwise he'd just have *her*."

32

THEY received a directive that "the booking of *all* air passages involving the expenditure of university funds must, in future, be made through Nigerian Airways." Joan argued herself into a panic in case they should have to change their tickets, because hers were paid for by the college at home, and Farquharson's weren't.

"Well, is it my fault Ibadan would only pay for me?"

"But if we have to change!"

"Believe me," he said, "I will get on the same plane with you. Oh, for the Lord's sake!"

Sudden quarrels, shooting up like fevers out of the heat. It was no help to have to think, "Now, in two months or so, I'm going to have to go home."

"I wish to God we'd come for two years," he said.

"Well, we didn't." And then she had to say, "Farq, I'm sorry."

Thinking of the Gangan, the Club, the palm trees and the bananas, and the lush, ungainly, frustrated landscapes, for a moment she astonished herself; she *was* sorry.

Florence's family, they heard, was letting the case go to court and not bribing anyone. Farquharson couldn't figure whether this was supposed to be conspicuous public virtue or a determined effort to teach Florence a lesson: *something* was supposed to be unusual about it. Jacob was disgusted. (That, Farquharson thought, was *his* virtue: portable moral disgust, easily kept away from his temptations. *Did* he steal eighteen pounds?)

Meanwhile Jacob did the ironing again, crushing Jamie's

367

shorts into damaged relief maps around the crotch. "He ironed well enough before we got her," Joan said. "Now look at it!"

It was Farquharson who thought of asking Stanley's Celina to iron for them. But Stanley took him aside, and with great care and the usual near-incoherence of rhetoric that in all great speeches threatened to keep him off the point, explained that though Celina was a good ironer and ironed for him (because she *had* an iron), yet it would not be proper for her to do work for pay in the same place where she "received"—and all the young formal guests who spent their mornings as un- or underemployed people paying calls in servants' quarters rose in a dignified vision, as stiff with etiquette as the Spanish Court, unanswerable. Farquharson thought that surely they would need the money, and was forced to bow to formality. But he was almost sure Stanley wasn't thinking of the money.

"*We* have guests," he said to Gail, "*she* receives. Twenty-nine people one morning between eight o'clock and lunch. Joan counted them. I think she resented every one of them."

He sat in his office, writing ingratiating letters to European hotels, feeling itchy and half forlorn. Oscar leaned against his inner doorway. "I hear your household is on trial for violence," he said.

"That was this morning. There'll probably have been another delegation at home before I get there."

"I haven't seen you here in the afternoon for a long time." Farquharson looked up at him, with an envelope raised close to his face, ready to be licked. "I often see your car—where are you?"

Farquharson licked the envelope.

"No offence. Very well." He raised his head. "Do you remember when your wife had to fill in the name of her tribe at UCH?"

Farquharson laughed and said, "She didn't do it." Surely Nigeria wasn't going to turn already into a series of "remember-when's"!

"Now, in the East," Oscar said proudly, "she wouldn't have to. We have just eliminated all references to tribes in all government documents or applications for employment. There are going to be no more tribes!"

Farquharson chuckled and said, "Tell that to the Yoruba, *or* to the Ibo."

"It is the Ibo, my friend, who are telling it to the rest of them. They can't say this is to favour the Ibo in the other regions—the East *is* the Ibo region. This is in favour of all the little foreign tribes, not of the Ibo!"

"When do you write the poem?"

"I have it in the office now. Come. Mr. Cord claims to be reading it."

"I haven't seen him in the *mornings*," Farquharson said.

Cord gave them the paper without speaking, and left the room. Oscar made a face after him, turned as if cringing and said, "Sit down, white man."

"I am not to write my tribe's name upon papers;
My government, taxes, my unemployment, the
        officialness of my existence
Are to have no tribe.
                    I have no family.
I the subject am a naked name.
Equal with other naked names?
Nwonkwo is not a man of the West;
Chukwuemeka is not a man of the North.
Do I need to name my tribe when my tribe is my name?
I am my history. Do not discriminate for me:
I am proud. I am Onitsha in my own person,
All its life. Or I am Umuahia.
Relieve me of the enforcement of having to name my tribe,
And all my tribe is free in me now to be a nation,
And I am nations. Give me the form."

Farquharson waited over it. He had to say something, but all he could think, after Mrs. Akinrinmade, was that this was the prelude to doing the same thing in all the country, and then who would profit but the diaspora of the Ibo?

"I don't know if this is the point of the edict," he said hesitantly.

"It will be the effect. This is the way to the end of jealousies. One Nigeria! No more of those strangers' ghettoes in the North; no Sabongaris.

"And no more Sabo in Ibadan?" (That, was naughty.)

"Oh, if the Northerners want to make themselves ghettoes in the South," Oscar said, "let them do it. They are in the Middle Ages! Come," he added, escorting Farquharson to the gallery outside, "you and Joan are to visit us Thursday night and meet a friend. You shall see what we are going to do in this new world of our new government."

Florence was fined ten pounds. A delegation apparently wasn't necessary. The janitor from the Arts Building appeared at the kitchen window to make sure about the job, since Florence was going to need four months' wages to repay the family for her fine. "And I think he almost tried to persuade me to raise her pay," Joan said.

She called Jacob to serve the dessert.

"So I'll have an amenable servant now," she said. "I think we can count on her family to see to that."

Farquharson said, "How are you ever going to go home?" and Joan was angry with him instead of laughing with him.

Florence wasn't recognizably more amenable when she came back, but, at least for a few days. she had no visitors. Jacob was more evasive than ever in finding ways not to carry the laundry out to her, or get it back, and there were displays of flouncing, sulks, and adamantine statuary in various places. Farquharson stood by the car on the third day and said to his wife, "I am studying the functioning of a slave economy."

"And if you walk into this house," she said, "flourishing a civil right ... !"

He ducked into the car. Exasperation made her comic, and then, having found words to make other people laugh, she couldn't hear what she'd said. "Stanley," he said, driving to work, "servants are a bad thing."

"Sir?"

"Yes, you shouldn't be able to say 'Do this' and get it done, because then you have to take what *is* done, because of your dignity. Or stand screaming."

"Farq does not want to dismiss his driver?"

"You're a professional, not a servant."

Pride said, "I thank you, sir."

Young lust drove cars and kept his house. If you didn't have to like a man to trust him, Farquharson thought, you also didn't have to trust a man to like him. Neither of them trusted the other, he felt, but as far as reason allowed, it seemed, they were friendly. They had driven side by side a great deal—that was the fact of eight months—they knew when the other breathed, or turned a head, or hesitated to say something. When Farquharson got into the car alone, and Stanley drove him, he could just relax and babble, justify himself repeatedly, discuss wealth, North American poverty, what he taught his students, and why he tried to teach it. He never acknowledged that he knew Stanley couldn't read. Stanley would come into the living room in the morning and wait, turning pages of *Life* or *Time*. They would give him *Life* when they were through with it. One payday Farquharson had seen him buy a big roll of Scotch tape. "Sir," Stanley had said, when he brought Farq back one noon, "I wish you to see this."

Picture after picture, taped to his wall, making a design of them: cars, landscapes, photographs of astronauts, of many cities. "All from magazines, sir, which you kindly give us." And in the middle a picture of the Toronto City Hall out of an advertisement, and a colour postcard of Ibadan, which he must have bought. Stanley pointed and said, "Jamie say this your home, sir." (Joan had showed it to Jamie: "That's a picture of our city," she had said. "That's where *you* come from." Farquharson could see Jamie taking the magazine to Stanley and saying, "That where *I* come from!" And Stanley would believe and honour it.)

371

Farquharson said, "That's like Mapo Hall." ("The kingdoms of the world," he thought, "and all the glory of them: the things I've seen and you won't, or that I *can* see.")

He looked at Celina, thinking, "My, she's pretty." Celina said, "Stanley do all himself, sir."

One day he had looked out and seen her pounding yams, standing bent beside the huge pestle, while Joan probably waited to criticize the noise. "Wait here," he said, and brought out Jamie. And Stanley and Celina gave Jamie permission to come and see them whenever he wanted to.

Now what should he do with the identical essays—tear them? To rip nine booklets simultaneously would be the kind of gesture that lacked quality. "What I tell you three times is true," he said, putting the booklets down in front of them, "but only the first time did it mean anything. Now," he said. "What's wrong with repetition?" He didn't manage, even after an hour's argument, to get them to admit that anything was wrong with it, even though he got them to say things about the nature of wisdom and authority, and the possible function of memory in a world of books. "As long as you hold your society in memory," he said at last, "knowledge is a ritual, and learning is conservation. But the book *is* memory. We've freed all those circuits, all that power— *now* what do you do?"

Memorize.

On Thursday night Joan didn't feel like going out. She said, "You go; Oscar wants *you* to meet a friend."

"No. We're supposed to see what they're going to do with the new world."

She looked at him, waiting for him to be himself.

"Well, I won't be late," he said.

"*Be* late. I've got an ache."

"In other words, 'Be mean; go.' What if I don't want to be mean?"

"Go anyway." She was lying on the couch; he loomed

over her. She took a dislike to his big silly dimpled chin. "Oh, get out of the house!" she said, laughing at him, and so he went.

Oscar's friend was a publisher. Farquharson had seen him before, drumming rhythms on the wooden arm of the chair. "Ah!" the friend said, pointing and coming to shake hands. "The white man—note what I call him: man." Poems in a heap were clustered where the flat arms of two chairs touched each other; Farquharson had entered a discussion of which of Oscar's poems to print. "You see," the friend said, "how we celebrate the new regime. Now there is no need to assert ourselves, to publish out of obligation because we have to assure an identity—against the British or anyone else. Now it is joy. Innocent Ikechukwu Iwuoha," he introduced himself. "Agent Three-I. 'I am Onitsha in its own person, all its life.'"

"That's fast to publication," Farquharson said.

"Life, sir, moves fast."

He was a little man, with a kind of sprightly dog's face, flamboyance and enthusiasm bedded in complacency. Farquharson took an instant half-liking to him, and watched it ebb into a rankling contempt close to disgust. The man was married. Mrs. Iwuoha sat in a couch on the far side of the room, bleared with tiredness, saying from time to time that she hadn't eaten, that she had been up almost all last night and driven miles today. "I tell her to eat!" Iwuoha said. "I, Three-I, tell her to eat. She says she is never hungry." He pointed to her. "You should cook better for yourself!"

Another couple, relatives of Victoria's, talked quietly to Victoria, leaving the men to their poems and publications and Mrs. Iwuoha to herself.

Iwuoha said, "*Zodiacal Light for a Military Dawn*".

"Too long."

"No title is too long if it can be read conveniently when the book is on the stalls. *Drums for a Military Dawn?*"

Farquharson said, "*Anxieties*".

Iwuoha thought of it. "That is the title for a poem. You have a

373

poem, have you not, my friend, called *Requiem for the First Republic?*"

"Ike, I want to sleep." A pretty, complaining woman, her face shiny with oil, her hair bruised into a Western hairstyle.

"Am *I* stopping you from going to sleep? Why should a man get married? All she does is want to go to sleep."

"I cannot go to sleep sitting in a chair. And when I have not had supper." She sat stupefied.

"Never does she eat when she should! Never! Victoria, I forbid you to feed her. She must learn! When it is time for me to eat, she eats. Now, my friends . . ."

Oscar and Iwuoha read poems back and forth, choosing and admiring, doing editorial work, sharing themselves with each other. Farquharson managed, after a long time, to be on his feet at the end of the room, near Victoria, standing with a glass of whiskey near the dazed, undozing Mrs. Iwuoha.

Certainly she had a stupid face: petulant, uneducated, sullen, as if she were owned, not married, and owned carelessly. Victoria was trying to talk to her. Her relatives had gone. They had offered to drive Mrs. Iwuoha, and she had almost got to her feet, but had been stopped.

"Who tries to steal my wife? That woman is mine: go!"

Victoria said, "She must sleep, Ike."

"Let her sleep: she has a whole couch. I'm sure Mr. Farquharson doesn't want to sit beside her." He bent forward over the poems. "Do you want to go home? Listen to her," he said to the rest, "she will say yes. Listen."

"Ike, I want to go home." Some minimal sulks, Farquharson thought, were worse than rage or hatreds.

"Well, you cannot go home." Then, to Victoria: "Oh, give her a sandwich; give her something for her mind. I cannot imagine why I married her, but since I have, she is mine. When I am finished," he said to his wife, "we will go home."

Oscar waited with another poem.

"We celebrate the new world," Farquharson thought, "and the new government, to be ourselves in joy." He didn't know what to say. He stayed by the bookcase, close to Victoria, reluctant to go home, embarrassed for Victoria, as if she were owned too, and if he moved he might show he knew it. The sandwich was refused.

Oscar and Iwuoha shuffled pages and rejected poems, carefully, under an appearance of self-indulgent enthusiasm. "It must be right," Iwuoha said. "This will be the first volume of poems published in the new era. It must embody hope, joy—and attentiveness. Wariness. Oh, for a title!"

Farquharson shouted, "*Cock-crow!*"

Iwuoha laughed. "They will call it the display of a political emblem and arrest me! NCNC is for the past, my friend."

Victoria, being a woman, waited, near the other woman, having no more real compassion or interest in a downtrodden flibbertigibbet, Farquharson guessed, than the girl's husband had, and knowing that if she spoke she'd show it. She did finally say, "Ike, you ought to take this poor woman home," but when she was denied, neither showed that she minded nor tried to raise the subject again. The room crawled, somehow, horribly, with embarrassment. It affected Oscar too at last, as if he knew that he was being judged badly, and wanted to make some composition, but had been caught in a male role.

Iwuoha said, "*Long Night, Swift Dawn.* That is what it is all about. Twenty-seven poems. Have I tormented you, my dear?" he added pleasantly, placidly, looking up and sliding the poems he was going to keep into a big envelope. "I think it is what she wants from me. If I am kind to her, she is so dull. Come. And when we are in our bed and I have been a husband, you can sleep at last. Sleep like a little foolish girl. Come. Walk! Wake up!" Out the door, into a white car.

Victoria walked Farquharson to the edge of the light on the grass. "Thank you for seeing it out," she said.

"What could I do?"

"You could have been part of the children's party. No, I shouldn't say that." He could feel her smiling, being fond of men, especially her own, and impatient with silly women. "Tell Joan if she needs to make another raid on the Clinic I'll give her a hand. And Henry . . ." They stopped. "Take care of yourself."

Joan was asleep. He looked at her. "Oh well," he said, "you wouldn't have liked it. I didn't."

Maybe he needed a reminder that this wasn't his country.

It was the last week of classes. Flame trees were in full flower; more of the queerly limited colours that seemed to be shared by everything that flowered—one red, one orange, one violet, one basic palish yellow, over and over again. Classes didn't so much run out as run down; the last one didn't even meet. Farquharson waited in an empty office, not wanting them to come. The Senior Common Room continued. They waited through a week for the exams to start, gossiping on the white furniture, commenting on the extraordinarily prolonged heat now following the extraordinarily prolonged harmattan—and the students had been distracted, of course, they explained to Farquharson. It wasn't a normal year.

Gail lay in his arms. He pulled her to him, rolled over, pushed himself in. He said, "Do you want it quiet like dreams or a little motor ticking over?"

Short, amused strokes and a rain of little kisses. She said, "I want to see you."

He went obligingly up to the length of his arms, stilled, then tightened whatever muscle it was that made the big shaft twitch and tease her. He could be pleased, and please, and have a placid face: somehow that delighted her. He said, "Putt-putt," finding a motion.

"Stop it!" she said, laughing. "You're tickling me!"

The little motor ticked over and grew suddenly into a big motor, the temperate happy game gone huge, but still nothing but temperate, and happy, and a game. To come that way was a game too, the tick-tock gentle rocking of the loins went on, and slowly he was nestling closer on top of her. And then slowly he pulled out, rocking still, and then suddenly was on his back beside her, clear eyes to the ceiling, his body looking somehow defined and unworn, as if it had been just made, and he put a big hand across her stomach, his fingers tickling her hair, and then moving down until they pressed against her folds and held her closed.

"You're a big tidy body of a man," she said. "It's a good body, Henry."

He said, "And *he* comes in." He was eased, peaceful. "That's the most extraordinary thing. Right here." He pressed. "Who does he come to? This is *my* mistress. Whose lover's he?"

She loved him. "Mine, when he's here? Does it bother you?"

"Oh, no. I can't give pleasure when I'm not here. And that's why I *am* here." He hesitated. "Among a lot of reasons."

"You do good things for me."

"I hope Bill does." He said, "Please say he does."

"Yes, he does, but it isn't the same." She lifted herself on her elbows: it was important to look at him, and to have him know he was being looked at. "I'm a—well, say, a busier person with him. He's a *handier* lover, somehow. I have to take care of him. He isn't nearly as big as you are." They hadn't talked this way before. "You've got a sort of repose you give a woman. Bill doesn't have it. Yet if Bill's here, even this way, after, I don't miss it."

"Do you trade tricks between us?" He felt ridiculous, and pleased for her.

"Of course I do, when you're in the right way. I bet some of it goes back to Joan."

"No."

There was a sudden little lonely frown on his face: she thought he didn't know he had it. "You've got more than enough for two women," she said. "You ought to spend yourself!"

"Ay," he quoted, "but I have a wife, and so forth."

"Then you can damn well fuck *her*." He thought she wasn't quite laughing at him.

"On the basis of future need?"

She said, "Because you're Jamie's father."

"Does Jamie's father have a mistress? Or is it just me does that?"

"Please," she said. "I love you when you're here, and I want that big prick of yours always to be happy. Oh damn," she said, "what'll I do when you go? Just be Bill's woman?"

Suddenly Uganda was the African country in the papers, while the government of Nigeria had a day of changing names. All political parties were abolished: the Society of the Sons of Oduduwa, the Ibo Tribal Unions, any little ones. The "former regions" were declared abolished. In their place (and with the same boundaries) were "territorial areas called provinces", and the word "Federal" was abolished from the "Federal Republic of Nigeria".

Farquharson tried, because he was Jamie's father, to seduce Jamie's mother. Unfortunately, he was too successful. He gave her the skyrocketing nerves, the violent, grabbing orgasm when two of her nails ripped his back, and the immediate dry rasping pain. She almost threw him out. "Sorry," he said. "I'm sorry."

He applied her hand. "Now would you help me finish, please?"

She didn't know what to do, so she just did things until she didn't have to.

The University Worker's Union went on strike. It was an ugly affair, tangled with old political alliances, and almost at once, as if by necessity, Ibo against Yoruba, with Mr. Sam Majękodunmi in the centre. As Mrs. Akinrinmade predicted, a party was trying to oust the over-mighty Bursar. Abruptly, as if for a change, expatriates spoke of empire-building, and how a man might have to surrender a month's pay or even more to get a job. Grace Spanier-Dodd said simply, "That man *would* be an NNDP Yoruba!"

"Well," her husband said, "Ogundele and Jack Okpata have a little empire at the Arts Building." Joan said, "You mean *our* servants ...?"

Farquharson watched Bill Garnett meet Gail at the far end of the pool: they seemed such strained, hungry people. They even shook hands. He thought, "I should have gone to their wedding, some time."

He didn't care about the Bursar. He had had his own meeting with Majẹkodunmi's extensions—it was only irony to think that they might have had to pay for their deaths with a month's or even a quarter's pay. How much had Stanley and Elias had to give? No wonder Jack Okpata came to the door in his finery of white and gold.

He contemplated the possibility that Majẹkodunmi was honest, and decided that with once-political factions now corrupting into a tribal simplicity they had never quite managed to have while the area of their politics existed, it wouldn't matter.

They met Bill and Gail outside the Staff Store. "We're for a war, of course," Bill said. "Majẹkodunmi's a man of honour. Let's all stand at the doors of our houses armed with frying pans."

Farquharson, jolted, wondered if he was supposed to wink at him.

Joan said, "Hasn't Africa made you two realistic about weapons?"

"A frying pan *is* realistic," Bill said, aggrieved. "Not as good as a matchet, but a damned sight better than a rolling pin." His face darkened into the familiar look of being lost and sorry. "I could have used one on the Abẹokuta road. Wham. Whee."

Farquharson said, "Wham, whee—*now* what?"

"Not in an enthusiastic cause," Bill said. "Come and buy a bottle with me." When they were inside, he said, "Sorry, Henry. You get to do *all* the things a man wants to do. I just got beaten up."

"I wonder what they're talking about?" Farquharson said when they came out the door.

Gail was being a swing, and swinging Jamie. Farquharson wished he had the nerve just to stare into Joan's face.

Somehow they were travelling behind Gail's Honda, going to have a drink in Bill's apartment. Bill rode hugging Gail, as if to pull her off the machine. Gravel fragments pinged against their metal.

Joan said, "Do you know Gail thinks you shouldn't stay in Africa?"

379

They had drinks on Bill's balcony looking at dull green tree-tops and a single blunt conical hill, under a grey ceiling that seemed to assemble itself as they looked at it. Jamie was held for a while, then taken down to play with Stanley. Bill got his frying pan then, and gave it to Joan and said, "Try it."

Gail said, "Bill, please!"

"No," Bill said. "I have daydreams of violence with a helicopter overhead." He was looking over the railing, at the ugly forest. "I wouldn't be a Nigerian," he said. "Who gives a damn what Majękodunmi does, if he does anything?" He raised his hand, shouted, "I laud his honour! He may even have some. Council discusses him Monday, you know. I recommend that Henry stay at home." He took the handle away from Joan and hit the frying pan with one hand. "I never thought to ask if they made a noise."

"Farq," Joan said. "I think we'd better go. When you don't have a steward," she said to Gail, "you have to cook."

The killing of the Ibos began in Kano.

The riot came. Farquharson set himself to look at it, having sent Joan and Jamie over to the Ormfords', and moved restlessly outside the house in the afternoon, listening. Some people were gathering in front of the language laboratory. He moved out towards Park Lane, and took up a station on the terrace in front of the theatre, below the parking lot. He saw a few big cars come up and let out, he supposed, Council members. Nothing was going to happen. He went around the corner, along the back of the theatre. Gail's Honda wasn't there.

He was in a buzzing nervousness, he supposed because he was waiting to be a spectator and there wasn't anything to look at beyond a few gathering people who looked at a building and each other. If he waited, he'd be asked why; he didn't want to say, "I want to see *you* hit each other!"

So he walked a diagonal trampled path to the Arts Building, looked at the irregular new roundabout filled with purple portulaca, and wondered if he could pick a few of the flowers and how long they would last. He had to breathe, and walk past the mosque into an open grove of trees like pines, planted in a grid. He would have liked to lie on the ground and be innocent—without reference to theories but because the world was. He moved aimlessly in shade, in the trees' rigid vistas. When finally something said it was time he walked back through Tower Court, and got into Park Lane just in time to see the ranked crowds break into a mob. One fight sprang into a dozen fights; there was a screaming commotion on the steps of the Senate Building. Farquharson, standing tall at the corner of the parking lot, saw a hand holding a grey stone rise and fall. Then it came up, at the end of a long straight arm, and came down again. He began to move.

Once again there were police, summoned somehow, unloading from a truck, interposing, as the just should, and Farquharson saw the man on the concrete (in patches, between black shoving bodies), lying face down, his arms out, and blood around his head.

Farquharson didn't will his feet to walk towards the steps of the Senate Building. He willed them to stop, and kept moving. Somebody said, "This not for you, big man," but Farquharson was on the steps. The crowd surged and the prostrate man was stepped on. Farquharson picked him up and carried him. No one stopped him then.

Nobody was in the Clinic. Farquharson carried the man as if he were a larger Jamie. He led a small unseen crowd to his house, told someone to get the key out of his pocket, carried the man into the empty bedroom, but him down bloody on the bed, sent someone to tell Victoria to get in a car and bring Garnett, drove the rest of them off, except a policeman who was making noises of authority, stationed the policeman on the patio, made sure he had his keys back, got boiled water and a clean cloth, and started to wipe a face.

Oscar was at the door, quarrelling with the policeman. "What the hell!" Farquharson shouted.

"Orders literally obeyed," Oscar called. "Victoria is gone. May I be of help?"

Farquharson said, "Sit down and guard my living room."

When Bill came the man was clean, and Farquharson didn't know what else to do. He was looking at Akinkugbe's Mongol moustache. He had bullied cushions and mattresses out of this man, been highhanded, as an *oyibo* could. Bill said, "What's *he* doing here?"

Farquharson didn't answer, watched Garnett study the man and look slowly sick. "God, what a butchery."

"You've got to admit," Farquharson said, "*I* do a better job."

33

OSCAR and the policeman were confining each other to the living room. Outside, presumably all around, people stood and stared. Farquharson and the doctor he had called in were alone with the furniture clerk. "I don't know," Bill said. "How can you mend that?"

"Do your men have a truck?" he said in the living room. "A lorry? Something to take him in?"

The law seemed unwilling to leave its one proved rioter.

"The people next door have a station-wagon," Farquharson said. "Suppose I get it."

He pushed through the crowd, uncertain for a moment how to get to the Ellis's. Then he went through the hedge.

Professor Ellis wasn't happy to know that his good automobile had to carry a bloody man, but Farquharson said, "Damn it, I don't want the man dying in my house!"

Farquharson saw a look of cold, unneighbourly understanding as Professor Ellis took out the keys, and said, "Do you want me to drive?"

Out one driveway, in another. They carried the man with about six people lifting him and Bill and the policeman giving contradictory commands. There was no reason for Farquharson to get into the station-wagon, but he rode to the hospital with the policeman in the front seat (and what seemed like a whole truck-load following them), to the displeasure, Farquharson noted, of the Ellis profile. Once at the hospital, Akinkugbe and his doctor quickly disappeared and Farquharson was left to the attention of a senior policeman while Ellis waited behind the wheel, disassociating himself.

"Why do you move this man?"

Did he have to explain?

"How can I investigate a case if the evidence is not left?"

"I can't say who hit him," he was saying. "There were too many people."

"I am not satisfied, sir, why you should be there."

Through a gap in the building he saw Ormford's car, wandering among the parking lots. He thought, "More help from Oscar."

"I went to see a riot," he said, "I saw a riot. It looked like a riot." He put his hands into the air and made signals at the meandering car, and was suddenly afraid that if Ormford saw him, he was going to honk.

"Why you lift up that man? Sir, I am not satisfied."

"Be unsatisfied then. You have my answers and my name. You can go home, Mr. Ellis, and thank you."

"I wish also to question this man!"

Farquharson stood massively among three policemen. It was extraordinary, Ormford thought, driving up, how huge that man could look. He had neglected Farquharson lately; he had had to, of course, to get away from Peg's gossiping. But why Farquharson should step in like a stretcher bearer into a clash by day . . . Were armies less ignorant if they could see each other?

"We thought you might bb-be in need of transportation," Ormford called.

Farquharson said, "You didn't for Pete's sake take Joan and Jamie home?"

"Why? Is it bb-bloody? They're at the Nwonkwos'."

Farquharson said to the head policeman, "May I go?" and had to dictate his address. "One Jaja Avenue. That is actually Eight El-Kanemi Road, but we don't use that. The *official* address is Eight El-Kanemi Road, but if you want to find us rationally you go to One Jaja Avenue." Suddenly (dangerously, Ormford thought) Farquharson was beginning to enjoy himself.

"It is not reasonable that I should write two addresses for one house!"

Ormford said, "Write Department of English, University of Ibadan, and let this man gg-go."

The Nwonkwos gave them supper. "Well," Joan said, "did you have your fun?"

"Did you realize," Victoria said, "that you have become a hero, Henry?" He looked blank. "You didn't know that you walked through the worst of the fighting, shoving people with stones in their hands out of your way? So your students say."

He thought, "Joan is afraid of me."

He said, "No. I thought the fighting was over. I just . . . Well, well. Am I a hero to the Ibo faction?"

"Not 'faction', Henry, please?" Oscar gave him another whiskey.

It tried to rain. The children ran laughing in the garden to be hit by the large drops. His hosts looked at him, he thought, as if they were sorry, not for what had been done, but that he had had to do it. The courtesy of their country was somehow impaired. Jacob chose the middle of dinner to come and say that he had washed away all the blood. When they were back in the house Joan examined the mattress. Farquharson said, "It'll look like the ones we made him take back."

"Well, you aren't a hero," she said. "Why did you have to go near them, anyway?"

He sang long quiet sad-songs to Jamie; for himself, too.

Gail appeared at the patio with the Honda. "I can't find Bill."

"He's at the hospital."

So they had a small visit, then Farquharson pushed the Honda up to the road for her. "Take care on that thing," he said. "Incidentally, she's going to watch us out the window."

"Let her . . . I suppose one day I'll be sorry you two weren't jealous of each other," she said. "Maybe then I'll know why I'm doing this."

He kissed her as for a goodbye, and let her go.

385

Joan was in the living room, mending something of Jamie's that she said the sun was ruining.

The note in his mail was a request to see the Bursar, signed by Bernice Funmilayọ. Mr. Gbadebọ had come specially to express his regard for the Professor. Mr. Gbadebọ's politics, Farquharson knew, had been Opposition politics. He wondered if by now they had become merely Yoruba politics, and wished he could be certain that Mr. Gbadebọ had not been one of the ones with stones.

Another student from Kuti Hall had said something formal and eager about humanitarianism. At least there wouldn't be any doubt about *his* politics.

Farquharson was hoping that Adebọwale hadn't seen him. Somehow he didn't want Brother Patrick knowing, *or* Mrs. Akinrinmade, should there ever possibly be a connection.

"Professor Farquharson," the mail clerk said, "Mr. Majẹkodunmi wish to see you as soon as you come, he say. I am to watch for you."

(Bernice Funmilayọ said, "Welcome, Mr. Farquharson.")

"Ah, my dear sir! Come in, come in." To Mrs. Funmilayọ: "You may go." He said, "I understand you have braved riot to be a Good Samaritan to Mr. Akinkugbe."

So this was Majẹkodunmi: shiny with good eating as if he were a balloon, bold tribal scars masking his face into an enduring happiness. (Farquharson was just starting to see that tribal scars were handsome.) But he had one informal scar, a large Y-shaped indented mark at the corner of his forehead, as if at some vulnerable time he had been almost killed by the corner of a metal box. He put his finger to it as he saw Farquharson look at it. He had dark trousers and a dark striped tie sprinkled with coats-of-arms. He stood up, offered a manicured hand to shake. Farquharson thought, "I know nothing but rumours. No facts."

He was thanked; he was made much of; he was confided in (by tone of voice). He was being angled for, as if he were an ally. "You cannot imagine," Majẹkodunmi was saying, "the difficulty of replacing good men, the Machiavellian scheming that certain groups will undertake, Why, last year, when we lost two men from the Maintenance Department in a motor smash: you have no idea of the difficulty—they were not replaced for *months*!" He stopped. "I cannot see that any union has the right to tell an authority *whom* it must hire."

"Have you heard," Farquharson said, "how Mr. Akinkugbe is?"

"No. I have not."

He couldn't rise to go; he was on his feet already. "Will you excuse me, sir?"

"This is *my* university," Majẹkodunmi said. "I am not accustomed to being ordered out of my own home. You knew, of course, that for yesterday's Council meeting I had been appointed to be secretary, in the absence of Mr. Lynch the Registrar. I was desired not to come! No, I assure you, Professor Farquharson, that if there were ever a time for diplomacy within this university, that time has passed. There is a time for force. You may not entirely have deprived us of a martyr, Professor Farquharson. May I, on behalf of those of us who are attacked, thank you again for your courage and your humanity?"

Mrs. Funmilayọ was coming in with a letter in an opened envelope. Farquharson thought there was something secret in the way she smiled at him.

"And I wish," Majẹkodunmi said, "I could know which side you are on, Professor Farquharson. It has always disturbed me," he added, "to know what men went to your house."

"He stared at me," Farquharson said to Gail, "awfully hard. I can tell you I got out of there fast!"

"What could he do to you?" she said. "His people aren't in power."

"Just the same, it was a bad moment. He obviously had some guess where his worthies went. I guess he can't get over the doctor's evidence that they were run over."

"Make love to me."

He made a noise like a parrot: "Duty *calls*! Duty *calls*!"

387

Jamie got diarrhoea. Joan felt she had to be chasing him, and changing him, all day. At the climax of the diarrhoea she discovered he had worms. Jamie was worried, and tried to be respectable, and went and got a cloth when he had an accident, and when Farquharson got home from lunch, fresh from having Mr. Adebọwale say, "Sir, I saw you Monday last," the worms had just been found. "I think if you had shown you noticed them," Adebọwale had said, "they would have hurt you. I can tell you, sir, myself—I would not have had the courage."

"I didn't see them." He sighed. "Don't make a hero out of a natural coward, 'Tunji," he said, finally using the first name that might show they were friends.

"Sir, you have taught me to disagree with what the Professor says."

"How did he get worms?" Joan said.

So he made a trip to town for worm medicine. Then there was a big fight to make Jamie take it while he gagged and spat. At suppertime everybody lost his temper at once, and Jacob was nearly sacked. Farquharson got violent heartburn. He suddenly took the car to see if he could get some antacid tablets in Ibadan, crunched about four at once, and then thought, almost horribly, that he had left Joan to put Jamie to bed and that it was too late to go back. He was lonely and angry then, and drove till he could feel better, then found himself on the road to the African night-club, whose name he didn't even know. He was early, but there were a few people going in. He said to himself, "That's Mrs. Funmilayọ."

Oh, what was he doing here? He drove away.

The diarrhoea stopped. Jamie eliminated worms vigorously. He said, "I no like worms!" and looked pathetic, and was hugged only after everything had been inspected and flushed.

Bill came over.

"Akinkugbe?" Farquharson said.

"What good are human vegetables?"

"Want to tell Majẹkodunmi that he *hasn't* been deprived of a martyr?"

At least his publicity had put the Ormfords back in the Farquharson's living room. They were drinking cocktails. The air through the windows was chill with rain.

"I've decided," Joan was saying, "that I am tired of Africans."

"I bb-believe," Ormford said, "that the American Peace Corps has people's psychological states in a gg-graph. The trough is supposed to be the end of the first year. Euphoria, seeming realism, and then Oh-my-Gg-god! You're at the Oh-my-Gg-god stage."

She said bitterly, "I can believe it."

"They listen to you," Peg said, "but they never listen to what you *say*."

"But I tell Jacob nineteen times the way he's supposed to clean. He says, 'I quite follow you, madam,' and does it *exactly* his own way!"

"Pity the poor gg-government," Ormford said, "which is also trying to exhort to virtue! People *must* work, people *must* be honest. Of course if they shout a politician's name in the street now, it's a political crime. Gg-given the vast overlap of Nigerian names," he said, taking his new glass, "there must be many poor women committing wh-whole series of political crimes simply by crying for their hh-husbands to come home." He raised his head. " 'Majẹkodunmiii!' "

Joan said, "Is *he* political?"

"You're not serious. You had an interview," he said to Farquharson. "He didn't tell you he'd bb-been sacked? I see a light in your eyes. Actually, with the Registrar away, he should have sent himself the letter, but I suppose they gg-got around that. Quite messy altogether, as I suppose he won't gg-go."

"You realize," Peg said, "that General Ironsi delivered a 'final warning' Monday," and she quoted: "If the disturbances go on, districts will be taken over as military areas."

Ormford said, "Nannies, with threats."

A good team, Farquharson thought, demonstrating Africa for strangers. "Will they do it?"

"The government of the East has appealed to people not to take the law into their own hands," Peg said. "I suppose you can take that any way you want, but it sounds like last time, except that the governments are looking at it instead of looking away. I don't suppose they can *do* anything, or why are they just saying 'Please!' "

The Bursar remained on the compound and came to work, but the appearance of a strike had almost vanished with the Council's decision to get rid of him in the most tactful, the most awkward, the most legal, and the most uncomfortable and damaging fashion possible. Factions fermented. Farquharson took Jamie to the sixteen-day cloth market simply that they might both breathe Africa. Four cabinet ministers were hanged in the Congo, in a public square. People who liked Africa felt badly, but said that was the Congo, and it was a long way off.

There were riots in Balewa's birthplace, in the North. The students wrote examinations. They had begun on Monday, when the strike exploded. Farquharson kept away from the office. He believed that professors should be seen around examinations only if they were invigilating, and Ormford's courtesy to him was that he had no work to do.

Postage rates went up. Rumours of massacre crossed the North; the Moslems in Kaduna prayed under armed guard. An editor printed the cartoon of a crowing cock with the caption "One Country, One Nationalism" and was arrested for the display of the badge of a political party. Ormford came over with the first set of scripts for Farquharson to mark and said, "To take off the bad taste, may I recommend an evening at the Gg-gangan tonight? I have always," he added, "damned the occasion of my bb-birth, but never more enthusiastically than when I have *these* around!" He waved the long booklets, and then set them high up in the bookcase. "Can you come? I wasn't planning anything, because

Peg was supposed to, but she forgot. Bb-by the way," he said, "I left my coat here."

The Gangan on a Saturday was a very different thing from the club they had discovered on a Monday. It was crowded to the walls, and the musicians seemed to have enlarged themselves to a nagging loudness. Ormford required them all to eat; the Farquharsons recommended scampi, and when they came they were little scant things obviously fit for a Saturday night. Peg launched a certain amount of drained, witty protest, but Ormford kept the table plied with wine and chat, and the shrimps had *some* flavour. He said it was *that* sort of birthday.

There were the Ormfords, some couple from Geology that the Farquharsons hadn't met before, and the Nwonkwos. Tables had been shoved together to make room for ten. "Not to worry," Ormford said, "they'll be late," and dealt with the waiter.

They had conversation in shouts that died in the middle of the table. There were varied dozens of people on the tiny floor around them; Ormford and Peg misbehaved dutifully, dancing or not. Oscar was proudly attentive to his wife, who seemed to glide orbiting at the edge of the crowd, changing shapes. Joan said, "That woman is the loveliest thing I ever saw."

Joan, wearing her gold-and-white and the malachite beads and the silver Christmas jewellery, and with no birthday except in the no-man's-land of August, wanted to have arms put around her and to be danced normally. Her husband did this, and looked at other people over her shoulder.

He realized when he saw the latecomers that he might have expected Ormford to celebrate, having decided to resume acquaintance, with an act of naughtiness. He said, "Hello Bill, Gail." But if he was expected to dance with women for Larry Ormford's pleasure, he would choose Victoria. One wineglass later, and with somewhat quieter music, they were on the floor. And his body chose that night finally, and absolutely, to understand what dancing was.

The lights went out; dim purple discs shone overhead: they

were in ultraviolet. Farquharson saw one man's socks, down by the floor, shimmering industriously. He pointed them out to Victoria, who was shining like a sun, pale gold and purple. Somebody bumped him behind. The very act of shifting himself was part of a dance. He thought, "This is what friends do."

"Henry," she said, "you have become a dancer."

He said, "No more hula." Not abandon: control, surrender to restraint, precision, and the existence of male life, heart, gut, and wit. The music left them in the ultraviolet finally, and they had to sit down again. He thought, "Peg isn't certain of me," and the bubbling entertainment of the thought made him take her too onto the floor and dance.

And since his doctor was dancing with his wife, that was the next thing.

The tablecloth seemed to pour blue light up onto the people's faces, and yet the light never reached them. Silhouettes of sea-weed-purple hands cut across its fluorescence looking dead and dirty. "Have I ever danced with you?" Gail said.

The couple from the Geology Department had been sixteen years in Africa and they no longer danced. One of them had a heart condition. It was as if they were leaving it to the world to guess which one of them it was. So because the Ormfords were dancing, and Victoria sitting to talk while Oscar found the washroom, and Bill and Joan somewhere on the other side of the floor, Farquharson and Gail rose and danced. "We danced on concrete, remember?" Farquharson said. "When Bill had the toe?"

Maybe, he thought, they were too serious, being lovers, to be dancers. They moved with ease enough, but half-alone, signalling but not catching echoes. They got ordinary light for it: plain light-bulbs and the continuing low candles on the tables. Somehow everything looked dim and garish.

They stayed on the floor. It was as if they couldn't get off until they had done something right. They were put back in ultraviolet. One whole party cleared off the floor to eat a feast at a far set of tables. Someone joined them in the ultraviolet, someone whose synthetic shirt damned him by not shining (Farquharson's collar blazed).

Bill said, "Your wife's in the can. May I cut in?"

They danced three together. There didn't seem to be any reason not to, and it was fun. Suddenly they were in a private circle, with snapping fingers and busy feet, but nobody really paid any attention until they had achieved something Central European, in a huddle with their arms linked around their shoulders, feet zigzagging, heel and toe, heads down then up, making a bit of valiant nonsense and manifestly proud of it. And the music dropped them right beside their table, and the lights went on.

Joan was back. Peg said, "Some kind of troika?"

Fortunately, the communal instinct held intact against embarrassment. Two of them unlinked arms—they didn't at first notice which two—and they fronted the table with Bill in the middle and sang "Happy Birthday" to Ormford, to the accompaniment of applause and some strenuous table-banging from the back corner. "Which," Bill said, sitting down, "is the fastest way of eliminating Africa I can think of," and having defined what they all were, he sat staring morosely into a candle and fiddling with the tails of his late shrimp.

It threatened then to be the sort of evening no one knew how to stop, but the thin couple from the Geology Department chose their own time for getting up from looking at the natives and each other, so there were all the formalities of thank-you's and well-wishes and departure, and Victoria asking suddenly for the outcome of Jamie and the worms (Farquharson blessed her for it), and everyone was outside and going. Gail put a white helmet on her head and the two went off on her Honda.

Joan said, "They go too fast."

"Good night, Ormfords. Forty-two more, eh?"

"Leave Ormford to his own embarrassments", he thought. "He asked for them."

They took the road in silence except for the car. From some anxiety Farquharson speeded until he could see the Honda. "I wouldn't drive one of those," he said, "I wish they didn't."

"Haven't you made a sufficient exhibition," she said, "for one night?"

"Oh, that."

"And don't you talk to me about states of innocence. I can see you thinking them."

"You should have joined us."

And she could tell that, flying through the dark, in pursuit of the Honda, he quite believed she could have. "Between who and who?"

"Between Bill and me. Naturally." He said, "We were dancing, weren't we?"

PART SIX

34

"FARQ," Joan said, "I'm being blown to bits." He had swung the ventilator window forward. He didn't close it.

"Sometimes I like to feel the wind in my hair," he said. "It makes me feel vee-rile." He said the word as if it had a hyphen in it. She didn't know who was being mocked.

A profile in the darkness, with the coxcomb of hair flapping as the hard air hit it. Nothing he could ever do could make him not pleased with himself, and yet sometimes she could catch him asleep with the whole of that forelock gathered into his fist, as if he were holding on, to keep safe. She saw Jamie sometimes sleep with his fingers against his head. "Well," she thought, "should I say it?"

He would make light of it, warning her.

She wondered whether her mouth moved.

He faced the dwindling white shape of the Honda on the road ahead as if to say, "Would you rather *I* talked?"

"Why did you have to dance with them?" she said.

"Bill came and danced with *us*."

If they were going to have a fight, he thought, *the* fight, they had better have it away from home. He saw the entry to the Ring Road and turned onto it. That way they at least had an imitation of a deserted road. "At least, if you had a mistress," he could hear her wanting to say, "you could have had her to yourself."

He could say, "*I'm* shared," savagely, and stop the car. He could feel the words in his mouth; she knew something stirred. He drew the car to a gentle halt and, as if he were a Nigerian, turned off the engine and the lights.

397

"And when you're finished having a temper," she could say, "you'll see why I'm right."

They sat in vivid, rather dreadful mental enactment of the fight they *could* have, and being closely married in many things, were lodged in almost the same fight, not knowing what to say that wouldn't start it.

"The crazy thing is," he was thinking, "*I* was the one who could have been celibate. And you couldn't."

They began to see each other. This man had sired a dying daughter and a living son: they both looked like him. And all the months when the hospital was fighting for the little girl, and she had been afraid and full of a dreadful hasty reluctance to lay herself open again to this man's seed—he had gone to the hospital three days a week without saying anything—until he came home, said, "Poor little fucked-up baby—no way to live," and then made her make love, had made her take his despair and make love out of it—and had put Jamie in her, somewhere in that time; Jamie, who was his father's total son, to whom she gave guarding and care for his little foreign sparkling industry and delight— "But," she thought, "I don't know him."

Nobody was going to take a father away from this son, certainly not this father.

He hunched over, near her, kissed her. Finally he said, "Hi, Jamie's mother."

Would he make her hungry for him, here on the road? She thought: "I've got to like him." She did, after all, like his clown's nose; she *was* safely fond of him, in some junior fashion. It was as if they had come to terms.

Showdowns, she thought, never showed the right things down, even if people spoke the words. You could travel in the dark, inventing words to the unforgivable quarrel, but when the time came and there was space to say them, one kissed the man, and was married to him, almost without valuing him. "Let the man play games," she thought. "It isn't as if *I* wanted him.'

"You know what I really mind?" she wanted to say. "It's that

398

you did all this in Africa. Because that wasn't what you came for.
You came to *do* something."

"I'm having an affair," he thought. "I mean to go on having it,
while it lasts."

He said, "*Ọmọ nâ dế!*" and took her to the other nightclub. Not
having had the fight, they had nerves to spare: they had to go
somewhere.

Drums, the moon, American wind instruments, the wall around
unreal and solid as if it were in a movie, while voices chorused
rude-sounding words. Joan said, "There's Bernice Funmilayọ."

"Why, Professor and Mrs. Farquharson," she said, "how very
pleasant."

Farquharson thought, "She's been an exile since she quit
Jeremy. She really means this."

They were made to meet a sullen half-drunk man in a damask
agbada. They couldn't keep Mr. Ogunsanwo from desiring to be
their host, but they managed not to dance; Mrs. Funmilayọ said
small indiscreet things about the university, teasing Farquharson
about his visit to her boss, so Farquharson asked her about Mr.
Sam Majẹkodunmi. She said, "He is in this office. I think he will
stay, you know. I come here very often," she added. "This is a
nice place."

Mr. Ogunsanwo sat measuring his beer into his mouth and
making adjustments to his sleeves. Mrs. Funmilayọ took him away
to dance after another bottle.

Joan said, "Let's go," and as the music swept up into hammer-
ing noise, they tiptoed out. "Poor Bernice!" she said. "What a pig
of a man!"

She put her hand under his arm. It was as if Mrs. Funmilayọ had
shown her what it was to be deliberately a woman, and she was
going to try it. After all, she was the wife of the man who had
that body.

Maybe it was the beer; maybe it wasn't. They got home, and
found Stanley's Celina in the living room ("Madam, he try not to
fall asleep, but I send him to bed") and faced each other, after
Celina, paid double, had slipped out, with their faces naked and

the room very much in focus. Farquharson said, "Well? Do you want me?"

It might have been the beer, she thought. She had to take him. But it was as if she couldn't feel him. He was a rubbery gouge without friction, and they had to labour in each other's arms for what wouldn't mean anything that way: sweat and wretched determination instead of—not fun, which she couldn't make herself expect, but the kind of brief, savage, shaming glory which she did know, and which was left to her. He churned, jerked, too long—as if he too had to feel himself and couldn't. He was a thing struggling to help, not kind, and not an instrument: a will, fighting, trying to be near. She hit him; she grabbed pieces of him; she dragged him to her; she forced a hand towards his balls as if she were going to drag them out of his body. And she couldn't come; she was marooned, debased, stuck in white friction with her head moving.

He was numb; he had to work. Recklessness finally dredged up the content of the nerves. He broke. He flooded her with a kind of hollow-stomached thoroughness, fell on her. She said, "More."

She thought, "He doesn't believe. He's angry."

"Hurry!" She drew up her legs.

So he thrust at her almost as if he were working with a broom-stick, and at last she came. "Okay?" he said.

He stayed inside, slightly moving, caressing her now from within, daring the pain. It came, but, thanks perhaps to the beer, not quite so much. Still, she said, "You'd better get out again."

He did.

She said, "It wasn't very good."

"Look at the clock."

"All right. We took a long time at it."

He was breathing deeply and shakily. Crises passed, she thought, not always to the end one thought for them. Now that he had been used as a lover, she wished he could sleep somewhere else.

In the morning she found the counterfeit sixpence lying on the closet floor under his grey trousers. "Do you put this thing in *every* pocket?" she said.

"I thought I'd lost it."

There were more outbreaks in the North. Farquharson finished marking his first set of questions, and discovered that he had failed almost three out of four of them. He went in a near-panic to Ormford to be told that this was about normal, and to make adjustments if he felt he had to, but otherwise let it by.

"Arveragus," Ormford read from the paper Farquharson was carrying at the time, "is a Briton knight who seeks fame and fortune at the court of King Arthur to which he can not bring his wife who is thus left at home pining and sorrowing to be courted by the 'squiyer' Aurelius who promises to remove the rocks so that he can make love to her while Arveragus returns home in safety on a boat. We are in no doubt as to what Dorigen thinks of this." While he read, Farquharson noticed, he didn't stammer.

Farquharson said, "I like passing people."

"That," Ormford said, "is a failing."

Farquharson made a face, and went back to work.

They had to start preparing to go back to Canada. WP2471 was taken to the Motor Transport Yard to be evaluated. Arrangements were made with a firm in Lagos to pack and ship their goods. Farquharson looked at his brick-red new jacket and said, "I'll wear that at home." WP2471 was declared to be in Good or OK condition throughout, except for the spare tire. Farquharson stuck up a notice on the Club bulletin board offering to sell. He finished all his questions, recognizing some handwritings and encountering a great many things he'd said.

Hausamen had been leaving them alone for a while, even the one they liked. Now they began descending for last assaults. Farquharson had a delighted set-to with one of his more constant and unlikeable ones over an orange-pink necklace set with tubular Venetian beads. One said it was coral; the other said it was glass. One valued it at two pounds, the other at three shillings, and after half an hour the Hausaman was waving a typed testimonial to his honesty and Farquharson was happily shouting, "You're trying to tell a man who has been in every glass factory in Venice what isn't glass?"

Joan said, "You have not been in every glass factory. Please be honest."

And the Hausaman chivalrously began testifying to the master's honour and honesty, together with his own virtue, until Farquharson had to pay an eventual nine-and-six to get rid of him. He hung the necklace on Joan's neck. "Yours," he said.

If they had come to some understanding the night of the Ormfords' birthday party, it didn't seem to be a friendly one. Farquharson made love to Joan with a scrupulous fairness, battling for her, but where once he would have nudged her or said, "Look" or "Hey", when Jamie did something like taking a cloth and polishing the furniture the way Jacob did, now he let her see it for herself, and at most looked halfway across the room towards her. The odd thing was that as he kept his privacy, he kept a shortness of temper with it. The neutrality between himself and Joan having been so roughly and abruptly marked out, he couldn't take his temper out on her but had to keep it, and when he couldn't keep it to himself, he found sometimes he was becoming sharp and curt to Jamie. Several times when they went shopping, Farquharson found that he had made Jamie cry.

Now the government announced that there was going to be a publicity campaign to explain the government's aims, policies, and principles to the North. Farquharson had visions of jeeploads of administrators meeting the striding orange camel of the postage stamps and trying to talk to it. The government announced also that there was going to be an inquiry into the Nigerian Railways, and the Nigerian Electric Corporation. Virtue was abroad again, preaching virtue.

An elderly man met Farquharson at the Club and said he might want to buy the car. The afternoon he was due to come to the house and see it, WP2471 was towed away to have its clutch replaced. "Fortunately," Farquharson said to the Nwonkwos, "he didn't come."

WP2471 came back, a considerable number of pounds later. Farquharson was wrestling, long distance, with the problem of getting enough money to go home on, and showing, for Joan, some of the first real tropical hysteria she had seen in him. "Two hundred and fifty pounds," he said, about the car. "I've got to get two hundred and fifty pounds for that."

"Are we suddenly broke," she said, "or have you just not been telling me?"

He said, "I just want to think about something other than money for the last month."

Then the college at home sent five hundred dollars to his bank, and they got travellers' cheques with it, half and half, his and hers. "You can leave me now," he said, and both of them wished he hadn't said it.

He saw her into the car and came back to get out his week's cash. The teller in the first cage waved him peremptorily over to the second and continued doing some bank business with a stack of cancelled cheques. Farquharson didn't need to look into the cage to know who was the second teller: the state of the line in front of him spelled Ogunsheye. Trying to be patient, or amused, he had to resign himself. He had missed Ogunsheye a great many times, largely by design; he had to get him sooner or later.

A little healthy-looking man, Mr. Ogunsheye, (with his name in front of him scorning the Yoruba under-dotted "ṣ") carried dreamy meticulousness to the point of rank hysteria. Whenever Farquharson or Joan sent Stanley to the bank, they knew by the length of his absence which teller he had had. Now Ogunsheye was again counting serial numbers on consecutive bills, comparing the numbers in opposite corners of the same bill, querulously refusing to accept careful lists of wanted denominations of notes and silver if even the crossing out of a figure, or the form of one, offended him. Farquharson wondered sometimes what a man trapped with such active, slaving rigour inside himself would

403

have to feel like to keep on, day in, day out, maddening his customers by the slow-motion pencil, the slow-motion eye, and the considering head. Joan was certainly going to be out of patience in the car.

It would have been useful to think of Joan, but one of Ogunsheye's qualities was that no one in his line could think of, or watch, anything but him.

One of the big Hausamen was ahead of Farquharson in a rage of dignity that would have done justice to an *ọba*. Ogunsheye was being reasonable, sniping with little pecking queries about what he was supposed to do. After a long time the next in line, a servant running errands, presented a paper. For once, Ogunsheye was quick. "What am I to do with such a piece of paper as this? Everything is wrong on it. Whose is this signature? This man will have to come here himself."

A moment of tongue-lashing. The servant—thin, in khaki—went away. Farquharson reached forward and shoved his cheque to rest in a U between the bars. To his annoyance Ogunsheye ignored all the waiting slips, took up something that had been slid through the wicket, and without looking at it lifted his head to stare through everyone. Suddenly he spoke in a light, happy voice, as if he were contemplating something between pleasure and content. "*When* I break down," he said, "I shall not come here for a *week*!"

And Farquharson loved him, and was still chuckling when he reached the car.

"*When* I break down," he said to the Nwonkwos, "I shall not come here for a *week*!"

He laughed all weekend over it, in between trying to get offers for the car.

Suddenly WP2471 became an object of hysteria. Panic, frustration, distaste—all the things in Joan's Africa that Farquharson had missed—had suddenly turned, embodied in that car, and, for no reason that Farquharson could see, dumped themselves on

404

Joan's husband. No one wanted to buy the car, except one ugly man whose offer seemed unrealistically low; no one offered himself at the Club or at the Kingsway (except one dealer, smiling and beaming untrustworthily at him). Stanley tried to round up a syndicate of buyers among his connections. Farquharson took the car back to the Bye-Pass and got, after much reluctance, an offer of two hundred pounds. ("Two hundred and fifty: I've *got* to have two hundred and fifty!") He came time and again back to the desk in the living room and worked out sums: bills, bonus on wages, the minimal costs in Europe going home. Then he would tear them up, watch Jamie play with the fairy castle and his cuddle toy, or with what was left of Gail's magic mountain with the cars. Then he would pick Jamie up and carry him, up and down in the house or around the grass—and Joan knew he was holding on, that when he lifted the boy up in a bear hug he was trying to cling to his temper, his amusement, to all the things he had suddenly (and, to Joan, for no good reason) lost. Then he would fling himself out of the house, and whether he went into Ibadan by himself, burrowing through the hot, humid streets, or to Gail's half-house with its huge furniture and windows choked by bougainvillaea, he came back the same: drained, irritable, ashamed only of his temper, and having had no respite.

Joan said, "I hate that car."

"All right. I've still got to sell it, don't I?"

They took it to a dealer on the far side of Ibadan, on a street Farquharson hadn't seen before. Five men examined it. Something in the engine was on the very verge of being seriously wrong: they disagreed on what. One hundred and eighty pounds.

"And to think," Farquharson said, "that one week ago somebody offered two hundred and forty, and I didn't like him and didn't take it!"

Stanley's coalition, including the mechanic, which Farquharson thought might almost be a good sign, arrived, inspected the car, pondered, and said they would come back.

And meanwhile the government of the West dumped, in a few days, every car that had been confiscated from the old regime.

Farquharson realized how panicky he was when he discovered that for four days he hadn't known about it. He wrote the figures down: Thursday, £240; Saturday, £200; Tuesday, £180; Thursday again, the last attempt, £160. "Well, at least it isn't just me," he said, several times. "They just shot the bottom out of the whole damn market."

Indeed, within a few days the government realized what it had done and tried to salve the damage by rationing the cars, and Farquharson threw the paper onto the couch and said, "Another virtuous announcement!"

By accident Joan and Gail came together at the Club bar. Farquharson was in the pool, swimming until his eyes were sick from chlorine. "That car!" Joan said. "All he can think about is that damned car! And he can't haggle any more."

On Friday a young man spoke to him outside the Staff Store, spent much time examining the car (WP2471, smug in its almost perfect tan-brown paint) and offered two hundred pounds.

Farquharson took his name (Mr. Igwe), and agreed.

Saturday morning, when Farquharson was out of the house, Stanley's coalition made an offer of two hundred and twenty-five pounds to Joan.

Farquharson had been lying on Gail's bed, wanting nothing but the air conditioning and a bit of quiet. Twenty-five pounds, when he came home and was told, was too much for honour.

That weekend was something he didn't want to think about, even as it was happening. He had signed, and had Mr. Igwe sign, a scrap-of-paper agreement about the purchase of the car. He tried to get it back. With Stanley driving, he chased all through Kongi trying to find out where the man worked; they found the house but not the man, and had to go out again and chase him to the cattle market. Farquharson's head was swimming in the heat, and he got a salt pill out of the glove compartment and forced it down, sweat in his eyebrows, wax all over his eyelids behind the steel-rimmed glasses worn for authority. He had rehearsed proper speeches about need and honour too much: all he knew was that he was ashamed of himself for trying to get out of an agreement, and that he was going to get out of it, no matter what he had to do.

They found Mr. Igwe beside the railway tracks, walking, easy. Farquharson thought he couldn't be more than twenty-two. He stuck his head out of the car window, and, disgracing himself to himself with every word (but not to Stanley, who was due to get a dash from the coalition, Farquharson guessed, if *they* got the car), ranted and orated, justified himself, noted how shocked the boy was at the destruction of the *oyibo*'s honour, demanded either an increase in the offer or an end to the agreement—and, when all he got was a shocked stare and a calling of his attention to his own honour, screamed out the window that he was going to repudiate the agreement, took his copy out of his pocket, tore it up, threw the pieces in the road, and told Stanley to take him home. All his humiliations, he thought, had to happen across from the cattle market.

And when he got home he felt sick and tried to refuse supper. Stanley's coalition came at suppertime, and he yelled them off the patio too and said, "I don't know!"

It seemed to be decided that because Mr. Igwe was just "a Calabar boy", they could do anything to him.

"You're being pretty disgraceful," Joan said, "do you know that?"

Mr. Igwe came, full of reproaches, on Sunday morning. He said, "I will give you the money Monday, sir, you will have to take it. I have your signature. You must be a man of honour, sir."

"Damn it!" Farquharson said to Joan. "I don't want to be beaten by *him*!"

Igwe was on the patio for Monday's breakfast. "All right," Farquharson said, "but if that money isn't in the bank by noon, the deal's off."

"*Yes*, sir!"

Stanley drove them over and left them in the bank, then took Joan to the Staff Store and back again. There was a long wait.

407

Finally Mr. Igwe came with a hundred and ninety-six pounds and counted them out to Farquharson, in a backwater close to the door. "We have to go to my house," he said, "for other four, or I can bring on Thursday."

"All the money by noon."

"Sir," he said, "not again. Not again, please."

"Oh, very well." Farquharson re-counted the cash, went to the first teller, made out his deposit form, gave in the money, watched the teller count it, looked back to see Mr. Igwe on a bench beside the door, and found Stanley, unnoticed, at his elbow saying, "Farq, I need a bob."

Taxi fare from the campus. Farquharson said, "The car?"

"It refuse to go."

35

So they let Mr. Igwe go, took the taxi to where Stanley had pushed the car, arranged to have it towed to the Motor Transport Yard the next morning, and Farquharson got a Morris Minor rented to him for the duration of his stay. "From tomorrow," they said.

He walked home under the sun, took two salt pills and then two cocktails.

"You've been putting on quite a display since last week," Joan said. "Are you going to stop?"

He stumbled on the fairy castle. "Damn!" he shouted, the vodka running down the back of his hand. "What the hell's that doing there?"

"Far' hit my castle!"

"Well you should have had it somewhere else!"

Joan shouted: "Farq!"

He was ashamed.

Jamie was putting the pieces of his castle on the desk, one by one; big tears stood in his eyes. Farquharson apologized, crouching.

"Far' hit."

Farquharson reached to pick up a pink turret.

Jamie said, "Mine," and took it away from him.

A long time later Jamie went into the bedroom and said, "You were *loud* to me."

Joan said, "Stanley's back."

"Is crankshaft, sir. Seventy-five pounds, he say, maybe more. Maybe they not get part." They stood looking at each other. "Sir, please, is this car of Mr. Igwe or you?"

So graduation morning, while Farquharson was waiting with his robes over his arm to go to Trenchard Hall, Mr. Igwe arrived, had the situation explained, was offered his money, refused it, and left seemingly convinced that this was another manoeuvre on the part of the *oyibo* professor to sell his car for the same higher bid he tried to get on Sunday. Joan said, "Don't be so noble you cost us our money."

"I'm trying honour. It doesn't seem to work any better than the other did. Who pays for the crankshaft?" He spread his hands. "When I break down, I shall not come here for a week."

To graduation, alone.

Apart from the guns, which today weren't there, the ceremony was like November, with a substitute for the dead Balewa (Dike himself), and many more people getting degrees. And again it was impossible to make out a word spoken. The Vice-Chancellor spoke with passion; the echo from the balcony confounded all he said, and the inhuman, rapid, precise syllables went on and on. Last time he was here, Farquharson thought, he had got a hard on.

He found a notice in his pocket that he had got with his mail days ago and not read because he was on his way to sell the car. To avoid the pelting syllables he spread it on his knee and let his eyes drop to it in snatches.

Press Release.

Mr. Sam A. B. Majekodunmi, Bursar of the University of Ibadan and Master of Independence Hall was directed by the Council of the University to proceed on leave as from 1st June, 1966.

Mr. Majekodunmi has remained.

(*"He is in his office,"* Bernice Funmilayo said. *"I think he will stay, you know."*)

In view of this open defiance of the constituted authority of this University, the Vice-Chancellor has been compelled to exercise his powers . . .

(*"If there were ever a time for diplomacy within this university, that time has passed."*)

. . . and has suspended Mr. Sam A. B. Majękodunmi from exercising any and all the functions of his office.

One word from Dike's speech began to detach itself from the chaos of echoes and rattle against his head: "tribalism".

Then he knew what the man had to be saying: "Don't let tribalism be strengthened by the education that should be destroying it. "The one clear thing in the echoes was the urgency of the voice.

Mr. Igwe wouldn't believe that anything was the matter with the car. Farquharson sent him to the Motor Transport Yard, but he came back still unconvinced.

Farquharson thought for half an hour, with Jamie playing so as not to disturb him on the further end of the couch, then said, "Well, here goes," and wrote a letter to the Motor Transport Officer, decided it was sufficiently snotty and legalistic to pass muster, and sent Stanley off with it.

When Mr. Igwe arrived on Friday still confident that he was going to receive the car, Farquharson gave him a carbon of the letter:

"Dear Sir: In view of the situation of the ownership of WP2471, I must ask that, as far as I am concerned, further work on the car be suspended pending the decisions of the new owner . . ."

"What? What is this?"

"I am no longer responsible for the nature of further repairs to the car, or for their cost."

"*What do you do to me?*"

"You chose to believe I was lying, Mr. Igwe."

Suddenly they were screaming at each other. Mr. Igwe stood there with the four pounds in his hand. "For the last time," Farquharson shouted, "*do you want your money back?*"

Eyes flashing, the "Calabar boy" counted the four red bills out, one by one, onto the patio. Farquharson picked them up.

The boy made a speech. It seemed to be unstoppable. It involved his dignity, his family, his honour, the words, "Sir, I am a man!" and once, fatally, "Sir, I assure you that I am willing to buy your car."

"Shit! *You have bought it!*" And then: "YOU ARE GOING TO BE QUIET AND LISTEN TO ME!"

Shaking, ready to stumble, he went finally into the house and started to close all the doors.

"I shall bring my brother, sir. I shall bring my brother!"

Face to face, flaring with wrath.

He ran into the bathroom and set the cold water thundering bubbles into the bathtub. Joan came to the door and said, "Jamie's been having hysterics for half an hour. How could you? Farq, you terrified him." She said, "*And* me. Farq, have you gone out of your mind?"

"What am I to do? Am *I* supposed to choose between a seventy-pound repair and a hundred-and-thirteen-pound one? He's screwed me once already. That's enough."

"Farq, I'm all for cheating that little man. But don't *justify* yourself!"

He went to his boy. Jamie was on his bed, clutching his cuddle toy, hiccupping—seeing, Farquharson supposed, the man with the frying pan. He knelt, naked, beside him. "Jamie," he said. "I'm sorry. I won't ever yell again."

"Go on," Joan said.

"Have a bath with me? Jamie, I'm all right, honestly." With all the passion and quiet he had he said, gently, "I didn't hit him."

"Never hit me?"

He crooned, "No, no, no, no. I just got tired and sad, and then I wanted to be mad at him." He lifted him up. "Let's cool off. Come?"

Joan heard the splash, thought, "Two elephants in the bathtub," and then, "Well, he'll have to clean up himself."

412

"Jamie," her husband had said, "I didn't hit him." *Why was he saying that?*

And finally, Jamie, standing between his father's knobby feet—wary, and as happy as he seemed to judge prudent—waded to Farq's hands and said, "Hug."

Joan said, "I'm taking Jamie to the Club. You can come when it's all over."

They went off in the tiny, half-broken Morris Minor. Farquharson waited under the fan, muttering, "I am tame, sir: pronounce."

But it was a quiet meeting of three, with the fortunately intelligent "brother" as referee. And Farquharson, remembering both that he was a white master and that he knew how to deal with Hausamen, hit a tone of reasonable asperity that didn't suit him but at least kept anything of his own emotions out of range. He managed in an hour to secure complete freedom from the car and a couple of comprehensive receipts at a cost of forty-five pounds as his share of the repairs. Igwe was still caught in his morning's speech, and he had to be told again by his "brother" that he had bought the car, and that his offers to go through with the obligation had gone past their time. Farquharson shook hands with them both at the door and made sure they had gone, and that WP2471 had gone also, for good, with them. "And in that car," he thought, "the dead rode to love."

Jamie: asking his father not to hit him. Farquharson sighed and thought, "He remembers. Oh damn, I wonder if he always will."

"Stanley!" he yelled.

"Farq," Stanley said, smiling, "that boy who was here. He not happy."

"Well?" Joan said.

"All over. And nobody yelled."

"How much?"

"I'm in for forty-five. He may be in for seventy."

413

"Now," she said, "let Stanley take Jamie over to the playground."

And she told him at length (he felt, implacably), how frightened Jamie had been, and how he mustn't do that again, or try to rush in love and gentleness as if it hadn't happened. "Let him get over it. And what did the two of you mean, about hitting people?"

"He saw me get in a fight once. I'm not proud of it."

He picked up a dog-eared old *Sunday Times* magazine and started to look at the coloured pictures. Joan said, "I see."

"No," he said, "you don't. But it doesn't matter."

Stanley and Jamie were sitting on the grass, solemnly holding conversation. Farquharson, watching them from the top of a small grass slope, felt miles off, as if he couldn't talk. "Lion—on—purple," Jamie was saying, speaking of his animals and his fairy castle together, to Stanley's loving bewilderment. "Cow on green. Cow has to be on green."

Stanley said, "Cow on brown."

Jamie said, "Man on red." He had a farmer or two among the plastic animals.

Man on red indeed, Farquharson thought. Knocked onto a red concrete floor, with a collapsed hollow in his head—but somehow the skin hadn't broken, and he had dragged him by the ankles around the dining room and the right armpit had jammed on the corner of the drinks refrigerator. It was funny to find himself thinking about having killed that one: "Far' *hit*." Of course: that was the one Jamie saw.

No sudden gentleness, he thought, and moved down the slope. "Hi, you two."

"Farq," Joan called, "I want to go to the store. Come with me?"

He hung halfway down. "All right," he thought, "two can play at that."

"Come to the store, Jamie."

"Got to talk to Stanley!"

"We talk of animals," Stanley said, looking proud.

"Nope. To the store!"

A sad little voice, a sort of clear meditation of protest: "Want to talk of *animals*!"

Joan said, "Are you going to bully your way to kindness? I told you not to."

Farquharson said, "Come on, Stanley. Talk of animals. We'll all go together."

But Jamie had stopped talking. He kept his animals, the colours of his towers, to himself, and Farquharson pushed him in a cart of his own around the almost empty store.

"Satisfied?" Joan said. "You made him happy, didn't you?"

Supper was over; Jamie was in his bed; Farquharson had sung him down for almost half an hour, and then suddenly Jamie cried as if he had to be forgiven, and Joan came in to hold him and said to Farquharson, "Fat lot of good your lullabies did. What is it, Jamie? Mummy's here."

"Oh God," he thought, "she's going to love him," and as if there were stark reason for it, he was afraid.

But Jamie was tending to his own needs. "Want Far'," he said solidly, through his tears. "Up!"

So Joan had to give him into his father's arms. Farquharson steadied him on his chest, then thrust him high into the air and made him a plane that banked and swooped. Farquharson shouted, "Africa!" Then Jamie called, "Plane fall *down*!" and Farquharson let him crash just excitingly enough onto the bed. "Now you go to sleep, sir," he said, and put him back in the crib.

"But what was he crying about?"

Her husband said, "Oh, for Pete's sake, shut up." At about a quarter to nine he said, "I want to go out."

"I'll be all right. I want to read."

He was on his way to Gail's house, and the white-blue Honda jumped past him with Gail and her lover on it. He forced the horn to one huge blast; the Honda went almost out of control and stopped. He backed up.

Bill was sitting behind Gail, looking shaken from the skid. "This is *my* night!" he called.

Gail said, "These things are tricky. Henry, what did you want?"

"What's wrong?" Bill said, and got off the Honda.

But he couldn't say that his wife and he had just found out that the one thing they had to do was struggle for their son, or that he had just a week to go. "Sorry," he said. So they took him to her house, where he stood irresolutely in the living room as they made a drink for him. There was the usual stage-model on the table beside the window: an eighteenth-century interior with a six-leaved screen and a tiny balsa chair. "For our historical collection," Gail said. "That's *The School for Scandal* in the original." She was a craftsman; pride and something more, a frank love of what she could do, spoke in her voice. She wanted praise from him.

Farquharson said, "Joan wants Jamie."

Being who they were, Bill thought, they couldn't comfort a man who was suddenly a week from irrelevance. He brought Farquharson's drink to him and said, "One good slug, and stop. Gail can either make you forget or make you remember, or we can all just sit here or you can go home." But he shook his head as if to negate all four.

"And if you're in trouble tomorrow," Bill said when he put Farquharson back into his car, "and need any form of comfort, come to us and we'll go on the town." He added, "I guess tonight *was* ours."

Farquharson left his rented car in the driveway. Everything was locked up. Suddenly he thought that he wanted to walk around the house, to claim it by perambulation, because he'd never done that. It was almost new moon: there was no one to watch him but stars and clouds. He set out along the left wall of the garage past the kitchen door.

Here was where Stanley and Celina had romped in the first few days. He hadn't seen Celina lately; he wondered if she was visiting. The house fell off into the distance on his right; Joan couldn't be in bed yet, surely. Like a Peeping Tom, he went up to his own bedroom window. The beds were turned down, like hotel beds. Joan wasn't there. He brooded at the big solid empty room, tinged green by screening. It was a far cry from watching Gail carry dusty books. It was odd that his wife had the figure a man was supposed to want in bed. If she saw him now, she'd be afraid. He felt his way along a narrow passage between the hedge and the house, blocked by a tree. Beyond that was the bathroom window, frosted glass closed and dark. Then Jamie's room, with light in it. He heard, "It's all right, Jamie. It's going to be all right. You tell Mummy and then it's all going to be all right. Farq didn't hit anybody, did he? He's your Daddy."

What did a man put his face at a window for? She was on the bed; Jamie was on her knee, being hugged and rocked. Farquharson could see his eyes and face, looking beyond the arms. And he realized that Jamie wasn't speaking, and wasn't crying.

He thought, "Go on, Jamie! tell her!"

And if she saw him?

"Your Daddy wouldn't hit anybody. If he did, he couldn't be the Daddy I know."

"Oh God," he thought, "that's my son. Sitting there."

"Two reflections in the one glass," he thought. "Just as he remembered it in the store window. One watched the other. Or watched over the other.

"Tell Mummy and it'll be all right, Jamie. Did you *think* he hit somebody?"

He thought: "You know I did. You've heard us. You just don't know who ... Tell Mummy, Jamie, and it'll be all right. Tell her, damn it!"

But Jamie was guarding his father by saying nothing. (And when the frying pan rose and fell, Jamie had gone into the same waking silence.)

If he could have struck his wife he would have done it. It didn't help that he was suddenly so abjectly and furiously sorry for her.

"I'd better come home," he thought. But he was afraid to move. How Joan hated the noise of invaders' feet going around that house, with pineapple, tomatoes, cloth, a basin for pickle bottles . . .

One dark window, beyond which was a bare mattress with the edge of a stain. Light in the living room . . .

He made a big noise with the door and cried out, "Yoo-hoo! I'm home!"

"He wouldn't sleep."

"Okay," he said, "let *me* try."

He lay on the small bed, holding Jamie beside him and singing to him. Joan stood in the door and watched. Farquharson wondered what the Yoruba was for "*She doesn't trust either of us.*" Without knowing what words he made he found that he had been singing, over and over, very quietly, "Up and down, in and out, hit and miss, time and again." Jamie was sleeping.

Joan said, "You made a *hit*, I see."

That did it. He said, "I was outside the window."

She shook it off. "He's worried, He's going to *have* to tell me, to get rid of it."

"What do you think I've done?"

"Hit somebody, I suppose. Probably some small, mean thing he's misinterpreted, but it's big to him."

"Some small, mean thing."

"You can be very mean," she said.

He had to go to bed in anger, a small sickening prolonged wrath like punk burning.

"Whatever I am," he said, in the middle of the night, since they were both still awake, "whatever I may have done, misinterpreted or not, I've promised Jamie never to hit any human being, and he knows I mean it. So don't dig below a shielding promise and pull everything out again. That's a direct order."

A cold voice in the dark: "I'll find out."

"Leave him alone."

36

HE went to say goodbye to the Ormfords, but it was as if a boat had already got out of reach of the dock. "Was it a *gg-good* year?" Did that have *any* answer?

They went into town, buying cautiously because they were supposed to be leaving within a week, and they couldn't find anything that could be said in the right way. It was as if they quarrelled all morning, all day, and yet never quarrelled, never really said anything. But Joan pushed Jamie around the Kingsway food department: Stanley was sent outside. And she kept her hand on the cart and made Farquharson bring her things.

Farquharson wondered if Jamie thought that his parents were in trouble with each other because of him—he kept making three-year-old stabs at tactful conversation. Language had been a superb complicated release for Jamie; now all the precocious words were set forth, and they didn't do any good; Farquharson could see guilt smuggle itself into his face all day, at intervals. He probably didn't remember a hand that struck, Farquharson thought; he remembered a whirlwind and a fall, and a father rushing huge out of it and first towering over and then swooping down to him—for something *he* had done?

They talked loudly at lunch, for Jacob in the kitchen, about very little. Jamie suddenly got into a talking jag, which not even his nap stopped. (They could hear, "Thank you, thank you. Have some beer." He was being a host.) He was rude, uncomfortable, unstoppable. Farquharson tried to calm him by launching into inane verbal games, but Jamie was in a runaway high-keyed state. It didn't help that Joan was looking at her husband steadily feeling him go wrong—and, if she could, without committing herself, pushing him to do one wrong thing.

He couldn't get away to go to Gail: he couldn't find how to.

At least they could go to the Club. But at half past four they hadn't been able to find Stanley. Joan said, "Well, we don't need *him* any more!"

Jamie said, "Hit him! *Mummy* hit him." He hit his father on the chest and said, "Drive *on*, Stanley!"

Farquharson turned his head to Joan and said, without humour, "I think you forgot that."

They had the Club to themselves. Jamie ran all over the lounge, until one of the bar boys asked them to hush their child because the manageress was there. Farquharson looked up into a hard, stale English face—and Jamie asked for a glass of water.

This often happened, and Jamie got a nice beerglass. This time, with a look at the manageress, the bar boy gave him a small plastic glass, so scratched it had become opaque, and looking as if it had trapped every germ in Africa. Farquharson refused it, raised his voice temperishly, demanded a proper glass, and staged an African tantrum when the woman said it was an invariable rule that children got only plastic glasses, because they broke glass ones. Somehow at the height of it he got a glass of water for himself, drank one mouthful and handed it to Jamie, while Joan glared at him and the manageress came furiously off the bar stool and to her feet. "We have a rule," she said, making her voice awful.

"You go to hell."

But at least Jamie drank.

Farquharson emptied the plastic glass against the flanges of the fountain, stepped on it, and dropped the pieces into a standing ashtray. "Now you think twice," he roared at the woman who, he was certain, was ready to swear at him, "before you make children drink out of contaminated glasses. I'm going to Dr. Garnett about this."

"Ahhh!" she said. "*Him?*"

Now Joan's and Farquharson's ill temper was out in the open.

They bickered steadily, through suppertime, even in front of Jacob, and Jamie became more and more a small bad boy, pushing for punishment. He got them both twanging with irritation, and their vindictiveness and his badness built, until Farquharson, goaded by a shower of pieces of fairy castle and the animals, and with Joan's glance of consent and even encouragement, picked Jamie up, said, "That's *enough!*" and put him across his knee and spanked him.

Jamie shrieked and fell onto the rug. Joan jumped out of her chair. Jamie put his hands into the air, his face wild with terror, and screamed, "Far' *hit!*"

Before Farquharson knew what had happened Joan had snatched Jamie up and was clutching and soothing him and staring at her husband as if she had never seen him before and never wanted to again, while Farquharson sat with both hands gripping the edges of the sofa cushions, as if to hold himself up.

"There, there," she crooned. "No, no, I won't ever let him hit you."

Jamie screamed. Horror started slipping like thick fluid into Farquharson's stomach and guts.

"You hit him, didn't you?"

He could hardly start his voice.

"When? How many times?"

"No," he said. "God, no!" He heard his voice as it must sound to her.

She said, "Jamie, I won't let him touch you."

Farquharson got up. Jamie shrieked and hid his head. He had spent words and patterns all day; all he had now were howls. But Joan wouldn't take him from the room: she had to confront the man who would do that to his own child, whatever "that" might have been. She screamed suddenly, a raw, stripped voice yelling at him, "What did you *do* to him?"

He turned his back on her. He was afraid; he wanted to strike her down. Jacob stared at them from the kitchen door. Jamie's crying changed suddenly to listening, heaving sobs. Farquharson

421

thought, "He's trying to stop!" "You think I beat him up," he said.

"When? When I was in hospital?"

"*Not* when you were in hospital."

"*When?*"

"Can you stand there and think I hurt him? Jamie, did I hit you?"

Tears rolled. The crying sounded different, he thought. But *she* didn't notice it.

She said, "That's *his* answer."

Farquharson saw Jacob standing in the kitchen. He pointed and said, "Out!"

"There, there," he heard. "Tell Mummy and it'll be all right."

Jamie wouldn't tell, not when he'd defended his father so consciously, for so long. "Jamie, you stop crying and tell me what he did. Now, you've got to."

Jamie was in the crib, holding himself together, crying almost without motion, staring at his mother.

She heard Farquharson come to the door. She said, "Keep out."

He caught her by the upper arm and dragged her into the hall. "What kind of everlasting damage are you trying to do?" he whispered. "That's *Jamie* in there."

Nothing else, probably, would have brought her to her senses. She stood looking at him with eyes almost as frightened as his own, and then let him go past her into the bedroom and followed him. Jamie was watching them as if he were afraid of both of them. "We're sorry, Jamie," Farquharson said. "Everybody got mad."

Jamie sniffed, and waited; then he lay down and put his thumb in his mouth, let his open eyes be watchful and miserable. They should have stood hand in hand, perhaps, where he could see them, but they couldn't do that: Jamie's eyes went between them. Farquharson started to hum.

"No, no," Jamie said, "no sad-songs."

Not calm of mind, Farquharson thought; and not passion spent—just sealed down. When he was asleep, a cold little lump that Farquharson covered, they left him.

"Well, if you didn't hit him," she said at last, "what *did* you do?"

One minute's silence meant that nobody was going to talk all night. Farquharson picked up a sitting tiger, a tortoise, and a deep-blue pointed turret, and sat fiddling with them. It was as if some engine inside him had set up a patternless slow vibration, hollowing him out. He couldn't think.

If he stayed in the room he was going to have to throw the animals out of his hand the way Jamie threw them.

"Where are you going?"

"Out."

He was in the kitchen, rummaging in the refrigerator for something to stop what wasn't hunger. She said, "There's some foil-wrapped cheese."

He pried a wedge out of the box and peeled it, using the frying pan for a waste basket. He put the cheese into his mouth in one piece and then stood there, his hand on the rim of the frying pan.

"You and Bill and the frying pan," she said.

It went over his head and down, clanged appallingly at their feet, and took a chip out of the floor. She was as shocked as he could have wanted her to be, and let him go past her, and it wasn't until he was trying to start the new car that she stooped, shaking, and picked up the frying pan.

"Was that just bad temper?" she said. The car jerked and left her.

"Come to us," Bill had said, *"and we'll go on the town."*

They weren't at Gail's place. He could still feel the frying pan leave his hands.

Bill's light was on. Farquharson went up the stairs two at a time. They were standing in the living room as if they were waiting for him. "Let's go," he said.

"Anything to say first?" Bill said. "Because if we go out, we're going to play."

"Nothing to say. I hit Jamie. Well, shall we play?"

423

Gail said, "Some kind of troika?"

"Any kind."

He kissed her, as if Bill were nowhere near. Bill kept his eyes on them and rubbed the end of his nose with his thumbnail. "Okay, let's go," he said when they'd had time. "You lead, we'll follow."

"I can take us all."

"No. I've become a Honda addict. I like the wind in my hair. She puts on a helmet and *whoom!*" He added, "I *do* make her put on the helmet."

For a moment they were a conscious triangle, then Bill said, "Toss you for it later."

He was in his car, moving. Where he would go, they'd go. He saw Joan going quietly into Jamie's room to put reasoned questions, but thought; "No. I shook her too much. She'll wait till morning."

At intervals he flicked his eyes to the rear-view mirror—they were busily coming up behind him. He fled into the dip at the airport, then up and on and into the turmoil of the settlement across from the cattle market. People seemed to be using the road as if it were a set of bridges. He bleated the horn steadily like a taxi and so cut through, getting a clear road with a lurching bump at the railway crossing, and drove soundlessly on, trapped suddenly, somewhere in the back of his head, in a world of Africans: "Oyíbó!" "Ògá, wá!" "Ẹ máa lọ,"—slogans on mammy-wagons: "Ọmọ nâ dé", "No King Is God"; the ads for worm medicine, anti-malaria pills, energy food, football pools; the house by Bodija with the inscription over the door saying "We are in the dark"— the Rational Book Store, the Hope Medicine Store, "Top People Drink Top"; New Court Road, Salvation Army Road—Ibadan; hills and hollows, swarming with people, hugged by the darkness, murderously laid out to daylight; antic Rome of arcades, unending traffic and meaningless metropolitanism; used-car dealers, the Modupẹ Club, the Ijẹbu Bye-Pass . . .

He was on the road alone . . .

He stopped, got out, looked back. He waited.

He went back to the Ọyọ road, thought suddenly that Bill and

Gail must be at the Gangan by now, raced out the Abẹokuta road, whining damnations after them, and then before he even planned it, swung onto the Ring Road and drove, thoroughly angry, to his own nightclub, and with his money in his pocket and his hand on it, went in.

Things were at a lull between bouts of music. He had to hunt a table and sit down and wonder what the hell he was doing there. He said, "Beer. Star," and waited. There were noisy black men and women, and two white couples trying to look sentimental. There was a woman by herself, looking at him. The music started in a cascade of drums, and he got up and danced with her.

This then was what he wanted: to move; to be set dancing, whole as a fish in water, checked and shocked by drumbeats, as if the drums could comb out the hurrying eaten-out restlessness inside him. He didn't have to be happy. He was frightened; he'd lost his friends. Joan was gone.

"You silent, man?"

"Always when I dance," he said.

He interested her for about five minutes. Then she went away. He didn't care where she went.

"Professor Farquharson! You're all alone?"

Bernice Funmilayọ.

He said, "I'm not supposed to be?"

"I should say not!"

He started himself dancing again as if he had to pump his way into it with his hips; she mocked him by imitating him.

He had to show off. He could feel, as if it were pushing up from the ground, the knowledge that he *could* show off. She danced with him, at him, beside him, near him, in front of him, with her head turned—any way he wanted.

There were two other women at her table. They all sat for a while, and the women talked in Yoruba: strident percussive voices. "We are talking about you," Bernice said.

"Say what you want." They were toys, not women.

"Ah," one of them said, "*Kí l'a fẹ́!*" and then the other woman

425

tittered and said something like "*Okó rè ha wé bí?*" to Mrs. Funmilayọ.

Mrs. Funmilayọ said, "Dance with her," but didn't tell him her name.

She was a little woman and looked rich and wicked. He felt as if someone were buying him, and didn't mind.

"No, he's for me," Mrs. Funmilayọ said to the third, and took him back, and kept her own eyes open.

"*Ǹjě ñkan tóbi,* Bernice?"

She didn't answer, and Farquharson had the convincing sensation that someone was looking at his crotch, and he thought he had better see if he had a zipper open. "Come, Farquharson," she said, "that can take care of itself when the time comes."

Then Farquharson sat islanded on his own language. Mrs. Funmilayọ said, "Ask him yourself," and there was a flurry of giggles, and then silence.

"Ask what?" he said.

"My friends are wondering," Mrs. Funmilayọ said, "whether you have a large or a small penis."

He put his glass slowly onto the table and held onto it, thought that they weren't the only people present who weren't real, and said, "Do I have to answer?"

"No," she said. She spoke to her friends, laughing with them.

"What do they want now? My balls?"

"*Ṣé a fé èpòn rè?*"

Delicate women's laughter.

"Why don't you give them an estimate?"

"Now, you are *not* offended."

"No," he said, and shrugged. "I thought it belonged to me."

"Oh come, that's the one part of a man that can never belong to himself. Are you really angry with them?" (Not "with me," he noticed.) Then, "Professor Farquharson, does your wife never wonder about African men?"

He said, "She doesn't have to."

"True," she said. "There was a naked man at Mọkọla today. It was a foolish question."

He pointed. "Do your friends speak any English?"

"Of course! They're shy."

Giggle. "Ladies," he said, "I'm big." (Yes, this was his show-off night.) "It's thick, and it's long, and it's strong. I'll match it against any good African, and it's damned big for a white man. Oh," he added, "the balls are all right, too."

They sobered to look at him, their heads in voluminous head ties, slightly out of style: they were obliquely offended, if not embarrassed. "Ó șe," the one said, and the other, more formally, "Adúpẹ́ o."

"Professor Farquharson, you are a brave man."

"Then dance," he said—and suddenly she saw how bleak he was, and said, "Come, you've been inventoried shamelessly. Show me what's left."

All right, he was Farquharson with the big prick: he could dig into the air and dance. And dance, time and again. He felt limber, sweated, strong, anxious. The inquisitive ladies were gone. "Yes," she said, "will you take me home?"

She was a big woman. Farquharson sat beside her, holding the key, hearing the music over the wall. "Where do I go?"

"You must forgive my friends," she said. "They had been drinking somewhat. They would not normally be so inconsiderate. May I give you a drink at my place? Or shall I go back in here and wait for another man?"

"Just tell me where to go."

Deep into town. They stopped somewhere on a hill slope. She said, "You lock your car."

The ground on one side fell off two feet below the pavement. "Quiet," she said, "and wait for the key."

A grey concrete unpainted hall, with a single light bulb. They went to the last door on the left. The door closed and locked, and she turned on a pink light.

He saw an iron bed, three cushions, a chair, a chest of drawers. "I also have the next room," she said. "Come into it."

A table, chairs, a small couch, all somewhat worn. A two-burner portable gas stove, and a tiny refrigerator like the one in his dining room. She gave him a glass of sherry. "This'll go bad with beer," he said.

"Don't," she said, "if you don't want to."

He raised the glass. "To boasting?"

She unbuttoned his shirt, and he took it off. She said, "White skin is strange." She turned and pointed up her back. "I always put the hook where I can't reach it."

He undid the hook. She pulled the top of the up-and-down over her head. He unhooked the brassière and she pulled it forward. Her breasts were smooth and heavy: he put his hands over them and drew her to him, moving his fingers. "Were you boasting?" she said.

"Yes, but about facts."

She untied her skirt. It fell. She took one of his hands and put it down between her legs and pressed it. He felt everything smooth and shining. Then she twisted out of his reach, laughing, and said, "Now you, my lover—prove the boast."

It was only partly up, stiffening in the little jerks of heart beats. She put her hands on him, and seemed to swarm down his body until she had her mouth on him, slipping and sliding with her tongue and lips until he said, "Easy! What do *I* do?"

He had never had love made to him with the fierce matter-of-factness of Bernice Funmilayọ. He liked it. It had the skilled efficiency of the dancing, as tense and sure to hold off as to come on. It was something he could match, clear-headed, and he let her lead only as long as he felt like it, then took over, then let her lead again. Her legs were clamping onto his body; she almost swung in the air beneath him.

As he'd said, he thought: thick, long, and tough. "No," he thought, "I said strong."

He stopped. "Did I say tough, or strong?"

He thought she snarled or growled at him.

Momentarily he had surfaced as a critical, puzzling mind. He threw himself down again, hunched, rolled with her. She started to make a high-pitched wavering noise. Her head lashed below him. Heat swarmed around his prick and he felt, when he stilled,

428

as if he were being pulled right into her. And then suddenly she seemed to throw him onto his side and pull away from him, and he was gasping with his rod sticky and high in air, and she said, "Now, *my* turn," and her head went down on him. Possibly it was the expected sign to go into the last high abandon, but it stilled him for a moment, and then he made it last for a long time until he said "Now!" and felt her head swoop like a long bird's, down and then up on him, until everything went and he felt her mouth scrambling about him to put him back to peace.

To have her fall passionately over him and cry wasn't what he expected.

A blue-black, solid, vigorous, proud, anguished woman. He thought he understood about her dead husband, but Jeremy Fisher? From this to the steward's niece? As if she was reading his mind she stopped crying, lifted away, her breasts dangling, and said, "Jeremy is rather small."

"How do I get home?"

They ended with the earthy mockery they had started with, and Farquharson stumbled down the stairs with instructions on how to get to the Kingsway.

"Thank you for a pleasant evening, Professor Farquharson."

"Tell your friends," he said.

"The boast? I shall say it was so little I had to squeeze it between my fingers."

He drove, bleared and aimless and full of peculiar life, the subsonic shaking inside starting again. Then he found a road he knew and set out for home. He had a rushing attack of conscience but he couldn't figure whom he had wronged, unless no longer caring what Joan knew meant that she was at long last truly wronged by what he *could* do. Mostly, there was a curious feeling that he had somehow been unjust to Dr. Garnett.

He could hardly keep the car on the road. "And calm of mind," he said, then giggled to his own surprise, and cried, "Fuck the Philistines!"

The railway crossing was a long diagonal. He was just bouncing over it when he saw a rather small pale object out of the corner of his eye. He left the car sitting in the middle of the tracks and ran on staggering feet over to where Gail's Honda was tucked into the ditch with its front twisted.

"Hey!" he called.

He shouted again and again. "The people on this!" he cried to shapes in the dark. "Where are they?"

Faces and flashlights. Headlights. Someone he knew. "Igwe! Come here!"

"Good evening, Professor."

Dead silence. Farquharson said, "Were they killed?"

"They lose control, sir, on the tracks. I cannot say how they go. They take to UCH."

And as the light of a train started to show against the trees, Farquharson got his car off the railway tracks and drove like a man condemned down to the hospital.

"Dr. Garnett," he said at the office, "and Miss Gail Johnston, are they all right?"

"What is your name, please, sir?"

Fidget, stare, wait. An intern came in. "Oh, Professor Farquharson," he said, "how is your wife?"

The nurse returned, annoyed.

They went through corridors and verandahs in the night, in sultry air. "Through here, please."

Bill Garnett in a private bed, his head wrapped up. "You disappeared."

"Gail?"

"Oh, I don't know. Unconscious. That helmet's no damn good." He looked up and sniffed. "Do you know you're a bastard, Farquharson?"

"Miss Johnston?" he said to the intern.

The man shrugged. "A broken wrist." He then said several learned things about concussion, and contrived to suggest that coma happened only if you diagnosed it.

And finally Farquharson had to stand helpless and trembling, at four o'clock in the morning, while Joan opened a door for him.

She let him stand reeling in the middle of the room and locked the door. Glass and metal made a dead hungry bang. He suddenly realized that all the way through the hospital he must have stunk of love-making. Joan looked half beside herself, cold with desolation and raw sick anger.

She said, "How was Gail?"

37

SHE was going to cry; she was shaking and ugly. He said, "They wouldn't let me see her." He looked away from her. "Bill's all bandages. His toe's been cut again." She was staring at him. "He said the helmet was no damn good, They smashed. I lost them."

But she said, "You stink like a billy goat."

"That's something else entirely."

He started down the hall. "Don't you dare wake him. And take a bath."

So he was the man who could watch his wife cry, hopelessly and horribly, and not even touch her. He could look at her. She had her hair buttoned down with bobby pins, to make beauty; her lips were faded. Was he invited to take charge of this? To love and cherish a prying, miserable woman who should have stayed in Canada? He said, "Joan, my wife," and feeling wretched and sick about it, left her there.

She followed, refused to plead. She watched him undress, folded his clothes, and stood in the hall for a long time, forcing herself to be stony-headed, while her lungs shook. When she got back to the bathroom she was just in time to keep his head from slipping under the water, though she couldn't wake him.

She tugged and hauled, and knew no other way to keep him from sliding under again but to get into the tub and kneel on one of his legs to keep it straight, then to fumble behind her for the plug and yank it out even though his foot was on top of it. The water ran sucking out, lowered around him, and an accidental spurt from the swivelling pipe scalded her arm. She started, Farqu-

432

harson's body shoved towards her, and she fell on top of it. The last of the water went out with an obscene noise of satisfaction.

His eyes were open. She didn't care how she stepped over him to get out of the tub. Her nightgown clung. If she didn't do something, he was going to look gentle and damaged until he woke up. She picked up the bottle of boiled water beside the toothpaste and shook ice water over him from head to foot.

He didn't yell. She said, "You were trying to drown yourself." He scrambled upright.

And as if it was the last way left by which she could insult him, she took off the nightgown and without bothering to dry herself sat on the lid of the toilet seat and took off the bedroom slippers she had gone into the bathtub wearing. She had waited till now, in seven years, to show him the body that didn't care whether it was clothed or not, the unerotic nakedness that apparently had to be what the soul was about, if they were going to have souls. He could make her join him now, he thought, on accident, or he could let her go. Intuition wasn't wanted; he saw the Honda; his flanks were nastily wet; he used the towel.

He was obsessively awake, but as if for a moment only. Joan went into the bedroom to get another towel, and used it there. When he came in she was sitting naked at the dressing table, with a stiff mouth, taking the bobby pins out of her hair. She said, "They're too uncomfortable."

He hung over her. "Tomorrow I'll have to go to the hospital, and wait."

"I know that." She was digging the brush into her hair. She said, "I didn't wish *this* on you."

He said, "I picked up a woman," and before she could think what to say back, because she had to take strokes with the brush, he had turned his back on her and gone to sleep.

She stared in the mirror at the buttocks, the stiff legs, the groove in the back, the shoulder muscles, the stubble glittering where the base of the skull met the neck.

Jamie was afraid of him.

She dreamt, waking, of what it had been like to drain bathtub water away from a drowned man. It was as if she could see his hair, dragged back by water, dry and spring forward. And she lay there afraid, not that he was going to die, but that therefore she was, and there was going to be no forgiveness.

Gail was unconscious for almost thirty hours, and because she was in a ward, Farquharson couldn't wait beside her except at visiting hours. He could only go, ask, and go away, or walk over to see Bill, who was in the old morose luxury of contemplating his injuries, his left arm held bracketed in what seemed a queer position.

"It was the tracks," he said. "We bounced and somehow or other the wheel got turned. I think I ended up in a fence. I'm told I was pulled out of one. Actually, Gail isn't as messed up as I am. She just hit her head. Carsten thinks she may have hit it on the rail, but the way we were going she'd have been dead." His eyes were blackened. "But I guess you know that sort of thing." He looked at his toe: "I wonder how long it's going to take this time."

On Monday, Jamie looked seedy and thoughtful, and brought Farquharson all his animals in a box with the fairy castle, as if making anxious amends for having thrown them so long ago into all that trouble. Farquharson had to play, with great caution, as Jamie played. Joan found him later, about to go to the hospital, sitting in the Morris Minor, as if it too were a toy he couldn't fit, staring through the windshield. He sniffed when he saw her and had to fuss over starting the car. She sighed and said, "Put Stanley in the back. He can take me shopping."

When Stanley got in he looked subdued, and only faintly proud. There was no smoke coming from his kitchen. Joan said, "Where's Celina?"

"She go to the Mid-West, madam."

He took Jamie onto his knee as if he were something new, and held him.

Bill was waiting for him, an apparition looking ridiculous in bandages. He took Farquharson's arm and said, "She's awake."

434

As they went along the high verandah he said, "As a medical observation, you were pretty rank the other night." They stopped to look over the railing for a moment at the forest-covered hillside across the highway. "It's always hard to think that the noisiest part of Ibadan's just on the other side of that," Bill said.

"Well, I guess they got my noise Saturday. I screwed her sixteen ways to Christmas and then she did a blow-job." Their words dropped silently into the air. No one would have heard them ten feet away.

"I hope not one of the local harlots, or I'm going to have to turn your genitals inside out and scrub them."

"Mrs. Funmilayọ."

"Oh, she'll be clean. Just the same I'd better check you over when I get back to base."

Farquharson disliked them both, acutely, for a moment.

"Hell, come on. We'll be past the time."

Gail was bandaged differently, and her eyes were purple and green, but the two lovers, side by side, as if they were his hosts (as, he thought, they had been, for how long?), looked very much like each other, as if they had decided to be the same person, but didn't know it yet. He felt something inside him creep away in a small, lonely resentment, and kissed Gail gently, afraid to hurt her face. "He thought we were on the town," Bill said, "so he was. Headache?"

She said, "Bad."

"Do you want to marry me?" He pointed. "After he's gone?"

"When does he go?" She'd forgotten.

"Friday. Today's Monday."

"No," she said. "I don't think so."

Farquharson felt himself a curiously isolated compound of all the ages of a man in love: the boy, the old man, the lover, the weighty husband—all put aside. It hurt. "You can let him come home, you know," he said. "We'll take care of him."

She put her hand up, as if she were shielding her eyes. Farquharson saw the ring he had given her sitting on the bedside table, without its stone. She said, "I want to see you some time."

Bill said, "Now I'm going to sign myself out. See you later."
So the Farquharsons had Bill in their house all that day.

Meanwhile, Joan was packing. She had it all clear in her mind how she was to do it. The documents and money were all ready in the desk, with the travellers' cheques. Farquharson went at the due time to the hospital and found Gail asleep, so while the women in the next beds looked at him and talked raucously he sat beside her, put his hand over hers, and waited, a big, still figure looking almost like a doctor himself. She had had a strong workable whole life away from him—teaching, costumes, the miraculous little stage models—she was a scholar in her way, and a good one, and she didn't know it yet. Dear Gail: he liked her.

She didn't wake until it was almost time for him to go, and there he was, somehow immersed in time, larger than normal, with grave, still eyes and the round metal-rimmed spectacles forgotten on them: schoolteacher, small boy, athlete, lover; the bright, huge ring on his hand. "What day is it?"

She said, "I wish you could lie beside me, but this bed's uncomfortable."

Sorting and packing was sick work. He did it all day Tuesday, broken by intervals of trying to pin some official down to lend them sheets and dishes, but they didn't have the Ormfords or Grace Spanier-Dodd to help them. Finally Farquharson went to the Nwonkwos and got some dishes and a frying pan and a double-boiler. And then Joan took Stanley and came back a half-hour later with bedding from the Baloguns, whose luncheon they had never returned and who thus hadn't been seen since fall. She said, "I had a lovely chat with Mrs. Balogun and she got her steward to get me everything we'd want, so that's that." Farquharson saluted, and disliked her.

By supper they were all ready, with ordered piles of clothes, and the animals and the cuddle toy set aside for Europe, with the fairy castle. Joan looked at her husband then and said, "Maybe they have after-supper visiting hours. Go on."

She let him thank her. "I'll put Jamie to bed," and when she saw him suddenly look worried, she said, "No, I won't ask him. But I had to try."

He picked Jamie up and hugged him and was hugged. He said, "Has he got a fever?"

"No."

He and Gail had foolish reminiscent talk, holding hands. When he left she said, "Can you bring me some soap? they haven't got any."

Sparse rain dotted the windshield, sparked in the headlights. They sat with newspapers, their belongings piled up, even the cushion covers off the cushions. "Remember what a time we had," Joan said, "getting the right mattresses?"

He said, "I remember Akinkugbe bleeding all over one of them."

Crack and thunder of lightning. Rain beating up the roof and garden. They had ten brown moths clinging to their ceiling above the fan. The lights went out and they had to find where Jacob kept the candles this time, but Jamie didn't wake up when Farquharson left a candle in his room and the storm was still crackling and rumbling, and the rain falling like lead, when Farquharson fumbled his way to the bathroom, somewhere around one a.m.

Only partly awake, not wanting to finish waking up, he sat on the toilet with his head hanging over and one hand guiding the stream of water so as not to make a noise with it, keeping a cotton-headed silence in the middle of the rain.

Absolute lightning struck as if into the bowl of water under him, the high bleaching light obliterated by the immense un-echoing crack of sound. He was on his feet, in the middle of the bathroom, unable to hear, not knowing where the door was. All the superstitions about lightning seemed to strike, lethal as the lightning itself. He couldn't breathe. Jamie was screaming. Farquharson ran, staggering, calling, "Jamie? That was a *big* one!" and when Joan came, crying, asking what did it hit, she had to see Farquharson in the chair, and Jamie kneeling on his naked thigh with his shoulders and his head crushed behind his father's arms—

437

and she could hardly recognize Farquharson because she had never seen anybody *scared* of death.

The great storm suddenly moved away. They took Jamie to sleep between themselves, on one side or another of the crack between the beds, and Joan said, "He *has* a temperature."

"I said he had."

With daylight the air misted and then grew very clear and hot. Jamie seemed listless, but Joan, with work to do and a country she didn't want to stay in, said that he was worn out by his fear of the storm, and when he started in valiantly handing Jacob every piece of the morning laundry she decided that at least he was going to have to be all right for the day, and busied herself. The packers appeared in the middle of the morning, and Jamie had much to watch as everything disappeared into cardboard boxes, among clouds of ivory-coloured paper. When it was all done the men squatted waiting and played with him, so he trotted this way and that, being formal as if the honour of the house were his. When everything was all on the truck the men waved to him or rubbed his head, the truck went around the corner of the garage, and he turned around to an empty house with white cushions on the chairs and gave himself up to the luxury of feeling miserable. Joan marched him off to a nap and came back saying, "He's got a big fever. I feel awful. What are we going to do?"

Farquharson said, "Bill. Now."

"He's in no condition!"

"You want *Foley*?"

Bill looked pirate-like, with his arm in the same queer braced cast. He examined Jamie, looked up and said, "Henry, have you had mumps? Well, hope that you have. He does." He demonstrated with his free hand on himself. "He's sore in all the right places."

"*Mumps?*" Joan said.

"He's going to balloon. You can't go home."

But Joan protested.

Bill said, "I'm not going to let you land in Italy with a child broadcasting mumps. Keep him here." He looked at Farquharson.

"Better go to the customs office and get your tickets changed."

Joan said, "But we can't stay here!"

"Have *you* had mumps?"

"No," she said, "but that's got nothing to do with it."

Farquharson came back from the Customs and Passage office, said, "Three weeks," and shouted, "Stanley! You're on to the end of the month. Change of plans."

"What did you have to do that for?" Joan said.

"Because he doesn't cost as much as a couple of weeks of Rome hotels."

Jamie's face swelled. There was no point keeping him in bed; they let him play if he wanted to, consoled him, gave him cooling drinks (even Jacob said, "Jamie, you like a cooling drink?"), and were kind to him, forgetting to wonder whether the servants had immunities, while every day Joan looked more strained and angry.

Gail was let come home, and Bill, since all the neighbours had gone away, moved in to take care of her with one hand while she, with two hands, tried to take care of him. Farquharson would go and visit them when he could get away in the afternoons. Then one day Bill said, "I'm going out," and they were left alone.

"Can we lie down?" Farquharson said.

"Henry, I can't make love. My head hurts."

He said, "I want to hold you."

Gathered into his arms, she shunted into the most comfortable place, and his lips brushed against the edge of her hair. Bill found them sleeping that way, and sat down and looked at them, then tiptoed out of the house again and went over to Jaja Avenue to tend his patient, and the mother.

He thought for a moment that Joan was doing imaginary housework: she was standing in the kitchen lifting a frying pan between her hands, and looking at it.

Joan was tired and in a wretched temper; Jamie was fretful and miserable. Farquharson was also tired, deeply tired, every day, as

439

if something essential had disappeared suddenly from his bones. Actually, he supposed, it was nothing more than anticlimax, but he was bound to the house. Oscar hadn't had the mumps, so Farquharson couldn't visit there. Then one morning he looked at Joan and saw that the side of her face was up. He said, "You've got it."

"No," she said, "it's just something with my ear. I don't feel good. But I do *not* have the mumps!"

Jamie was lethargic, but his face had gone down.

The government's pursuit of virtue, and advertising of it, was beginning to sound hysterical as the platitudes and the pictures of the government leaders came out in the papers day after day. Farquharson remembered the publicity campaign bounding along on its jeeps in the North, still talking, he supposed, to camels and to Kano. Joan, seeing that Jamie was all right, told Farquharson to take him for a ride, but instead he took him to the Zoo, finally, as he had long ago promised to. It was a little zoo: a few cages and pens on a small rectangle of land slanting down to a running creek in the bush and a trench-surrounded bare pen for a pair of very young elephants. It had chameleons on a bush in a glass box, a refreshment stand that sold peculiar candies, lots of monkeys in a monkey house in the middle, and an aviary. And there were a hyaena with a cut foot, cranes, and a huge ugly warthog. Jamie shrieked at the monkeys, wanted the cranes, oddly admired the warthog. They stood on the stile-like steps looking down on it while the beast, who looked like danger given a body and lumps, snouted and pushed against the walls of its pen.

Joan's method for handling the mumps was to close the house, let no one in, and keep herself in her room, with a scarf wrapped around her face. Her head swam in a kind of rational delirium that came on her mainly when she lay down. She made Farquharson take Jamie out of the house and go, it didn't matter where, and Farquharson took compelled farewell drives through Ibadan until he remembered that he wanted Joan to have an up-and-down, and he and Jamie bought some stuff in the CFAO and took it to the dressmaker, and the result of that was that Lebanon Street became again for a few days a kind of drug, and Farquharson carried Jamie on his hip (with his head wrapped in a handkerchief), and haggled lovingly, but as if there were no meaning in it.

He made his visits to Gail and Bill with Jamie on his knee. Gail's head came out of bandages and she put on an African head tie. She said, "I've had half my hair shaved off." Bill had had his head shaved too and now was stubbly with new growth around what was going to be a scar. Farquharson knew that these two people slept together, now and he guessed chastely, every night. He was walking around with a hunger in his balls he didn't know what to do with. He thought of going to the Bursar's office and seeing Mrs. Funmilayo—but didn't, because of a kind of raw, shamed gratitude to her that somehow he didn't want her to know about. Besides, he wanted to lie in Gail, motionless and immersed, as if it were possible to leave her everything he was, and go home some form of a new man who didn't matter. Joan with the mumps was a nasty woman.

He was sorry for her. He stripped his bed and slept in the spare room because she wanted him to. She was alone, with her various hurting glands and her pride, and then she would sit on the stool in front of the dressing-table mirror, constructing images of the frying pan, and Farquharson, and explanations of why Jamie was so terrified, all unclear, and indicating only that she should be angry at him. The mumps held her head in a vise; she dragged through the days; and the frightening possible violence of her husband was the one thought that she couldn't get away from.

Bill materialized in her bedroom, insisting he had to look at her. She filled in time by telling him how childish and selfish her husband was, that he had tantrums, that he picked up the frying pan and threw it right on the floor in front of her and that as far as she could figure out he must have done the same thing in front of Jamie because when he came near him in certain ways the child shrieked that he was going to hit him—and on and on, fishing for an answer, since Bill talked about frying pans too. Farquharson was a coward; a little boy who hid things from her; he didn't even bother to be faithful; she didn't believe in the great love for Jamie.

What had he ever done for Jamie except carry him around and look proud? She said, "I *work* for that child!"

So he told her about the frying pan, and about what Farquharson had done for Jamie, and some home truths; his honour and his love of the man made one great repayment of loyalty—and Joan saw Farquharson kill to protect his son and had her mind rubbed further into the danger of Akinkugbe's rescue, and was left alone, with a stern medical lecture about lying down, to face the fact that her husband was a killer, that there was no excuse for him, that Jamie had seen him kill a man, and that she had to defend herself and her son from such a man and get away.

She took her rings off and hid them in a suitcase.

Her neck was sore; she wanted to press her hands against her abdomen. Her murderer was out with Jamie. Hurting internally, her head in a sick imperceptive clamour able only to reason, not to imagine anything, she put her suitcase into the locked pantry, ignoring Jacob's stares, then took Jamie's suitcase, crammed his toys and his clothes into it, half-dragged it down the house, took her jewellery, her make-up, more of her clothes, random untidy things, the toothbrushes, half-filled the third suitcase, had to get Jacob to carry it to the pantry, and then openly, or so she thought, stole her passport, two of the airplane tickets, her papers and vaccination books, her travellers' cheques, put them all into a purse, and held onto that, remembering that Jacob stole. When no one looked she locked it into the desk drawer. Stanley was in his quarters: she tottered over to them. "Dirty little room," she said.

"I want you to be here tonight. Don't say anything to anyone, anyone at all. I want you to be here tonight. I'll call you."

He said, "Yes, madam."

38

FARQUHARSON and Jamie came home happy from Gail's, laughing at foolish words between them. Joan sent word that she felt awful and didn't want to eat, but that she'd get them supper and watch them eat it, and that was what she did. She watched them. After their appetite had gone she sat in the living room watching them some more, and then she tripped and had to be carried to bed, and when Farquharson went back to look at her she was lying on her back talking vehemently to herself about safety and protection and "you ought to tell me to run away".

"Jacob," he said, "tell Stanley to get Dr. Garnett."

So Joan finished her mumps in a private room in the Hospital, where she should have been for days.

Gail stayed with Jamie, while Farquharson took Joan away.

The staff doctor said, "Absolutely no visitors, even you, Professor Farquharson, for at least three days."

Joan said, "Do as he says."

Stanley asked if he could go. "Madam say to be in." Farquharson said good night to him.

"Why don't you take Jamie for a trip?" Gail said. "Go to Akure, or something. You might as well, you've been ordered off. And Joan'll be all right. They'll just make her rest."

"Brother Patrick," he said, "I wonder. Adebọwale's in Ilesha."

"I ought to make love to you," she said. "I just feel tenderly moral since I've been wounded"—it was Bill's word; she smiled at it—"and Joan's sick."

He put his hand to her chin, and raised it, "I love you," he said.

443

"Love the country," she said. "Love Nigeria."

"Your ring broke."

"Oh, my poor Henry."

But he said, "Poor Joan. Damn. I guess I'm a married man."

He made himself a double cocktail, and wondered why the pantry door was locked. The drink half done, he came and opened it, and found the suitcases. He was kneeling over their contents, under the light-bulb. Joan's dresses, Jamie's toys. He ransacked the house then, in an agony lest Jamie wake, and finally had to break open the desk drawer because he couldn't find the key.

After midnight he was still looking at her passport and wondering what he could do when Jamie's name was on that passport, and not on his. "*Madam say to be in.*"

He said, "She did, did she?"

Adebọwale in Ilesha?

He searched the kitchen. The hollow night moved with him: tins of fruit and meat; bottles of sterilized milk—Joan always kept a lot—bread. "Foil-wrapped cheese," he said aloud, and thought he sounded contemptible. Bottles of water. Squash. Alcohol. An escape pack, to eat on a road.

So they went to Akure, going very cautiously because Jamie was sitting all by himself on a small, thick cushion borrowed from Victoria. Jamie sang, Farquharson sang; they bounced; they had a good time. They were on a road in a peaceful country. When they wanted to, or when they had to, they got out of the car, played and stretched, or Farquharson pissed at the side of the road while Jamie teased him, remembering, and said, "Far' pee!"

"You're damn right I do."

Ifẹ burst on them like a busy jabbering mouth. They went right through it. From time to time Farquharson made a sandwich, or stopped to let Jamie have a drink.

"Mummy rest."

"M-hm. For about a week, I guess."

Once, imperiously, Jamie demanded to go into the trees and be left alone, and Farquharson gave him a couple of tissues and watched him trot into the middle of a cocoa farm, pull down his pants, and squat. "My God, somebody's been looking at Africans!" Farquharson thought, and turned tactfully away and stood singing *Vissi d'arte* by the road.

Ilesha. He didn't remember it. He asked at a store after Olatunji Adebọwale, but without success. In the end he drove straight on to Akurẹ, turned in to Brother Patrick's school, and in the kind of twilight that tried to pull his eyes out of his head blew the horn and called for Brother Patrick, and then went looking for him. Jamie was wide awake and somewhat apprehensive.

"I'm afraid you've missed him," a voice said in an Irish accent. "He's in Ibadan."

Nevertheless they were made at home, given a meal and a bed, and kindly thought of. Their host spent half the next day showing them through a Government Experimental Farm on the other side of town, so that Jamie could watch animals. Then they would have thanked him, but he made them have another meal. They went back to Adebọwale's store for squash and pop—and candies, because they wanted candy—and were recognized, and greeted. Then they tried unsuccessfully to get a chalet at the rest house for the night and weren't recognized.

"Okay, Jamie," he said, "we'll sleep in the car. You can sleep in the back seat, and then you can tell Mummy all about it."

Jamie said, "Mummy in hospital—*she* can't hear."

"Oh, she'll come home."

"Then Farq go away?"

"No," he said. "No."

"Never *both* go away?"

"No," he said.

Sunset, dangerous twilight, the dark. They sat drawn off the road, with the lights on, and ate sandwiches with new bread, candy, pineapple, and soda pop (Farquharson spiked a Fanta). They were cozy, tired, very happy people and when supper was over and Jamie had walked into the dark crying "Jamie pee!" and come back, he curled up in the back seat as obediently as was desired and was huddled into slumber almost at once. Farquharson was able to drive the car.

He'd had his dream: he'd had Jamie and Africa all to themselves for two happy days. Anxiety waited in Ibadan, and from then on, he supposed. For the moment he was happy among the milestones going by. He went slowly through Ifẹ, hoping Jamie wouldn't wake: it was a noisy city.

Suddenly, far in front of him, he saw a crowd, but as the headlights plunged into them, men started to scatter and run away. He saw the cloth stores shuttered for the night, and brown people at the edge of light, too far away to be seen clearly, or to have their shouting connected with them—and then an empty road, but not quite empty.

There were three dark lumps in the narrow pavement, catching the headlights. He had to go slowly to get past them; he mustn't wake Jamie with steering or rough engine noise, or with the bump of going over one. One was by the wall, easy to pass, with shoulders flat to the road and arms spread sideways, the rump stuck into the air as if balancing. This side of the neck there were great stains spurting. The head was a stony ball on the other side of the road with white eyes one above the other in the headlights. He would go down the road to the next lump leaving blood marks with every turn of his tires.

He could sense people watching him pass, from between the buildings, could see them out of the side of his eye shrink back or peer forward at the edge of the shadow of his lights. He kept his eyes straight ahead and moved the car, delicately, as if his senses were in the front tires and how they turned. The second body was face up, lying with its feet towards him. He saw light-grey trousers and the soles of trim narrow shoes, and had almost to stop, wondering how to get around it. There was a huge stain of burning and blood at the crotch.

The third body was only a few feet away to one side. He was going to have to drive over at least part of one of them. He knew no more streets in Ifẹ, and he didn't want to gamble on what would happen if he tried to back up. He picked his way: over the elbow of one body with his right wheels, over the upper legs of the second with his left (it was face down; he couldn't see anything damaged except the signs on the road of a surge of blood from the throat). The car jounced, slowly, and then he stuck. He imagined himself ripping the surface off the back of the dead thighs, and knew that he had never in his life been closer to screaming. He let the car stop.

Faces, back in the dark, three or four together. He spoke out the window, gently, "I can't move." At least the road ahead was clear, if he could get past. If Jamie woke there would be nothing in the lights but a road and houses. He pointed to the back seat. "Ọmọ mi ńsùn. Kò dára kí ó jí."

(*My child is sleeping. It is not good that he wake.*)

If they would kill him, he would have to wait for them. He sat as if he were stuck on a stone in the road, and hadn't seen anything.

"Oyíbó? Kí l'o fẹ́?" A jurist's voice, also quiet. *Peeled man, what do you want?*

"Mo lọ s'ílé mi. Mo fẹ́ lọ s'Íbàdàn." He hoped he had it right: *I go to my house; I want to go to Ibadan.* (He had made that phrase out of his book, it seemed years ago; he had been proud of it.)

"Don't wake the boy," he added. "He mustn't see this. Kòyẹ kí ọmọ nâ kò rí" (Was it "rí"? see—*It is fitting that this child not see*— how to say *these things?*) "ìwọ̀nyi."

"Bẹ́ẹ ni, bẹ́ẹ ni." They were saying *Thus it is, thus it is*: Yes.

Jamie had been moved by the bump, but he was still asleep. The men were like shadows, standing on Farquharson hated to think what, lifting the back of the car. If the drive wheels could just move, gently, over the thighs. They had let him go. He called "Adúpẹ́," just loud enough to be heard. There were two long-robed Northerners in the headlights ahead of him.

Jamie said, "Bump. Bi-ig bump!" and hunched over and was asleep again. Farquharson wondered if he had even wakened up.

He passed the spot where the road signs marked the ancient wall. Now there was a man running down the road ahead of him, in a curious galvanized shamble, as if his arms and legs hadn't been attached properly. When the lights struck him he ran even more wildly, and fell down. Farquharson stopped the car beside him and threw the door open.

He had to say, "I'm white. Get in."

The man scrambled to his feet and blundered towards the car. in the reflection of the car lights Farquharson could see that he was young, that he had been scraped in several places, and that his shirt was torn.

The door closed; the car started. Jamie was asleep. "I do not know why they want this," the man said, "why they do this to us. We go to Onitsha. We do not want to live here. But this is one Nigeria!"

"Don't wake the boy," Farquharson said. "He slept through that."

The man shifted and looked back over the seat. Farquharson said, "How many of you?"

"Sir, four. We see what happen to each other. But when the light come, I run away."

"Where do you want to go?"

"Sir, I must go back to Ibadan."

"Okay, stop talking and let me drive."

But for a long time it wasn't possible to make the man stop talking. Farquharson was able to keep him off the details of what had happened to his friends, but then had to listen to him talk about the Ibo and what *they* had done, and about himself. "Sir, I am educated man, able to hold any job. I am bookkeeper, sir. I can be steward." And he began to bargain for a recommendation to a steward's job, since Mr.—"I am sorry sir, I do not know your name—" being widely travelled, must know many people, and furthermore must of nature retain interest in this person whom he had benefacted (that was the word). Farquharson found his resilience and pushy energy as distasteful as his simultaneous shocked desire to be describing his friends' butchery. Finally he said, "Go to sleep, let me drive," more harshly than he wanted to, and the man fell silent. And when Farquharson could cast a glance at him, he was staring into the night with eyes that obviously were seeing only fire and matchets.

He didn't know how far into the night he was, or how long the road was. He drove it, and the road was blearing in his eyes. He stopped. Jamie murmured; the Ibo, fallen almost asleep, woke in fear and Farquharson reached around in the back for the water bottle and slapped water over his face and chest.

And then at a turn in the road when he had slightly slowed, one of the back tires blew and the car seemed to stumble askew towards the edge of the road and stop in a wall of bushes. Jamie woke to the flapping tire and the crack and swish of a lot of hard spindly plants, and was bounced into the narrow space behind the back of the driver's seat. He started to cry very hard.

The man in the passenger's seat forced the door open against the grabbing branches, pushed himself out, and reached into the back, saying, "Here your Daddy, boy," while Farquharson was shutting the key off and getting onto his knees with his head cramped to reach down behind the seat.

"We blew a tire," he said. "We're perfectly okay, Jamie. This is a passenger."

He put in a good ten minutes making Jamie feel that the accident was almost a privilege, and fun. Then the Ibo said, "What we do, sir? I look in the boot, your spare is flat."

Farquharson went back to check, and crouched by Jamie. They looked at each other in the red tail-light glow. Farquharson winked. He said, "I saw a sign just before we went off the road."

So they felt their way a hundred feet back along the road, without a flashlight. The headlights tangled in incandescent branches behind them. Jamie said, "Dark. Dark!" Farquharson saw the milepost glimmer, felt the back of a sign beside it, and lit a match. They read the name of a village. Farquharson said, "That must be less than a hundred yards ahead of where we went off the road. Let's lock up and walk."

The Ibo said, "Sir, I stay here."

"You'll be all right with me." But he wouldn't come.

Farquharson took out a carton of soft drinks and the bottle

opener. Then, having opened a bottle for his passenger, he turned out the lights, and while Jamie pressed close to him, locked up the car by feel. "All right," he said, his voice loud on the road. "Good night."

He picked Jamie up, and with the bottles in his free hand and the opener in his pocket, walking by the smoothness under his feet, he started for the village in pitch darkness. He sang one of Jamie's sad-songs and felt all right again, secure with the small and intact person who hadn't seen the street in Ife.

He knew he was at the village when the air on his face had the sense of having widened. "Well," he said, and called in a clear but ordinary voice, "anyone home?"

He saw an unfocussable hole in a dim wall, and was feeling his way to it when without any sound except from the suddenly placed leaves, the rain started. In seconds it was a cloudburst. A single flash of lightning showed him the doorway, and he plunged into it, ducking so as not to bang Jamie's head, and the rush of water followed him. Someone inside struck a match.

A man scrambled to his feet from a mat on the floor, fastening a cloth around him. Two men were looking at them, one naked, putting the match to a light. Lightning seared the room past them. Farquharson let Jamie slither to the floor and stood holding his hand firmly. "English?" he said.

"Yes, master. Why you here?" A dim red room, stained with black and the shadows of sleeping people. The man in the covering cloth closed the door. Farquharson explained about the car, the blow-out, the flat spare. Was there a tire pump in the village?

Rain came rocketing down. He wondered about the partially injured Ibo in the bush. A woman in the corner woke up and called something. Rapid explanations crossed the room. She said something irritable and definitive. "Master, if you like to sleep till morning," the man in the covering cloth said, while the naked man went back to his bed and lay on it, "she say sleep here. Master, there is pump. We fix. My bed, sir, please."

He could hear Joan in the hospital ordering him to keep that child out of that bed. "Can I have some cover for the boy?" he

450

said. He took off his shirt. From somewhere back in the dark the man brought a folded cloth. Farquharson lowered himself onto the mat—it was a thin, hard mattress—pried his sandals off his feet, opened the folded cloth and adjusted it as a sort of papoose sleeping bag, undressed Jamie and tucked him up, placed him like a package on the mat, took his clothes over to where he saw a shelf and spread them out on it, the man helping him by moving the few things to one side. Then Farquharson put his hands on his shorts and said, "Wet," and the man said, "Master, my cloth. For morning," unknotted it and gave it to him. So Farquharson stepped out of cold cotton shorts and lay on the bed with a print covering cloth spread over him, tucked a very silent and wide-eyed Jamie into the familiar place beside his arm, and lying on his back said "Good night." The man blew out the light.

It was strange that he could forget about murder in the streets, and just let warm sleep come over him, but he lay in the complete dark, under the shouting rain, humming almost silently to Jamie until Jamie slept. The flashbulb lightning outlined the shutters and the door, crowding the air with blackness; it was as if the sound of the rain were all that could ever go past him. He was safe, sheltered whole and intact in a box of earth and roaring metal. He relaxed, was dazed and at peace, and finally sound asleep.

"Ẹ̀kárọ̀, Ọ̀gǎ."

It was a woman's voice. Daylight glared in a tall box shape behind her. Farquharson found the covering cloth spread neatly over his chest as if someone had made a bed. Jamie was still asleep. He levered himself up and disengaged his arm, which was cramped. He said, "Ẹ̀kárọ̀."

"Ẹ fẹ́ jẹun?" She showed him food in a dish, some form of yam, he supposed.

So when Jamie woke Farquharson had some strangely tasteless, semisolid pale stuff chewing in his mouth. He got up with the covering cloth gathered around him and brought Jamie a bottle of lemon soda, and then had to go back to his still wet shorts and find the opener. Jamie sat, naked and very dignified, drinking out of the bottle. Farquharson, being left alone, hastened into his clothes, shivering under their chill, got his sandals on, and made Jamie stand into his shorts and put on his shoes. And then hand in hand they walked into the sunlight—they must have been let sleep a long time—and found a group of men under the palm-roofed shelter taking turns on an old bicycle pump, pumping up his tire with a wide calabash full of water beside them, and an old tire-mending kit in a rusty canister. Farquharson breathed deeply, and was very happy. "Soon, master!" they said. "Soon!"

It was starting to get hot. The men seemed jubilant. Farquharson wondered which of them was the man who had given him the cloth the night before, or whom he ought to dash for putting him up for the night. Then he thought to feel in his shorts pocket to see if anyone had got his wallet. When they saw him with it in his hands they laughed at him. "No, master!" they said. "No! We no take you money, master!" They laughed, chuckled, mocked him about it. He waited with the wallet in his hands, feeling foolish, then went back to the thick-walled house he'd spent the night in and looked for the woman, to give her something, but there were many women in a group, and again he didn't know which she was.

Then finally he said, "*Fún ilé yí?*" (*For this house*) and held forward a five-shilling note. Giggling, a woman came up and took it. "*Ó ṣe,*" he said. And they imitated him with eager smiles.

"Ready, master?"

He held the rest of the money then until he was back at the car. They went almost in a parade, with two men bowling the wheel. He thought he had locked the car, but it had been pushed out of the bushes, and unquestionably one of the doors was open. They had taken the jack from the front seat, and the car was balancing on it. They put the tire back on, kept themselves busy around Farquharson, and wouldn't let him touch anything. And finally one of them knocked the hubcap on with a jaunty thud or two of the tire iron.

Farquharson said, "I had your cloth last night? Your bed?"

He dropped the tire iron through the window into the driver's seat, opened the wallet, took out a pound, heard them say, "No, master, please!" so they had their dutiful argument, like haggling in reverse. Then they waited for him to go.

Suddenly he said, "I had a passenger last night. Did you see him?"

"Master, he go!"

Farquharson imagined the impudent, unlikeable, frightened man creeping on the road between the houses of the village in the dark, and running on through the bush. He got in, shifted the tire iron, let one of the Yoruba lift Jamie into his seat, saw beyond them between the thin tree trunks of a cocoa farm, then shoved the weapon under the seat without looking at it, said, "Wave to the men on my side," and drove off, with Jamie waving and being waved to. The accelerator hit the floor, and he fled bounding on the pavement past the house that had sheltered him. He'd seen his passenger on his back among the trees, not even hidden, battered and dead—and he knew that they had done it with the tire iron and had probably washed the blood off in the calabash with the tube.

He got to Ibadan in the middle of a still Sunday morning, and put Jamie and himself into a huge tepid bath. Then he went to the hospital. She was pretty in the bed.

He said, "Joan, I want to go *home* now."

39

It wasn't possible. The Farquharson's plane was flying to Rome in the small hours of the early morning of the twenty-ninth. It would take longer than that to change their tickets again. Meanwhile, the doctors kept Joan in hospital.

So he had his friends, his house, and he had Ibadan: four persons (five, with Stanley), a set of stripped concrete rooms, and a sprawling mess of bleak, gaudy houses and vindictive anger-ridden sly people dressed for show and making him feel, when he looked at them, as if little swallowed bits of blood were riding in his stomach. He could believe that the dead boy had been obstreperous and smug, but what did he do with the contented faces that gave him his tire iron back? He clung to Oscar and Victoria as sane, pleasant people, haunted their house, often with Jamie, and talked to them, as if he were trying to shape his year into being something that hadn't happened to him.

"I'm sorry that you had to see all this," Victoria said.

He looked at her delicate, young, vigorous face, with the hair dragged back into the single short spike of pigtail, and the eyes that were fierce and gentle at the same time, and always half amused. He said, "Did you get your spoons back?"

"No, never."

"I taught three people," he said. "That's about the level of a good year, but it does seem small."

She liked him. She gave him several suppers that were in no sense accommodated to the European palate, and he took that for the honour it was meant to be. And when he came back from the hospital and found Stanley and Jamie playing wisely together in the living room, he put a hand on Stanley's shoulder before he picked up Jamie and flew him about the room. (And the Nwonkwo children, still shy after the whole year, led Jamie off to their toys, or to a chase of raindrops, in the front yard.)

Oscar tried to tell him that what he had seen was one of the death spasms of the First Republic, inevitable perhaps, but essentially meaningless, and something which had already ceased to happen in the North. "We have turned the corner," he said. "We have put our Time of Troubles behind us. Now it is in truth 'One Nigeria'."

Jacob, to Farquharson, came and went like an automaton. They disliked each other, and Farquharson was in no mood to regret the unfairness that, he knew, caused this: he favoured Stanley. Joan in hospital held herself back from him so far now that it wasn't even married kindness to go and talk to her. So Farquharson would sit on Stanley's bed at night and talk to him or to whatever friend was there with him, bringing beer to accompany them, trying partly to explain himself, partly, he thought, just to be.

It was his last week, and he hadn't yet sunk himself into that still, absolute, final long love-making that, curiously, he was looking forward to.

"I'm trying to get rid of being in love with you," Gail said. "You've got to help."

She wanted one violent finish. Night after night he was there, slow, huge, giving her everything he happened to be in that half-hour, the casual, whole self with never a repeat. And yet he wasn't happy: he was a wretchedly angry person waiting to go back to Canada. Bill had to be very kind to her.

Going home, Farquharson would have to pass Bill, sitting on the front doorstep, his bandaged head held waiting over narrow shoulders, his bandaged toe sticking conspicuously out of the old cut-open shoes—but Bill wouldn't get up until Farquharson was in his car. Joan came home Monday the twenty-fifth.

Farquharson said to Bill, "One more time."

455

"There," he said (it was noon, on Wednesday), "now go down, and take me."

He had to carry her to the bed, take her clothes away from her, strip himself without help, enter her, and make her climb like fire. Their last time wasn't long, or stately, but a kind of violent untidy mess, dragging them in tumult and unsteadiness until she was sobbing and he was thrusting like an animal with his arms locked under her back. And when they were over, they were over suddenly, with a ruinous empty clarity that couldn't make caresses, and he got the hiccups. They lay so long then without talking that they heard Bill come in and shut himself into the kitchen to make lunch.

Embarrassed at last, Farquharson kissed her like a young, nervous man and tiptoed out of the house. Joan was waiting for him with her lunch eaten.

"Jamie's full of how you took him for a long drive and he slept in the car," she said.

"You want to pack tonight or tomorrow morning?"

"I am packed."

They hadn't said anything about the suitcases in the pantry that Farquharson had unpacked. He wondered if she remembered.

"Look," she said, "I'd better get another bottle of this prescription before we go. Why don't you get it now?"

"Can I have a nap?" He said. His loins dragged.

"You've done everything for yourself," she said, "now you can do this for me."

And they were in a futile, empty fight about everything. Finally she shouted, "You never talk to me!"

"About *what*?"

But if she was going to say, "What about the men you killed?" she was stopped by a university car turning into the driveway. "Oh for heaven's sakes," she said, petulant, "get out and get that stuff. Will you for once do something kind?"

He was standing at the back of the shop, waiting for the drug, when he wondered about a dark-blue Peugeot with no one in it

456

but an African in khaki. The pills were put into his hand. The cashier said, "Are you all right, sir?"

He didn't speed. He felt too numb and scared, and he held in front of himself the picture of Farquharson coming into his own house, and Jamie in the living room running to be lifted up. Cars passed him: one blue Peugeot driven by a woman in a huge scarlet head tie. The gates of the university's defence were wide open. His people would be there, sleeping for siesta. The living room doors were open. "Joan?" he called.

Jacob was gone.

"Joan? Jamie?"

A cry that ripped the house: his son's name, to empty rooms.

Drawers hurled open. The passport gone, the tickets: all as it was before. "*Jamie!*" Out on the patio, bellowing like a man half killed.

The airport.

No quiet driving now: the Morris Minor crashing over the road as if it had no springs and no control. The airport closed, not sealed, a couple of adolescent Nigerian children talking in the waiting room, "Woman and a little boy; did they take a plane from here?"

Cool looks, no answer: querulous shaking of heads. He took the car out of the parking lot and stuck at the roadway.

The Motor Transport Yard. "Sir, this office closed now! Come back tomorrow."

"Did you send a car to take my wife and boy down to Lagos?"

"Our records are inside, sir."

The glass door would be fine to break: a tire iron . . .

What was he doing, *telling* everyone? WP2471, under the shed roof, with its engine hanging on shiny chains, looked out at him.

Not to Gail's. He couldn't.

They weren't at the Club.

No one. The manageress, sitting at the bar, drinking, scorning to look at him.

Not in the Staff Store. Who did Joan know? Who were her friends? *At the Nwonkwos'?*

"Henry!" Victoria said. "What's wrong?"

He said, "I can't find Joan and Jamie."

"Your driver was looking for you."

"Farq!" Stanley met him, hangdog, handsome as pity. "Mrs. give me this," he said, holding an envelope.

White glare. He couldn't read it for the sun, walked into the house, stood under the unmoving fan. He breathed as if each breath were a clamp he was using to hold himself together. Flat, handwritten, unkind, hurt words. She was gone to Lagos. By killing a man he had lost the right to raise his son. She would go where she wanted to as soon as she could change the tickets, and he couldn't stop her. When she saw him—because she would have to see him—they would discuss it. And a list of what belonged to the Nwonkwos, and the Baloguns, what of their leftover household goods was to go to Jacob and Florence (the iron), what was owed in money to Jacob and Florence (no word about Stanley), and would he see to it. And she wouldn't be staying in a hotel, so he wouldn't find her.

Victoria and Oscar were on the patio.

"Henry," Oscar said.

Farquharson shoved the letter at them. Victoria took it and folded it without reading it and gave it back. Then in dull quiet words he told them what the letter was.

"Killing?"

"October, the day of the incident." He told them that, too.

"And your love affair?" Oscar said, while Victoria tried to stop him.

"She didn't even mention it." He bit his lip and looked between them. He said, "I want my boy. I don't want her." He said, "I'll never want her again. I want Jamie."

"Then go to the Lagos Airport," Oscar said, "now. She must come there. Then take your son."

Victoria said, "Oh, the poor boy!"

She threw silence over them. Then Oscar said, "Did you *really* kill?"

"And if Joan knew Jamie was alone in the house when they came in," he said, "I'd never get him."

Abruptly practical, Victoria said, "Did she leave you money?"

He searched the bedroom and his clothes. "Just what I had," he said, "and the travellers' cheques."

Slowly a pattern settled. He was to pack, dress, write cheques for the servants' wages. Victoria would see that everybody got the right equipment. Oscar would drive him down to Lagos, lend him the car, and stay with friends, or leave him at the airport with the car, and come and get it when he was told to—they wrote a telephone number out for him there and put it with his vaccination certificate, in his pocket.

Victoria scoured the house for objects. Farquharson packed. "Henry," she said. "Come here. Look." The malachite necklace was in the toilet bowl. One of the beads had cracked off the string. He had to grope for it. He shoved the whole wet lot together into his coat pocket. He had wet his cuff.

"Are there a couple of silver bracelets?" he said. "Or did she like them?"

They had packed his suitcases. The house was bare.

"If there's anything Stanley wants, he can have it." He pulled out the malachite beads. "I wanted to buy these," he said. "I bought them because I wanted them. Would you want them, Victoria? Mend the one bead and have them, or if you don't, give them to Gail? Give them to Bill to give to Gail. Oh, if I get Jamie, I'll come back!" Then, "Keys," he said. "Here."

Oscar brought his white car around. Stanley put the suitcases into it. Suddenly Farquharson saw him standing unhappily at the white car. "I never wrote you a letter," he said.

There was some paper in the desk. He wrote, rapidly, as honest a good letter as he could, signed it and folded it. Then one for Jacob, less honest, more conventional, and put Jacob's cheque with it. He gave Stanley his letter and cheque, said, "Mrs. Nwonkwo will see to everything." Then, "What is it?"

"I pray God may give you your boy, sir," Stanley said.

"I'll write."

Stanley shook hands with him.

Victoria bent to the car window and kissed him. Oscar made the car heave and turn. The last thing Farquharson saw was Stanley, heavy-eyed, with his cheque in his shirt pocket, staring after him.

No university gate; no airport; no Mọkọla roundabout. When they came abreast of Dugbẹ Market, Farquharson suddenly said, "I never went into that," and stared at where all the buses stopped as if their being there was a measure of how little truth he had of the country he'd been in. No Ibadan now: out onto the road south, the legendary Lagos-Ibadan road of all the car wrecks. Oscar drove at great speed, and there were in truth car wrecks, of all ages and degrees of ruin, two every three miles, never removed, in one place three within sight at once, one very old. Mrs. Kayọde's Cortina, presumably, was somewhere here.

The road was wide, with immense shoulders. Farquharson counted wrecks—anything to push him, if it could, nearer to Jamie. Towns went by like blind faces. The jungle grew denser beside the road. Water appeared in the dusk, then in the dark. The pavement shrank suddenly to a one-lane swamp bridge with head-lit cars coming the other way.

If eyes could force the dark . . .

"Ikeja," Oscar said. "We are here." He was steering along a wide trafficked street dotted with lit blocks of flats. "Soon the airport, Henry."

Farquharson had a lump in his throat like an egg of vomit covered with a glass shell. He tried to swallow.

Then as soon as they were in the parking lot, he ran from the car into a white building of many windows and a long one-storey wing. He waited, panting, at a wicket. "Has anyone come in with the mate to this ticket?" he said. "To change a flight? A woman and a small boy?"

"Name?"

"Farquharson." Spelled. "F. A. R. Q. U. H. . . ."

Pause. "No. They are booked on the same flight, Mr. Farquharson."

"Give me a pen and paper."

"You may write over there, sir, where is a magazine stand."

Farquharson bought a postcard, asked to borrow a pencil, was refused, bought a blue Biro, wrote, "Don't. Please. Please don't. Please," cursed himself for being a fool, bought another postcard, stood hesitating with it. Oscar, finding him, said, "Ask her to phone you," and dictated the number. "My friends are not far away."

It was Oscar who bought an envelope, addressed it to Mrs. H. J. Farquharson, and gave it to the official at the wicket with a careful African explanation about attempted child theft and a heartbroken father, but the man stared past Oscar's head and said, "Where is this man? I do not see him!"

Farquharson, hollow-eyed, was counting the faces to find those of his own people. Oscar didn't quit the wicket until he was satisfied that it would be impossible for the ticket to be changed without the person who changed it being directed to the envelope. He thought of adding a rider that the ticket seller should phone, but had already left the counter so he shrugged and promised himself to do that after he had made Henry eat.

But he could hardly get his man to leave the airport.

Oscar, scared by having to deal with a dazed man, went to another wicket to see if his friend could get a room at the Airport Hotel, but there weren't any.

"Suppose she doesn't phone? Suppose she didn't change the tickets, just bought new ones? I mean, there was such a rigmarole ..."

"You will make yourself sick. Wait." And he went back to ask of every other flight between now and then, made an important fuss and threw the university's name around, and found, finally, after much angry time, that no Mrs. Farquharson and child were on any flight between then and the one in question. And this time he gave his friend's phone number and said, "Let us know," and gave money.

Farquharson let himself be taken to the car and driven, first to the friends to leave a message, then to the Airport Hotel to have a meal—and when he saw the little lobby with the steps across it he

461

went to the desk to find his wife and son. They weren't registered.

Oscar couldn't force Farquharson to eat, but he wanted to conceal his own appetite by offering lavishness (beer, chicken-okra stew glistening on the plate, comforting in the belly: "My friend, I cannot let you starve yourself")—and watch him take the fork in his hand, and try.

Farquharson found that hunger asserted itself, even against dread or whatever it was that stalled a man hurrying where time raced and stopped. He had his mouth burnt by the pepper sauce, and swallowed.

A sweet, coffee, the bill paid. He was walking back to the lobby, to the desk. He turned aside and looked out across the wide courtyard that had been his first Nigerian earth. "Do not stay here, Henry. Please, to my friend's house."

"She has not checked in, Mr. Farquharson. And the hotel is full."

To Oscar's friends.

"Josephine Uka. David Uka. Professor Henry Farquharson." Hands shaken. "What a pleasure."

Telephone on the corner table. By the couch. If he could sleep there . . .

"His wife is sick . . ." Fast explanations behind him, *in English.* Somehow he felt that if he were taller he would be through the ceiling: the wet, heavy air buoyed him. They had come from the hotel in a drenching fast weeping rain. It was dying away. He was in an upper flat somewhere: where? Oscar and the husband had gone from the door; he had the wife in the room, moving, a marionette on strings, swinging her bottom because she couldn't help it. Would he sit down? she said.

Beside the phone, stiffly, with his hands meeting each other and tensing. She smiled and left him. There was a balcony across the room from him. Blackness and lights. He got up to stare.

Mrs. Uka saw his back from the kitchen, rock-solid sloping shoulders pulling the suit coat tight. She called, "Take off your coat!" in the imperious voice of students saying, "I have a complaint, sir." He let the coat slip off his back. A big steady man, she thought, sprung and weighted with good full muscle. "You will find your wife," she said.

An odd voice said, "Thank you," and then, "and my boy?"

She opened doors. The last rain hung windless. "Lagos," she said, pointing out, Farquharson thought, across water.

The men brought his suitcases. "Henry, may I go into Lagos and ask questions?" Oscar said.

"I'm sorry," Farquharson said, knowing husband and wife were moving gently behind him not to disturb him. "I'm a bad guest." He came back in and sat. He wanted to put his hand on the telephone.

The man said, "I don't see how you can help it," and Farquharson looked at both of them and saw a short couple, formal, dressed like Americans and handsome because of good health and food.

Farquharson said, "Could I have a drink?"

He could not have had kinder people. He knew that, and he was enraged with himself that he couldn't be polite and talk to them, but if he tried he saw the telephone not being watched and felt that it mightn't ring. They let him wait. They wondered if it would be kind to try to make him talk about his boy, but they hadn't the heart to, so they talked past him so that he could attend or not, as he chose, and when Oscar got back and said, "It is almost one o'clock, why do you not all sleep?" they were making stilted conversation about the government. Oscar launched into a jubilant cadenza on the arrest that day of the former Minister of Finance of the Western Region and the former chairman of the Western Nigeria Development Corporation, charged with having stolen in their heyday "five hundred thousand pounds, *at least!*" he said.

"This country," Farquharson said. "This *God-damned* country!"

His tongue was loosened. They argued into the cramped stifling depth of night, adding beer to beer, letting the wife retire and reappear with a tray of small-chop. Farquharson said, "Ordering universities now to turn out sixty per cent science graduates, that sort of thing. Do they control the mind?" He quoted the papers on

463

Ironsi: "I know nothing of laws. I shall give orders, and they will be obeyed."

The phone rang in a small ugly silence.

Josephine said, "At *this* hour?"

The phone was held towards him, on the end of its cord, two black closed holes. For five seconds after he'd taken it he couldn't make his voice work.

"Hello?" he said.

"I speak from the airport." An important, very loud voice. Everyone in the room could hear it, as Farquharson had to lift the receiver away from his ear.

"Yes?" he said.

The voice from the telephone was like thin sparks spitting: "... has collected it. Yes. A woman and a boy." A pause. They heard the voice complain, "He has gone away."

"No," Farquharson said, getting started again. "Were the tickets changed?"

The sputter became more confidential, and the three in the room lost the words of it.

"You don't know where they're staying?"

Oscar took the receiver from him almost reverently and hung it up.

"He told her he couldn't change two of the tickets without the third. I don't know what you said to him, Oscar, but thank you." He shook his head. "Thank you."

"Doesn't her residence permit give as her reason for entry into Nigeria 'accompanying husband'?" David Uka looked triumphant in a bright, printed chair. "Isn't that what they always say?"

But Farquharson said, "She took him to an airport at two-thirty in the morning, pulling him along by the hand." He had the forefinger of his fist pressed into his lower lip.

"She couldn't go to bed and leave him," Josephine Uka said. "I will make coffee." She disappeared again, and the men let him sit and went out to the balcony to talk, with the rumble of voices no more than just turned on.

464

After a long time, Farquharson came out on the balcony with them. He said, "She must have read it."

"She will phone at breakfast."

"Will she?"

"Coffee," Mrs. Uka was saying. "David, you must go to sleep. This is not a weekend."

"I'm sorry," Farquharson said.

Silence, and the phone rang.

"Hello? Joan?" An extraordinary radiance, and a cracking voice: "*Jamie!* ... Hi. No, I'm all right. No. I got a ride down. No, in a *white* car. You sleep now. Sad-songs tomorrow. Yes. Yes. Good night." A long pause. "Joan? Where are you? Please. Well, because I want to know." He pulled the receiver away from his ear, almost as if to look at it. The other men heard the words, "At the airport."

"All day tomorrow? What's the point? I've been so scared. *Please.*"

They heard her voice viciously bite off the words: "*Don't. Please. Please don't. Please!*" And then she hung up.

40

July 28–29, 1966

JOAN rode in the back of the Peugeot with a complaining and increasingly tremulous and worried Jamie asking where his father was. She explained that Farq and Jamie had had a trip, and now Mummy and Jamie were going to have a trip—and she saw every town they went through as unfriendly to her. She had made the driver take the Abẹokuta road. She had money; she had righteousness. She was horrified at the clinging, castor-oil quality of her sentimentality, but she had Jamie, and so how she felt didn't matter much: every milepost at the side of the road justified her.

It didn't help that the one thing Jamie was willing to talk about, long after they had passed Abẹokuta, and the air was getting low and sticky, was his trip with Farq, as if that alone was giving him confidence on this trip—or that he was articulate and insistent, and couldn't help making her see the perfect picnic, and contentment, and the unexpected scary-lovely night in the village house, and the happy authority of the way he thought of Farq. Joan had justification: she was trying to use it in place of courage. She was a temperish, frightened woman when she was brought to the Lagos suburbs and asked where she was supposed to go. And because she knew only one place, she went to the Airport Hotel and tried to get a room, and couldn't, and tried in panic to scold her way to one, and wouldn't bribe for one, and didn't get one, and then cried. So while the driver waited she got them supper in the restaurant and made Jamie eat—that at least she could do—and then there was a cancellation. The clerk called to her, gave her the room, openly commanded gratitude, and was suddenly given three pounds and ordered not to tell anyone she was there. Recklessly she promised five pounds more before she went. He said, "I will be faithful, madam."

She made the driver take her to the airport once, to ask about times and tickets. They promised to see what they could do, and then the driver took them back to the hotel, and left for Ibadan. She put Jamie to bed. He wouldn't go to sleep. She tried singing one of his father's songs to him, and he wouldn't have it. Finally, she turned the light out and sat in the dark, staring out of the open window. When Farquharson stepped into the entry to the court-yard, she saw him.

There was no peace, no rest. She was married to a man who killed people and had a son, and rather than run from both she was running from only one of them, grabbing one half of a being to get away from its other half, and it didn't free her that everything in her suddenly, morally loathed him—not out of fear, but out of cold, necessary disapprobation. The mood might have been born out of the obsession of the mumps. Certainly she had been half out of her head in the hospital, and she was obsessive still, but the mood was born, it was hers, and she was going to have it.

He had taken Jamie alone through Africa, while she was sick.

Deep in the night, the phone rang. "Mrs. Farquharson? Sorry to disturb you. There has been a difficulty with your ticket. Perhaps it could be cleared up if you could come here right away. There is a morning flight perhaps available. Also there is a message for you."

"Read it to me."

"I must not open it, madam."

"If I get on that morning flight, will I be able to come back to the hotel and sleep?"

"Yes, madam. But, please, there is a difficulty about the tickets . . ."

She phoned the desk. "Get me a taxi."

She had to shake Jamie awake and get him into his clothes again. The taxi charged too much (with an idle meter), and she went into the building with her eyes as sharpened with sleep-lessness as if she had been half drunk, was given the envelope and

467

told, "The holder of the third ticket must change his ticket too, madam."

"You're lying."

"Madam?"

"Why the hell did you get me out of bed for this?"

Jamie dragged her hand.

The man turned away and went off to consult someone, leaving her with an envelope in her hands, in a handwriting she didn't know. She had to drag it open in little jerks.

"Madam, I am very sorry. The places I thought were available have been taken." Then he shook his head again. "The three tickets, they must be changed as a unit. This has to do with the price, madam."

She said, "Who's bribing you?"

He called his superior and explained, scolding, that he was being accused of taking bribes and lying. She heard the words, "... stolen from the father ..." Somehow she got back to the hotel. As soon as he got in the taxi, Jamie pulled his hand out of hers and sat on the far side of the seat. And so finally she phoned Farquharson. She would have Jamie, at least, all day tomorrow.

"Look at him," she thought, almost hating him, after he had been speaking to his father, "sleeping happily!"

She hadn't lost her determination, her righteousness, or her justification: they had simply been taken away from her. She took a sleeping pill. It fought sleep, and finally she took another.

Jamie was awake long before she was, crying with fright and hunger, Her head ached.

Then she spoke like a tourist: "We're going to see Lagos, Jamie."

Mrs. Uka let Farquharson sleep on her couch until well after noon. She had given him a pillow for his head, and he lay crumpled with his back to the room, his shirt tail pulled out, and his fawn-coloured trousers creased every which way, his feet in bright-red socks. When he woke she said, "Sit around. Rest. Use my husband's razor if you want to shave."

He saw himself in the mirror, over the lather, with his eyes smudged and heavy, and he thought his hair looked like dry grass in a drought. Large hard ears, with the razor next to them. Sharp wings to his nose. That crazy clown's-rubber-ball look on the end of it. With the safety razor at his neck, for a moment, a tiny little wash of fright stuck in memory: a car heaving over obstacles, one wheel at a time, then being lifted over. He wouldn't think of it; he was going home. Somehow he was getting out of this country with his son and wife, suitcases . . . He would stand in St. Mark's Square with Jamie on his shoulders, listening to the band.

He washed the razor carefully, put it where he had taken it.

"*Vissi d'arte: vissi d'amore. Non—*" What? It ought to be something like "*Non ho fatto mal a nessun . . .*" only it wouldn't fit. "*Nessun*" what? He wanted to say "*personne*", but that was the wrong language. *I have done no harm to any . . .*

To any what?

He called, "May I take a bath?"

Swift cool water, ready for him. Out of his clothes; fold them; lay them on the floor. Make water, shake away the end drops, cup his balls, straighten his tie. . . Climb into the water; sit.

Wait, with two loud children in the flat, his suitcases ready, his coat folded on top of them. Oscar sent word that he was going back to Ibadan about ten o'clock; he'd drive Farquharson to the airport before then if he wanted to go, or he could take a taxi. Farquharson said, "People are good to me."

Mrs. Uka said, "No," chiding and simply, because she found herself fond of the big awkward man, whose restlessness grew steadily more courteous the worse it was. Before supper he took the children down to the grass outside and played with them, throwing the ball and catching it, and falling down when he missed it, sometimes. He had two small boys to laugh at him.

He ate supper, worried about his own boy, smiled, and grew steadily greyer and more anxious. "Come," Josephine Uka said, "would she truly leave you?"

Rain came over with the dark, drifted, and left them washed

469

and stifled. Oscar came in as if he wanted to be jumping up and down.

"Taxi, Henry?" he said. "Or do you want to wait in the airport until the concrete grows to your shoes?"

David Uka pointed. "Sit that man down and give him coffee and a liqueur."

"I'll go to the airport," Farquharson said.

"Not yet! I have cherry brandy. Please."

So they all sat down. The children had shaken Farquharson's hand good night. "All right," he said, "One cherry brandy, one coffee, calm, and then run."

"And then wait, wait. Henry, this is not Rome Airport, or London. This is Lagos!"

He said, "I wonder where they are!"

"You go to sleep, Jamie," Joan said. "I refuse to take us to the airport one minute before I have to."

"Want Farq," he said. "I've had no fun all day." It was the most grown-up sentence she had ever heard him make.

"Why, we saw all sorts of pretty things," she said. "Shops, and streets . . ."

Jamie said, "Good night!"

Goodbyes, handshakes. "May I wish you happiness?" Josephine Uka said.

"I wish you would. Thank you for putting up with me."

Roads of cars. Everyone drove at night. Taxis honked. Trucks honked. "The Mogambo nightclub," Oscar said suddenly, at a turn. "We should have gone there." Then he said, "Do you want to leave our country so very much?"

"I can't think of that. I want Jamie safe in my hands, and to know what to do with his mother. What's Nigeria? I want to get out before anything else happens here. I'm tired of bodies. The next body I want is my own, thank you very much."

"Henry, you saw too much of the wrong thing."

"It was there," he said.

"We will come to the Second Republic, my friend, and then you will see. One Nigeria, in fact, as it has been pretended. No tribes, no enmity. Oh," he said, "freedom to sneer at a Northerner or a Yoruba, if I want. But no killing, Henry. A strong government and no killing. I promise you."

Farquharson said, "Send me a poem about it."

Oscar insisted on carrying his suitcases through the door. "And now goodbye, Henry," he said. "I have a long way to go."

"And give my love to Victoria. Jamie's too."

"That will be safe, with you gone. Any word for Gail Johnston?"

"Yes," he said. "Tell her I found Jamie, even if it isn't true." He wondered, sluggishly, whether there were anything else to say. He said, "We said goodbye." Oscar was standing like a good salesman, alertly aware of where he was, conscious first and foremost of his own body, a full, whole, closed self. He had to be let go home.

"Your address, Henry. I must send you a copy of my poems." Farquharson scribbled for him.

Briefly, the two men surveyed each other. Then Farquharson felt a handshake, and Oscar was gone with the kind of pride, Farquharson thought, that should have been wearing an *agbada*, and been Yoruba; and he was delighted momentarily, before his insides went grey again, at how insulted the man would have been if he had said that to him.

He settled down on the bench to wait. Slowly the crowd thickened. The people seemed to be mostly African and Italian. He bought a coloured postcard of Ibadan to give to Jamie, an aerial view of New Court Road, with the Kingsway and the blue church, and Mapo Hall far away at the right margin, but he couldn't really follow Lebanon Street because of the angle of the picture.

He wasn't prepared to be suddenly stricken homesick for Ibadan, or to feel that least wanted of emotions cross him like a fever.

They hadn't come yet. If he watched, hollow-chested, hollow-skulled, with no guts, he could find them. They would come in that door and go by, when the plane was called. He went to the weigh-in counter. He trusted Joan to come. And yet he'd been afraid all day, ever since she'd phoned. Empty and sick. But that was for Jamie.

"Here you are, sir." He could go through.

"Can I wait for a while?"

"Yes. The plane is delayed."

"How long?"

"One, one and a half hours. We have informed the passengers at the hotel."

"I see."

He should have walked up and down. He just stood and watched the door.

One, one and a half hours.

They had to come. The crowd pushed him around the corner. He wondered if there were two planeloads at once, both delayed, one going somewhere else.

Without his suitcases he now felt stark, as if he had become not himself, and had only pockets and clothes hanging on him. Passport, permit . . .

"What can I do with this, Mr. Farquharson? This is a photostat! You must have your paper, sir. This is not a legal thing!"

He thought, "All to do again." But after ten months he knew how: raise your voice, bully, make a nasty, efficient row, and just let your temper go. He didn't expect that there would be so much temper, or that it would go so far. He stormed, coldly, as if he had had Mr. Igwe on the patio but had known how to do it. "I was admitted with that paper," he said, in an interval. "If it was good enough to get me into the country it can be good enough to get me out again. Do you find any fault with my passport number on it, perhaps?" And on, and on.

What was a crowd at the entrance thinned here and beyond into a sparse trickle of people. The rage worked finally, as soon as the despair in it won, cracked, and made him grin. "Am I supposed to go back to Ibadan," he said, "and find the man who never turned up to give me the original on September the thirteenth, nineteen sixty-five? I wouldn't make the plane!"

"You are leaving Nigeria?"

"For good."

"This can not be so, sir. This permit does not expire before September, nineteen sixty-seven."

Farquharson thought suddenly that the man looked like his late passenger, and said, "Are you an Ibo?"

"The Professor knows," the man said, "that there are now officially no tribes in any government services?"

"I know that. I just thought I recognized something."

Some kind of pride struggled with bureaucracy and won. "Through those doors, sir." They had a bond.

He entered a huge ugly lounge, sown with scattered people, and waited on foot, to watch, visible to the Immigration man he had just passed. To have recognized an Ibo must have been worth something. He should have dashed the man. Joan hadn't come.

He saw a man in a blue shirt talk to the Immigration man; then the Immigration man nodded, the other went away, and the Immigration man beckoned to him.

"Telephone, sir, for you."

"Where do I go?" The heart leaped.

"In the office, sir. They will show you. Around the corner, sir. I will know when you come back that I have let you through."

Farquharson thanked him and ran. Sure enough, around the corner he saw a door open behind the cages and the luggage counter, and a man in a blue shirt looking to him and signalling. He was almost thrown into an office and left alone, with the door closed.

"Hello, Joan?" he said.

"This is Mr. Amele, the Assistant Furniture Clerk at the University of Ibadan. Your driver Mr. Ademu and I have been trying to locate you all day, Professor Farquharson."

473

He listened thunderstruck, rage spilling into his ears. "You *what?*"

"Sir, I have been to your house Eight El-Kanemi Road, with your driver, and we have searched the place high and low. You have not returned the pillowcases. Sir, we must have those pillowcases."

He roared, "You wouldn't lend me any!"

"Professor Farquharson, it is on our list—pillowcases. You have to unpack those pillowcases, sir, and send them back."

"Even if I had them, my suitcases are now checked through to Rome. I could hardly recover them and unpack." But there was more insistence. "Is Stanley there?"

"He is, sir."

"Put him on."

He steadied himself dangerously. "Stanley? Did we borrow pillowcases?"

"Sir, in the first term."

"Those were returned."

"So I have believe, sir. We take them back."

"And you told him that?"

"Yes, but he says is written, sir, that we have not return."

"Call me Farq, will you?"

A suddenly different-sounding voice, Stanley as a man: "Farq, you have your son?"

"I'm waiting for him, if I can ever get off this God-damned phone." There was some kind of disturbance or argument outside the office, near the ticket counters.

Stanley said, "Sir, goodbye. Mr. Amele now. Greet Jamie well for me."

But Mr. Amele still wouldn't believe there were no pillowcases, and they were each shouting into the phone, until Farquharson realized that he was enjoying himself too much, and not being able to stand it another second slammed the phone down, and thought in the moment of aftermath that the room was shaking with the sound he'd made.

Something was shaking. Not echoes or a plane: trucks and cars.

474

Farquharson broke out of the office, saw suddenly in front of him, on the other side of the ticket cages, helmeted soldiers in green, and a few people beside the window, standing very still. He said, "Excuse me," and ran.

Some word was said behind him. Somebody yelled. There were more soldiers in front of him. He went around the corner and saw the Immigration man, ashen behind his lectern, looking sidelong at a bayoneted rifle barrel. Farquharson stopped. There was another armed soldier, almost beside him, and a man in officer's uniform, by the window, with the face of a Hausaman and a revolver in his hand.

The Immigration man cried to him, "Sir! sir!" and pointed a shaking hand to the doors: "Your wife!"

Joan: that meant Jamie.

Farquharson started to walk; past one soldier, then the other, who still had his rifle trained on the Immigration man. But Joan and Jamie were in the departure lounge until the plane. He had them: they couldn't get away. So he turned towards both the soldiers, glanced at the officer, and said, this being Africa, "What are you doing to this man?"

"Dear God," Farquharson thought, "I know how to deal with Hausamen."

One of the rifles wavered. The officer said sharply to Farquharson, "Go through that door."

But the dangerous taste for quarrelling was still with him. "I want an explanation for what's going on in here," he said, the rage about the pillowcases running like little tacks under his skin.

The officer pointed, using his gun.

The Ibo Immigration man cried, "Your wife's permits were all in order, sir. You go that way!"

A yelling man suddenly ran around the corner and then seemed to be lifted sideways with a thunderclap, a jet of blood flying out of his mouth.

The Hausa officer said, "No expatriates will be hurt, sir. Go in there."

Jamie wanted him. But Farquharson had had a ten-second

friendship with a man, so he said, "Leave him alone," and took the Immigration man by the arm. "Come," he said.

Shaking, the Ibo came. Farquharson put a sheltering arm over his shoulder. For a few seconds it seemed that they were going to get to the doors, Ibo and *oyibo* between Northerners. Then the Ibo lurched forward, screaming, Farquharson's hand closed convulsively on the shoulder of the coat, and the man would have spun crashing to the floor if he hadn't been controlled for a second by the bayonet in his back. Then the soldier shoved him down and tried to lever the bayonet out again. Pink blood frothed after it. The Ibo's hands clawed at the concrete floor, and through the little window in one of the doors, Farquharson saw Joan standing in profile at the far end of the lounge. Her face was tiny, but it was clear that outrage had blanketed any fear she could possibly be having. She might have been beside him, telling him what his country was. He wanted to slap her face.

The soldiers gave a great tug on the Immigration man's legs and yanked him into the middle of the floor. Farquharson caught the movement and followed it. He saw two guns carelessly held, an indulgent officer by the windowsill, a slack mouth trailing blood on the floor, and one eye whose eyelid beat. Then the clean bayonet went into the Ibo's waist and Farquharson heard the point screech on the concrete. The soldier was jolted off his balance and Farquharson jumped him. Before the man knew what had happened he was knocked away from the gun into a hard sitting fall. He yelled. The rifle stood in the wound for an instant as if balanced on the bayonet point. Then Farquharson plucked it out and turned to the others, holding the rifle like a tennis racquet at the ready. He had a moment of terrified nostalgia for the frying pan.

Revolver and rifle fired together into his stomach, clubbing him backwards. For a second, he didn't feel it. He was hanging against a teetering Immigration lectern, caught on it because it had snagged his armpit, and his hand had locked onto something below. He seemed to rise into the air as his feet shoved, and then he came toppling forward and sprawled on the floor near the

Immigration man, on his side but turned slightly down. One leg drew up and pushed out, drew up and pushed down again.

Officer and private looked at each other as if to check what they'd done, then the officer, suddenly cautious, hurried over and started pulling everything out of Farquharson's pockets, stuffing them into his own. He saw a huge white-metal ring on the man's hand, pulled the hand away from the edge of the body and wrenched and twisted the ring off. "Identifiable," he said, and pushed the hand into the spillage under the stomach.

There was still shooting, away over to one side.

Farquharson was burning. Agony was some part astonishment, and he was extraordinarily alive, unthinking, and hurt. He felt the ring go from him and tried to call out, and made some noise in the middle of the noises he hadn't known about, that were also his. His round glasses had been broken, and he had blood in one eye and an arc of thin metal frame across the other. But he saw one of the big blue doors open, and he heard somebody yell beyond it, and call a child to come back.

Large, very solemn-eyed, Jamie stood in the doorway, looking for him. They saw each other. Farquharson tried to be quiet, and not frightening, but his leg still moved, and he couldn't hold his breath to stop making sounds. Jamie stood gravely, not allowing himself to come forward lest he should cause trouble. Farquharson forced himself to think "Don't cry now, Jamie, please," and Jamie didn't cry. They knew who they were.

"Little boy!" The officer waved the ring and came near. Jamie stood still for him, too. "Here's a toy. Now go back, go in. This man will be quite all right."

Farquharson couldn't talk. He was light, and drifting somehow, warmth creeping over and into his squeezed hands. Jamie had taken the ring and gone away. The door was fastened with the soldier standing against it. Nobody else was going to come around the corner. They were in control.

"And now," the officer said, "before we are interrupted again, and with your pardon, sir."

Farquharson felt something cool and hard shove into the base of his skull behind, where it met the neck; then the touch wavered, ceased, came gently back again. He forced all his attention on to it, and it wouldn't stay still.

"We are not going to get into trouble," the man said privately, "over this sad accident."

Jamie had the ring shoved into his pocket. He sat on the floor with his back to the closed door, drawing his mother to him by staring at her. She had seen her husband's head through the glass, briefly; he wasn't there now. Then she saw the look on Jamie's face, and his thumb, hopelessly too small, shoved into Farq's silver ring. She heard the report of a revolver that destroyed half a face. And forever and forever she hated Henry Farquharson.